FROM A FAR LAND

JABEN'S RIFT, BOOK 1

G. David Walker

ISBN-10: 145363116X
ISBN-13: 978-1453631164

www.gdavidwalker.com

Dedicated to my family, who put up with my highs and lows as I chased a dream through the land of Teleria. Special thanks to K.B. and everyone else who offered their advice and suggestions.

Every day, every moment, is another step on the journey.

CONTENTS

Prologue

The ancient structure crouched in the middle of the Scottish woods. For centuries, it had waited…

The sound of crunching leaves broke the late afternoon stillness as a solitary figure pushed through the tangle of brush toward the building. Mesmerized by his discovery, Jason Bennett shrugged off assaults by vines and brambles battling to hold their hard-won territory. The teenager stopped as a particularly stubborn bramble won a skirmish with his sleeve, a victory heralded by a loud rip.

"Oh, man!" He scowled at the suntanned skin peeking through the hole in his new shirt. *Mom's gonna kill me*, he thought.

With a sharp jerk, he freed his sleeve and forged ahead. A few more steps brought him to the entrance. He eyed what was left of the door lying beside the building, almost obscured by weeds and grass, then looked at the gaping maw where it had hung. His gaze slowly traveled around the crumbling edges of the opening. *Maybe this isn't such a good idea*. Almost before the thought could register, he stepped inside.

Overhead, the roof had fallen in at several spots, splashing the dirty floor with rubble-strewn patches of sunlight. Vines and creepers covered portions of the walls, and a large section of one wall in the front room had collapsed. The musty smell of mold and decaying leaves filled the air. He kicked a clod of dirt, watching it shatter into dust as it hit the wall. It was just an overgrown ruin, similar to the old, decrepit shacks he had seen back home, the only difference being that this one was made of stone instead of wood.

He explored a few of the rooms, but found nothing except more dirt and dead leaves. It was beginning to get dark, so he decided to head back to his great uncle's house. As he turned to leave, the lengthening shadows revealed a glow coming from somewhere deeper inside the building.

Intrigued, he went in search of the source of the light, the approaching dusk forgotten for the moment. He followed the flickering radiance to a room that appeared to have weathered the passage of time better than the others. The light came from a doorway on the other side of the room. It looked like it opened to the outside, although he would have sworn he was in the middle of the building.

Maybe there's a courtyard or something like that, he thought. *The light might be coming from something out there*. Ignoring the small voice of caution in the back of his mind, he stepped through the door.

The light disappeared. The building was empty once more.

Something has changed. The being raised its head as a ripple in the ether disturbed its self-contemplation. Was it time? For centuries the being had waited, sometimes watching the interaction between the points of light and darkness that traversed the flowing colors of the vista before it. At other times, it would turn its attention inward, pondering its own existence for decades at a time.

Now, another moved along a dark thread toward the intricate ballet the being had observed for so long. Yet this new addition was neither light nor dark. It shifted between one end of the spectrum and the other, a rainbow condensed into a single point of existence.

A whispering echo broke the silence. "So, he has found the way at last."

The being knew it was not supposed to interact with the dancers, and, for the most part, it had observed the Covenant. It remembered how easily the points of light now twirling before it could be extinguished. But now it reached out and, ever so slightly, shifted the end of the dark thread upon which the newcomer traveled. *The others will not know*, it thought.

"And so it begins. A new song for the dance."

Then it watched as the rainbow point of light approached the end of the dark thread…

1
Doorway

Where am I? A black void surrounded Jason. There was no sound, no sense of motion, nothing. *Am I dead?* His heart pounded against his ribs, and the coppery taste of panic filled the back of his throat. Then a tiny glimmer of light appeared, a lonely star in an empty sky, bleeding streaks of color into the darkness. The colors swirled and eddied around him in a fluid kaleidoscope of ever-changing hues. He saw shapes beginning to form. With each passing second, the shapes became clearer and more distinct, until he found himself standing outside a small stone building in the middle of a forest glade.

He spun around, but the door he had just stepped through was nowhere to be seen. *What the...?* Running a shaky hand through his hair, he gazed about. He jerked back to face the cottage as he heard footsteps inside. Before he could think, the door opened and he was staring into the eyes of an old man.

The man searched Jason's face with eyes that brought to mind slate gray storm clouds just before the rain begins. Then a wide smile spread across the old man's face as he grabbed Jason's arm and pulled him inside.

"Welcome, traveler! Be welcome in my home. You are from the Far Planes, are you not? Your garb is much different from those who live here. Let me look at you." He stepped back, his eyes taking in every detail of Jason's appearance.

Jason studied the old man in turn. He wore a simple green robe that brushed lightly against the floor. Wispy hair the color of new snow grazed the man's shoulders, held in check by a headband of shimmering metal. *He should have a long white beard*, he thought in the back of his mind.

The man looked him up and down. "Hmm. Ah well, in any case, it matters not where you are from. I am simply pleased that you are here."

At this point Jason had regained just enough composure to ask, "Excuse me, but where, exactly, is here?"

The man's eyes widened. "Do you mean to say you do not know? You, my boy, have the pleasure to be in, and I apparently have the honor of welcoming you to, the world of Teleria."

Hold it! Did he just say 'the world of'? He started to repeat his question with slightly more emphasis on the word 'exactly' when the man's eyebrows flew up and he said, "Oh dear. Where are my manners? I have not even introduced myself."

He bowed. "I am Reyga Falerian, Emerald Loremaster, *saiken lo*, and Elder of this province, but it would please me if you would simply call me Reyga. Please, sit down and let me get some refreshments. Then we will talk."

Without waiting for a reply, he turned and left the room. Jason stared after him for a few moments and then looked around.

It was a modest home, with shelves of books and stacks of scrolls taking up every available space. He glanced at one lying on a small table beside him, but couldn't decipher the symbols covering it. An ornate staff of dark wood, crowned by a green crystal the size of Jason's fist was propped in a corner. In the fireplace on the far wall, an energetic fire burned. He frowned as he looked at it. The cheerful blaze danced on a single small stick. *Huh. That's kinda weird.*

As he scanned the rest of the room, his eyes focused on a large mirror on the far wall. Then he realized it wasn't showing the room where he was sitting. As he watched, the image rippled like the surface of a pond. He was about take a closer look when Reyga came back into the room, carrying two large ceramic mugs and a platter loaded with various fruits. Reyga handed one of the mugs to him and, after grabbing a few pieces of fruit, sat down.

"Now, tell me your tale, young man. Where are you from? How do you come to be in Teleria?" He waited for Jason's answers with a look of anticipation dancing in his storm-cloud eyes.

Jason lowered himself into a chair. "Well, uh, I'm from Missouri."

The old man looked shocked. "Misery? What a dreadful name! Is that the name of your world?"

"No, not 'misery.' Mis*souri*. And that's not the name of my world, just the part where I live. My world is called Earth." *And this is a conversation I never thought I'd be having*, he added to himself.

"Hmm. And what do you do in Miz-*oor*-ee?"

Jason shrugged. This had to be a dream. "Not much. I go to school. I'm on my school's basketball team."

"Basket-ball? What is that?"

"It's a sport," Jason said. "We go up against other schools."

"Ah, you do battle to establish dominance over these others."

"Well, not exactly. I mean, sure we want to dominate them. But not the way I think you think...I mean...I think." Jason shook his head. "Well, in any case, it's just a game."

Reyga nodded slowly. "I see. Well then, tell me how you came to Teleria."

"I'm not really sure." He pretended to study his mug as he thought about the chain of events that had brought him here.

He and his parents had been visiting his great uncle, Nyall McFarland, outside Aberdeen, Scotland that summer. Uncle Nyall was rather well to do and owned a sizeable piece of land in the Scottish countryside that had been in the McFarland clan for generations. Jason and his family hailed from slightly more modest accommodations, namely a medium sized ranch-style home in the Missouri Ozarks.

His parents had planned this vacation so that Jason could see his family's ancestral lands. As soon as they arrived, they and the McFarlands started talking about old times, long lost friends and relatives, and what seemed like the entire lineage of their family all the way back to the Roman Empire. His father loved family history, and he figured his dad was practically in heaven discussing it at length.

He endured for almost an hour before excusing himself. He didn't want to make a bad impression on their hosts by dozing off right in the middle of a riveting story about how great, great, something-or-other McFarland had fallen asleep in the middle of milking a cow, and cost his wife first place in the county baking contest because she didn't have any milk for her muffins. He'd decided it was a good time to see his family's ancestral lands on his own.

While strolling the grounds, he had spotted some woods not far from the house. A trail led through them. He'd felt an irresistible urge to follow that trail.

Then he found the building, and the doorway that led to this place. *This world.*

He looked up from his mug to see Reyga watching him expectantly. He shrugged again. "There's not much to tell. I was taking a walk, found an old building, and when I walked through one of the doors, I came here."

Reyga studied his face. "Very well," he said finally. "Perhaps you would like to know a little of our fair world?"

"Yeah, sure," he said, more from a desire to redirect the conversation away from himself than anything else.

"Well." Reyga took a sip from his mug. "Where to start, where to start? Hmm. I suppose, as with any story, the best place to begin is, of course, at the beginning! Listen, and learn of our world.

"To begin, this world is called Teleria, as I mentioned before. But the Teleria you see today has not always been as it is now.

"Ages ago, according to legend, our world had reached the pinnacle of technological achievement. The ravages of aging and of disease had been vanquished, hunger had been abolished, and wondrous technology even allowed men to venture beyond this world. No one wanted for anything. It was a time of peace and prosperity. This was the First Age of Teleria. Then came the Devastation.

"Most of the records of that time have long since crumbled to dust," Reyga said. "The bits and pieces of information that we do have were almost lost until the system of Loremasters was established." He waved a hand. "But I get ahead of myself. First, let me tell you what is known of the Devastation, and then I will tell you what came to pass afterwards."

He leaned forward to grab a few more pieces of fruit before settling back more comfortably in his chair.

"Unfortunately, we have not been able to learn who started the Devastation. Of course, I suppose at this point in time that information is rather unimportant. All that is important for us is that someone struck the first blow.

"That day saw weapons unleashed of incredible destruction, the likes of which we can only imagine. In the end, it did not matter who started the War, for it was over in two days. The surface of our world had been decimated, and mankind had destroyed itself. Thus ended the First Age of Teleria."

Jason shook his head. Then he blinked his eyes a few times and shook his head again.

Reyga leaned forward. "Are you all right, my boy?"

Jason pinched himself. "Oh sure. No problem. I'm just trying to wake up. That's all."

The old man looked confused. "Forgive me, but did you say you were trying to wake up?"

"Yep. Sure did," he said. "I'm sorry, but this can't be real. I'm not really here and neither are you. This whole thing is some sort of weird dream. I've either passed out in that old house, or a stone came loose and knocked me out, or maybe I got a whiff of some hallucinogenic mushroom. I don't know." He tilted his head. "On the other hand, I might never have taken that walk at all. I might still be in bed dreaming this whole thing."

"Why do you believe this to be a dream?"

"Why? *Why?* Because this sort of thing doesn't happen, that's why! It's impossible! This is like something you'd see on some late night sci-fi show on TV. In real life, you don't just step through a doorway and find yourself in another world. It just doesn't happen!"

"Ah, I see," Reyga said. "While I do not know what the words 'sigh-fy' or 'teevee' mean, I believe I am beginning to understand. I am afraid this is no dream, my young friend. Tell me, does your world not have portal abilities?"

Jason gritted his teeth and slapped himself. Blinking through watering eyes, he was disappointed to see that there was still no change in his surroundings. His ears ringing, he muttered, "No. I don't even know what a 'portal' is."

"Then I am certain it has been quite a shock for you to find yourself transported to a completely foreign world."

"Yeah, if I thought this was real it would be a shock. Since it's just a dream, though, it doesn't bother me at all. In fact, the only annoying thing is that I can't seem to make myself wake up."

"Of course. Tell me… I am sorry, what was your name?"

"Jason. Jason Bennett."

"Tell me, Jason Bennett, can one feel pain in their dreams?"

He thought about it. "Well, I've always been told you can't feel pain in your dreams. That's why people always want someone to pinch them to make sure they're awake. But it sure didn't feel too hot when I smacked myself." His face brightened. "Maybe that's because I did it to myself. Yeah, that has to—"

The calm expression on Reyga's face gave no warning as his hand flashed out in a blur, and was just as suddenly back in his lap. Stars briefly obscured Jason's vision as a shock of pain exploded across the side of his face.

"OWW!" He grabbed his cheek. "What was *that* for?"

Reyga leaned forward. "Please forgive me, Jason Bennett, but it was necessary. It is vital that you understand that this is no dream. Teleria is a pleasant mistress to all who know her, but there are things in our land that make short work of those who believe they are dreaming, and I would not see you meet such an untimely, not to mention unpleasant, demise."

He stood and walked over to the window, glancing outside. "Perhaps you have learned enough of Teleria for today. The night will soon be upon us. I will prepare a place for you to rest tonight."

The mention of nightfall brought Jason to his feet. "Night? If this isn't a dream, then my folks are probably going nuts by now wondering where I am. I need to get home." He looked around. "How do I get back?"

Reyga's expression gave way to one of profound sympathy. "I am very sorry, Jason Bennett, but there is no way for you to return. Teleria is your home now."

He stared at Reyga, mouth agape. "No way back? What do you mean there's no way back? I can't stay here. I have a family, and friends. I have to get home!"

Reyga shook his head. "Would that I could send you back. But while we have the ability to create small portals within the confines of our own world," he gestured toward the object Jason had originally mistaken for a mirror, "we do not have the power to create portals to other worlds. Our wisest and most powerful *saiken* have been attempting to do so for many years, but thus far we cannot."

"No, no, no, no..." He paced back and forth. When Reyga paused, Jason looked at him with desperation in his eyes. "Listen to me. I have to get back. I've got a date next Friday with Tracy Jacobson. She's a cheerleader. No, she's *the* cheerleader! My SATs are coming up, and...and my eighteenth birthday is this Tuesday." He grabbed the front of Reyga's robe, fixing the old man with a wide-eyed stare. "I can't stay here! *I can't!*"

Reyga's expression became one of sympathy mixed with steel as he made a small gesture. A chair shot out from the wall and slammed into the back of Jason's legs, forcing him to sit. As he tried to get back up, Reyga gestured again. It felt as if iron bands were wrapped about his arms, chest, and legs. Try as he might, he couldn't move from the chair. He started to protest, but with another motion from the old man, he found that no sound would come from his mouth. After several seconds of silent shouting and struggling to break free, he collapsed back into the chair and glared at Reyga, panting from his exertions while occasional drops of sweat ran down the side of his face.

Reyga bent and looked into his eyes. "Listen to me. I will help you in any and every way I can, but you must understand two very important things. First, and most important, this is not a dream. It is very real, and the first time you are out in our land and you forget that may very well be your last. Second, there is no way back to your world, at least not yet. We are trying with all of our resources to create portals to other worlds, but we have not succeeded. That is not to say that we will not succeed, merely that we have not succeeded *yet*. Do you understand what I am telling you?"

At first, he just glared at the old man. After a moment, he slumped back into his chair and nodded.

"Very well," Reyga said. "I am going to release you from this chair. If I feel you are losing control again, I will put you back into it. Do you understand?"

He nodded again, and Reyga appeared to accept that as sufficient. Reyga stepped back and made another small motion with his hand. Jason felt the invisible restrictions fade away.

He started to stand up. "How did you..." Before he could complete his question, his vision blurred and the room began to swim and spin around him. Everything seemed out of balance and the floor tilted underneath his feet. He heard Reyga saying his name, but it sounded as if the old man was at the far end of a long tunnel. With one last swirl of color, he fell into a blackness even more complete than the one that had brought him here.

Reyga was unsure how to proceed. He had been pleased to receive a visitor from the Far Planes after so long, but the more he interacted with this Jason Bennett, the more he sensed there was something unusual about the young man. He had not wanted to use *dimsai* on him, but the boy had appeared to be on the verge of hysteria, and he felt there had been no other recourse.

To use *dimsai* on another person could be an uncomfortably intimate, and sometimes even dangerous, experience. Usually nothing happened. Sometimes, however, the person's deepest thoughts and emotions were revealed. And if the person had any significant *dimsai* ability of their own, the results could be unpredictable. *Dimsai* backlash had felled more than one *saiken* in years past. For this reason, one of the first things Reyga had been taught as a student was not to use his power on another sentient creature unless it was absolutely necessary.

This time, he sensed something in the young man. It was as if some nocturnal beast, disturbed in its slumber, had sleepily opened one eye, glanced about, and then drifted back to its mysterious dreams. It had been a somewhat unnerving sensation, and one that Reyga had not experienced before.

When Jason Bennett fainted, he knew he would not be able catch him. So, he used his power to prevent the young man from being harmed when he hit the ground. Again, he felt the sensation of something on the verge of awakening. It had been most unsettling, and he resolved that, barring the direst of emergencies, he would not use *dimsai* on Jason Bennett again.

After getting the boy into the spare bed, he walked back into the main room and sat down to consider the situation. He picked up a nearby scroll and stared blankly at it, tapping it on his knee as he considered his next steps. After a few minutes, he roused himself with a small shake of his head. This was accomplishing nothing.

He walked over to the portal on the wall and touched a spot on the frame. The image in the portal rippled, and then changed. He waited patiently until a figure stepped into view.

"Greetings, Loremaster," the figure intoned as the head inclined briefly. "May the mantle of wisdom ever rest upon your shoulders."

He bowed. "May your power be exceeded only by your honor, High One."

Formalities complete, both he and the High One assumed more relaxed poses. The High One was a tall, lean man who, even when relaxed, conveyed an aura of subdued power.

"Hello, Reyga," the High One said with a warm smile. "What can I do for you? I hope you are well?"

He returned the smile. "Oh, I am quite well, thank you." His smile faded. "I have received a visitor."

"Indeed? And since you felt it necessary to contact me, may I assume we are talking about a Far Planer?"

"Yes, High One. It is a young man by the name of Jason Bennett."

The High One hesitated for an instant before answering. "Interesting. This would be the first in several years. We had almost decided the Far Planes visitors to be at an end."

"I was rather surprised myself," he said. "Nevertheless, I was quite pleased to receive the young man into my home. But I have encountered something rather peculiar."

"Peculiar, eh? It must be more than just peculiar for you to have contacted me about it. Tell me."

He told the High One of the arrival of Jason Bennett, and their conversation. He recounted his visitor's rising agitation until he had been forced to use *dimsai* to restrain him. Then he mentioned the strange sensation he felt both times he used power on him.

"So you see, High One, I decided to seek guidance regarding what to do with this young man. I had originally intended to take him to Drey's Glenn and entrust him to the village leaders, but when I had this most unusual experience, I became unsure as to the wisdom of that course."

The High One nodded. "You were right in coming to me with this. Tell me, did this Jason Bennett show any signs that he might have any *dimsai* ability himself?"

"No more than any other Far Planer. But I only conversed with him for a short time before he fainted. No doubt from portal sickness."

The High One considered for a moment, then said, "Proceed with your original plans, but after introducing him to the local authorities bring him here. While no Far Planer save one has yet to show any *dimsai* ability, until we know what caused your unusual experience it would not be wise to allow him to roam freely in our land.

"Do not use a portal for your transportation. It may unsettle him again, and the time spent on your way will allow you to learn more of him. I will send Captain Gatlor to accompany you. While you travel, I will consult with the Circle and see if there is anything I can find in the ancient texts that might help us to determine the best course of action."

"Thank you, High One. You are most wise. Tell me, if he should ask questions, which he almost certainly will, how much should I tell him? I have already given him a general history of our world."

"Hmm. We dare not give him too much information until we know more about him. On the other hand, we do not want to arouse any suspicion on his part, and create an enemy where none may exist."

He was silent for a moment, then continued. "Very well, you are free to tell him anything he wishes to know about our society and its laws and customs. You may also tell him of the different races of Teleria. But unless he asks, make no mention of *dimsai,* and do not use any more power in his view. I have no doubt that he will ask how you restrained him, but tell him only enough to quench his curiosity, then change the subject if possible. Do not tell him any more about *dimsai* than you absolutely must."

"I will do as you say, High One."

"One more thing, Loremaster Reyga. Do not mention our adversary to him. Until we know more about him, we cannot be sure where his loyalties will eventually lie."

2
A New Day Dawns

Misshapen trees with gnarled, twisted trunks surrounded Jason. He thought he saw tortured faces in the bark, frozen in expressions of horror and despair. *Where am I?* He didn't see anyone else, but the primal sounds coming from the shadows told him he wasn't alone.

He spun to his left at a sudden blur of motion. Nothing was there. Lightning flashed overhead, but not the bluish-white lightning he knew. The incandescent streaks tearing at the dark sky above him were garish shades of red and purple.

He couldn't see a way out in any direction. *How did I get here?* His breath came in hard, short gasps, and his heart felt like it was about to burst from his chest.

A glimmer of light caught his attention through the dark trees. A voice called his name. *That sounds like Dad!* If he could only get to the light, all of this would go away and he would be all right.

He crashed through the underbrush toward the light, fighting his way through the vines and creepers. Branches tore at his shirt. The voice calling his name grew louder as he got closer. After what seemed an eternity, he broke into a small clearing where a bonfire clawed at the darkness, illuminating everything within its reach with a fiery, orange glow.

A figure stood silhouetted before the fire. His father! He ran forward, almost overcome with relief. As he reached out, the figure turned toward him. He found himself staring into the slate gray eyes of an old man who began laughing maniacally, while shrieking Jason's name over and over again.

Jason jerked upright, drenched in sweat, looking into the same gray eyes as the ones in his dream. Hands grasped his shoulders. He knocked them away, expecting to hear the insane laughter again. But these eyes weren't filled with the lunacy from the dream, but with concern and compassion.

"Jason Bennett." The voice in his dream.

"Jason Bennett," Reyga repeated. "Wake up, my boy. You were having a bad dream."

He shook his head and took a deep breath, blinking to clear his vision. Once he was sure he was awake, he looked around the room. It was small, with little more in it than the bed he was in and a couple of chests. Against one wall was another bookshelf filled with books and scrolls. A small window let in a cool breeze.

"Oh, man," he groaned, "it wasn't just a dream."

"No, Jason Bennett, that was most definitely a nightmare you were having."

He flopped back on the bed. "I was talking about being *here*. Until just now, I had been hoping this was all a dream and I would eventually wake up in my own bed." He looked at Reyga. "But that's not going to happen, is it?" It was more a statement of harsh reality than a question.

"I am afraid not," Reyga said. "This is your home now. At least it will be unless and until we find a way to open portals to other worlds and dimensions. And we have been trying to do that for many, many years."

Jason was silent as he tried to assimilate the fact that he was trapped on another world, separated from his family, friends, and everything he had ever known.

Reyga stood up. "Come. The morning is half spent and we have a bit of a journey ahead of us. It is time to get up. I have brought you something to eat while you get ready."

The mention of food brought a wave of nausea. "Please don't mention food. I think I'm gonna puke."

Reyga cocked his head. "Puke?"

His stomach churning, Jason replied miserably, "Yeah, puke." At Reyga's blank look he said, "You know…puke. Barf? Hurl? Blow chunks? Toss your cookies?" Still seeing no sign that Reyga understood, Jason added, "Um, throw up? Be sick?"

At last, recognition dawned in the old man's face. "Ah, finally I understand, Jason Bennett."

"It's just Jason. Bennett is my last name. You can just call me Jason. Anyway, what the heck did you do to me?"

"Do to you? What do you mean?"

"I mean, how did you knock me out like that? Whatever you did, I've got one whale of a hangover from it."

Reyga looked confused again. "Hangover…hangover…ah." He nodded. "The way you feel right now is not due to anything I have done, Jason Ben...pardon me...Jason. You are suffering from what we call portal sickness. It is harmless, and will pass soon, but it is not a pleasant experience."

"Portal sickness?"

"Occasionally, a first time traveler will find his system upset by the trip through a portal. It is similar to the problem some people have of becoming ill while on a boat, although a bit more intense."

That's the understatement of the year, he thought. The only time he could ever remember feeling like this was when he had developed a case of stomach flu, a sinus infection, and mono all at the same time.

"When you fainted," Reyga continued, "I realized what had happened, and, anticipating your condition this morning, I brought you a particular fruit to eat that is a known cure for portal sickness." He held out a small tray with five or six slices of something that looked like a miniature grapefruit on it. "Here, eat this. It will help you recover more quickly."

Jason didn't reach for the plate.

"Please. I promise that within the hour the way you feel right now will be nothing more than a memory."

He took the tray, frowning at its contents.

Reyga muttered something under his breath, picked up one of the slices of fruit, and took a bite from it. From the look on his face as he ate it, Jason guessed this was one of Reyga's favorite foods. The old man's pleasure was evident as he chewed slowly, his eyes half closed and a slight smile on his face.

After he swallowed, Reyga sighed in obvious contentment. Then he looked at Jason once more. "Again, I ask you to eat. You have nothing to fear, and I assure you it will make you feel better. After all, had I wished you harm, I did have all night."

He couldn't argue with that, so he slowly picked up a slice, and, with one more look at Reyga, placed it in his mouth. Trying to hide his trepidation, he bit down.

Instantly, succulent juices exploded into his mouth. The plate almost fell to the floor at the intense flavor of the fruit. It tasted like a cross between an orange and a lemon, but without the sour bite one would expect from such a combination. A hint of sweetness served as a counterpoint to the tangy citrus, while weaving in and out of the other flavors was an echo of mint. The mint was more pronounced in the odor, which filled his nostrils and immediately began to clear the fog from his head. Reveling in the unexpected flavor, he got completely lost in the experience.

He came back to reality when his hand reached for another slice only to find that he had already eaten them all. He looked at the empty plate, and then looked at Reyga, as if to accuse him of stealing the other pieces while he wasn't looking.

The amused look on the old man's face seemed to confirm his suspicions. He was about to say something, when Reyga's face broke into a broad grin. The old man's eyes opened wide as he leaned forward. "At last, Jason Bennett, *I have you!*"

At Jason's recoil and alarmed look, Reyga burst into laughter. Between guffaws and snorts, he managed to say, "Peace, Jason Bennett, peace. I merely jest with you."

Reyga's merry laughter continued for several seconds. At last, his mirth began to subside. As he wiped the tears from his eyes, he took a deep breath and exhaled noisily. With one last stifled giggle, Reyga regained his composure and said with a twinkle in his eye, "Please forgive me, Jason. I am sorry for alarming you, but you seemed so certain that I meant to poison you with the calintha fruit that I simply could not resist."

As Jason sighed in relief, he tried to look annoyed with the old man, but the lingering taste of the fruit on his tongue refused to allow such a mood. Almost against his will, he grinned sheepishly.

"Ah, Jason, at least now I can be sure that you no longer believe yourself to be dreaming." Reyga looked at the window. "In any event, we must prepare. I trust you are feeling better?"

He had to confess that Reyga had been right. The fruit had dispelled his feelings of nausea and sickness as if they too had been nothing more than a dream.

"I'm feeling better," he said, "but would it be possible to get some more of that?"

"I am afraid I do not have any more," Reyga replied. "It is a very rare fruit that can only be harvested one sixday out of the year. It is only given in cases of portal sickness, such as you experienced, and for occasions of state. And even in the state occasions, each guest is allowed only two pieces. What I gave to you was the last I had."

"Ah. Okay."

His disappointment must have been plain to see, for Reyga said, "Perhaps we will see if we can get a bit more. After all, it is not every day that we get a visitor from the Far Planes. I suppose that should qualify as a special occasion."

As Jason climbed out of bed, Reyga gestured toward the chest by the window. "There is a basin of water for you to wash and refresh yourself, and I found some clothes that I believe will fit you. The ones you have on, besides being rather unusual for Teleria, are somewhat damp from whatever you experienced in your dreams. If the clothes I brought do not fit as well as you would like, they will at least suffice for now. We can find other clothing on the way."

Jason went to the basin, removed his shirt, and splashed water on his face and arms to wash away the drying sweat from his nightmare. He picked up a small towel lying beside the basin. "On the way? Where are we going?"

"There is a village not far from here. We will go there first, where I will introduce you to the village leaders, and you may get some more exposure to our culture and society. We can also purchase some clothing for you if you wish, and we will need to secure supplies for our journey."

"Journey?" Jason dropped the towel and picked up the rough cloth shirt Reyga had supplied. "Journey to where?"

Reyga hesitated a moment before answering. "There are some people who wish to meet you. It has been several years since we have had a visitor from one of the Far Planes, and they would like to find out more about you and your world."

"Yeah? How'd they know I was here?"

"I apologize if you wished your presence here to remain secret. But, as a Loremaster, it was my duty to report receiving a visitor from the Far Planes. So, after getting you to bed last night, I contacted a colleague of mine to let them know of your arrival."

"Oh. How?"

"I used the portal. Do you remember me telling you last night that we had been able to create successful portals within our world?"

"Yeah."

"It was through the portal you saw in the front room that I made contact with those who wish to meet you."

"Are they, um, what did you call yourself? Loremaster? Are they Loremasters too?"

"Yes, there is a group of Loremasters that wishes to see you, and to learn about you and about your world."

"Can they help me get back home? You said that there were some people who were working on portals to other worlds. Is that them?"

Reyga shook his head. "No, those that are studying portal creation do not reside at Lore's Haven."

"Well, I want to meet them. If there's any way for me to get back home, I want to know."

"I understand your desire to return home," Reyga said, "but we must first meet with the Loremasters at Lore's Haven. After that, we may be able to meet with the others."

"So, what is a Loremaster anyway? Are there a bunch of you guys running around?"

"Let us finish preparing," Reyga said. "Then, while we travel to the village, I will tell you of Loremasters."

As he walked through the bustling halls of Lore's Haven, Tal Vardyn, Pearl Loremaster and the High One of the Circle of Nine, did not need to consult with the ancient texts. After studying them for decades, he could recite all twenty-three volumes from memory. What had come unbidden to his mind the night before filled him with foreboding, and had been a constant theme winding its way in and out of his restless dreams.

It was a prophecy given over eight hundred years before by a seer named Taleth…

From a far land, Jaben shall come.
The last to arrive, he will already be here.
Powerful and powerless,
Our hope and our doom are in his hands.

His destruction is our hope.
His denial is our doom.
For our land to live, the far land must die.

When Reyga mentioned Jason Bennett's name, the prophecy leapt into Tal's mind like a Beja cat pouncing upon its prey. And like the feline hunter's finger-long claws, the words of the prophecy sank into the High One's thoughts and refused to be dislodged.

Even with his head muddled from the futile attempts at sleep the night before, Tal knew that his actions regarding this young man could very well determine Teleria's fate for generations to come. He spotted a page and gave him instructions to assemble the Circle.

He also knew that he would be unable to make any rational decisions with his thoughts racing as they were. He found a relatively quiet corner, closed his eyes, and concentrated upon stilling his mind. After a few moments, he opened his eyes. Better. He would have time for a more thorough period of meditation later.

"At least I hope I will," he said to himself, and headed for the Circle chamber to prepare.

The sun was climbing into the clear morning sky as Jason and Reyga walked out the door. The first thing Jason noticed as he stepped outside was the multitude of odors filling the air. He looked upwind, and then slowed until he finally came to a complete stop. He had seen plenty of backyard gardens before, but this was surely the king of all gardens, if there was such a thing.

There were at least a dozen different species of plants, each bearing a crop that would be the envy of any farmer back in Missouri. Some looked a little like tomato plants, but the fruits that hung from them were as large as soccer balls. He wondered how they kept from collapsing under the load.

He heard Reyga chuckle behind him. "Ah, I see you have noticed my modest attempt at gardening."

'Modest' was not the word he would have chosen to describe Reyga's garden. "Are you kidding? We have neighbors back home that would give their right arms to be able to grow a garden like this!"

Reyga smiled. "I must confess that I too am pleased with how it turned out this year. Gardening and growing things has long been a…well, a hobby of mine, as it were."

"Man, if this is what you consider a hobby, then you give the word a whole new meaning."

"You are most kind, Jason," Reyga said, bowing his head slightly. "Now," he continued, "we must be on our way. There is an escort awaiting us in the village."

"Escort?"

"Yes. Those who wish to meet you have sent some people to accompany us on our way. Their presence is merely for our protection."

"What about the portals? Didn't you say you have stable portals in your world? Isn't there a portal to where we want to go?"

"There is, but considering your first portal experience, it was decided that this route would be better. This will also give you a chance to see more of our world and our culture."

He wasn't sure he agreed, but didn't say anything. Now that he knew what to expect, especially the tasty fruit, he didn't think a portal trip would be all that bad.

"How do the portals work anyway?" he asked.

Reyga started to answer, and then stopped. "I am afraid that is a question better answered by others," he finally said. "Perhaps when we get to Lore's Haven, someone there will be able to explain the process to you."

"Oh. Well, okay."

Reyga strode off toward one end of the glade. Jason noticed a small trail there. As he fell in behind the old man, he gazed about, taking in his surroundings. The trees surrounding them were clothed in robust foliage. Most of the leaves and shrubs were the various standard shades of green, but here and there, sprinkled among the green, were plants with leaves of delicate teal, vibrant purple, or even an occasional pastel pink. A bright blue sky peeked down at them through the leaves and branches, and a light breeze playfully ruffled Jason's hair.

The woods were unmistakably full of life. Screeches, tweets, and trills filled the air. They seemed to blend together into one harmonious song, like an orchestra playing an intricate concerto. He was about to remind Reyga of his promise to tell him what a Loremaster was when he heard the flutter of wings. With a startling gust of air beside his ear, a bird the size of a small hawk landed on his shoulder.

Sharp talons gripped his shoulder through his shirt. He came to a stop. "Um, Reyga?"

Reyga turned. When he saw the bird, his eyes widened. He seemed to be at a loss for words.

Out of the corner of his eye, Jason tried to get a look at his unexpected passenger. The bird was yellow, with a burst of red and blue on its chest. The beak less than two inches from his eye had a cruel hook that marked this bird as a predator. It returned his gaze without blinking,

He tried not to flinch as the bird shifted. "What should I do?"

Reyga's glance wandered from the bird back to Jason's face. "Hm? Oh! I apologize. I was rather surprised to see a bird, especially one of this kind, on your shoulder. Be at ease. You are in no danger."

He relaxed, and then stiffened once again as the bird tightened its razor sharp grip. "Okay," he said. "That's good to know, but how do I get this bird off me?"

Reyga slowly began walking toward him. As the Loremaster approached, the bird screeched as if to warn him away. After holding its ground for a few moments, it launched into the air and winged its way toward the clear morning sky, giving another offended screech as it flew. They watched as it came to roost at the top of a tall tree. Once more, the bird sounded its defiance.

"What was that all about?" Jason asked, rubbing his shoulder. "I thought for a moment you forgot how to breathe when you turned around and saw that bird."

"Hmm?" Reyga responded, his eyes still on the bird. Then he turned his attention back to his companion. "Please forgive me, Jason. It is somewhat unusual to actually see a bird of this species. They are rather rare. I can recall only two other times in my entire life when I have actually seen one in the wild."

"Really? What kind of bird is it?" Jason asked. He looked up at the top of the tree where the bird still watched them.

Reyga looked at the bird again. "It is a carilian, although it is more commonly called a fortunewing."

"Why?"

"Legend has it that one's experience with the bird can predict their future. To hear the call of the fortunewing as it is perched is said to be a good omen, but to hear its call in flight is considered a bad omen."

"Uh huh. So what kind of omen is it when it lands on you?"

"I do not know," Reyga said as his gaze returned to Jason. "I have never heard tell of one actually landing on someone."

Then, with one last glance at the bird, he said, "Well! To be sure, it was an interesting experience to begin our day, but we need to continue on. We still need to buy supplies for the journey, and our escort is, by now, no doubt awaiting us."

"Okay," Jason said, as they began walking again. "You were going to tell me about Loremasters. What is a Loremaster? How does someone become one? Are there a lot of you?"

Reyga walked for a few moments before answering. Finally, he said, "A Loremaster is a man or woman who has chosen to be the caretaker of a certain area of knowledge. It is the responsibility of the Loremaster to preserve the knowledge in his or her area of expertise, and to add to that knowledge whenever possible.

"As they start getting on in years, they select an apprentice to whom they will pass on everything they know. When the old Loremaster becomes too feeble to retain the post, or when they pass on, the apprentice takes over and the knowledge is preserved. And no, to answer your last question, there are not many Loremasters. There are nine on the Circle to be precise."

"And you're one of them."

"Yes."

"What, one day you just said, 'Hey, I think I'll be a Loremaster'?"

Reyga chuckled. "Oh no, Jason, there is much more to it than that. Each Loremaster has a group of young men and women who share an affinity for the same area of knowledge. They assist him in his studies. They will serve together working with the Loremaster for many years. From this group, one will be chosen to be the Loremaster's apprentice. It has been this way since the system of Loremasters was established almost fifteen centuries ago."

"Alright. You said you were the Emerald Loremaster. What is that? What are you the Loremaster of? And where are your people?"

"My assistants are at Lore's Haven, where we are headed. The place we just left is my home. I was taking a few days of rest, when you arrived. Your timing was fortuitous, for I usually spend more time at the Haven than I do at home."

"Lucky for me, I guess. So what's an Emerald Loremaster? What exactly are you the Loremaster of?"

"Each Loremaster is given an insignia, or symbol, signifying their office. It was decided long ago that the symbols would incorporate gemstones, to indicate the beauty and desirability of knowledge. For my office, it is the emerald, as you see in my staff. Other Loremasters will have different gems depending upon their area of study."

"Okay," Jason said, a little impatiently. "So, once again, what is your area of knowledge? What does the emerald stand for? What are you the Loremaster of?"

Reyga looked somewhat embarrassed. "The Emerald Loremaster preserves the knowledge of plants and agriculture."

Jason stopped walking. "Sooo, the garden…" he began.

"Is not quite so impressive an accomplishment as it would have been had it been grown by someone else." Reyga finished, turning back to the path with a slight smile on his face.

"Not exactly a hobby then, is it?" He'd caught the smile as Reyga turned away. He thought about the garden and the earlier incident with the calintha fruit. "You're an ornery, old goat, aren't you?" he muttered under his breath

Reyga turned back to him. "I beg your pardon? What does it mean to be an 'ornery, old goat'?"

As Jason stammered for an answer, he mentally filed away the fact that Reyga must have exceptional hearing. Trying to keep his face from turning red, he said quickly, "It's, ah, a term of, um, respect. Yes! It's, uh, something we say back home to people we admire, that's all." He hoped he sounded convincing as he watched to see how Reyga would respond.

Reyga considered his words for a moment, then smiled and inclined his head. “I thank you then, Jason, for your kind words.” Then he turned back to the trail and resumed walking.

Jason breathed a sigh of relief and vowed to himself never to say anything about Reyga unless the old man was nowhere within a two-mile radius.

After a few minutes of walking, he spoke up again. “So, let’s go back to what you were talking about yesterday. What happened after the war? If they had all this technology, why didn’t they just rebuild everything?”

“Indeed, why did they not just rebuild? That is the obvious question. Very well, let me think. Where did I stop yesterday? Hmmm...” Reyga paused for a moment as he thought, and then his eyes brightened. “Ah yes,” he said. “Now I remember.” As he resumed walking, he continued his tale from the previous day.

“In the days before the Devastation, we have learned that our world had a population of over seven billion people. After the dust had settled, it is estimated that there were less than thirty million left alive.” He gave a heavy sigh. “Over ninety-nine percent of the population dead, with many more to die in the sixdays and spans following. Mankind, once dominant on our world, had been reduced to a mere shadow of what he once was.

“The planet also paid a high price for our foolishness,” he said. “Because of the terrible weapons used, large sections of our lands were rendered uninhabitable for generations. But even that paled in comparison to the effects of the most devastating weapons.”

The light breeze suddenly felt cooler, and a solitary cloud obscured the sun, casting a pall on the forest around them. Reyga didn’t seem to notice as he went on with his tale.

“While we do not know what they were, we have learned that the combatants had developed frightening weapons. These terrible devices could literally tear rifts in the very fabric of space, essentially opening holes into other dimensions.

“From what we have learned, the rifts would usually collapse upon themselves within a matter of moments. A small number, though, did not close, and began to let in forces and energies completely alien to our world. It was one such rift that ended the Devastation.

"It happened on the second day of the war. A rift opened up, and some type of energy began pouring into our world. The energy that came through this rift nullified something the ancients called 'electricity.' Apparently, all of their amazing technology, from the greatest machine to the smallest, depended upon this force for its operation. With it gone, all of mankind's technology was rendered useless.

"Within the space of a few hours, mankind had gone from being master of the planet, to being just another contender for survival, with less natural skills than the plants and animals we had dominated for so long."

As the sun re-emerged from behind the cloud, Reyga paused to glance at the sky. He took out a cloth to wipe his face and neck, and then turned to Jason as he continued the story.

"To be sure," he said, "this rift is quite probably the only thing that allowed anything at all to survive the Devastation. With the electricity gone, the rulers found it impossible to use any more of their weapons. So, as suddenly as it began, the Devastation was over, with only the lingering effects of the weapons remaining. Those lingering effects, however, changed our world forever."

Reyga glanced around at the lush foliage surrounding them. With a sorrowful shake of his head, he continued. "The days following the end of the Devastation were full of confusion, anger, and despair. With our world in ruins, no one knew what to do, where to begin rebuilding, or if rebuilding would even be possible.

"As the people began exploring the tattered remnants of their lands, they mapped out the areas of the greatest desolation in order to avoid them. They marked these on whatever maps they could find or make. Eventually, they found places where they could begin the slow process of rebuilding."

Reyga began walking once more as he went on with his tale.

"As the survivors began to spread out and explore, reports started circulating about strange and bizarre creatures. Stories were told about areas where the world seemed almost alien. There were even rumors about visitors from other worlds.

"At first, of course, these tales were dismissed as nothing more than dreams, or the ranting of the insane, or perhaps words spoken from the depths of a bottle of spirits. Some, however, did not discount these stories. They went out in search of the things they had heard about.

"These explorers came back with strange creatures," he said. "Animals were found, and sometimes people, with extra limbs, or sometimes even an extra head. Some had become extremely sensitive to light, or to heat. Most eventually died out without ever passing these traits to offspring. But not all. Of those that survived, a few became the progenitors of some of the races in Teleria today.

"These were all explained away as strange mutations. But then other creatures were found, creatures that seemed almost to be some sort of merger between two different living things. These could not be explained by mutation.

"The most horrific unions were the ones where one of the living beings was, or had been, a human. In most cases, the creature produced from these unions was quite insane and either very violent, or almost catatonic from despair. No one knew how these shocking mergers had happened, or what to do for these unfortunate souls. Eventually, a few that survived their change also became the forefathers of new races."

When Reyga stopped talking, Jason said, "So there are more than just humans here?"

"Oh yes. There are quite a number of races living in Teleria. You will see some of them during our travels."

The rest of the journey passed uneventfully. Reyga pointed out various plants and animals, and told Jason about some of the different races of Teleria. Reyga told him about the Ferrin, a cat-like race of people, and about the Grithor, a folk that found light to be extremely uncomfortable and so had become a nocturnal race, living mainly underground. He told Jason about several other races as well, including one called the Shanthi, who were able to alter the pigment in their skin and hair in order to blend in with their surroundings. Unique physiology in their hands and feet also gave them the ability to cling to walls and other surfaces.

"We will have one of the Shanthi accompanying us on our journey, although you may never see her," Reyga said.

"Her?" Jason asked.

"Yes, a young woman by the name of Lenai."

"So why won't I see her?"

"The Shanthi are a rather secretive people," Reyga replied. "This was not always so, but with their abilities of concealment, some of the Shanthi turned to, shall we say, less honorable methods of providing for their needs. They became a mistrusted and misunderstood people, which caused them to isolate themselves from the other races, especially humans. You may occasionally hear people refer to them as 'shifters.' It is not a term I would advise using should you ever find yourself in their company."

He made a note of Reyga's warning, and they continued on their way, with Reyga changing the topic from the races of Teleria to its history and customs. This was just a little too close to his dad's discourses for his liking.

At the thought of his father, he felt a pang of homesickness. Bruce Bennett was a moderately successful businessman, whose penchant for teaching his son all about his lineage was, at times annoying, and usually terminally boring. *I'd give anything to hear one of Dad's history lessons now*, he thought.

He wondered what his parents were doing, and what they thought had happened to him. Reyga said there was no way back, but he wasn't going to give up until he found a way.

As Reyga's oration on Telerian history continued, he let his mind drift, giving the occasional grunt or 'uh, huh' to show that he was still listening, even though his thoughts were a world away.

3
First Impressions

In time, their path joined a broader road, which came to a village Jason assumed was their destination.

"This is Drey's Glenn," Reyga said. "It is the largest village in this province."

Jason looked at the buildings around them. They were a variety of shapes, sizes, and colors, some made from stone like Reyga's home, some from wood, and some a combination of both. They ranged from simple cottages to larger buildings with intricately carved wood and stone architecture.

Not much further along, they approached a market area. Vendors hawked their wares at the tops of their voices, women exchanged gossip and compared recipes, and buyers and sellers engaged in spirited bartering sessions. For the most part, the people looked human, although their clothes reminded him of a renaissance festival he'd been to about a year before.

Interspersed among the others, he saw people that didn't quite fit the mold of what he thought of as typical humans. Nearby, a slender man who looked about eight feet tall walked along a line of stalls. He had pale, greenish skin, and moved with a willowy grace that didn't seem possible for someone of his proportions. A little further away, haggling with a merchant, was a creature with a stocky build, canine features, and a layer of short brown fur covering its face and body. It reminded him of a werewolf from one of those late-night 'B' movies. Try as he might, though, he couldn't remember ever seeing one where the Wolfman quibbled over the price of beets.

Children ran here and there, playing the typical games of catch and tag. The sound of their happy laughter floated above the clamor of the market. As they entered the central square, he spied a group of children playing catch with a ball about the size of a volleyball. He slowed. *Something doesn't seem right about that game.* He squinted to get a better look. Then he realized the children weren't actually touching the ball. Just as it would get close to one of them, they would hold up their hands as if to catch it, but it would stop a few inches from their hands and reverse course, flying back toward one of the other children.

He stopped, blinked hard a couple of times, and looked again, but what he saw confirmed his initial impression. He stared at the group until the ball bounced off one boy's head and away between the houses. The children laughed and ran after it. He was still looking after them when a hand grabbed his shoulder.

"Whoa!" he exclaimed as he spun around. He saw Reyga standing with his hand grasping air where Jason's shoulder had been. "Geez, don't *do* that!"

"I apologize for startling you," Reyga said, "but we need to meet our escort and finish preparing. We still have to introduce you to the village leaders as well."

"Yeah, okay." He glanced back toward where the game had been. "Hey, did you see those kids over there?"

"Kids?"

"I mean children. Did you see them?"

Reyga looked around. "I see many children. To which ones are you referring?"

"They were over there between those buildings." He pointed toward where he had seen the group.

Reyga's gaze followed Jason's finger. "I see no children there," he said.

"Well, they're gone now. But they were playing a game with a ball, only they weren't touching the ball."

"What do you mean?"

"They were playing a game of catch, but they didn't actually catch the ball."

Reyga looked confused. "You mean they kept dropping it?"

"No. The ball would come to one of them, and then, without them touching it, it would fly back to one of the others."

"Are you sure?" Reyga asked. He looked back toward the building. "Perhaps there was a string or twine attached to the ball and you just did not notice it."

Jason shook his head. "I don't think so," he replied. "That ball was flying on its own."

"Well, I do not see the children you are talking about."

He sighed, defeated. Suddenly he remembered the chair from the previous night. "Hey!" he exclaimed. "That reminds me. How did you—"

"Oh, look," Reyga said. "There is our escort." He headed across the square. "Come, Jason. Quickly!" he called back over his shoulder.

Jason looked in the direction Reyga was walking, but didn't see anything that resembled an escort. He didn't want to get lost in the crowd, though, so he gave one last glance to where he had seen the odd game and then hurried after Reyga.

After several moments of twisting and turning through the crowd, they made it to the other side of the square. Reyga stopped. "There they are."

Jason looked, but at first didn't see what the Loremaster was pointing at. Then he saw them, and, having seen them once, couldn't understand how he missed them the first time. They stood in front of a small stone building in an island of calm amidst a sea of bustling bodies. Even in the crowded square, there was an open area around them, as if invisible barricades were keeping passers-by at arm's length. Two appeared from this distance to be human, but the third was definitely not. He stood at least as tall as the pale green man, but was built like a juggernaut.

At first, Jason thought the giant was wearing some sort of brownish armor under a leather shirt. Then he realized the 'armor' was actually the man's skin, which looked as solid as steel plating. The scar-covered arms were as big as Jason's thigh, and his head appeared to sit directly on his shoulders, without any interference from something as trivial as a neck. Looking at him, Jason was pretty sure he could take on an entire professional football team and come out of the fray needing nothing more than a toothpick and a nap, and he wasn't entirely sure about the nap.

The goliath didn't move as they approached, but his deep-set eyes watched them steadily from under the overhang of his forehead. Peeking out over each of his massive shoulders was the handle of a weapon, but Jason couldn't tell what kind. Underneath the unwavering gaze, he didn't feel quite bold enough to ask.

As they got closer, he tore his eyes from the mammoth figure and looked at the other two men. One wore soft, russet-colored leather and metal bracers on his wrists. He appeared to be picking rather sharp-looking teeth with a short white blade as he leaned against the front of the building.

When they walked up, he stopped his oral hygiene, stretched, and yawned. It was then Jason realized that the 'blade' was actually a claw, which retracted into his fingers along with the others Jason saw. From what Reyga had told him on the way here, Jason decided he must be a Ferrin. The fangs he saw and vertical black slits in the middle of gold-colored eyes seemed to confirm it.

No weapons were evident on him, but Jason was sure that the claws would more than suffice. His amber eyes regarded them with a gaze that was part boredom, and part amusement, as if he had a secret that only he knew.

Jason looked at the third man, who appeared even at close range to be human, although Jason got the impression that he might be the most dangerous of the three.

His ice-blue eyes, which had rested on them briefly when they stopped, constantly swept the crowded surroundings. He had an athletic build and a cruel double scar down the left side of his face. He wore hard leather armor and boots, and looked to be carrying an entire arsenal of blades. Jason could see four short daggers in a bandolier across his chest, a sword strapped to his back jutting over his left shoulder, a shorter sword at his waist on his left side, a long dagger on his right, and another knife strapped to one boot. He also carried an ornate bow, the arrows for which showed over his right shoulder.

Jason wondered how many more weapons he was carrying that he couldn't see, and perhaps even more perplexing, how he could walk with that much metal strapped to him. *I'd love to introduce this guy to an airport metal detector*. As he imagined the security guard's reaction, he couldn't suppress a giggle that forced its way from his lips.

The man was instantly in front of him, glacial eyes boring into his own. "Something amuses you, boy?" he asked in a voice that promised bloodshed if Jason gave the wrong answer.

For the second time since his arrival, Jason was unable to speak. This time, however, it was because his tongue had a stronger sense of self-preservation than his brain did. It adamantly refused to relay any of the amazingly witty comments his brain was sending. He could only stand there, eyes wide, hoping Reyga would be able to save him from what he was sure was certain death, or at the very least, permanent maiming.

Reyga broke the tense silence. “Peace, Gatlor Bortas. This is Jason Bennett, the one with whom the Circle wishes to speak.” The subtle emphasis he placed on the last phrase implied that to harm Jason would be to incur the wrath of the Circle.

Without removing his gaze from Jason, Gatlor replied, “My apologies, Loremaster Reyga. Please forgive me for my hasty reaction.” Jason didn’t think he sounded very sorry. *Probably shouldn’t push it, though.* At last, the man looked at Reyga, and he stepped back. He bowed his head briefly to the Loremaster.

“I am commissioned to bring you both to Lore's Haven. Upon my honor and by my blood and blade, I will see that you arrive safely,” he said. He turned to Jason. “So, you are the one the Circle is so eager to see? The Far Planer?”

Jason shrugged. “I guess so.”

Gatlor studied him. “We have been sworn to bring you safely to Lore's Haven, and this we will do, but mark my words: if one of us tells you to do something, even if you do not understand why, do it immediately and ask any questions later. Your life may depend upon it. Hopefully, we will have an uneventful journey, but nevertheless, do not forget what I have said.”

A bit uncertainly, Jason nodded his agreement, and Gatlor continued. “Now, allow me to introduce my companions.”

He walked over to the cat-man and said, “This is Seerka. He is Ferrin, in case you are unfamiliar with the different races of Teleria.”

Seerka briefly bowed his head. Jason noticed that the man’s slightly pointed ears sat rather high on both sides of his head, and appeared to be able to swivel.

“It is an honor to meet someone from the Far Planes,” he said in a silky voice, rolling the ‘r’s.

“Nice to meet you,” Jason replied.

Gatlor moved over to the behemoth. “This is Calador. He is a member of the Dokal race.”

Calador gave a slight nod of his head, and intoned in a voice that was deep, but surprisingly smooth for his appearance, "Far Planer."

Jason nodded back. "Dokal."

Calador stared at Jason for a moment, then a low rumble started in his chest. Jason was alarmed at first, until he realized the giant was chuckling.

"You have spirit, Far Planer," Calador said. "That is good, in its place. Spirit is like a blade. It can save your life, or it can turn and cut you. Be careful when you display it that it does the former rather than the latter."

"I will," Jason said. Feeling suddenly bold, he added, "And my name is Jason, not 'Far Planer.'"

Calador chuckled. "Jason, then."

Something flew over the crowd and landed at Calador's feet. The warriors tensed, but then relaxed as they saw that it was a child's doll.

A little girl's voice rose about the dull roar of the market. "That was mean, Tyrdan! How will I find Lyra now?"

The owner of the voice burst through the edge of the crowd into the middle of the group, blonde curls flying. She stopped as she saw the three warriors.

"Oh!" Her brown eyes grew large as she looked up at the huge Dokal warrior. Then they dropped to the doll resting at the giant's feet. It was obvious she was torn between a fervent desire to run for the cover of the crowd, and her intense longing for her plaything. She fidgeted under the gaze of the group.

Calador bent down and picked up the doll. In the slab of his hand, it looked even smaller than before.

"Is this yours, little one?" he asked gently.

Unable to speak, the girl nodded, tears welling up in her tormented eyes.

The huge warrior squatted down and held the doll out to her.

"Here, child," he said. "Do not be afraid. No one will harm you here."

She shuffled forward. Slowly, she reached out and took the doll from Calador.

"Thank you, sir," she said, hugging the doll to her chest.

"What is your name, little one?" Seerka asked.

"Liana," she said, staring at the ground.

"That is a lovely name," Seerka said.

"And that is a lovely dress," Calador added.

As she heard the compliments, the girl peeked up at the warriors with a bashful smile tugging at the corners of her mouth.

"Thank you," she said shyly. "My mama made this dress for me."

"Your mother is clearly skilled," Seerka said. "It makes you look very pretty."

At this, the girl giggled.

"Who is Tyrdan?" Calador asked.

Her little brow furrowed. "My meanie big brother," she said. "He is always being mean to me."

"Liana! Where are you?" A woman emerged from the crowd, and then stopped as she saw the little girl surrounded by the warriors. A brown-haired boy trailed close behind her.

"Liana," the woman said, as she saw the girl in the midst of the warriors, "why are you bothering these men?"

"Please," Reyga said, "do not be angry with her. She merely came to retrieve her doll, which had apparently gained the power of flight." He cocked his eye at the boy, who edged behind his mother's skirt. "At least, temporarily," he finished.

"Tyrdan threw it, Mama!" the girl proclaimed, pointing at the boy, who suddenly looked very guilty.

Calador looked at the boy. "You must be Tyrdan. Come out where we can see you."

The boy crept out from behind his mother's skirt. She put a protective hand on his shoulder as the Dokal warrior stood up.

From his full height, Calador fixed the boy with a firm gaze and rumbled, "You should be nicer to your sister."

The boy's eyes grew wide as he looked up at the huge warrior staring down at him. "Uh...uh...uh...yes, sir," he finally managed to stammer out. Then he ducked back behind his mother, missing the conspiratorial wink Calador gave her.

Well, he won't forget that *anytime soon*, Jason thought, as he turned away to hide an amused grin.

The mother tried to suppress her own smile as she realized the warrior's intent.

"Thank you, sirs, for finding my daughter," she said. "We come here once a month from Brayden Fenn and I would hate to lose her."

"In truth," Seerka said, "she found us. We merely found her doll."

"You have a lovely daughter," Reyga added. "You should be proud of her."

"Thank y—" the woman started, just as her 'lovely' daughter stuck her tongue out at her brother. She sighed, rolling her eyes at the warriors and drawing chuckles from the escort. "Come along, children," she said, as the three disappeared into the crowd.

After they had left, Jason looked around. "I thought you said there'd be a Shanthi with us?"

"Lenai will join us after we leave the village," Calador rumbled.

Seerka added, "The Shanthi do not enter human villages, and rarely socialize with humans at all. Humans do not trust them; therefore, they do not trust humans."

Gatlor said, "There are a few of the Shanthi that have chosen not to accept what they have been told about humans. While they understand that most humans distrust them, they do not believe it is true of all humans. They are still very cautious," he continued, "and it is difficult to win their trust. But once you have their trust, they are boon companions. Betray that trust, and they can be lethal enemies. Lenai is such a one."

"And you've earned her trust?" Jason asked.

Gatlor shook his head. "Not I," he said. "She accepts me because I have sworn a blood oath to serve the Circle. It is Loremaster Reyga that has earned her trust. I do not know how or where. You would have to ask him."

As Jason looked at Reyga, the Loremaster shook his head. "I am sorry, Jason, but that is one tale I cannot tell you. To do so would be to betray Lenai's trust in me, and that I will not do."

Jason thought about it. "Okay," he said. "That's cool. I understand about keeping confidences. I can respect that."

Reyga inclined his head. "Thank you, Jason. I am glad you feel that way. Perhaps you may be able to win her trust as well. Then I will be able to share this tale with you."

"I would not get your hopes up, young one," Seerka said. "I know several Shanthi, and they are notoriously distant to those whom they do not know, particularly humans."

Jason digested the Ferrin's words for a moment, then said, "Well, we'll see. Stranger things have happened, I guess."

Gatlor grunted. "Not many."

Then, turning to Reyga, Gatlor said, "I have procured pack animals for our journey, and basic food items and supplies. If there is anything else you wish to purchase, you should do it this afternoon. We leave at first light."

Reyga nodded. "We will be ready. Thank you for your preparations. We will meet you here in the morning." He inclined his head to Gatlor, with the warrior reciprocating with a nod. "Come, Jason," Reyga said. "We must secure lodging for the night, purchase some additional supplies, and I still must present you to the village leaders."

After the young man and old Loremaster left, Gatlor turned to the others. "Well? What do you think?"

"I think this may be one of the more interesting assignments I have received from the Circle," Seerka said.

"Oh, aye," Gatlor agreed, with more than a touch of sarcasm, "it will be most interesting." Then, more seriously, "Of course you know we were being watched?"

"When are we not watched?" the Ferrin replied. He showed his fangs in a feral grin. "We are very popular."

"Perhaps, but the attention we received today was for the boy, not for us. What about you, Calador? What are your thoughts?"

The giant warrior considered for a moment, and then said, "I believe there is more to the youth than is readily apparent. I find myself liking him. I would not like to see him or the Loremaster harmed on this journey."

"If he does as told, he should be safe," Gatlor replied. "But I sense a rebellious spirit in him that could get him into trouble."

"Yes," Seerka agreed. "I see a little of the Ferrin in him. Accommodating when it suits them, but following their own choices when it does not."

"Perhaps," Calador said, "but knowing that will simply serve to keep us more alert."

Calador chuckled at the disgusted looks from his companions, then, turning serious again, he asked, "Did you see who was watching us?"

Gatlor scanned the busy square full of people. "No. Whoever, or whatever, observed us was well concealed. I am certain we will be followed."

"All the better to be alert," Calador said. As his companions rolled their eyes at him, he began to laugh again.

Jason followed Reyga as the Loremaster purchased supplies for the journey, including, after a rather lengthy search, a couple of pieces of calintha fruit. Even knowing what to expect, the invigorating flavor and aroma still surprised him. He tried to chew slowly, as Reyga had done, in order to draw out the experience as long as possible.

Then they found a small garment shop where they purchased some clothing and soft leather boots that fit a little better than what Reyga had supplied. After brief introductions to the village leaders, they found an inn and got a room for the night.

As they entered their room and Jason saw the beds, all of his strength seemed to drain down through his feet and disappear into the cracks between the floorboards. He flopped down onto the nearest bed with a groan.

"Man, I'm beat," he said. "I thought I was in better shape than this."

Reyga smiled. "I am sure you are more fit than you feel right now. Remember, this is only your second day. You are still acclimating to our world. That alone can be very draining for some."

"For some? So there have been others that have just popped in from other worlds?"

"Oh, yes," Reyga said. "Centuries ago, it was not at all uncommon. They usually arrived through one of the large rifts, although their journey through the Riftlands was almost always more unsettling than the journey through the rift itself." He sat down on the other bed. "Over the last century, there have been fewer and fewer. It has been several years since our last one. We thought there might be no more until you showed up. Tell me, how did you get from the Riftlands to my home without learning where you were?"

He rolled onto his side. "I didn't," he said. "I walked through that door I told you about, and then I was standing at your place."

"Do you mean to tell me that you came here through a chaotic rift? I had assumed you arrived in the Riftlands, where most others do."

"I don't know. Is that what you call it? A chaotic rift?"

"That is the only way I know of for you to have appeared at my door as you describe." Reyga's brow furled in thought. "But the odds of anyone coming safely through a chaotic rift are astronomical. There has been less than a handful in our recorded history. You are very fortunate indeed."

"So what is a chaotic rift?" he asked, and then opened his mouth in a huge yawn.

"I think perhaps that is a topic for tomorrow," Reyga said. "You are very tired, and we have quite a journey ahead of us. You need to get some rest."

He didn't have the strength to argue. As he closed his eyes, he asked, "How long will it take to get to Lore's Haven?"

"With good weather, and no delays, it is a five day journey."

"Okay, sounds good..." he mumbled as he drifted off to sleep.

From the shadows underneath a tree across from the inn, two pairs of eyes watched the light go out in the upstairs room where the old man and youth were staying. They had seen the escort arrive that morning, and had observed the subsequent meeting with the two who now slept across the road. They had known instantly that the young human was a Far Planer. That by itself was enough to warrant further observation. The fact that he traveled overland with a Loremaster and an escort from Lore's Haven made it even more intriguing.

One of the watchers shadowed them that afternoon as they went about their errands. The other reported what they had seen to the Master, who commanded them to continue watching and reporting. In the darkness, they received new orders from the Master. One scurried off into the dark night, while the other returned its attention to the room above. There was nothing they could do other than watch and wait, at least for now.

4
A Matter of Opinions

Jason woke from a dreamless sleep to someone shaking him. As he pried his gritty eyes open, he saw Reyga.

"Oh, did I doze off while you were talking?" he asked with a yawn. "Sorry about that. What were you saying?"

"No, my boy, it is time to get up. You have slept through the night, and now we must meet our escort and get underway for the Haven."

He stretched, and rubbed his eyes. "Are you sure? It doesn't feel like I slept all night."

"Oh, I am quite sure," Reyga said with a chuckle. "And if I know Gatlor, he and the others are already waiting for us even now."

"Okay, okay." He struggled to his feet. "I'm up." He looked around for the clothing they had purchased the previous day until he realized he was still wearing it. "Is there anything to eat?"

"We will eat as we travel," Reyga replied. "Time is of the essence. If we are late you will find that Gatlor's tongue is every bit as sharp as his blades."

They gathered their supplies and headed out into the pre-dawn darkness. Jason was glad Reyga was with him. He would have been totally lost otherwise. The deep shadows made everything appear eerily different from what little he remembered. The Loremaster seemed to know precisely where he was going, and soon Jason saw the stone building where they had previously met their escort. The three warriors were waiting for them as if they had never left, this time with gear and animals. They arrived just as the first signs of light crept across the sky.

Jason saw Gatlor glance up, and then turn to Calador. He heard a clinking sound, and the rumble of the giant chuckling. As they put their supplies down, Gatlor turned to them. "Well," he said, "a promising beginning, although you have already cost me coin."

"Indeed?" Reyga said. "And how have we done that?"

Seerka snickered and said, "Gatlor had, shall we say, 'concerns' about young Jason's fortitude. He was not convinced you would make it here by first light. Calador had no such concerns, and now has Gatlor's coin."

Although Calador said nothing, he jingled the coins in his massive hand, and Jason again heard the giant's rumbling chuckle.

"Oh," Jason said. He looked at Gatlor. "Sorry."

Gatlor scowled. "Aye, well, it was worth it. I would rather get a timely start to our journey than take coin from this great lout's purse."

Calador and Seerka laughed.

"Do not let him fool you," the Ferrin said. "Gatlor despises losing bets."

"I also despise falling behind schedule," Gatlor said pointedly, "and we are wasting time with this idle chatter." He turned to Reyga and Jason. "I have secured several charnoths for our journey. We have left one unburdened for you to load your supplies on." He gestured toward the animals standing nearby.

Reyga turned to Jason and said, "Would you please see to the supplies? I need to have a word with Gatlor." Then the Loremaster walked off with the warrior, speaking to him in tones too low for Jason to hear.

Seerka walked over to Jason. "I will assist you," he said. "You do not want to approach the charnoths without being properly introduced."

The cat-man grabbed one of the bundles and walked toward the unloaded pack animal. Jason followed, carrying the remaining supplies. The animal looked like a rhinoceros, minus the horn, and stood about five feet high at the shoulder. Its legs and feet were like the legs of a big cat, complete with claws, and two wickedly curved tusks emerged from its mouth. The hairless gray skin looked thick enough to stop a bullet.

"Not so glamorous as horses, perhaps," Seerka said, "but these will also serve to guard our camp during the night. Come, we must introduce you."

They moved to the lead animal. Seerka held Jason's hand up to its nose. The animal snuffled at it for a moment, then studied Jason's face with what looked to be more than the usual animal curiosity.

"Are they intelligent?" Jason asked, returning the animal's curious gaze.

"More so than most other animals. That is one reason they are preferable to horses on a journey such as this. They can be fierce fighters when confronted by an enemy."

The beast blew a short gust of breath at them and tossed its head. The other charnoths turned to look at Jason, and then they too tossed their heads before turning their attentions elsewhere.

"There," Seerka said. "You have been accepted. The charnoths know you are part of our group, and will defend you with their lives should the necessity arise."

"Well, that's good to know," Jason said. *I'd hate to have one of them mad at me*.

Gatlor and Reyga returned as Jason and Seerka were finishing. While Reyga checked their supplies, Gatlor motioned for Seerka and Calador to join him.

When they had moved out of earshot, Gatlor told them, "We have been instructed by the Circle to use no *dimsai* in front of our young visitor unless we are in jeopardy of our lives."

"Interesting," Seerka said. "And did they tell us why?"

Gatlor shook his head. "No, and I did not ask. If the Circle thinks we need to know the reasons for their actions they will tell us. My oath is to serve, not question the orders of the Circle."

"True enough," Calador rumbled, "but I do not recall the Circle ever giving an order such as this. It does make one wonder as to the reason."

"You may wonder all you like," Gatlor said, "but see to it that he does not see any power being used unless and until the Circle gives us leave. Understood?"

As the others nodded their agreement, Gatlor looked over to where Reyga and Jason were waiting. "Something tells me I am going to be very glad to be rid of this Far Planer by the time we get to the Haven."

Tal Vardyn sat in his chambers mulling over the meeting of the Circle the previous day. The gathering had started out civil enough, but as he related what Reyga had told him about the young Far Planer, he had seen a myriad of emotions running across the faces of the Loremasters. Then he mentioned the prophecy. *That may have been a mistake.* Almost before he finished, several Loremasters were on their feet. He leaned his head back against the chair and closed his eyes…

"He must be killed immediately!" Chon Artel, the Obsidian Loremaster, bellowed. "The prophecy is clear! His destruction is our hope!"

In a smooth voice that seemed to glide through each part of the chamber, Seryn Shal, the Diamond Loremaster, said, "We must not do anything rash. Now is not the time for ill thought out action. We need to meet this young man, and ascertain for ourselves what manner of person he is. The prophecy is not as clear as we may think."

As Chon glared at her, the gathering dissolved into pandemonium, each Loremaster trying to be heard over the others. Tal watched the scene for a few moments, and then, with a blast of *dimsai* that cast a glare over the entire Circle, he roared at the top of his voice, "*ENOUGH!*"

Silence filled the room.

"We are Loremasters," he said sternly, "and we will conduct this assembly, and ourselves, with the dignity and honor that our office demands."

In a lower, yet no less authoritative voice, he went on. "The next one among you who displays another outburst like that will answer to me." He gave them all a hard look. "Now, everyone sit back down and let us discuss this in a calm, rational manner as befits civilized people."

He watched as the Loremasters took their seats. "I realize it is no small shock to suddenly find ourselves in the middle of a situation that, if it is what the prophecy refers to, may very well determine the future of our world. While we are all familiar with Taleth's prophecy, I am certain none of us expected to be living it. Nevertheless, that is the path fate appears to have given us, and it is up to us to walk it as best we can."

He paused for a moment to study their faces, and then went on. "Loremaster Reyga is bringing the young man here. They are coming overland, so we have a few days to discuss our options. I personally agree with Loremaster Seryn. I believe that we should meet him. After that, we can decide what to do with him. Until they arrive, I believe we need to devote ourselves to studying the prophecy to see whether or not we can divine exactly what it is saying."

Chon stood up once more, although with somewhat more dignity than the first time. He was a short, stocky man, with a thick black beard and bushy eyebrows. "As I said before, High One," he said in gruff voice, "the prophecy seems clear enough to me. 'His destruction is our hope' it says. That seems easy enough to understand." A couple of the other Loremasters nodded thoughtfully as he sat down.

Seryn stood. "The prophecy also states that 'for our land to live, the far land must die.' What land would that be?" She looked around the Circle. "It does not sound so clear to me when you consider the entire prophecy instead of just one line," she finished, looking directly at Chon, who favored her with a scowl.

Jarril Breth, the Amber Loremaster stood. He was Ferrin, one of only two non-human Loremasters on the Circle. His bright green eyes scanned the faces of the other Loremasters as he spoke. "Something else to consider: Taleth also said that although Jaben would be the last to arrive, he would already be here. What are we to make of that? Are there two of him? Will he have an accomplice? No, I do not believe the prophecy is clear at all. We must study her words and meet this Jason Bennett. Perhaps after we speak with him, we will be able to understand the prophecy better. Or we may decide that this young Far Planer is not the Jaben of Taleth's prophecy at all."

For the next hour, the Loremasters took turns expressing opinions and asking questions. Finally, Tal stood up.

"I believe we have discussed all we need to today," he said. "We all have much to think about, both concerning Taleth's prophecy, and also each other's words. Let us adjourn for now, and we will meet again in three days." He looked at each Loremaster in turn. "I urge all of you to seriously consider each position and opinion that has been presented here, even if it differs from your own. Only by exploring all of our options can wisdom prevail. May the mantle of wisdom ever rest upon your shoulders," he concluded.

"May your power be exceeded only by your honor, High One," came the formal reply from seven voices as the Loremasters stood and began to file out…

On the whole, he thought as he opened his eyes, although it had not gone as well as he would have liked, it also had not gone as badly as he had feared. Perhaps the meeting two days hence would not be too trying of an ordeal. He opened another of the texts and resumed his studies.

From this vantage point, the world spread out before her like an intricately woven tapestry. A chill breeze whispered against her cheek. She didn't notice the cold, immersed as she was in secret thoughts of her own.

"I see you're up here brooding again."

The dark-haired woman didn't need to look behind her to know who was speaking. Without turning, she replied, "What you call 'brooding,' I choose to call reflection."

"Call it whatever you like. It accomplishes nothing, and it changes nothing."

The woman stood and turned to the speaker. A dark figure faced her, cloaked in shifting shadows. Only fiery eyes blazed at her from the darkness surrounding the head.

"Oh, take off that silly disguise," she said. "There's no one else around, and you know it doesn't impress me."

"Really?" the figure responded. "Don't you think it makes me look taller?" As he finished, the shadows faded until a handsome, wavy-haired man stood smiling mockingly at her. "So tell me, my dear, what were you 'reflecting' on?"

Tilting her head slightly, she said, "Actually, I was thinking about when we first met so very long ago. About how different we are now from how we were then."

"You mean, of course, how we were when we were like *them*." With a disdainful toss of his head the man indicated the vista behind the woman.

"Yes, that. And more."

"Well, I for one prefer what we are now."

"And what is that?"

"Gods," he said. "Or at least the closest thing this world has ever had to them."

With a wistful laugh, she replied, "Gods. Funny, I've always thought of God as a benevolent father figure, watching over His creation." She shook her head. "We act more like petulant children, fighting over a toy that none of us wants to share."

"My, we are in a mood today, aren't we?" he said, raising an eyebrow. "Why do you do this to yourself? Why, after all these centuries, can you not accept the simple fact that we have been given a great gift? That we have been raised above what we were, what they still are."

"Is it a gift?" she asked. "Or is it a curse?" The man rolled his eyes and turned away. "Think about it," she urged him. "Look at what it's done to us. We were all friends. We all loved to be together. Now, we can barely be on the same planet without the Covenant keeping the peace between us."

He spun around. "Has it ever occurred to you that perhaps the Covenant is part of the problem?"

"What? The Covenant was the only thing that kept us from destroying this world after we were changed. It's the only thing that's kept us at peace with each other for over a thousand years."

Holding up his hands, he said, "Okay, I'll grant that in the beginning, before we learned to control our powers, the Covenant was necessary. I'll give you that." He shook his head. "But now, the Covenant is like shackles, taking our freedom from us. We may as well be in cages."

"That would seem only fitting, since cages have long been used to keep people safe from dangerous things."

His eyes narrowed. "We are not animals, and I am tired of being caged. And I'm not the only one who feels this way."

"What are you saying?"

"The time for the Covenant has passed. There was a time for it once, but no more. The time has come to abolish the Covenant and make other arrangements."

"Other arrangements? Such as what?"

"Such as being given our due as the most powerful beings on this planet. Such as stepping out of the legends and back into the world."

"As gods, you mean."

"Why not?" he asked. "Compared to them that's what we are."

"No. We are not gods, and I will never think of myself that way."

He softened his tone. "My poor, dear Alayn—"

"No! Don't ever call me that!" she interrupted. "When this first happened to us we agreed that we weren't the same as we were before. We reversed our names to remind us that, even though we didn't know what we had become, we were human once. In that respect, I still agree with you. We aren't the same as what we once were. Once I was Alayn, but no more. Now I am something else. Now I am Nyala. Alayn exists only in the past."

"In the past? How can you say that?" He spread his arms and spun in a slow circle. "Everywhere I look, I see Alayn. After all, Alayn is largely responsible for how this world came to be as it is now. How we came to be as we are. Or had you forgotten?"

"How can I forget? It still haunts me to this day." She drew a shaky breath. "So many died. Just two short days, but they've become the longest two days of my life."

"Yes, I know," he said. "And that's why you can't simply accept this power for the gift that it is, choosing instead to carry a ridiculous load of guilt throughout the centuries." He shrugged. "So now you are Nyala. Nyala, the Brooding One. Do you remember when they used to call you the Sparkling Goddess?"

She stared into the distance. "Of course. And they called you Regor the Shadow Lord." Her eyes came back to him. "A name I'm sure you would like them to know again."

"I wouldn't object to being called that again. But what about you? Don't you remember saving that child's life? Wouldn't you like to be able to do that again? Just think of all the good you could do now that you have so much more control of your power."

"Her name was Lisa," she said, remembering. "And I'm glad that I was able to save her, but even after saving her life, she and her parents were still afraid of me. Even after all these centuries, the fear in their eyes still pierces my heart."

"But this is a different world," he said. "They didn't understand the power back then. Now it's just another part of life. It would be different now. It would b—"

"No," she said, turning to him. "We are not gods, and I will not agree to any new 'arrangement' that implies that we are."

He searched her eyes. Then he was cloaked in darkness again, eyes blazing at her.

"I know," he said. "I didn't think you would agree to it. But I think it's only fair to warn you, you may not have a choice."

Then she was alone once more, with nothing but the chill breeze for company.

She scanned the horizon and the sky overhead, sensing that he had truly gone and was not just hiding.

"Do you know what you're doing, husband?" she whispered. "Because I do."

5
On the Road

"So, what's a chaotic rift?" Jason asked. They were sitting in a small clearing, taking a short rest break to have lunch.

Reyga chewed his food for a moment, then swallowed and said, "Most of the few remaining rifts are stable. In other words, they are anchored at both ends. Where the rift is today is the same place it was yesterday, and the same place it will be tomorrow. Such anchor points do not bind a chaotic rift. One or possibly even both ends fluctuate constantly. A path that led to your neighbor's house yesterday, may lead to another world today. Thus the name."

"Okay," Jason said. "You seemed to think it was pretty amazing that I had come through one. Why? Am I the only person to ever come through a chaotic rift?"

The three escorts had been listening. When Jason asked this question, Seerka answered, "No. There have been a fair number of travelers who have come to Teleria through chaotic rifts."

"Aye," added Gatlor around a mouthful of food, "but most of them did not survive the journey."

Jason looked at Reyga. "Is that true? Most people who come here through a chaotic rift end up dead?"

"I am afraid so," Reyga said. "It is an unfortunate truth that for most of those who have come to our world through a chaotic rift, the trip has proven to be fatal."

"Why?"

Reyga thought for a moment, and then said, "Consider our world. The surface upon which we stand is but a small fraction of the total area occupied by the planet. There is all of the area below the surface, and the oceans, as well as the atmosphere. Because chaotic rifts are not anchored, they can open up anywhere at all. You were very fortunate that the rift you came through chose to open up at ground level."

Jason felt rather thick headed as he said, "I'm not getting you. What are you trying to say?"

Gatlor tossed aside a small bone he had picked clean, and spoke up. "What he is trying to say, Far Planer, is that the rift you came through could just as easily have opened up far above the surface, deep underwater, or even somewhere inside solid rock. If it had opened up in any of those places, we would not be having this conversation right now, and I would be sitting comfortably in some tavern with my feet propped up, having an ale."

"Does that really happen?" Jason asked, shaken by the thought.

"Oh, yes," Seerka replied. "Gatlor usually puts his feet up when he has an ale," he finished with a wink.

Reyga gave the cat-man a look of exasperated amusement, and then turned serious as he answered Jason. "There have indeed been recorded incidents where the body of a Far Planer has fallen from the sky, or washed up on the ocean shore."

"And what he said about solid rock?" Jason asked, with a sick feeling in the pit of his stomach.

"Unfortunately, yes," Reyga replied. "In all of our recorded history, there have been very few that have come unharmed through a chaotic rift."

"How many?"

"We know of only two, now three, instances where a traveler has come safely to Teleria in this manner. Actually," he added, "tomorrow we will be passing through a village where one of them dwells. He arrived about thirty years ago or so. If we see him, I will introduce you to him."

"What about the other?"

Reyga hesitated before replying. "His arrival was much further in the past," he finally said.

"Oh," He thought about what it would be like to suddenly find yourself high in the air, or deep underwater, or worse.

Shortly, the brief respite was over, and it was time to get back on the road. As they walked, Jason glanced at the woods on either side of the road. He'd been trying all morning to catch a glimpse of the mysterious Lenai, with no success. He hadn't seen anything that gave any sign that the Shanthi girl was nearby. He was starting to think there was no one out there to be seen.

As if reading his thoughts, the Loremaster said, “She is there. She scouts ahead to ensure that we are not approached without our knowledge.”

Jason shot him a look. “How did you know what I was thinking?”

Reyga gave a little laugh, and replied, “You have spent most of the journey thus far peering into the woods. It was not difficult to surmise what, or should I say who, you were looking for.”

He felt his face growing warm as he heard the chuckles from the three escorts. He’d tried to be circumspect, but apparently, subterfuge wasn’t his strong point.

Eventually, the sun sank toward the horizon, sending streamers of gold and crimson stretching across the sky. As the shadows lengthened, Gatlor announced it was time to find a place to set up camp for the night. Not much farther along they came to a place the warrior deemed acceptable, and the company stopped. As the escort began unloading supplies, Reyga motioned for Jason to follow him.

“While the others are setting up the campsite, we need to find wood for a fire,” he said.

Jason didn't think he could take another step, but forced his aching feet to move as Reyga set off into the surrounding trees. Fortunately, there was an abundance of deadwood to be found, so in a very short time the two had accumulated an impressive pile of wood for burning.

He was sure they had gathered more than enough to last through the night when Reyga turned and headed back towards the forest. Jason was ready to drop. “Hold it,” he said. “Don’t you think that's enough?”

Reyga didn’t stop, but called over his shoulder, “One more trip should suffice. Come.”

Shaking his head, Jason wiped the dust off his hands and shuffled after him. As he entered the trees, he realized the Loremaster must have been walking faster than he thought. Reyga was nowhere in sight.

“Hey! Where’d you go?”

“This way, Jason,” Reyga’s voice replied from up ahead. “Come this way.”

He followed Reyga's voice, and soon found the Loremaster standing in the middle of a ring of large trees. "What's wrong? Why are we just standing here?"

"I want you to meet someone, my boy."

Jason looked around at the circle of trees, but didn't see anyone. He gave Reyga a confused look and said, "Um, are you feeling okay? I don't see anyone else here."

A slight smile played about the corners of the Loremaster's mouth as he said, "Lenai?"

"Yes, Loremaster?" said a female voice.

Jason spun around, almost tripping over his own feet. He looked in all directions as he regained his balance, but he didn't see anyone.

"Lenai," the Loremaster said with fondness in his voice, "would you humor an old man and say 'hello' to my young friend, Jason?"

"Only because you ask it of me, *ch'tasa*," said the voice. Jason was sure he was looking directly at the spot the voice was coming from, but he still could see no sign of the Shanthi.

As if a cloud concealing her from view had dispersed, the girl appeared. She stood almost as tall as Jason, and had a lithe, athletic build. She wore a sleeveless tunic and breeches that came down to the top of her bare feet, and had charcoal hair that dropped just past her shoulders. Jason gaped at her. He'd been looking at the exact spot where she had been, and he hadn't been able to detect her at all. Suddenly, he wasn't sure what to do. He'd been trying to catch a glimpse of her all day, and now that she was standing right in front of him, he couldn't think of anything to say.

"Greetings, human," she said. "I am Lenai." There was no welcome in her voice, and her dark eyes had a watchful, guarded look in them. Jason thought she looked fairly human, except that her skin shifted hues occasionally.

"Uh, hi," he managed, and then mentally kicked himself. *That was lame*.

Lenai gave him a slight nod, and then turned to Reyga. "Loremaster Reyga," she said in a friendlier voice, "if you require nothing else of me, I need to resume scouting the area."

"Of course, my dear," Reyga said with a smile. "Please return to your duties, and forgive me for the interruption."

"No forgiveness is necessary, Loremaster," she returned warmly. "I am always at your service." Then, with another cautious nod to Jason, she turned toward the woods and vanished as if she had stepped into a thick fog.

As soon as the girl disappeared, Jason found his voice. "You mean that's it? Just a 'greetings, human' and that's all?"

"For now. And even this was asking much of someone of Lenai's race. Most humans will live their entire lives without ever seeing a Shanthi. I was not sure if she would grant my request, but she too is very curious about you."

Jason snorted. "Yeah, she looked real curious. She couldn't leave fast enough."

Reyga chuckled and began walking back toward the camp. "Do you remember what I told you before about her people being very secretive? Had she not been curious, you would still be wondering what a Shanthi looks like. And she was correct in that she has other duties."

"I suppose. How did you know where she was? I couldn't see anything at all."

"I did not know where she was," Reyga replied. "I knew she would be near, simply because we were away from the campsite, and part of her duties as a member of our escort is to watch over us, you in particular. But I could see her no better than you. The Shanthi are masters of concealment and stealth."

Jason thought about that for a moment, and then asked, "What was that she called you? Shetasa? What's that?"

"*Ch'tasa*," Reyga said, giving it the proper pronunciation, "is a Shanthi word that is a bit difficult to translate into our language. The closest that I could explain it would be to say that it means friend, although it implies an intimacy that goes far beyond ordinary friendship."

"You mean you're like...together or something?" Jason asked. The idea alarmed him, although he wasn't sure why.

"Together?" replied Reyga. "I do not underst— Oh!" He came to a stop as comprehension dawned in his eyes, and then he burst into laughter. "No, no, my boy!" he guffawed. "Goodness, no! I am far too old for a girl of her age!" As his laughter abated, he took a deep breath. "Oh my," he chuckled, "let me see if I can explain this."

The Loremaster thought for a moment, and then said, "Things you would not do for your best friend, you would do for your *ch'tasa*, and secrets you cannot tell your closest family member, not even your own lifemate, you can tell your *ch'tasa*. It is more than both friend and family, and yet it is like neither. It is not a word the Shanthi use lightly and Lenai honors me greatly by using it with me. Long ago, the Shanthi believed that to consider another person as *ch'tasa* was to actually give them part of your own soul."

"Wow," Jason said, as he digested Reyga's words. "So how did you become Lenai's *ch'tasa*?" he asked, and then held up his hand as the Loremaster began to reply. "Wait," he said, "let me guess. That's part of that story you can't tell me, right?"

"I am genuinely sorry, Jason," Reyga said. "If I could tell you, I would, but…"

"Okay, okay." Jason gave up. "Maybe someday I'll hear it. It's not like I'm not going to have enough time, since you tell me I'll be here for the rest of my life."

"I truly hope to be able to tell you someday," Reyga said, "but right now we need to get back to the camp. No doubt they are starting to wonder what has happened to us."

With that, the young man and the old Loremaster headed back toward the campsite.

The next morning dawned bright and clear, and the band of travelers set out once more on their journey. After a few hours of walking, they approached another small village.

Gatlor turned to the group as they reached the outskirts of the village. "This is Gildenfell," he told Jason. Then he addressed the rest. "It is still somewhat early for the midday meal. However, this is the only village we will pass through until we are almost to Lore's Haven. We will stop at the inn in town to rest, eat, and replenish the supplies we have used thus far."

Gildenfell was considerably smaller than Drey's Glenn, and it had a much more relaxed air about it than had the bustling market town. The seemingly haphazard scattering of drab buildings they passed didn't show nearly the variety of the previous village.

As they walked along the packed dirt road that served as the main thoroughfare, they were met with curious stares from townsfolk along the way. Some gave them greetings, which the escorts and the Loremaster returned courteously. The children they passed were particularly fascinated by Calador. A few mustered the courage to greet the huge Dokal warrior, who answered their greeting with a nod.

Eventually, they came to a small wooden building that apparently served as a combination of roadside inn and tavern. A weatherworn sign swung over the door, creaking in the slight breeze, but Jason couldn't read the writing on it. He looked around as they went inside. The six or seven patrons that were present glanced up, and then did a double take as they saw the warriors. A few appeared to know who Reyga was as well, for they leaned over to their companions and began exchanging muffled whispers as they eyed the party.

The inn itself was rather nondescript. They were standing in a large central room with ten or so small tables scattered about. The wood floor had been worn smooth, with dirt ground into the grain that no amount of cleaning would ever remove. A rough wooden bar stood to one side, with a few aging barstools in front of it, and in the back of the room a staircase led up to the shadows of the second floor.

A balding, pot-bellied man Jason assumed was the innkeeper came out from behind the bar, wiping his hands on his apron. He clearly knew who Reyga was because he stopped in front of the Loremaster and bowed clumsily as he said in a rough voice, "Welcome to Carilian's Roost. I am Kellar, the owner. It is an honor to have you in my establishment, Loremaster Reyga. It is indeed. What can I get for you and your party?" He was a rough looking man, and it was obvious that had he been addressing anyone other than a Loremaster, the courtesy would not have been as evident.

Reyga nodded a greeting to the innkeeper and said, "Water and whatever your special of the day is will do nicely, thank you."

As Kellar bowed again and went to retrieve their food, the Loremaster surveyed the room until he found what he had been looking for.

"Ah, good," he said. "I was hoping he would be here. He usually spends most of his time here these days."

Jason followed Reyga's gaze, and saw, almost lost in the shadows at the back of the room, a figure sitting with his back to them. Jason hadn't noticed him when they'd entered the room. His clothing appeared to be the same drab brown of the woodwork in the tavern.

"Who is he?"

"Remember me telling you yesterday that one of the other people who came to Teleria through a chaotic rift lived in this village?" As Jason nodded, Reyga said, "That is he. His name is Brusha. Come, and I will introduce you."

While the escort took seats at one of the tables, Jason followed Reyga over to the lone figure. When they drew close, Reyga said, "Greetings, Brusha."

Without turning, the man replied in a voice ragged with age, "Reyga? Is that you? It is good to hear your voice. Please, sit with me a while."

Jason thought the man's voice sounded familiar, but couldn't decide whether he had actually heard it somewhere, or if it was just a voice from a dream.

"I would enjoy that," Reyga said, "but it will have to be another time. I have brought someone I would like you to meet. He is a young Far Planer by the name of Jason Bennett."

At the sound of Jason's name, the man stiffened, and his drink, which he'd been raising to his lips, fell from his hand, spilling across the table. He struggled to turn around in his seat, his voice quavering. "Bennett? Jason Bennett? Can it be? Jason, is it really you?"

As the man turned toward them, Jason felt the blood drain from his face, and his ears began to roar. He thought he might pass out again. This couldn't be! It was impossible! The frail man who now faced him had to be in his nineties, perhaps even older. But there was no denying what his senses were telling him. As their eyes met, he knew it was true. He knew this man. He had seen those eyes every day of his life, since the day he had been born. Even though he felt like he couldn't breathe, he forced one word out from between his numb lips...

"Dad?"

6
Reunion

Time stood still for Jason. He wasn't even sure if he was breathing. From the edge of his vision, he could see Reyga staring at him in confusion. The three warriors watched him with expressions ranging from intrigued curiosity to wary suspicion. All of this was a footnote in the back of his mind as he tried to comprehend the fact that his father, now an old man, was standing before him in a world that wasn't their own.

For his part, his father seemed like he couldn't decide whether Jason was real or a hallucination. After blinking his aged eyes several times, he hesitantly reached out a trembling hand. As his fingers touched Jason's sleeve, the elderly Bennett drew a ragged breath that collapsed into a sob, and he drew his son into his feeble embrace.

"Jason, it *is* you," his father managed through his tears. "Oh, Jason, I never thought to see you again."

"Dad? What are you doing here? How did you get here?" But even as he asked, a part of him realized that he wasn't alone in this world any more. Somehow, his father had found him. His arms slowly went around this frail, old man that his father had become, and he held to him tightly. In his father's embrace, the feeling of loss that he'd been holding at bay finally broke loose, and tears flowed down his face as well.

Eventually, they regained their composure and separated themselves. The elder Bennett, however, refused to release Jason's hand, as if afraid that if he let go his son would vanish once again.

Jason repeated his earlier questions. "What are you doing here, Dad? How did you get here?"

Before his father could answer, Reyga interrupted. "Please forgive me, Jason, but are you saying that Brusha is your father?"

"Yeah, but his name is Bruce, not Brusha. Bruce Bennett."

The Loremaster frowned. "But how can that be? I have known Brusha...Bruce, as you call him...for longer than you have been alive. He arrived in this very village almost thirty years ago!"

"I don't know. Why is he so much older now? He was in his forties when I left." Then a thought occurred to him. "Is Mom here too? Did she come with you?"

His father let go of his hand and dropped his gaze to the tabletop. "Your mother is not here. I'm afraid she left me. We have been divorced for many years now."

He stared in at his father in shock. *What? What do you mean 'divorced'? You were happily married three days ago!* The word echoed through his mind. *Divorced...divorced...* His parents had always been the epitome of the "match made in heaven." He sank into a chair.

"What happened? Why did she leave?" Then what his father had said hit him. "What do you mean, years?" he asked. "Dad, I've only been here three days!"

Bruce Bennett shook his head as he gazed into his son's eyes. "Oh, Jason," he said, sitting down. "Oh, my dear son. You disappeared fifty years ago."

Jason was stunned. "Fif..." he breathed. It was hard to think. *Fifty years?* How could that be? He couldn't grasp what he had just heard and decided to set it aside for the moment. There were more important questions he needed answered. "Why did Mom leave?" he repeated.

"It was my fault," his father said. "When you didn't return that night, we were frantic. Along with the McFarlands, we searched the woods for hours, thinking you might be injured or unconscious. We called the local authorities, who organized search parties to comb the area. We searched for weeks, but the only sign we ever found were your footprints in the dust of that building in the middle of the woods. They led to a doorway and simply stopped. We never understood that."

"That's where the rift was that brought me here."

His father nodded. "I didn't discover that until many years later. Eventually we had to return to the States. Every chance I had, I returned to Scotland to keep looking for you. The travel expenses drained our savings. I sold my business and used the money to keep searching. After almost two years of this, your mother finally accepted the fact that you were gone. I, on the other hand, wouldn't allow myself to give up hope, and refused to quit looking. You were everything to me, and I wasn't going to stop searching until I found you or died trying."

He rubbed a shaky hand over his face. "Finally, your mother had had enough. Three years after you disappeared, she told me she couldn't take it any longer. She said that she couldn't live in the past with me anymore. Either I would get on with life with her, or she would get on with life without me." He spread his hands. "You see the result of my decision."

The two were silent for a few moments, and then Jason asked, "So, how did you get here?"

"After your mother left, I sold everything and moved to Scotland. The McFarlands had plenty of room and allowed me to live with them. I got a job in a local pub at night, and spent the days searching the countryside for any clue to your disappearance. I spent hours and hours researching records and histories of the area. Ten years after you vanished, I came across a reference to someone else who had disappeared in those woods three hundred years before. I was surprised to learn that he was one of our ancestors, Bothan McFarland."

Out of the corner of his eye, Jason saw Reyga stiffen, but he was too involved in his father's tale to wonder about it. He searched his memory, dredging through fragmented segments of his father's half-forgotten history lessons.

"I kinda remember the name, but I don't remember you ever saying that one of our ancestors had disappeared."

"I didn't know he'd disappeared either," his father replied. "I'd always been told he got drunk one night and fell into a well. I asked Uncle Nyall about that, and he said that's what he'd been told as well, so I started digging into the local records from that time."

"And?"

"Bothan apparently went out hunting one day and never returned." He paused, and then added, "All they ever found of him was his hunting gun."

Jason knew that tone of voice. It was the voice that said 'go ahead and ask me.' Looking intently at his father, he asked slowly, "Where did they find his gun?"

“I think you can probably guess,” his father replied. “They found it leaning against a wall inside that building.”

“So that building…”

His father nodded. “When I read that, I knew that somehow that building held the key to your disappearance as well. I bought a tent and began sleeping in the woods beside it.” He chuckled. “Your great-uncle thought I had gone completely around the bend, and I believe he was about to have me committed. I told him what I’d found and begged him to let me live in those woods. After an hour, he finally relented, and said I could do what I wanted. I imagine he thought it would be easier to simply let me do that than to try to drag me away to some asylum.” He shifted in his chair to a more comfortable position. “So, I began my life in the woods. When I wasn’t working at the pub, I would sleep in shifts, a couple of hours at a time, and explore the building when I was awake. I learned every square inch of that building. I became quite the talk of Aberdeen. 'The galoot from the States.'" He laughed and shook his head. “I can’t say that I blame them. I would have thought the same thing.”

“How long did you live in the woods?”

“Ten years,” his father sighed. “Ten years of watching and waiting, without even knowing what it was that I was watching and waiting for. Then one day, it was like I suddenly woke up. I looked at myself and thought, ‘I’m a sixty-five year old man, living in the middle of the woods, looking for a son who disappeared twenty years ago.’ I did a lot of thinking after that, and decided that your mother had been right all along. It was time that I got on with what was left of my life, just as she had done. But, after investing so much time, I couldn’t just pack up and leave. It was the middle of summer, so I decided to wait until the end of the year, and then I would give up the search.”

“So what happened?”

“Three weeks later, just after dusk, I looked out from my tent and saw a glow inside the building. I thought my heart had stopped. I wondered if perhaps I *had* finally gone mad. I went into the building, and followed the light until I came to a room. *The* room. It was the one where your footprints had stopped. The glow was from the doorway on the other side. I’d been in that room a thousand times, and I knew what was on the other side of that door. I knew that beyond that door was another empty room just like the one I was standing in, yet when I looked through the door, I saw a forest. I knew this was where you had gone, so I took a deep breath and stepped through. Everything went black. At first, I thought I had made a terrible mistake, but then I found myself in the same woods I'd seen through the door. I had arrived in Teleria."

Jason shook his head, confused. "But I don't understand why you're so much older. How could you have come here thirty years ago, but not stepped through the rift for another twenty years?" he asked.

His father shrugged. "I don't know. From my point of view, you disappeared fifty years ago, but here you are, still seventeen."

Reyga spoke up. "There can be only one explanation," he said. "The rifts are not simply doorways through space and dimensions, but through time as well. Amazing! It simply never occurred to us. This will certainly give those studying the rifts something to think about."

They sat in silence until Kellar returned with their meal. After they had all eaten, Reyga said, "I think it would be best, Brusha…I mean Bruce…that will take some getting used to. I think it would be best if you accompanied us to Lore's Haven. The Circle will want to hear your story."

Before getting back on the road, they found an outfitter where they replenished their food and water. They rearranged the supplies so Jason's father could ride on one of the charnoths, and set out once more.

"This is a remarkable world, Jason, don't you think?" his father asked.

"It's something else," he answered. "I've seen some pretty wild things already."

"The *dimsai* is truly amazing," the elder Bennett said.

"The what?"

"The *dimsai*," his father replied. At Jason's blank look, he said, "What we would call magic in our world. Almost everyone here has some ability with it."

He shook his head. "I don't know what you're talking about. I haven't seen any magic." Then he stopped. "Or have I?" He looked at Reyga.

Reyga met his eyes and sighed. “Yes,” he said, “you have seen people using *dimsai*.”

“The game of catch?”

“Yes. And the chair that first night you arrived.”

“Why didn’t you tell me about…what did you call it? *Dimsai*? That seems like a pretty big thing to leave out.”

“I am sorry, Jason,” Reyga apologized. “I was following the orders of the Circle. You were not to know of *dimsai* just yet.”

“Why wouldn’t the Circle want Jason to know about *dimsai*?” his father asked.

“I cannot say anything other than that we were unsure as to what kind of person Jason was. If he turned out to be an enemy, we did not want to reveal too much to him about our world,” the Loremaster explained.

Jason crossed his arms. “And just when were you going to decide whether or not you could tell me about this *dimsai*?”

“After you met with the Circle. The meeting was for us to learn about you and what manner of person you were.”

“And if you’d decided I couldn’t be trusted? What would have happened to me then? If you turned me loose, I would have found out about *dimsai* eventually if everyone has the ability to use it. What would the Circle have done?”

Reyga shook his head. “I do not know. But please believe me when I tell you that there is much more that you need to know.”

“Like what?” Jason demanded.

“I cannot say,” the Loremaster said. “It is not my place. When we get to Lore's Haven, the High One will tell you what he thinks you should know.”

“Well, I may just have a few things to say myself to this High One,” Jason replied.

“Please, Jason,” Reyga said. “I can only speak for myself, but I do not believe you to be a threat, and if it were up to me, I would tell you anything you wished to know. However, the Circle has not met you yet, and I must follow their directives. I know this is not fair to you, but I ask you to restrain your anger until after you meet with the Circle and the High One.”

He had to admit that if their roles had been reversed, he might have done the same thing. Still, he felt as if he had been deceived. "I'll try to stay open minded," he grumbled. "But I'm not happy about this."

"I know," Reyga said. "I am not altogether pleased with the situation myself. I thank you for your forbearance." He gave Jason a formal bow.

"Yeah, yeah, whatever," Jason muttered. Then, slightly embarrassed by Reyga's bow, he turned back to the trail.

They walked for about another half hour, when the woods around them fell silent. The only sound was the whisper of the breeze through the trees. Gatlor signaled the group to halt. As soon as they stopped, Lenai appeared in front of Gatlor and said, "Prepare!"

In a blur, Gatlor and Calador drew their weapons and scanned the trees around them. Seerka's ears laid back, and Jason could hear a growl from deep in his throat. The Ferrin's claws were fully extended, and he looked ready to leap on the first thing that approached the camp.

Jason glanced around nervously, not knowing what to expect. The forest, so cheery with birdsong just a moment ago, now seemed threatening and dangerous in the ominous silence. He jumped as the sound of something crashing through the underbrush broke the stillness.

"What approaches?" Gatlor asked.

Lenai held a wickedly curved dagger. "A large band of Trellin raiders. I have never seen so many together!"

"Trellin?" Seerka said. "What are they doing this far north?"

Before Lenai could answer, a raspy hissing sound filled the air, and the raiders burst from the woods around them. As the warriors raised their weapons, the girl took one step towards the approaching creatures and vanished.

"Jason!" Reyga said. "We must get your father down. The charnoths will fight."

Several of the charnoths were already tearing at the ground. One or two gave screeches that Jason could only compare to the sound of a hundred fingernails scraping across a blackboard. They got Jason's father down and into the center of the warriors and animals just as Jason heard the first clash of metal. He turned to see what was happening.

Gatlor, sword in one hand and long dagger in the other, was fighting a creature that looked part human and part reptile. The creature's scaly skin was a dark mottled green, almost black in some places. It wore dark leather armor, and carried a jagged-edged, double-bladed short sword in one clawed hand, and a thin black dagger in the other. *Lizards with swords. Now there's something you don't see every day.*

He pushed the thought aside, and watched as Gatlor countered the raider's attack with dazzling speed. The flash of sunlight on steel turned the warrior's parries and blocks into a blur of gleaming metal and leather. Then the creature sank to its knees, dark blood flowing from a gaping wound in its neck, courtesy of a blow almost too fast to see.

Jason turned to see how the others were faring. Calador had engaged several Trellin. He wielded a large axe in one hand, and an equally large maul in the other. The weapons swung like pendulums of destruction at the ends of the warrior's powerful arms. Whenever one of his attackers would move too slowly, a devastating blow sent the creature flying away to crumble in a motionless heap wherever it landed, viscid blood soaking into the grass and dirt below.

As Jason watched, another creature darted in from Calador's side. Its sword came down on the huge warrior's forearm with a force that would have severed an ordinary man's arm. Calador roared as his plate-like skin absorbed the blow. A back swing of the maul crushed the creature's skull. Blood began to flow from his arm, but he didn't appear to notice as he turned back to his other opponents.

The smell of blood and beast was thick in the air as Jason turned again. Fifty feet away, Seerka moved with inhuman speed and agility, growling and screaming like a mountain cat. As the raiders swung at him, he nimbly dodged their blows, or blocked them with his bracers, and then darted in and slashed at the creatures with his claws. The Ferrin's acrobatic jumps, blocks, and rolls were a mesmerizing exhibition in deadly skill and grace. There were already two Trellin lying in dark crimson pools at the feline warrior's feet, their faces and necks reduced to scaly tatters.

Tearing his eyes away, Jason saw that the charnoths were fighting as well. He watched as two of them attacked one of the raiders and dispatched it with a ferocity that caused him to turn his head in nausea.

A heavy blow knocked him to the ground. Head ringing, he looked up to see one of the creatures standing over him. Just as it began to raise its sword, a streak of yellow flew into its face. It stumbled back as it tried to dislodge the furious bundle of feathers and talons attacking it. Jason couldn't be certain, but it looked like the same bird that had landed on his shoulder when he and Reyga were on the forest path.

He rolled over and started crawling away on his hands and knees, when the bird's screeching stopped. A rough, booted foot in the small of his back pinned him to the ground. The pressure vanished, and he rolled to his back to see the creature standing over him once again. He saw the bird struggling on the ground a short distance away.

He tried to roll out of the way, but the creature's feet were on either side of him, preventing his escape. He could only watch as the sword began its fatal descent. Just as the blade was about to split his skull, a greenish-white flash of light stopped the sword inches from his face. He looked over and saw Reyga standing with his staff pointed at the creature, the crystal in the end of his staff glowing like a small emerald sun.

Then a shadow passed over Jason, and, with a bone-crushing thud, the creature was gone. He got to his knees in time to see that Calador had crushed the raider's chest with his maul, and was now bringing his axe down. Jason looked away quickly, but still heard the sickening crunch of the weapon striking home.

He looked to the other side of the battle, wondering where Lenai was. He saw one of the raiders stagger as if a weight had fallen on it, and then clutch at a jagged gash that ripped open across its neck. As the creature sank to its knees, Lenai appeared behind it, blood-covered dagger in hand. Her skin had flushed to a dark maroon, and the look on her face sent chills up his spine. She scanned the battle and vanished again.

He watched another raider stagger. This one had faster reactions than the first. Quickly, it reached up over its head, grabbed a handful of air, and slammed its invisible load into the ground. A cloud of dust flew up and Lenai appeared, visibly stunned. She rolled unsteadily to her hands and knees, shaking her head. Her back was to the Trellin, so she didn't see it approaching her, sword in hand.

"No!" he yelled, and with a speed that surprised even him, he charged toward Lenai and her would-be executioner.

Lenai looked up at him blankly. It was clear that she hadn't recovered her senses yet. As the raider raised its sword, Jason dove over her and hit the creature with a tackle that sent them both tumbling.

He jumped to his feet and ducked underneath the first swing of its sword, but he wasn't quick enough to dodge as the creature plunged the dagger in its other hand into his shoulder. He backed away, clutching his shoulder. As the raider moved toward him, raising its sword, the hilt of a dagger appeared sticking out of the side of its neck.

It staggered back, clawing at its throat. Jason turned to thank Lenai, but she was still on her knees trying to clear her head. He looked past her and saw Gatlor running toward them, one slot in his bandolier conspicuously empty.

Gatlor grabbed the front of the creature's armor. "What are you doing here?" The only answer it gave was a last gurgling hiss as it died in his grasp.

Clenching his teeth against the pain in his shoulder, Jason turned to survey the battle and saw one raider still alive. It was running for the protection of the trees. Gatlor saw it as well and shouted, "It must not escape!"

His sword clanged to the ground as he took an arrow from his quiver and nocked it in the bow that was suddenly in his other hand. He raised the bow and released the arrow. There was a hissing roar of pain as the raider fell to the ground, the arrow protruding from the back of its leg.

"Take him alive!" Gatlor barked, as Calador and Seerka went to retrieve the fallen creature.

He examined the dagger buried in Jason's shoulder. "That was a foolish thing to do," he said. "Oh, aye, brave enough, I suppose," he conceded grudgingly as he turned to help Lenai to her feet, "but foolish."

He turned back just as Jason lightly touched the dagger. "No!" he snapped, grabbing Jason's wrist. "You must not remove the blade. We must get you to Lore's Haven at once. Loremaster Reyga!" he called as he turned away from Jason.

"I think I'll be okay," Jason said. "It hurts, but not as much as I thought it w—" He gasped and fell to his knees as liquid fire ran through his shoulder. It felt as if the dagger had become a red-hot brand piercing his flesh. As he struggled to catch his breath, the burning crawled from his shoulder down his arm, and then to his chest and neck. Fiery tendrils of pain spread to the rest of his body like magma flowing down a volcano. He collapsed to the ground and could do nothing but lie there, writhing in agony. It felt like his entire body was in a blazing furnace.

Spots danced in front of his eyes as the pain intensified even more. He turned his head and saw Reyga making mysterious gestures with his hands, and then the air shimmered in front of him. Past the shimmering, Jason saw a small blur of yellow rising toward the sky. He thought he should know what it was, but couldn't focus through the searing pain. He heard his father saying, "Jason. Jason, hold on." The last thing he felt was the Dokal warrior lifting him, then the pain became too great. With one final agonized cry, he blacked out.

A hooded figure stepped out from the concealment of the trees as the last of the party stepped through the portal. It watched the portal winked out of existence, then it slowly walked through the array of reptilian corpses on the ground.

"Well, and well, Gatlor. I see you and the others have not completely lost your fighting skills." Thin lips smiled underneath the hood. "No matter. This was merely a test. How interesting that Brusha is the pup's father." With a gesture, a portal opened up. "Aye, 'tis very interesting indeed." A moment later, the portal vanished, taking the figure with it.

7
Lore's Haven

Reyga stood before the Circle. As soon as he and the others arrived at Lore's Haven, he had gone to the High One's chambers. Minutes later, he followed a grim-faced Tal Vardyn back out into the corridor. Grabbing a nearby page, the High One ordered an emergency meeting of the Circle. As the Loremasters gathered, almost without exception they expressed surprise to see the Emerald Loremaster.

"You were not expected for another three days," Chon grumbled as he spotted Reyga.

"I will explain everything as soon as we are all assembled," Reyga said.

Once they had all settled into their seats, the High One stood. "Loremaster Reyga and his party were attacked."

A collective gasp filled the room. Delani Morn, the Amethyst Loremaster, demanded, "Where? By whom? Who would dare attack a Loremaster?" Her auburn hair and hazel eyes seemed aglow with indignation at the mere thought that someone could attack one of their own.

"It was a band of Trellin raiders. It took place shortly after they left Gildenfell."

"Impossible," Chon said. "That is less than four days from here. The Trellin do not come this far north."

"Nevertheless," the High One replied, "Jason Bennett even now lies in our healing area with a Trellin bloodfang in his shoulder. Captain Gatlor has already sent trackers to see if they can determine where the attackers came from. Loremaster Seryn, I know you wish to hear what will be said here, but I must ask if you would personally see to the young man. While I am certain your assistants are most capable, we dare not take any chances at this time. Loremaster Reyga or I will answer any questions you have once he is out of danger."

The Diamond Loremaster rose immediately. "Of course, High One. With your leave, I will go tend to his wounds now."

"Thank you, Loremaster Seryn. Please see to your patient."

Once Seryn left, the High One turned back to the Circle and said, "Loremaster Reyga will tell you of what has transpired this day."

Now, Reyga stood before his peers, wondering how they would take the extraordinary news he would be giving them. Chon, of course, would bluster and bellow. Delani would think of nothing except defending the honor of the Circle. Seryn and Jarril would want to take time to consider the options. The High One, as always, would ponder how today's events fit in with history and prophecy. Of the remaining three, he was not sure.

His gaze wandered around the chamber. The circular walls were made of polished white marble, with a domed ceiling arcing overhead. There were fourteen high-backed seats, each exquisitely crafted from dark blue chola wood. He had always admired the subtle touches of gold filigree accenting the head and arms of the chairs. The High One's chair was opposite the main entrance to the room. Four chairs sat to either side for the remainder of the Circle. The last five chairs faced the Circle from behind a modest stone podium in the center of the room, where he now stood. These were for guests, or anyone summoned before the Circle. Set into the wall near the ceiling and circling the room were nine intricate designs of iridescent tiles, each surrounding a large gem corresponding with one of the nine Orders.

The Loremasters were watching him expectantly. "I have many things to tell you today," he said. "As you have already heard, we were attacked by Trellin. Why the Trellin attacked us or, even more disquieting, why they have come this far north, we do not know. We did manage to capture one, and we will find out as much as we can from it. What you do not know is that before we stepped through the portal, we counted the bodies." He paused, and then said, "There were sixteen dead Trellin, and one alive. The raiding party consisted of seventeen Trellin."

Kalen Dristal, the Topaz Loremaster spoke up. "How can that be? The Trellin never travel in groups larger than five."

"I do not know," he replied. "But that is how many there were."

He looked around the chamber as the Loremasters whispered to each other, and then said, "The next thing you should know is that Jason Bennett came to Teleria through a chaotic rift."

Several raised their eyebrows at this, but none seemed overly taken aback at the news.

Jarril said, "While that may be unusual, Loremaster Reyga, it is not unheard of. Although, he is a fortunate young man to have arrived unharmed."

"True enough. However, his father also came here through a chaotic rift."

"What?" Chon said. "You did not tell us his father came with him. Why did you not mention this before?"

"His father did not come with him," he said. "His father arrived in Teleria thirty years ago."

The Loremasters looked at him in confusion. "What deception is this, Reyga?" Chon demanded. "We were told this Jason Bennett was a boy of less than twenty years. How could his father have arrived here thirty years ago?"

"There is more," he said. "From his father's point of view, he did not step into the rift until twenty years *after* Jason had disappeared from their world."

Brin Jalasar, the Ruby Loremaster said, "This is madness, Loremaster Reyga. Did his father come to Teleria before or after his son?" The Ruby Loremaster was a tall, broad shouldered man, with a hawk-like gaze.

Ignoring the question for the moment, Reyga said, "Not only did his father come to Teleria through a chaotic rift, he came through the same chaotic rift that brought Jason Bennett to us."

At this, there were a few outbursts of "Impossible! Ridiculous!" The room dissolved into a buzz of conversation.

T'Kel Sho, the Sapphire Loremaster stood. "Loremaster Reyga," she said in a soft, lilting voice, "you know as well as we that by its very definition, a chaotic rift does not appear twice in the same place. How can you explain this?" The Sapphire Loremaster was the other non-human Loremaster on the Circle besides Jarril. She was F'aar, an amphibious race that could function equally well on land or underwater, although they preferred their watery home to the land. As she spoke, small gill slits on either side of her neck fluttered.

She went on. "And what of Loremaster Brin's question? How can you explain the apparent contradiction as to when this boy's father came to Teleria?" T'Kel resumed her seat as she finished speaking.

"Obviously we have made a mistake in our definition of a chaotic rift. Either that, or there is yet a third type of rift that we have just now encountered," he said. "As far as the discrepancies regarding Jason's father, I believe it may be possible that the rifts not only traverse space and dimension, but also time. It would appear to be the only explanation."

"Preposterous," Chon scoffed as the Loremasters once more began to talk amongst themselves. "Traveling through time? I suppose next you would have us believe trees can talk."

"I understand that what I have proposed sounds unbelievable. But what I have told you is not all. There is yet more you need to hear."

Chon crossed his arms as the rest of the Loremasters quieted.

Reyga took a deep breath. What he was about to tell them would send the room into chaos. "When Jason's father was telling him about how he came to be in Teleria, he told Jason that he had found records indicating that one of their ancestors had also disappeared some three hundred years earlier. This ancestor had apparently entered the same rift as Jason and his father, which, one would assume, would have brought him here."

As several of the Loremasters began to speak, he held up his hands and said, "Please. Allow me to finish."

When they settled back, Reyga said, "Jason's father—I have known him for many years as Brusha, but Jason tells me his name is Bruce—in any event, his father told him that the name of his ancestor who had disappeared was… Bothan."

There was a moment of stunned silence from the Loremasters, and then they were all on their feet trying to make themselves heard. Even the High One seemed startled by his last statement, staring at Reyga as if he had just transformed into some fantastic creature.

Then the High One regained his composure and stepped up to the podium. His staff came alive, crackling with *dimsai* and getting the attention of the Loremasters. One by one, they stopped talking and resumed their seats.

Once the room was quiet again, the High One said, "Loremaster Reyga, you did not mention this when you came to my chambers."

"I know, High One, and I ask your forgiveness. But you left to summon the Circle before I could tell you."

The High One did not answer at first. Finally, after several moments, he said, "So, considering that you felt it was necessary to mention this young man's ancestor, should I assume that you believe his ancestor to be the one we know as Bodann?"

"I believe it is, at the very least, a distinct possibility."

"You realize, of course, how extraordinary this chain of events would be if that proves to be true?"

"If it is true," he replied, "and it is my own personal belief that it is, then that would mean that Jason Bennett is almost certainly the Jaben of Taleth's prophecy."

"Then we are indeed at a critical point in the destiny of Teleria. Let us go see this young man." Turning to the assembly the High One said, "This meeting is adjourned. Think about what we have heard today, but say nothing of this to anyone. We will meet again tomorrow after Firstmeal. May the mantle of wisdom ever rest upon your shoulders. Come, Loremaster Reyga." The High One turned and strode from the chamber without waiting for the formal reply from the Circle.

Jason was dreaming he was back in Drey's Glenn. The village was in flames and a hooded figure stood in the marketplace, arms raised to the sky. The figure laughed as terrified townspeople scrambled to find shelter. Crackling tendrils of lightning danced on its fingers.

Occasionally the figure would point at a building or a person, and lightning would shoot from its hands, setting the target ablaze. Jason saw the burned corpse of the tall, green man he had seen. Over there was the body of the werewolf, the fur burned off its body in patches.

He saw his father come out of one of the buildings and walk toward the figure. His father had stepped out of the building as a man in his forties, as Jason remembered him. With each step, however, Bruce Bennett grew older and older.

He tried to run to his father, but his feet wouldn't move. He yelled at his father to get back inside the building, but couldn't make himself heard over the pandemonium. As Jason watched helplessly, the figure turned toward his father. One hand came down to point at the now elderly Bennett. A torrent of lightning shot forth, and his father disappeared in a flash of light.

Dad! No!! Jason screamed in his dream. Then the figure turned to face him. The hands came up and pushed back the hood of the robe, and Jason found himself staring into his own laughing face.

He opened his eyes with a start. He was on a cot in a large room. He tried to lift his head, but the effort brought a wave of pain, as if he hadn't moved in weeks. He gasped and let his head fall back to the cot. As his eyes focused, Reyga appeared.

"Jason?" the Loremaster asked softly. "Are you awake?"

His throat was dry. "I think so," he managed. "Where are we?" He tried to shift his head, but even that tiny movement caused him to grimace at the pain.

Reyga put a light hand on his uninjured shoulder. "We are safe in Lore's Haven. Try not to move," he said. "You have not yet fully recovered from the bloodfang."

"The what?" he whispered.

"The dagger the Trellin raider used on you. The bloodfang is a lethal weapon. Its blade is hollow and filled with a particularly virulent poison. Once imbedded in flesh, it slowly releases the poison into the victim. As you discovered, it is a very painful process."

"Then why wouldn't Gatlor let me pull it out?"

"A bloodfang must be removed almost immediately," Reyga explained. "They are crafted in such a way that if one waits even a few moments to take it out, the blade will break off in the wound. This releases all of the poison at once. Had you removed it, you would almost certainly have died. Even as it was, enough of the poison had been released into your body that Seryn had to use all of her skills to keep you alive."

"Seryn?"

"Seryn Shal serves as the Diamond Loremaster, who preserves the knowledge of the healing arts," Reyga said.

Jason thought about how close he had come to pulling on the dagger, and how lucky he had been that Gatlor had stopped him in time.

"What were those things?" he asked.

"They are called Trellin," Reyga told him. "They are a particularly ill-tempered race, who generally spend more time fighting amongst themselves than attacking others. Because of their adversarial nature, they have never traveled in groups larger than five."

He winced as a spasm of pain ran through his shoulder. "It sure looked like there were more than five when they jumped us."

"Indeed," Reyga agreed. "There were seventeen Trellin in the party that attacked us. We have many unanswered questions. We do not know why there were so many together, or why they were so far north. We also do not know if this was merely an aberration, or if the separate tribes have declared a truce. If they have banded together..." The Loremaster shook his head. "Well, we will have to wait to see if there are any more reports of large groups of Trellin. Meanwhile, we will see what we can find out from the one we took captive."

"What about the others? Is everyone okay?"

"Yes, we are safe."

"And Lenai? She's okay too? That thing threw her down pretty hard."

"I am well, human," a voice said from his other side.

Startled, he gritted his teeth against the pain and forced his head to shift in the direction of the voice. He saw the Shanthi girl standing by the wall about twenty feet away. As he struggled to turn his head toward her, she took a few steps away from the wall, but stopped short of coming all the way to his cot.

"Lenai has not left this room, or slept, for the last three days," Reyga told him.

"Three days?"

Reyga nodded. "We returned to Lore's Haven three days ago. You have been unconscious since then."

"But why has she been here all that time?"

"You saved my life," Lenai said. "A debt such as that must be repaid."

"Repaid?" he said. "Hey, listen, I just didn't want to see that thing split your head open, that's all. You don't have to repay me for anything."

The girl shook her head. "Honor demands it."

He was too weak to argue with her. He noticed the fatigue that showed in her face and stance. "Well, we can talk about that later, I guess," he said. "Since it looks like I'm going to live, you should get some sleep."

She raised her chin. "I am well. I will stand watch until you are recovered."

He sighed and looked at Reyga, pleading with his eyes. Reyga appeared to understand. "Jason is right," he said to her. "You do no one any good by denying yourself needed rest. I will watch over him."

"It's not like I'm going anywhere," Jason added.

She looked like she was about to protest, but when the Loremaster lifted an eyebrow at her she relented. "Very well," she said. "But I will return after I have slept."

"Fine," he sighed.

She walked to the door and hesitated, as if unsure whether she should really leave or not. Then, with a final glance back at them, she walked out, closing the door behind her.

After Lenai had left, he looked at Reyga. "What was that all about?"

"It is as she said," Reyga replied. "You saved her life."

"Well, yeah, I guess so. But can't I just say 'forget about it' and have it over with?"

"Do you remember when I told you about the Shanthi? How some of them had used their abilities for dishonest gain, and that this was why the Shanthi were a mistrusted people?"

Jason nodded as much as his pain would allow.

"Well," Reyga continued, "most of Lenai's race do not use their abilities in such ways. Due to the actions of the less scrupulous few, however, for the majority of the Shanthi honor has become of paramount importance. If they feel they are indebted to someone, they will not rest until they feel that the debt has been repaid, and neither will Lenai."

"Please don't tell me she has to save my life to feel like we're even."

Reyga chuckled. "While that would certainly settle her debt to you," he said, "it does not necessarily have to come to that. When she returns, ask her what she feels would be adequate repayment. Often the Shanthi will offer their services to those they feel indebted to until they feel honor has been satisfied."

"Services?"

"Not as a slave, but as an equal, freely offering assistance."

"Gotcha."

"May I offer you a piece of advice?" Reyga asked.

"Sure."

"This is an opportunity for you to learn about the Shanthi, and about Lenai. It is an opportunity very few humans ever get. Do not lightly dismiss her determination to repay you for your deeds. Your words and actions will determine how much you will learn about her and her people."

"What do you mean?"

Reyga looked him in the eyes and said, "Do not insult her by asking her to do menial tasks. And do not offend her by asking her to do things that are, shall we say, inappropriate. Honor her desire to repay you, and treat her with respect as an equal."

"Okay," he said. He was having a hard time keeping his eyes open.

"But enough for now," Reyga said. "You need more rest. Sleep now, and someone will be here when you awaken. Oh, and one more thing, Jason."

He forced his eyes open again.

"I wish to thank you for what you did for Lenai. I would have missed her greatly indeed, had you not acted when you did."

He nodded groggily, "Sure, no probl..." Then he drifted off to sleep.

When Jason awoke, a pale light streamed through the lone window in the room. He cautiously moved his head, and, feeling no major pain, tried moving his arms and legs. Movement caught his attention. Lenai stood by the wall, looking like she had never left.

"You are awake," she said. "I will tell the others." Without waiting for a reply, she left the room.

He looked around, getting his first look at the inside of Lore's Haven. It was a large room with a high ceiling. There were other beds, all empty. Against the far wall, he saw a long table and a set of shelves. The table and shelves were loaded with books, containers, mugs, and various other items.

The door opened and the girl returned, accompanied by Reyga and a flaxen-haired woman wearing a circlet about her head. The circlet held a clear stone the size of a robin's egg. Bracelets on both of her wrists contained smaller versions of the stone. As Lenai returned to her post by the wall, Reyga and the woman came to the bedside.

Reyga spoke first. "Are you feeling any better?"

"Yeah," he said. "There's still a little pain, but at least now I can move without feeling like my head is going to fall off. How long did I sleep this time?"

"Only through the night," Reyga replied with a smile. "And now, Jason, I would like you to meet Seryn Shal, our Diamond Loremaster."

The woman bowed her head and said, "It is an honor to meet you, Jason Bennett." Although her voice was soft, every word seemed to resonate throughout the room.

"Nice to meet you." While Seryn had a gentle manner, and there was an air of kindness about her, he sensed an intensity behind her sky-blue eyes that made him think that he would not like to be on this woman's bad side.

"Reyga tells me you're the one who kept me alive," he said.

"With the aide of my assistants," she explained. "I served in more of a supervisory role."

Reyga shook his head and said, "Loremaster Seryn is being modest. She is the most accomplished healer in recent generations."

Seryn smiled. "Reyga flatters me. I do what I can, and simply hope that my efforts will be sufficient."

"Well, I owe you one," he said. "Thank you."

Seryn bowed her head once more, and then said, "I need to examine you. May I?"

"Sure, go ahead. Do what you need to do."

Seryn raised her hands, and then hesitated, looking at Reyga.

"Jason knows of *dimsai*," Reyga said.

She nodded and closed her eyes. After a moment, her hands began to glow with a silvery-blue light. She opened her eyes and stepped towards him. Suddenly, he wasn't sure if he wanted to be examined after all.

Reyga said, "Do not fear, Jason. You will not be harmed."

He tried to relax as the woman's hands got closer. Seryn's hands stopped about six inches from his head. She kept them at that distance as she moved them down over his chest and arms, and from there over the rest of his body. He felt warmth emanating from them that eased the pain wherever they passed. When she finished, the glow faded from her hands and she stepped back.

She nodded in satisfaction. "The last traces of poison from the bloodfang have dissipated. You should be able to leave the healing area by tomorrow."

"Wow," he said. "That was amazing. All of the pain is gone."

She smiled politely at the compliment. "I am pleased that you are feeling better," she said.

"I feel great. Are you sure I need to stay here until tomorrow?"

"While you no longer feel the pain of the poison, your body is still in a weakened state. I would like you to stay here for one more night. Then, tomorrow you may go to the quarters that have been assigned to you."

He sighed. "Okay, one more night isn't that big of a deal, I guess."

"In the meantime, I will let your father know that you are awake. He has been very anxious during your time of healing," she said.

After she left, Reyga said, "The High One has been waiting to speak with you. With your permission, I will tell him that you will be able to speak with him in the morning. Or would you prefer to meet with him this afternoon?"

He thought a moment, and then said, "Let's wait until morning."

"I will tell him."

The door opened again, and the elder Bennett hurried into the room. Reyga nodded his farewell and left father and son to themselves.

8
Beginnings

Jason's eyes flew open. The window showed nothing but darkness outside. Several candles provided a pale flickering light. He looked around the room, and saw Lenai standing against the wall again. She appeared to be studying something at her feet. As he watched, her skin ran through a parade of different hues and shades. At times, parts of her body would vanish completely, and then reappear while another part disappeared in its stead.

After a few moments, as if she felt his gaze, she lifted her head and looked at him. Her skin and clothing returned to their normal colors, and Jason could almost feel the wall going up around her.

"That was cool," he said. When she didn't answer, he continued. "How do you do that?"

"Do what?"

"Make your skin and clothes change colors like that."

"All of my people have this ability," she answered, but offered no further explanation.

"Well, that's quite a talent."

After a few uncomfortable moments, he tried again. "You know, you don't have to stay here like this. I'm fine."

"As I have said before, honor demands that I repay my debt to you."

"Even if I tell you it's not necessary?"

"Even so."

"Well," he said, "I think it's only fair to tell you that I don't plan on going one-on-one with any more lizard men. Come to think of it, I'm pretty sure I'm not going to throw myself in front of a rampaging charnoth any time soon either. So how long do you think this is going to take?"

"It will take as long as need be."

"Until you feel like this debt you think you owe me has been repaid?"

"That is correct."

He thought about Reyga's advice. "Well, since I don't plan on giving you any opportunity to save my life in the near future, maybe we could work something else out."

Her eyes flared. "Have a care what you ask of me," she warned.

"No, no," he said quickly. "It's nothing like what you're thinking. Well, at least nothing like what I think you're thinking," he added.

She eyed him. "Very well, human. What would you have of me that you would consider fair payment for my debt to you?"

"Well, first of all," he said, "would you please, please, *please* stop calling me 'human'? My name is Jason. I would really like it if you would call me by my name."

She didn't answer for a moment. Finally, she nodded, "Very well. I will call you by your name. But this is not enough to consider my debt paid."

"Yeah, I figured you'd say that. So, how about this? When they let me out of here, you show me around Lore's Haven. Who knows?" he added. "Maybe you'll get lucky and keep me from falling out a window. That would make us even."

"If the Circle allows, I can show you the Haven and grounds," she agreed. "But that still does not satisfy my debt."

"Well, there was one other thing I was going to ask."

She waited for him to continue.

"I was hoping maybe you could tell me more about yourself, and about your people."

He could see her tense up. "Why do you wish to know about my people?"

He sighed. This was turning out to be harder than he expected.

"Reyga told me your people are misunderstood," he said. "He said humans don't trust the Shanthi, and the Shanthi don't trust humans. But he also said most Shanthi value honor more than anything. I just want to learn about your people so I don't offend you or any other Shanthi I might meet. That's all."

She studied his eyes as if they would reveal a different truth behind his words. He was sure she was about to refuse, when she nodded slightly.

"Very well," she said. "I will call you by your name, show you around Lore's Haven, and tell you about my people."

"And about yourself."

"And about myself," she agreed, after a brief hesitation. "You would consider this sufficient to repay my debt to you?"

He shook his head. "I don't feel like you owe me anything at all. The question is: do *you* think this is enough to make us even?"

She thought about it. "What you ask is difficult for someone of my race, but I will agree to this as repayment of my debt."

"Good," he said. "Now, I was wonder—" The girl held up her hand, stopping him mid-sentence.

"Rest now. It is still several hours until first light," she said. "The High One wishes to speak with you immediately following Firstmeal. After you meet with the High One, I will show you Lore's Haven."

He thought about arguing, but his better sense won the day. He let his head drop back onto the thin pillow.

"Go back to sleep, human," she said. As he started to sit up to remind her of their agreement, she held her hand up once again.

"My apologies," she said. "Go back to sleep, *Jason*."

Satisfied, he closed his eyes and went back to sleep.

Lenai watched the young man as he slept. She was not sure what to make of him. When she had been given the assignment to join the group escorting him to Lore's Haven, she was certain she knew what to expect.

First, he was a Far Planer. Although she had not had the opportunity to meet very many Far Planers, they all tended to be the same. Without exception, every one of them turned out to be either ignorant, naïve, self-centered, or some disagreeable combination of the three.

As if being a Far Planer was not enough, he was also a human, and not just a human, but a human male. With very few exceptions, one of whom being Reyga, every human male she had ever met had been boorish and crude. She knew human males found her attractive. More than once, she had been forced to teach them proper courtesy. One had even gone so far as to put his hand on her. She had instructed him in the correct manner in which to treat a Shanthi female. He survived the lesson. Barely.

There was no reason to expect this one to be any different, no matter how much the Circle wanted to see him. When he first mentioned working something out, she was afraid she was going to have to kill him on the spot, and risk the wrath of the Circle later.

However, his requests were not what she had expected. This bothered her. She prided herself on being able to discern what type of person someone was, and human males were the easiest of all to read. The things he had said and done had taken her by surprise.

She did not like being taken by surprise.

First of all, he had saved her life. When the Trellin threw her to the ground, she had been knocked almost unconscious. Though most of her recollections were vague, there were a few things that were clear. She remembered him running toward her. She immediately assumed he was in league with the Trellin and was now coming to finish her off. She had been too groggy to defend herself, and could only wait for his killing blow.

Then he leaped over her. She managed to turn around just in time to see the Trellin plunge its bloodfang into his shoulder. She realized then that he had just saved her life. She felt an uncomfortable mixture of surprise that a Far Planer would sacrifice himself for a stranger, irritation that she was now in a human's debt, and a guilty relief that he would not survive long enough for her to have to repay that debt. A wave of shame washed over her as she recalled that feeling of relief. It had not been an honorable reaction.

And just now, his requests had also been unexpected. She had studied his face and eyes when he asked for information about her people. If there had been even a hint of deception, she would have refused. No matter how hard she tried, she could sense no ulterior motives in him.

She felt another unusual mixture of emotions as she watched him sleep. Part of her was annoyed that his words and actions had caught her off guard. Another part was apprehensive as to what the days ahead would bring, and how much she could safely reveal about her people. And then there was still another small part of her that wondered if Jason Bennett was one of those rare humans that was actually worth knowing.

The only thing she was certain of was that she would have to be on her guard with him. Perhaps he was just what he appeared to be, but her Shanthi nature also had to consider the possibility that this was all an elaborate deception, staged for reasons known only to him.

She studied him. When she was satisfied that he was asleep, she resumed the self-discipline exercises he had interrupted.

The High One was sitting at a large table with several thick books spread open in front of him when Jason was escorted into the room the next morning. Jason thought that if it weren't for the robe and staff, he would look like any number of farmers back in Missouri, with their salt-and-pepper hair, and silent scrutiny of anything new or different. Despite his rather ordinary appearance, the air of authority about him was unmistakable.

With a gesture, the High One dismissed the Warders and Lenai. Then he came around the table.

"Welcome," he said. "I am pleased to see you up and about, young man. I hope you are feeling no lingering effects from your ordeal?"

"I'm okay," Jason replied. "That lady Loremaster, Seryn, she's something else."

"Yes. Seryn is a credit to her chosen path, and we are fortunate to have her among our numbers. Please allow me to introduce myself. I am Tal Vardyn, Pearl Loremaster, and High One of the Circle of Nine." He gave Jason a formal bow.

Jason tried to be civil. "Yeah, nice to meet you."

Tal raised an eyebrow. "Yes. Loremaster Reyga mentioned you were somewhat displeased when you learned of my instruction to withhold certain information from you."

"'Displeased' is hardly the word for it. I was mad. I still am a bit. Why didn't you want me to know about *dimsai*?" Jason asked, his irritation beginning to show. "What's the big deal?"

"That, my young traveler, is what we are here to discuss," Tal answered evenly. "I make no apology for my decisions. I only hope that once you hear what I have to tell you today, you will understand why I felt it necessary to withhold certain information."

He returned to his chair, and motioned for Jason to take another.

"Please," he said, "be seated and be comfortable. Are you hungry or thirsty? I can have refreshments brought in if you like."

Jason shook his head as he sat. "No, thanks. I'm fine."

"I understand Loremaster Reyga has told you of our world and a bit about our society," Tal said. "Tell me, how much have you learned about Loremasters?"

Jason thought for a moment. "Well, Reyga said a Loremaster is someone who studies a certain area of knowledge, and that they spend their whole lives trying to discover new things about it. From what I can see, it looks like Loremasters have some sort of authority or prestige to go along with it."

Tal nodded. "Indeed," he said. "And is that all you have learned of Loremasters thus far?"

"He didn't go into a whole lot of detail."

"Very well then," Tal said, "let me tell you a bit more about the Loremasters and the role we play in our world." Without waiting for a reply, he settled more comfortably into his chair and began.

"In the year 97 PD—that is, Post Devastation—a man named Agathon Saltor realized that, without intervention, all of mankind's knowledge not already lost in the Devastation would soon vanish. If that happened, man would find himself thrust back into ignorance and darkness. It was Agathon who developed the system of Loremasters. He began to search throughout the land for men and women who possessed certain qualities.

"First, they had to have an extraordinary desire to serve and protect our world and its people. He was seeking a willingness to do whatever was necessary, even to the point of self-sacrifice, to defend Teleria against any dangers.

"Next, they had to possess a strong intellect. They had to be able to learn, comprehend, and retain vast sums of knowledge.

This needed to be combined with a quick mind, able to assess any situation instantly.

"Finally, they had to be among those who possessed the strongest emerging talents for the use and control of *dimsai*."

"Emerging talents?"

"*Dimsai* is not native to Teleria," Tal explained. "It entered our world through one of the rifts. Over time, some of the races developed a certain control over this mysterious power. From among those who have the strongest abilities, the Loremasters are chosen.

"After searching for almost ten years, Agathon finally found nine men and women whom he thought would be able to undertake the task of rediscovering the knowledge mankind had amassed over the centuries. He charged them to devote their lives to the discovery of new knowledge in their selected fields, as well as to the protection of that knowledge."

That sounded odd to Jason. "Wait a second," he said. "Why would they need to protect knowledge from anyone?"

"This question has been asked before," Tal said. "In order to give you a complete answer, let me first explain that the Loremasters do not hoard knowledge, but instead see that it is passed on to those who will use it to benefit the people of Teleria. A craftsman who uses wood," the High One gestured toward the table, "would be given training and assistance in woodworking techniques, both old and new, that would help him or her provide the highest quality products to our people.

"Now, as to who would try to take such knowledge, suppose a forging technique were discovered that would produce superior weapons or stronger armor than anything we now know. And suppose only one person knew about it. If that person were to fall into the hands of a warlord bent upon conquest, what would prevent this warlord from overrunning Teleria and assuming control? That is our purpose, to see that such knowledge does not fall into the hands of those who might use it for their own gain.

"In the case of our hypothetical forging technique, the Loremaster would take this knowledge and pass it on to the artisans and craftsmen who deal in metalwork. Thereby, the knowledge is preserved, and used for the greater good of Teleria."

"Okay," Jason said, "so Loremasters are the good guys. But that doesn't explain why you didn't want me to know about *dimsai*."

Tal was silent for a few moments, studying Jason. "I am not entirely certain how much I should tell you," he said. "Although, I suppose you should know that Loremaster Reyga has told me he believes you can be trusted."

"Well, it's nice to know that somebody here trusts me. But it's not like I asked to come here or something like that."

"True enough," Tal admitted. "But what we, and by 'we' I mean the Circle, are trying to determine is whether or not your arrival in Teleria is truly nothing more than an accident, or something more."

"What do you mean? What else could it be? Do you think I came here deliberately, or someone brought me here on purpose? Why?"

Tal's fingers tapped upon the table. At last, he said, "In order to answer your question, I must give you some information that I must confess I am not entirely comfortable revealing to you. However, as Reyga has spent more time with you than any other, out of respect for his wisdom and council I will proceed." He leaned forward and clasped his hands.

"There is a prophecy that was given over eight hundred years ago. According to this prophecy, a person named Jaben would come to Teleria, holding the fate of our world in his hands. As is often the case with prophecies, names and phrases can be somewhat different from what they actually turn out to be. When Loremaster Reyga told me your name, I found it uncomfortably close to the name given in the prophecy."

"So you think I'm this Jaben person? That I'm some kind of savior or something?"

"Or destroyer," Tal said, looking him directly in the eyes, "if indeed you are the Jaben of the prophecy. In truth, we are not certain what role Jaben will play. That is why we have been so cautious with you. Should you be Jaben and prove to be false, we did not want you to have any more information than what was necessary to reveal."

"And if this Jaben is supposed to save your world instead of destroying it, did you ever wonder how he'd react to your suspicion of him?"

"Of course," Tal sat back. "Therein lies our dilemma. How would we know which path Jaben would follow? And would our actions toward him affect which path he chose? As High One of the Circle, the decision on how to proceed fell to me. I decided to err on the side of caution. If Jaben's path is to lead to the salvation of Teleria, then I could only hope that he would understand, and forgive us."

He thought about what the High One had said. It made sense, presented that way, but he still couldn't help feeling annoyed.

Finally, he said, "So, this whole situation is all just because of my name? Because it sounds a little like this guy in your prophecy?"

"Not entirely," Tal responded. "There is, of course, the fact that you are a Far Planer, the first one we have had in recent years."

"And?"

Tal laid his hands flat on the table. "Understand, Jason Bennett, that what I am about to tell you I say only because of Loremaster Reyga's trust in you. I want you to know that."

"Okay."

"Very well. There is also the experience Reyga had when he used *dimsai* on you."

That startled him. "What experience?"

"Occasionally, when one uses *dimsai* on another sentient being, certain things about that being are revealed to the one using *dimsai*," Tal explained.

"What things?" he asked, suddenly feeling very exposed.

"Different things," the High One replied. "Thoughts, emotions, sometimes plans and intentions. It is generally considered an unwelcome intrusion, and that is one reason why we try to avoid using *dimsai* on other sentient beings. Additionally, if the intended target is able to use *dimsai* as well, the events can be unpredictable, sometimes even disastrous. However, because of your distraught condition when you arrived, Loremaster Reyga did not see any alternative, although he found the experience rather disquieting."

"Why? What happened to him?"

Tal leaned forward again, studying Jason intently. "Loremaster Reyga sensed something in you," he explained. "It was something he had never experienced before."

"What was it?"

"He did not know," Tal answered. "He could only describe it as the sense of something on the verge of awakening."

"Awakening?" He thought about that, and then asked, "Did Seryn say she sensed anything?"

Tal shook his head. "No. It is doubtful that she did. Those who choose the path of the healing arts spend years training their minds in order to prevent such an intrusion. Because the use of *dimsai* on others is essentially a requirement of their Order, they must learn how to shut out anything that may be revealed about their patients. It is an extremely difficult discipline to master. However," he added, "even if she were to sense something, the oath she took upon becoming a healer would prevent her from revealing such information except under the most dire circumstances."

Jason tried to stay calm, but the thought that there might be some unknown 'thing' inside of him, whatever that meant, filled him with apprehension. *If I had just stayed at Uncle Nyall's house*, he chastised himself. He heard the High One draw a breath as if to speak, and looked up.

The High One wasn't looking at him, however, but over Jason's shoulder. "Nyala!"

Jason turned and saw a shimmering being, seemingly composed of thousands of iridescent sparks, stepping into the room from out of thin air. Jason could see two shining white orbs where the eyes would be as it turned to them.

"High One," it said in a whispering voice that echoed throughout the room, *"I would speak with this one."*

Before he could react, the being stepped toward him, and he found himself inside a glimmering sphere, mesmerized by the creature's gleaming eyes.

He didn't know how long he stood there waiting for the creature to speak, when it said, *"You will remember when it is time."* With a silent flash, the sphere surrounding them disappeared, and they were standing in the High One's chambers.

The creature turned to the High One and said in its echoing whisper, "*A word of advice, High One. Treat this one justly. He is all you hoped...and all you feared.*" Then, as suddenly as it had appeared, the being was gone.

In the silence following the creature's abrupt departure, Jason and the High One simply stared at each other. After a few moments, Jason shook himself and took a deep breath.

"What was *that?*" he asked.

"What did she say to you?" Tal asked in a shaky voice.

"She?" he said. "That was a 'she'? How do you know that? What was she?"

Tal waved off Jason's question. "*What did she say to you?*" he demanded.

"She didn't say anything," he said, taking a step back uncertainly. "Well, she said I'd remember when it was time, but that was all."

The High One scanned the room as if expecting the being to reappear at any moment. "You will remember when it is time...when it is time," he mumbled to himself absently. His brow furrowed in concentration as his gaze dropped to the floor. "It has been centuries," he whispered. "Why here? Why now?"

"What is she?"

"What?"

"That thing," he repeated. "What is she?"

Tal's troubled gaze returned to Jason. "Oh yes, yes." He smoothed the front of his robe. "She is called Nyala," he explained. "She is one of a small group of very powerful beings called the Altered. From what we can gather, stories about them began shortly after the Devastation. None of the few fragments of records that we have recovered from before the war makes any mention of them. They have not been seen in centuries, and most have decided them to be nothing more than myth and legend. I only knew who Nyala was from the descriptions that have been passed down."

"There's more than one? How many?"

"According to the tales we have heard, there are seven Altered. They do not, so far as we know, intervene in our affairs. However, legends say that in the years immediately following the Devastation, they were much more involved in our world. Apparently, the results of their involvement were not always what we would consider to be positive. From what I have been able to learn, you are fortunate that it is Nyala who has taken an interest in you. The others would not have been as gentle. Now," the High One continued, looking at Jason intently, "I must ask again. Are you certain she did not say anything else to you?"

He shrugged. "It's not like she had much time to say anything. She just said I'd remember when it was time, and that was it." He shook his head. "Nothing else."

Tal gave Jason an odd look. "Jason," he said, "how long do you believe you were with her?"

"I don't know. Not very long. A few seconds, maybe a minute, tops."

"Young man, in the time that Nyala spoke with you, I could have traversed the whole of Lore's Haven and returned with ease," Tal said.

"No way!" Jason was shocked. "There's no way I was in there that long."

"Indeed you were. And obviously, whatever it was that Nyala said to you, she does not feel the time is right for you to remember it. This is most puzzling."

"What did she do? Could you see anything?"

Tal shook his head. "I am afraid not. You both were totally hidden from me while you were in the sphere."

"Did you try to get me out?"

"Any such effort would have been wasted. According to the tales told of the Altered, the power of the entire Circle combined is no match for even one of them. I did not wish to test that today and risk incurring their wrath. I could do nothing other than wait and hope for your safety."

The two stood silently for a moment. Presently, the High One said, "Well. I had planned on speaking with you longer, young man, but I believe we could both do with some time to think about this morning."

He couldn't argue with that, and simply nodded his agreement.

The High One continued, "There is a feast planned for this evening in your honor. I hope you will find it enjoyable and the food to your liking. The Circle would like to meet with you the day after tomorrow. Perhaps after that we can continue our conversation."

"Yeah, that's fine with me," he said, still thinking about the shimmering being.

"Very well." Tal opened the door. "I will see you at the feast tonight. You are welcome to look around and familiarize yourself with the Haven. I am sure there is much you would like to see, and Lenai can answer any questions you may have. Until this evening, then."

Jason nodded at the High One and walked out into the corridor, where Lenai was waiting for him.

9
Friends, Food, and Fear

The rest of the day, Lenai showed Jason around the Haven, telling him about the different areas they passed through.

Everyone they met showed the utmost courtesy and respect to him. He couldn't believe people actually bowed as much as they did. Before long, he found himself bowing in return. *It sure is different from back home.* It wasn't just the fact that almost half of the people he saw weren't human, but that everyone seemed to be genuinely concerned for his well-being and comfort. At every turn, it seemed like he was being offered a freshly baked roll or a piece of fruit. One woman even gave him a tunic she had just finished making.

“I couldn't accept this,” he protested.

“Nonsense,” she replied. “You are new to our world. Please take it as our family's way of saying 'Welcome to Teleria.'"

Behind her, a man he assumed to be her husband beamed at her. A little boy rode on the man’s shoulders, apparently the couple's son. The boy grinned down at Jason from his lofty perch. Jason smiled back, and examined the garment. It was a beautiful piece of craftsmanship, with an intricate pattern embroidered at the shoulders and waist.

“Are you sure?” he asked. “It looks like you've put a lot of work into it.”

“Absolutely,” she said. “I can always make another.”

He bowed awkwardly, and said, “Then I'll wear it to the feast tonight. Thank you.”

The woman smiled, clearly pleased. She returned his bow, although much more gracefully. “You honor me.” Her husband watched with a look of pride on his face that touched Jason in a way he couldn't quite understand.

“That was kindly done,” Lenai said, as they walked away.

“Well, it’s a really nice shirt,” he replied. She didn’t say anything else.

Later in the day, a group of small children playing in a commons area accosted them. When they spotted the two, the children ran toward them as fast as their little legs would carry them. Short, downy hair covered their heads, and each had large buckteeth underneath a small, button nose. The only thing he could think of was a cross between a human and a chipmunk.

"Lenai! Lenai!" they shrilled as they approached.

They were suddenly waist deep in a sea of small furry bodies, all waving their hands in the air as they tried to get the Shanthi girl's attention.

"Lenai!" yelled a chorus of young voices. "Fly me! Fly me!"

She looked at them fondly, but said, "Children, children! Can you not see that I am accompanying a visitor about the Haven?"

The children quieted and turned to him. Each bowed and said, "Hello, sir. Be welcome in Lore's Haven." Some added, "We are very sorry for bothering you."

Lenai looked at him over the heads of the children and said, "Please forgive them. They do not mean any disrespect. We will go on."

He resisted the urge to pet the children on their fuzzy heads. He grinned at them instead, which won him a few shy smiles in return. "No, it's okay," he said. "Take care of them. I'll just sit over here and watch."

Lenai raised an eyebrow. Then she turned back to the children.

"Very well," she told them. "But only for a moment."

"Me first! No, me! Me!" echoed a chorus of voices.

Lenai scanned the eager upturned faces, then said, "Garen, you first."

One young boy came forward with a toothy grin as the other children backed away, giving them room. Lenai picked the boy up and held him up over her head. Then she vanished.

"Look at me! Look at me! I'm flying!" the boy crowed, seeming to hang in midair.

Jason laughed as he watched the boy 'flying' around the commons area. *Garen, the wonder chipmunk.* He tried to spot any sign of Lenai, and then shook his head in amazement. He couldn't see anything at all underneath the boy.

Several of the adults nearby yelled encouragement. Clearly, this was a favorite game in this quarter, and everyone seemed completely at ease with the Shanthi girl as she played with the children.

When Garen's turn was done, Lenai reappeared and selected another child. After every child had been given a turn, she walked back over to him.

"Thank you for your patience," she said. "Are you ready to continue?"

"Sure," he answered, climbing to his feet. As they left the commons area, he stopped. "Tell me something."

Lenai didn't say anything as she came to a halt. She looked at him impassively, waiting for his question.

"I understand that you can change the color of your skin," he said. "I get that. But what you were doing then didn't look like just camouflage." He could see she didn't understand. "Camouflage just means changing your appearance to blend in with your surroundings," he explained. He shook his head. "But you looked like you were totally invisible back there, not just blending in."

She didn't respond at first, then she gave a slight sigh. "You are correct," she said. "While my people can change the color of their skin, that is not the extent of our abilities."

"You can make yourself invisible?"

"Yes, although it takes a bit of effort, and no small amount of self-discipline."

"So, right now we could be surrounded by a whole group of Shanthi and not even know it?"

"No. If there were any other Shanthi near us, I would know."

"How?"

"The Shanthi also have the ability to sense others of our race," she explained. "I will demonstrate. There are currently two other Shanthi within Lore's Haven." She looked at a point over his head and her face took on a distant, unfocused look.

After a moment, she said, "One is in the west tower, the other is in the training yard. There are none that I can sense outside of the Haven." Her eyes refocused and came back to rest on Jason.

"Wow," he said. "That's pretty impressive. So how close do you have to be to another Shanthi to sense them?"

"It varies from one Shanthi to another," she replied. "I can detect any Shanthi within ten stones' throw distance, although the most sensitive among my people can sense another Shanthi within a quarter day's journey."

She glanced at the sky. "We should return you to your quarters. You will need time to rest and prepare for the feast this evening."

He nodded and they headed back toward his room.

An hour later, Jason watched from his window as the sun slowly dropped below the distant horizon. From this point, he could see that the keep stood on a plateau. Not far away the land dropped off toward a forest below. A knock at the door pulled his attention away from the picturesque view. When he opened his door, he saw Reyga and Lenai waiting for him.

"Are you ready, Jason?" the Loremaster asked.

He nodded.

"Good," Reyga said. "Shall we go?" He started down the corridor, with Jason falling in beside him. Lenai followed behind.

"That is a beautiful tunic, Jason," Reyga said. "Is that Aliea's work?"

Jason shrugged. "A lady gave it to me earlier today. I don't know her name."

Lenai spoke up. "Aye, it was Aliea. She offered it to welcome Jason to Teleria."

"And a fine welcome it is," Reyga said. "She does extraordinary work. I have one or two articles of clothing from her myself, as do several others on the Circle. She is truly gifted."

As they passed through the halls of the Haven, Jason admired the intricate tapestries lining the walls. Some were merely colorful designs, but others depicted various scenes and pictures. There were woven patterns showing heroic battles, simple forest scenes, and the occasional depiction of village life. The halls themselves were filled with people strolling this way and that. Just as earlier with Lenai, anyone they met stepped aside to let the party pass, bowing or nodding courteously at the trio as they went by.

Eventually, they arrived at a large set of double doors. Pages on either side swung the doors open with a flourish as they approached.

His jaw dropped as they walked through the doors. He felt as if he had stepped into the dining hall of a giant. The banquet hall was in the shape of a semi-circle at least five hundred feet across. A raised dais stood at the straight side, directly across from the doors they had just entered. He stared in awe at the soaring arched ceiling overhead, reaching its distant apex directly above the dais, with banners and streamers hanging from it in a gala of colors and patterns. Along the wall behind the dais towered intricately patterned stained glass windows whose colors matched the banners. He saw people entering through two other sets of double doors in addition to their own.

Several rows of curved tables followed the contour of the walls. The overall effect was of a group of arcs nestled one inside the other. The guests sat facing the main table on the dais, while the servers moved along the inside of the curves, keeping goblets filled, and replacing empty trays of food. Two aisles radiated from the center of the dais, separating the room into three sections, and allowing the guests and servers to reach their places with ease. The room looked like it could easily seat at least a thousand people if not more.

A page stationed just inside the door announced their arrival. "Emerald Loremaster, Reyga Falerian! The esteemed Jason Bennett of the Far Planes! Honored member of the Circle Guard, Lenai of the Shanthi!"

About a third of the seats were already filled, with more guests arriving by the moment, each guest's arrival being announced equally as stridently as had been their own. The drone of dozens of conversations filled the room.

"We will be sitting at the main table in the front," Reyga said.

He looked toward the dais and saw that his father was already seated at the table, waiting for them to join him.

After several stops for introductions and small talk, they made it to their seats at the main table. His seat was the second seat from the podium, with his father beside him in the third seat.

The High One took the seat beside the podium, and Reyga occupied the seat next to Jason's father. The remaining members of the Circle filled the other seats.

He noted a number of different races dispersed among the crowd as the guests found their places. The servers were human, for the most part, with a few of the 'chipmunk' race he had seen earlier as well. Lenai said they were called Rodinn, but he couldn't get the chipmunk image out of his mind.

Once everyone had been seated, with only a couple of stragglers hurrying to their places, the High One stepped to the podium. The murmur of conversation died to silence as he waited.

"Welcome, friends and guests of Lore's Haven," Tal said. "We gather this evening to welcome a new arrival to our world, and a new friend, Jason Bennett."

After a round of polite applause, Tal continued, "Enjoy your meal, and afterwards please come and bid Jason welcome to our fair world." With a nod to the room, Tal returned to his seat.

The sound of clinking silverware and spirited conversation filled the air as the guests turned their attentions to their plates and dining companions. After a first hesitant bite, Jason's appetite reasserted itself, and he set to his meal with enthusiasm. He found the food delicious, even though he couldn't identify most of it. His father apparently had no culinary objections either, judging by the gusto with which he attacked his plate.

Halfway through the meal, Reyga rose from his seat and raised his goblet. As they noticed him, the other Loremasters and guests quieted. When the room was silent except for the whispery sounds of the servers, Reyga spoke.

"High One," he said, "in view of all of these gathered here this evening, I would like to honor you in the same way as young Jason honored me during our journey to Lore's Haven."

Jason reviewed their journey as he chewed, trying to remember exactly how he had 'honored' Reyga during their travels. Tal smiled graciously and, along with the other dinner guests, raised his goblet, waiting for Reyga to finish his toast.

Jason's eyes widened as he realized what the Loremaster was about to say, but it was too late to stop him.

Reyga smiled broadly and proclaimed, "You, High One, are an ornery old goat. You—"

The sudden sound of spluttering and choking interrupted him. He looked down to see Jason coughing and red-faced, with part of his meal dropping down his chin onto his plate, while his father pounded him on the back.

"My dear boy!" Reyga exclaimed. "Are you all right?"

With one last cough, he wiped his face with his napkin, cleared his throat, and said, "Yeah, I'm okay. I just, um, swallowed something the wrong way, that's all."

He glanced sideways at his father, who was looking at him with his lips pursed and one eyebrow raised suspiciously. He gave his father a sheepish smile and a shrug, and then found something profoundly interesting to stare at on his plate.

Reyga finished his toast and sat down. The rest of the meal passed without incident. Later, after an hour or so of introductions, welcomes, and small talk, Jason finally made his way back to his room. As he collapsed onto his bed, he renewed his vow to watch his tongue around Reyga.

As Lore's Haven slept, ten days' journey to the south, the village of Brayden Fenn also slumbered, peacefully nestled among the ancient trees of Faedor Woods. A dog dozing outside one of the houses was awakened by rustling in the branches and leaves overhead. The dog growled softly as the sound came closer. Before it could react, a silken net dropped from the canopy above and ensnared it, jerking it up into the trees. There was a barely audible yelp, and then all was silent again.

Scores of shadowy figures descended on glistening silken ropes into the village. Without a sound, they began entering houses, one after another. Muffled screams and final rattling gasps were the only indications of what was happening behind the doors.

Then, a piercing scream shattered the darkness, as one woman managed to evade her attacker long enough to alert the village. Her scream cut off, but not before the windows of several nearby cottages lit up.

Men came out, swords drawn, to investigate the scream. Their wives, some of them armed as well, gathered children together. Two of the men met between their homes.

"What is it, Koryn?" Cale asked. He scanned the village, sword at the ready.

"I do not know," Koryn answered.

Just then, from the door of the house across the lane, a shadowy form seemed to flow out the door.

As they spotted it, both men gasped in horrified shock.

"Brayden's blade!" Cale exclaimed. "A Manarach!"

"Manarach? None have been seen in years."

The creature looked around, head cocked, as it listened to the sounds of the village awakening to the threat. From the waist up, it had the appearance of a human, but below that was the hairy body and legs of a spider the size of a pony. Its face was human looking as well, except for the two large, ebony orbs where the human eyes should have been, and the six smaller orbs encircling the rest of its head.

"Well, there is one, as sure as we stand here. They are attacking the village," Cale said. "We cannot stand against them. The Circle must be warned. Come!"

Cale turned toward the town center, where the contact portal to Lore's Haven was, with Koryn right behind him. Cale had only taken a few running steps, when he heard a shocked gasp. He felt a hand brush down his back and saw Koryn's sword slide past, the metal blade kicking up sparks as it scraped against the rocky path. Cale turned to see Koryn on the ground, a silken rope entangling his ankles, with a monstrous Manarach pulling the other end of the rope hand over hand.

Koryn frantically tried to free himself, but the strand would not come loose. As the creature dragged him backwards, he waved Cale on. "Go! Go! The Circle must be warned! Do not stop!"

Cale was frozen by indecision. He knew Koryn was right, but he could not bear to leave his friend. Then it was too late. Koryn was in the creature's grasp. The Manarach's hands trapped Koryn's arms behind him, and one pair of its legs imprisoned him about the waist. The creature raised its head up, as if looking into the branches overhead, and Cale saw a pair of fangs as long as his hand emerge from folds of skin in its neck.

"Cale, please!" Koryn cried. "In the name of all that we hold dear...*GO!*" Then he stiffened, lips pulled back over his teeth, as the creature's fangs pierced his back.

With his friend's final look of agony seared into his mind, Cale sprinted toward the center of town. All around him he could hear the horrific sounds of men, women, and children screaming as the Manarachs' relentless slaughter continued.

He turned the last corner and saw the meeting hall. Even though his village was lost, if he could alert Lore's Haven, the Circle would be able to meet this threat. Reaching deep inside, he somehow found the strength to increase his speed. Finally, after what seemed like an eternity, his foot hit the first step to the small building.

Just as he reached for the door, a net of sticky strands enveloped him. He felt himself rising off the ground, being pulled into the foliage overhead. "Goodbye, father," he whispered, just before he felt the vicious fangs drive home.

At the same time, three days' journey to the east of Brayden Fenn, on the banks of the Shonta River, the village of Dronnin was meeting a similar end. Instead of the silent Manarachs, however, Dronnin's fate came at the hands of scores of hissing Trellin.

Because the Trellin did not possess the stealth of the Manarach, the men and women of Dronnin were able to mount a defense of their small fishing village. It made little difference, however. The onslaught of reptilian warriors quickly transformed the dirt streets of Dronnin into a bloody quagmire, oozing down the riverbanks to form a dark crimson cloud staining the clear waters of the Shonta.

10
Loss

"So, do you have any brothers or sisters?" Jason asked Lenai the next day as they continued their tour of Lore's Haven.

"My parents had a son before me, and another daughter after me," she replied.

"Where are they?"

"My sister lives with my parents in our telosh. My brother left home four years ago."

"Telosh? What's that, your house?"

"No. It would be what humans call a village, although, unlike human villages, Shanthi teloshta are not exposed for all to see."

"Are they invisible?" he asked, remembering the previous day's conversation.

She shook her head. "No, just concealed. Some of the dwellings may be underground, while others might be in the trees. We fashion our dwellings to blend in with the land around us. If built correctly, you could walk through the midst of a Shanthi telosh and never know it was present."

"Wow."

A little while later, he stopped to examine a large design on the wall. "What's this?"

"This is a focus point for one of the primary portals," she said. She indicated the wall opposite the strange design. Across the corridor stood an arched doorway made of highly polished wood. However, instead of leading to another hallway, what showed between the doorjambs was nothing but a blank wall. Armed guards kept vigil to either side of the frame. They had a relaxed manner, nodding pleasant greetings to passers-by, but their eyes took in everything around them.

"What's a focus point?" he asked. "And what's the difference between a primary portal and any other portal? And why is this door frame built on a solid wall?"

From behind them, a voice said, “A focus point is what enables travelers to come to Lore’s Haven from anywhere in Teleria.”

Jason turned to see a pleasant-looking man dressed in a yellow robe, with a round face and thinning brown hair, smiling amiably at them. A torq with a large yellow stone in it hung around his neck.

“Loremaster Kalen,” Lenai said. “I apologize. I did not realize you were behind us.”

The Loremaster waved off Lenai’s apology. “No, no,” he said. “I was passing by, and I saw you and our guest discussing the focus point. I thought I would stop and introduce myself.”

He turned to Jason, and, with a formal bow, said, “Greetings, Jason Bennett. I am Kalen Dristal, *saiken lo*, and Topaz Loremaster. I am pleased to meet you at last.”

Jason awkwardly returned the Loremaster’s bow. *I’ve got to practice bowing.* “It’s an honor to meet you, sir,” he said.

“Please, call me Kalen. ‘Sir’ sounds so formal, does it not?”

“I suppose.”

“So,” Kalen said, rubbing his hands together. “You have questions about the portals? Perhaps I can help explain a little about them. What would you like to know?”

“Well, before I ask about the portals, what's a *saiken lo*? Reyga said the same thing when he introduced himself.”

“Ah, yes,” Kalen replied. “A *saiken lo* is a high master of *dimsai*. The word ‘*saiken*’ simply means 'knowledge of *dimsai*,' and *'lo'* is an indication of rank. All of the members of the Circle are *saiken lo*, as are many of the other independent scholars, and even some tradesmen throughout Teleria.”

“So there are other ranks of *saiken*?”

“Oh, yes indeed.”

Kalen glanced around at the bustling corridor, and then indicated a relatively open area to one side.

“Let us step over here, out of the way, and I will explain,” he said.

Once the trio was out of the middle of the busy hallway, the Loremaster straightened his robe and took a deep breath. “Almost everyone is born with a latent ability to use *dimsai*,” he said, “although children are instructed not to use their power until they have received proper training. At the first sign of power, usually around a child's tenth birthday, a boy or girl becomes *saiken fel*, which means they have power but have not yet received any formal training.

"Sometime after their fourteenth birthday, the child and his or her parents will choose a trade. Then, they will find a master, a *saiken tek*, in that field that is willing to take on an apprentice, a *saiken cho,* for training. Formal training generally takes anywhere from five to seven years."

"What then?"

"When an acceptable level of control over *dimsai* has been demonstrated, the student may become a *saiken cha*, a tradesman, or they may choose to become *saiken li*, a *saiken* who has chosen to continue his or her quest for knowledge, hoping to one day earn the rank of *saiken lo*. This ongoing study can be done by either joining one of the Orders or through independent research," Kalen explained.

"What if they never get to an acceptable level?"

The Loremaster's expression became somber. "If, after the seventh year of training, the student still has not demonstrated enough mastery of *dimsai* to fulfill the apprenticeship, they are declared *saiken ri*. They are forbidden to use *dimsai*, in order to prevent them from harming themselves or others. Fortunately," he finished brightly, "it is extremely rare for anyone to be declared *saiken ri*."

"Uh huh. So, what does a Topaz Loremaster take care of?"

"I preserve the knowledge of atmospheric phenomena and anything related, such as weather cycles, storms, and the like." He made a slight gesture, and a sudden breeze ruffled Jason's hair and caused his tunic to billow up.

"Cool," Jason said with a grin. "Okay, so, going back to our first topic, how does a focus point allow people to get to Lore's Haven from somewhere else?"

"First," Kalen said, "I should explain that a focus point is only required if a traveler is not at a travel portal. In that instance, they can create a portal that comes to this doorway, or to either of two other doorways located in Lore's Haven."

"How?"

"Each portal in Teleria has a unique focus point associated with it. A traveler wishing to come to the Haven through this particular portal need only concentrate on this glyph." Kalen indicated the pattern on the wall. "Then, providing they have the power, they will establish a portal to this doorway. Should they wish to travel to a different location instead, they simply concentrate upon the focus point associated with their desired destination."

"So why doesn't someone at a travel portal need a focus point?"

Kalen pointed toward the sides of the doorframe. Two columns of crystals with designs etched into their surfaces were set into the reddish wood, one column on either side of the doorway.

"These are focus crystals," Kalen explained. "When we wish to set up a travel portal to a certain location, a *saiken lo* will take a number of these crystals to that location. Once there, he or she will use *dimsai* to imprint the location onto the crystal. The crystals are then set into frames, as you see here, to serve as anchor points for the portals. So long as the traveler possesses enough *dimsai* ability, they need merely touch the crystal representing where they wish to go in order to create the portal."

"Cool. So, how do they turn the portal off?"

"Once the person who established the portal steps through it, the portal closes. For that reason, if there are several people traveling together, the person who creates the portal must be the last one through. Otherwise, those behind would be stranded. Or, if the creator of the portal does not plan to come through it, he or she can also release it, allowing it to close."

"Alright, so what's the diff—"

"Oh, dear," the Loremaster said suddenly. "I am terribly sorry, Jason, but I must be going. I was on my way to confer with a colleague when I stopped. I meant only to introduce myself, but I am afraid I got rather involved in our conversation."

Kalen gave him a hasty bow, and started down the hallway. "I hope we can talk again, young man," he called back over his shoulder. "I truly enjoyed the few minutes we had." With a final wave, he turned a corner and was gone.

"Well," he said, after the Loremaster disappeared around the corner, "that was interesting."

"Loremaster Kalen is an honorable man," Lenai told him, "but he sometimes loses track of time. Particularly when he is involved in a conversation."

"Gotcha. So, how do the crystals get imprinted?"

Lenai shook her head. "My people do not possess enough power to create portals," she said. "Therefore, we have no interest in the manner of their creation. You will have to find someone else to answer that question for you."

"Oh, okay."

Lenai nodded toward the portal. "Travelers are coming from Orrin. Watch."

He turned to look at the doorway. The wall between the doorjambs wavered like a distant mirage on a hot summer day. Then, an iridescent shimmer flashed along the doorframe, and he was no longer looking at a blank wall. Another room was visible through the doorway.

The guards, who had been standing at relaxed attention before, had stepped back. They watched the doorway closely, with their hands resting on the hilts of their swords.

From the newly visible room, a couple and their young son walked into the hallway. As soon as the man cleared the threshold, the room on the other side winked out of existence with a silent flash of light, and the wall was back once more. The guards relaxed, nodded a greeting to the family, and then resumed their former positions.

"Man, I wish we would've had one of these when we drove to California last year for vacation," Jason said.

At Lenai's puzzled look, he shook his head. "Never mind. So, how did you know someone was coming? And where they were coming from?"

"When a portal is about to be activated from a travel portal, the focus crystal associated with that travel portal will begin to glow," she explained. "If no crystal glows, then we know the portal is being created from somewhere else."

"Okay, so how d—"

"I have told you all I can of portals. As I said before—"

"Okay, okay," Jason said, holding up his hands in defeat. With one final glance at the portal, they continued down the hall.

Not much later, they were walking down a little-used corridor on one of the lower levels of the Haven. No one else was around when a rift opened up beside them. A voice said, "Come, laddie. It's high time you and I had a wee chat!" Before he could react, a dark figure leaned out of the opening, grabbed the front of his shirt, and dragged him through the portal.

"No!" Lenai yelled, leaping forward. With a silent concussion of power, she slammed back against the wall of the passageway and slid to the ground.

"Sorry, lassie," the figure said, leaning out of the shimmering opening, "but I dinna think ye have an invitation." Extending his hand toward the prone girl, tendrils of power snaked out and crawled over her still form.

With a low chuckle, the figure retreated back into the portal, which silently winked out of existence, leaving the passageway empty except for the limp body of the Shanthi girl lying on the cold stone floor.

An insistent knocking coming from the door to his outer chamber dragged Tal from his slumber. He squinted at the window in his room as he tried to blink the sleep from his eyes. The darkness outside told him the sun had not yet given thought to rising. He yawned and untangled himself from the warm cocoon of his bed sheets.

When he opened the door, he saw his apprentice, Radyn, standing outside along with a Warder. His student's dark hair stuck up on all sides of his head, and puffy circles under his eyes showed that he had been peacefully sleeping not too long ago himself.

"Please forgive this interruption of your rest, High One, but Lenai has been found unconscious. It looks as if she has been attacked."

"What?" Instantly awake, Tal's mind began to race. "Where was she found? When did this happen?"

"She was found in one of the lower passageways. Warder Garris found her while he was conducting the nightly patrol." Radyn indicated the man behind him.

Tal turned to the Warder. "Do you have any idea what may have happened to her?"

Garris shook his head. "No, High One. She was unconscious when I found her. We searched the lower levels, but found nothing unusual."

"Where is she now?"

"She is in the healing area," Radyn said. "One of Loremaster Seryn's students is treating her, and the Loremaster herself is being notified as we speak."

"What of Jason Bennett?" he asked. "Lenai has been escorting him about Lore's Haven these last two days. Where is he?"

Again, the Warder shook his head. "We do not know. She was alone, and we did not see any sign of the Far Planer on any of the lower levels, nor in his quarters. His bed has not been disturbed. We are expanding our search to include the rest of Lore's Haven and the surrounding area."

"Good, good." He stroked his chin as his gaze wandered across the floor. Who could have done this? He looked at the Warder. "Notify me at once if you find anything else." He turned to his apprentice. "Awaken Loremaster Reyga, and have him meet me in the healing area. I will be there as soon as I am dressed."

"Yes, High One. I will go at once," Radyn said. With a bow, he and the Warder left to carry out Tal's orders.

After getting dressed, Tal headed for the healing area. As he reached it, he saw Reyga hurrying from the other direction. He waited for the older man.

Reyga stopped and bowed quickly, breathing hard. "High One," he said, "how is she?"

Tal knew of the special bond between the elder Loremaster and the young Shanthi. "I do not know," he replied. "I just arrived myself."

When they entered the healing area, Lenai was lying motionless in one of the beds, a thin sheet covering her from the shoulders down. Her eyes were closed, and had it not been for the almost imperceptible rise and fall of the sheet, Tal might have thought she had already passed.

A young man and woman tended her. When they looked up and saw the two Loremasters, they stopped what they were doing and bowed formally. He waved off their bows. "Now is not the time for formalities. What word of Lenai?"

The young woman stepped forward. She had a slight build, and solemn, dark eyes. "High One," she said quietly, "I am Elira. Lenai's injuries are healed, but we cannot awaken her. I considered probing more deeply, but decided to wait for Loremaster Seryn to arrive. She should be here momentarily."

Reyga was studying the still figure on the bed. "She is in no danger?"

"No, Loremaster Reyga," she replied. "Her injuries no longer pose a threat, and she appears whole. I do not know why she does not awaken, but she is in no danger that we can see."

"And what of Jason?" Reyga asked. "Is he well?"

Elira looked confused by the question. Tal turned to Reyga. "I am afraid no one knows where the young man is," he said. "He was not with Lenai when they found her, and he has not slept in his bed. He has apparently vanished." He could not keep a note of suspicion from creeping into his voice.

"High One, surely you do not believe he is responsible for this?"

"Loremaster Reyga," he said, "I realize you have developed an affinity with the young man. Considering what you have already been through together, I must say I can hardly blame you." His glance fell to the floor for a moment, and then he looked Reyga in the eyes. "I, however, do not have such a luxury. I cannot rule out any possibility, regardless how unlikely it may seem."

"But, High One…" Reyga began. Then he stopped and looked at Lenai. After a long moment, he nodded. "Of course, High One. I understand. Forgive me."

Tal placed his hand on the older man's arm. "I am sorry, my friend. I truly hope that Jason is innocent of this. I know your trust is not easily given, and I hope your faith has not been misplaced."

Reyga looked once more to the figure on the bed. "As do I, High One," he breathed. "As do I."

Just then, the door to the healing area opened and Seryn walked in, moving quickly to the bed. She glanced at Lenai, nodded briefly to Tal and Reyga, and motioned to her assistants.

"What is her condition?" she asked them. Although her face was calm, it was clear that she was completely focused.

Elira said, "Loremaster Seryn, her injuries are healed, but she will not awaken. I was about to probe more deeply, but since she no longer appeared to be in danger, I thought it best to await your instruction."

Seryn looked over Lenai's still form. "Well done. Proceed with your examination. I will observe."

Elira turned back to Lenai. She bowed her head and closed her eyes, preparing herself. As Elira gathered her focus, Seryn walked over to Tal and Reyga.

Reyga stepped forward, and said in a low voice, "Perhaps you should deal with this, Loremaster Seryn?"

"Have no fear. Elira is my best pupil. In truth, I plan on naming her as my apprentice at the Gathering's End Festival this year."

Tal raised an eyebrow. "Apprentice? Is she not rather young for such a position?"

"Perhaps," Seryn said, "but she is my most talented assistant, regardless of her age. And the fire that burns in her heart for those in her care rivals my own."

"I find that difficult to believe," Tal said with a smile. "Nevertheless, if you believe she is capable, then it must be so."

Seryn lowered her voice further and leaned toward them. "If I am not mistaken, I believe she and Tor will also be announcing their betrothal at the festival." She indicated the young man watching Elira attentively, ready to assist if she needed him.

"Indeed?" Reyga said. A slight smile played across his face. "Well then, the festival this year will be a most joyous event."

They fell silent as Elira opened her eyes. She glanced at Seryn, who gave her an encouraging nod. The young woman took a deep breath and raised her hands, which began glowing with soft argent light. Then she began slowly moving them above the length of Lenai's body. As she examined Lenai, she told them what she was seeing.

"The internal injuries are fully healed," she said, her head bowed in concentration. "There is no bleeding, nor blockage of blood flow." Her hands moved up Lenai's body. "The heart is strong and steady. Her air passageways are clear." Her hands continued to move up the girl's body, until they hovered over Lenai's head.

"The injury to her head is healed, and…wait…there is something." She closed her eyes once more, brow furrowed. "It is difficult to tell." She tilted her head to the side, eyes still closed, a look of puzzlement on her face. Then, with a sharp breath, her eyes flew open. Like the sound of a giant whip cracking, a glaring arc of power exploded from Lenai's body, hurling Elira across the room.

"Elira!" Seryn and Tor cried out. Tor and the three Loremasters ran to where Elira had fallen. She did not move as Tor dropped to the floor beside her, lifting her up and cradling her in his arms.

Seryn's power flared as she fell to her knees and began ministering to the still figure. As the moments passed, her eyes closed, and tension flooded her face from the strain of her efforts. "No!" she hissed. Her breathing became labored, and her hands blazed even brighter as she intensified her power. The gemstones in her circlet and bracelets came to life, adding their fire to the glare.

Tal and Reyga moved to either side of her and laid their hands on her shoulders, placing their power at her disposal. The moments passed as Seryn struggled to heal her soon-to-be apprentice. Tal could feel her strain as she drew on their power.

"No!" Seryn repeated, her voice breaking. Her hands and gemstones blazed like small suns. Tal had to squint his eyes against the piercing radiance. The glare cast their shadows into sharp relief on the stone walls of the healing area. He could feel the power draining from him as she demanded more of his resources to save her assistant.

Just as he was sure he could give no more, Seryn cried out and collapsed, the light vanishing from her hands like a snuffed candle. He blinked his eyes as the room appeared suddenly dim, and looked to where Seryn had fallen. She lay face down, her head resting on her forearms, her back heaving from the exertion of her efforts. Without lifting her head, one hand crept towards Elira's still form, moving up to lie on the girl's hand. Tal knelt beside her, with Reyga looking on over his shoulder.

"Seryn, are you injured?"

"No," she replied, in a ragged voice. "I am not injured, High One."

She raised her head. Sweat and tears streaked her face as she looked at Tor, still cradling Elira in his arms. His tormented eyes were fixed on her face. "Loremaster?" he asked in a small, pleading voice.

"Oh, Tor," she said. "I am so sorry. Her injuries were too severe. I—" Her voice broke. She took a shaky breath. "I could not save her." She bowed her head, unable to watch as Tor's once-happy future crumbled, leaving behind only bitter dust of loss.

For a moment, Tor did not appear to understand. Then he started trembling. Finally, with a cry of a soul in torment, he bent his head over the woman that would have been his lifemate, pulling her tightly to him. His anguished sobs of grief were the only sound in the room as he rocked her lifeless body.

Tal was stunned. How could a situation that had seemed so promising just a few moments before have turned into such tragedy? He knew using *dimsai* on another sentient being could sometimes have dire consequences, but the severity of such results was usually determined by the amount of power the target possessed. Most of the races of Teleria, Shanthi included, did not possess enough *dimsai* for this to be a concern. What could have triggered such backlash from Lenai?

The sudden change in outcomes denied coherent thought. It was impossible to focus on the questions spinning in his head. Instead, he bent to help Seryn to her feet. Beside them, Tor's grief had subsided to quiet tears.

As Seryn regained her feet, Reyga took a step forward. An expression of confused grief drew deep lines in his face. "Loremaster Seryn," he said. "How? Surely that was not backlash? Not from a Shanthi?"

Seryn wiped away the lingering tears and glanced sadly at Tor. "No, the Shanthi do not possess enough power to cause backlash of that magnitude." Then her eyes turned to ice, and she turned to the table. "I must examine her myself."

Tal stopped her as she stepped toward the bed. "Do you think that wise?"

"Wise?" She laughed bitterly. "On the contrary, High One, I am certain it is not," she said. "Nevertheless, it must be done.

We must know the 'how' and the 'why' of this, in order to answer it."

From behind them, a grief-ravaged voice barely recognizable as Tor's broke in. "*Find out who did this!* Then I will hunt them down! I will avenge Elira!"

Seryn turned back to look at the young man, his face filled with the passion of his anguish. "Peace, Tor," she said softly. "We will find out why this happened. I promise you that much." He did not reply, but his desolate eyes said that he would hold her to her oath. Seryn nodded slightly, and then turned back toward the bed.

Tal fell into step beside her, motioning Reyga to her other side. "Our power is at your disposal, Loremaster Seryn," he told her. "We will do what we can to assist and protect you."

Seryn gave him a half-smile that vanished as quickly as it appeared as she moved into position beside the bed.

As they had done before, he and Reyga placed their hands on Seryn's shoulders while her head bowed and the silvery-white aura bloomed around her hands once more. Tal's other hand took on a faint cream-colored glow as he extended it toward the still form on the bed. On Seryn's other side, Reyga mirrored his stance. A sparkling green light danced lightly across Reyga's fingers.

Seryn positioned her hands above Lenai's shoulders, and began moving them upwards toward the young woman's head. She focused intently on Lenai as her hands moved, watching for any sign of a repeat of what had just happened. Slowly, her hands moved over the Shanthi's neck, and then hovered above her face.

"I am going to probe more deeply now," she said. Tal prepared himself as Seryn forced her power deeper.

"Yes," she said. "I see what caught Elira's attention." She frowned. "I have never seen anything like this." The glow about her hands increased as she probed more intently.

Suddenly, like her former assistant, Seryn took a sharp breath. Instantly, power sprang from Tal and Reyga's hands. Iridescent pearl and verdant green joined to form a crackling shield between them and the girl on the bed. At almost the same instant, another bolt of power sprang from Lenai's body, attacking the shield with explosive force. The concussion knocked all three Loremasters back, but they managed to keep their footing. As suddenly as it had appeared, the burst of power vanished.

Tal regained his balance. "Is anyone hurt?"

The other Loremasters indicated that they were unharmed.

"By Agathon's scrolls!" Reyga said, shaking his head. "If that was what struck Elira, it is small wonder she was unable to withstand it."

"That was not what struck Elira," Seryn said.

"What?" Tal asked. "What are you saying?"

"That was merely an echo of the power that struck Elira," Seryn replied. "Before the *dimsai* struck us, I was able to get a glimpse of what has been done to Lenai."

"What is it?" Reyga asked.

Seryn studied the still form. "She has been made a trap," she said. "I have never seen anything such as this. I can only imagine the skill and power it must have taken." She shook her head. "The only thing I am certain of is that this was meant to kill the first person to trigger it. Even had it been myself, I would not have been able to withstand it."

Reyga looked at Lenai. Concern and frustration filled his eyes. "Is there any way to undo this?"

Seryn shook her head once more. "What has been done to her is beyond my skill to remedy. However," she added, as Reyga began to speak, "as I said, this was but an echo of the initial force. A reserve of power has been placed within her. How, I do not know, but I believe that each successive time the trap is triggered, the *dimsai* in her will be diminished. It should be possible to drain the remaining power away safely, if adequate precautions are taken."

Tal frowned as he looked from Seryn to Lenai and back again. "Who could have done such a thing?" he asked.

"I do not know, High One," Seryn replied. "There is no one that I am aware of in Lore's Haven, or in the whole of Teleria for that matter, who has the power or the skill that would be required."

His mind went back to the encounter with Nyala. "Is it possible the Altered have decided to intervene once more in the affairs of Teleria?" he asked.

Seryn sighed. "I suppose anything is possible, although I cannot fathom what the purpose of such an attack might be. However," she said, turning to look at Reyga, "it might not be beyond the abilities of anyone who has this much power to conceal their *dimsai* from others."

Reyga gave Seryn a troubled look. "So, you believe Jason to be responsible for this?"

"I do not know, Loremaster Reyga," she said. "But considering your own experience with the young man, you yourself must have your own suspicions."

"I understand your concerns," Reyga said, "but I find such thoughts difficult to entertain. He very nearly sacrificed himself for Lenai. I can scarce believe he would use her in such a way, even if he did possess the ability to do so."

Seryn looked back at the still form of Elira, and at Tor, who had fallen asleep beside her, one arm across her and his tear-streaked cheek resting on her shoulder. "Loremaster Reyga," she said solemnly, "you know I have always held you in the highest regard. I know that you are a man of honor, and that you have chosen to give your friendship to this young man." She turned to Reyga, her eyes burning with an inner fire. "I truly hope he is all you believe him to be, but you should know this: Should we find that Jason Bennett is responsible for what has transpired this night," her voice gained a dangerous edge, "I swear to you he will wish the bloodfang had slain him."

Tal and Reyga said nothing as the she turned back to her patient.

11
Muddy Water

Jason stared into the murky shadows of the ceiling above him. His jumbled thoughts harassed him as he tried to make sense out of the events that had brought him to this situation. Just a few hours before, he had been certain he was in mortal danger. Now, in a comfortable bed underneath a warm blanket, he reviewed the past few hours in his mind…

"Come, laddie. It's high time you and I had a wee chat!"

The voice came out of nowhere, and before he knew what was happening, he landed harshly on a rough stone floor. An explosion of stars blurred his vision as his head struck the stone.

Through the ringing in his head, he heard Lenai's exclamation, and then a concussion of power blinded him again. The man said something he couldn't quite make out, and then the portal closed.

A cloaked figure stood over him. A cowl covered the man's head, obscuring his features. Jason blinked away the spots dancing in front of his eyes, but still couldn't make out the face hidden among the shadows of the hood.

"Well, laddie," the man sneered down at him, "welcome to my humble home. I hope you enjoy yer stay." Low laughter sent chills up his back.

He struggled to his feet. "Who are you? What do you want? And what did you do to Lenai?"

"Yer little shifter is alive. She's of no use to me dead, so you needn't be worryin' yourself about that." The man sat in a nearby chair. "And as for what I want, it's as I said. I want to have a few words with you. Anythin' wrong with that?"

"I guess not, but—"

"Good!" The hooded figure gestured, and a chair shot out from the wall, slamming into the back of Jason's legs. He fell into the chair. *Wow, déjà vu*, he thought, remembering his first encounter with Reyga.

"Comfortable?" Before he could answer, the man leaned forward in his chair. "Now tell me, boy, why is the Circle so interested in you? Are you the one they think will best me?"

"Best you? Who *are* you?" Something about the man's voice seemed familiar, but he couldn't quite put his finger on it. The throbbing in his head wasn't helping any either.

"I am Bodann," the man said, in a tone that implied Jason should quiver with fear.

"Who?"

The man straightened. "Do you mean to tell me those bletherin' Loremasters have not told you about Bodann?"

He shrugged. "Sorry. Maybe they were saving it for a special occasion." *Bletherin?* The phrase seemed out of place, but before he could give it much thought, Bodann leaned forward until his hood was only inches away. Damp, putrid breath invaded Jason's nostrils, almost gagging him. Light from the wall torches caused the man's eyes to glitter through the shadows of the cowl.

"Mind yer tongue, laddie," Bodann whispered, "before someone minds it for you."

Jason gasped as he felt a noose around his neck. It felt like frigid, dead flesh pressing against his skin, cutting off his breath and sending a chill through his blood. He thought his neck muscles must be turning to ice as fingers of frost crept up the back of his neck and down into his shoulders. Just as shadows were gathering at the edge of his vision, the constriction eased and he drew in a wheezing breath.

Bodann leaned back in his chair. "Now then," he said, "perhaps we can talk without yer flip tongue gettin' in the way."

"Uh, yeah. Sure."

"Alright," Bodann said, "here's how it will be. I'll ask questions. You will answer them." His voice took on an ominous tone. "And you'll want to keep this in mind." For a brief instant, Jason had the sensation of an ice-cold snake gently gliding around his throat. He couldn't suppress a shudder as Bodann finished. "If I think yer not tellin' me everything, you'll know it. Now, I'll ask again. Why is the Circle so interested in you?"

He shook his head. "I don't know. Reyga just said I was the first one to come through a portal in several years, so the Circle wanted to talk to me."

"Why did they take you to Lore's Haven overland? Why not use a portal?"

"My first trip through a portal made me sick. Reyga said the Circle thought it would be better to bring me overland to keep me from getting sick again."

"Go on. What else?"

"Well, we were attacked on the way to Lore's Haven. Some creatures called Trellin. They looked like big lizards carrying swords."

"And would that be all? There's nothin' else you think I might be interested in knowing?"

Alarm bells went off in Jason's head. Trying to appear calm, he shrugged and said, "No, that's pretty much it."

A blazing corona of power enveloped him. It felt as if the skin was being ripped from his body, and he couldn't suppress a scream. As suddenly as it began, the power disappeared, leaving him gasping in shock. Beneath the memory of the pain, he felt something else, a tingling sensation he couldn't identify. Bodann leaned forward once more.

"I warned you to tell me everything," he said. "You seem to have forgotten about your father, laddie." At his startled look, Bodann nodded. "Aye, I know about him. I know you picked him up at Carilian's Roost in Gildenfell, and that he's been here in Teleria for nigh on thirty years."

"How do you know that?"

"I have ways that are none of your concern, boy. But then, you'll find there's very little in Teleria I'm not privy to."

His mind was racing. How much did Bodann know? Was it even worth the effort to try to hold anything back? And what would the man do the next time he caught him holding something back?

"Now then, let's continue our chat. And remember, I know more than you think. It'd be a sair fecht indeed if I find that yer still tryin' to hold anythin' back."

A sair fecht? Suddenly he knew why Bodann's voice sounded so familiar. Before he could stop himself, he blurted out, "You're Scottish?"

Bodann didn't answer at first. Then he said, "Aye, I called Scotland home for a time. From the day my mother bore me until the day I came here." He studied Jason for a moment, and then said, "So, you're from back home. An interesting coincidence, but it changes nothin'. You'll give me the information I'm wanting, or I'll drag it from your bones."

Like puzzle pieces, several bits of information came together in his mind. He stared at Bodann with his mouth hanging open.

"What is it, boy?" Bodann asked. "You look like you've seen a spirit."

"You wouldn't be… I mean… Are you…?"

"Och! Out with it, already!"

He took a deep breath and said, "Are you Bothan McFarland?"

Slowly, Bodann stood up. "I haven't heard that name in many, many years," he said. "How would you be knowin' it?"

Heart pounding, Jason said, "Well, um, if you're Bothan McFarland, you're one of my ancestors."

Bodann reached up and pulled the hood back from his head, revealing a shock of unkempt auburn hair and mutton chop sideburns surrounding intense sea-green eyes. Jason gasped for air as the icy rope again encircled his neck.

Eyes blazing, Bodann towered over Jason. "Do you take me for a fool, boy?" he snarled. "Yer name's Bennett. I know that much. You should have told those foolish Loremaster friends o' yours to come up with something a bit more convincing. More's the pity you'll never have the chance to tell them of their blunder." The noose tightened.

Jason's body screamed for air. "I'm not lying," he managed to choke out. "My father's name is Bennett. My mother is a McFarland. Her family is from Aberdeen."

The constriction around his throat eased almost imperceptibly, but it was just enough to allow him to draw a whisper-thin breath. Bodann stared at him with an expression he couldn't decipher.

"Aberdeen," he said. "Alright, you've got my attention. But mind you, if you make even one wee mistake, it'll be yer last."

Although the frigid noose was still uncomfortably tight, Jason went on. "My great-uncle Nyall lives outside Aberdeen. We were visiting him."

"Touching. But it proves nothin'. You'll have to do better than that."

"Uncle Nyall lives on some land that has been in the McFarland clan for generations."

"Go on," Bodann said.

Jason shivered from the chill around his neck. As the cold seeped into his neck and jaw, it was growing difficult to talk. "There are some woods near the manor house. I went for a walk and found an old stone building in the middle of the woods. I was exploring it and ended up here."

The pressure on his neck faded away. "A faerie glow inside the building just after twilight," Bodann said. His voice sounded distant as he stared at a point over Jason's head. "Look through a door, and instead of a room there's a wood as green as any I'd ever seen. I couldna stop myself even had I wanted to. I had to go. Forgive me, Morna. I had to go."

Eventually, Bothan's gaze returned to Jason. Jason leaned back in his chair, away from him.

"So," Bothan said, stroking his chin, "you have McFarland blood in you. Do you know what that means?"

"Uh…no?"

A broad smile broke across Bothan's face. "Why, lad!" he exclaimed. "It means we're kinsmen! C'mere!" Grabbing his arm, Bothan pulled him out of his chair and into a bear hug, pounding his back with enough force to drive the air from his lungs again.

Just as he was sure Bothan was about to crack a couple of ribs, the man stopped his pounding and held him at arm's length.

"Oh laddie," he said, "please forgive a suspicious old galoot for his harsh treatment. I thought you were another pawn sent by the Circle to destroy me. Can you ever forgive me?"

Caught off guard by the sudden change in the man's attitude, Jason said, "Uh, yeah sure, I guess."

"Good! Good! That's a good lad," Bothan said. "A forgivin' heart, that's a true sign of the McFarland blood flowin' in ye."

"Um, I guess so," Jason said, still cautious. "So, if you don't mind my asking, why does the Circle want to destroy you? If you don't want to talk about it, that's OK," he added quickly.

Bothan sat down. "No, no. You deserve to know, after what I've put you through. To be honest, lad, I kinna tell you, for I don't truly know myself." He motioned for Jason to sit down as he went on. "It wasn't always like this. There was a time when I was a friend to the Circle. A time when I believed them to be noble and upright, defending the land from anyone or anything with evil motives. I even lived at Lore's Haven."

"So what happened?"

"I found out what the Circle truly stood for."

"What do you mean? What do they stand for?"

"They want to have control over all knowledge. They don't want anyone havin' any knowledge without their leave."

"Well, sure," Jason said. "That's what they told me too. They want to protect the knowledge from anyone who might use it in ways it shouldn't be used."

"A half-truth is what that is, lad," Bothan replied. "Aye, they want to protect knowledge. But they also want total control over it. They want the final say-so as to who gets taught what, while the rest of the people become ignorant, dull-witted sheep."

"Uh, that's not exactly how it was explained to me."

"Of course not!" Bothan snapped. He stopped himself and made a visible effort to relax. "Sorry, lad," he said. "Whenever I hear the lies of the Circle it makes my blood boil. Like as not, that's why they'd just as soon be seeing the end of me. Because I'm no longer blind to their ways."

"Sorry," Jason said. "Didn't mean to make you mad."

"It's not your fault. You only know what those smooth-tongued Loremasters have told you." Resting his elbows on his knees, Bothan leaned forward in his chair and looked into his eyes. "But I'll warrant they haven't told you everything you need to know either."

"What do you mean?"

"Well, for instance, they didn't tell you about me, did they?"

"Well, no, but maybe they were waiting for the right time," Jason said.

"Aye, perhaps. But tell me some of the other things they've told you, and I'll let you know if they've forgotten any of the details."

He wasn't sure how much he should say. *But then again, he probably already knows about everything I'd say anyway*. He decided to chance it.

"Well, they told me about a prophecy," he said.

"Aye, that would be Taleth's prophecy no doubt. Did they tell you what the prophecy said?"

"The High One said someone named Jaben would come, and that he would have the fate of this world in his hands. He said they thought I might be this Jaben person because my name sounded a bit like it."

"Anythin' else?"

"He said they weren't sure whether Jaben would be a savior or a destroyer, so they had to be careful with me not to reveal too much information about themselves or Teleria. That's why they tried to keep me from knowing about *dimsai*."

"Ha! The fools." Bothan laughed. "You can't keep someone in Teleria from knowing about *dimsai* any more than you could keep them from knowing about air." He shook his head. "What else did they tell you about the prophecy?"

"That's it."

"That's all? Lad, you're not serious!"

"Yeah," he said. "That's all they told me. Is there more?"

"Only the most important part." Bothan ran a hand through his shaggy hair. "Alright, laddie, brace yourself. You're not goin' to like what you're about to hear. This is the part that should concern you. Part of the prophecy says 'His destruction is our hope' and 'For our land to live, the far land must die.'"

Brow furrowing, Jason asked, "What does it mean 'His destruction is our hope'?"

"Just what it says," Bothan replied. "They've got plans for you, lad. Dark plans."

"What?"

"Aye, and that's not all. Did you catch that other line?"

"The other line? Well, sort of. What was it again?"

"It says 'For our land to live, the far land must die.'" He nodded as Jason's eyes grew wide. "Aye, lad, you see it now, don't you? They're goin' to go to our world and destroy it."

Jason went over the conversation again and again in his mind. They'd spoken of other things as well, but the words of the prophecy echoed in his thoughts. Had Reyga lied to him? Was it all just a front? And what about Lenai? Was she really repaying a debt to him, or had she been told to keep an eye on him? Was he in danger? Was Earth in danger?

There were too many questions that needed answers, and each time he pushed one aside, two more popped into his head. Finally, he gave up and closed his eyes. Before too long, he drifted into a troubled sleep.

The appetizing smell of breakfast greeted him the next morning as he awoke. He yawned and stretched, and then looked around the room. He'd been too distracted the night before to take note of his surroundings. It was a comfortably decorated room, with tapestries on the walls and warm sunlight streaming through a large window. He swung his feet over the edge of the bed. A cool breeze from the open window lightly tickled his toes. He stood up and stretched once more before shuffling out into the main room.

"Ahh, you're awake then." Bothan set a steaming tray of meat on a large table. Bread, fruits, and other foods sat on the table. Two plates waited as well, apparently for Jason and his host.

"Come, lad, have something to eat." Bothan gestured to one of the chairs. "Eat as much as you like. I know when I was your age I could put away most of a good-sized cow." He gave Jason a wink. "Well, that's what my mother always liked to say."

The mention of Bothan's mother sent a pang through Jason. He ducked his head to hide the unexpected tears that came to his eyes. Bothan looked puzzled, then his eyes widened and he slapped his forehead.

"Och! Bothan, ye bletherin' idiot. Curse ye for a fool. Laddie, I am so sorry. I didna think before I opened my mouth." He shook his head. "I've been here long enough for my loss to fade and be replaced by more cheerful memories. But you, you've only been here a few days, and the wound is still fresh." He laid his hand on Jason's shoulder. "I am truly sorry, lad. I didna mean to cause you pain."

Jason wiped his eyes. "It's okay. I'm fine," he said. "So, you had a hard time when you first got here too?"

"Aye, lad, that I did," Bothan said. "It'd be fair to say I almost drove myself mad trying to find a way back. They told me there was no way, but I wouldn't believe them. I tried for months, even years, to find a way back home."

"To Morna?"

A slight twitch at the corner of Bothan's mouth was the only sign that the remark had affected him. "Aye. Morna was my wife, but she's not all I left behind. I also had three sons and a daughter, as well as my parents and a brother that I haven't seen since setting foot in this world."

"I'm sorry," Jason said. "I shouldn't have said anything."

"It's all right, lad. As I said, I've had time to accept my fate, and can look back on the memories of my kin with fondness instead of tears. You'll get there too eventually. It will just take some time."

"I suppose."

"And look on the bright side. You've got your father here, and now you've found another kinsman in me. Truth be told, having you here lightens my heart, it does."

"There is that," he said. "I guess things could be a lot worse."

"That's the spirit, laddie! I know it will be a tough go at first, but you'll be fine. Just give it time."

"Yeah, you're probably right."

"Of course I am. Now, let's eat! A good meal does wonders to lift a broken spirit."

With that, the two sat down and began breakfast.

With a stifled yawn, Reyga stood up from his chair. He put his hands in the small of his back and pressed, grimacing at the barrage of pops and cracks. He and the High One had assisted Seryn as she triggered the trap again and again, each time being met with slightly less force. Finally, she deemed it safe to allow her assistants to finish the work.

Before bringing her assistants in, they moved Elira's body into another room, out of view. Tor, looking broken and frail, shuffled out without a word. After that, the High One returned to his chambers while Reyga remained in the healing area. He wanted to be there if and when Lenai awoke. He sat in a chair by the wall, watching the students work. Now, the latest trio, a young man and two young women, turned away from Lenai's still figure.

"Loremaster Seryn," said the young man. "The power appears to be drained. We no longer get a reaction from our probing."

Seryn had not left the healing area either. Shallow circles under her eyes were the only sign of her fatigue as she walked over to the bed. Reyga tensed as light blossomed about Seryn's hands and she examined Lenai. He relaxed as she stepped back, apparently satisfied by what she saw.

"The remaining power has been expended," she agreed. She turned to the trio. "Well done. Go back to your quarters and get some rest. Return after midday meal." Together, the three bowed, first to Seryn, then to Reyga, and filed toward the door.

Just as they reached the door, the young man turned back to the two Loremasters. "Loremaster Seryn? May I ask a question?"

Although obviously exhausted, Seryn nodded. "Of course, Teryl. What do you wish to know?"

Teryl looked at the two young women with him, and then took a tentative step back into the room. "Loremaster Seryn," he hesitated, and then continued. "It is common knowledge that Elira is the most gifted student in the Diamond Order, but she was not here this night. Is she well?"

Seryn looked at the ground, steeling herself for what she had to say next, before meeting their eyes. "No," she said quietly. "Elira is not well."

The girl to Teryl's right stepped forward. "What is wrong with her?"

Seryn studied their faces for a moment before answering. "Elira was the first to trigger the trap within Lenai." The girl's hand flew to her mouth, and she shook her head, clearly not wanting to hear Seryn's next words.

"Elir…" Seryn's voice broke, then she steadied herself and continued. "Elira's wisdom is no longer with us."

At this news, the two young women began to cry quietly. Teryl sniffed and wiped his eyes, trying to maintain his composure.

Seryn said, "I will be announcing this to all of the students later today, and the High One will tell the people of Lore's Haven. I would ask you to keep this news to yourselves until then if you can. It is a terrible tragedy, and I do not want rumors and speculation springing up before I have a chance to tell everyone."

Teryl cleared his throat. "Of course, Loremaster. We will not reveal what we know."

Seryn nodded, and the three turned and left the room.

"Will they be able to conceal their knowledge?" Reyga asked.

Seryn shook her head. "No. Even if they do not speak of it, their tears will proclaim it."

Reyga turned back to the still form. "How long will she remain asleep?"

"I do not know," Seryn replied. "I have no way of knowing what effect having such power placed within her will have. We can only watch and wait for now." She studied Reyga's drawn face. "You should rest," she said. "Please. I will send someone to you as soon as there is any change."

"I cannot rest until Lenai is recovered and I know what has happened here."

Seryn looked toward the room where they had taken Elira's body. "Nor can I."

Tal's face was grim as he listened to the report from Warder Thom. First, there was Elira's tragic death combined with Jason Bennett's unexplained disappearance, and now this.

"Who brought this to your attention?" he asked. They were in the courtyard surrounded by a small group of Warders and residents of Lore's Haven. He had been taking his usual morning walk when Warder Thom stopped him.

A thin-faced man stepped out from behind Thom and bowed deeply. "I did, High One," he said.

Tal searched his memory. "Gerrid Carr, yes?" he asked.

A look of surprise crossed the man's features. "Yes, High One. We met at the last Gathering's End festival."

"Of course," he answered, nodding. "Your chola wood carving won top honors in the craftsman competition as I remember." Gerrid smiled, clearly pleased that the High One remembered him.

"I hope we see more of your work this year," Tal said. "Now, please tell me again what happened, and start from the beginning."

Gerrid's smile faded. "Yes, High One," he said. "I have a friend who lives in Brayden Fenn. On the first day of every sixday, we speak with each other through the contact portal. This morning it was my turn to open the portal, but when I did there was no one on the other end. I could see the wall of the portal room, but nothing else. This is not the first time that this has happened, but usually someone will come to the portal within a short time."

"And this time was different," Tal said. It was not a question.

"High One, I waited half the morning for someone, anyone, to come to the portal." Gerrid's voice shook. "Something has happened at Brayden Fenn, High One. I just know it has, and I am afraid for my friend and his family."

Although he found this news disturbing, even more so now that Jason Bennett had disappeared, Tal tried to keep his expression and voice calm. It would not do to start a panic among the people. "Be at peace, Gerrid. We will find out what is happening at Brayden Fenn. I am certain there is a perfectly good explanation for their unusual absence from the portal room."

"I suppose so," he said. "You are probably right, High One." His expression did not match his words.

"We will try to contact them throughout the day, and if, for some reason, we are unable to do so, I will send someone to check on them. Now, what was your friend's name so that we can tell him of your concern?"

"Thank you, High One. His name is Cale. Cale Jalasar."

"Jalasar?"

"Yes, High One," Gerrid answered. "He is Loremaster Brin's youngest son."

Tal's face did not betray the sinking feeling he suddenly felt in the pit of his stomach. "Ah, yes. Of course," he said. "Well, Gerrid, thank you for bringing this to our attention." He motioned for Warder Thom. "And now I am afraid I have other duties I must attend to, but rest assured, we will look into the matter."

He turned and walked back toward the door leading into the Haven, with Thom falling into step beside him. As soon as they were out of earshot, he said, "Find Captain Gatlor and have him come to my quarters. Tell him I have an assignment for him."

12
Decisions, Decisions

"I think I should go back," Jason said. He'd been mulling the matter over in his head throughout breakfast. He didn't want to make Bothan angry, especially after experiencing his temper, but he didn't feel right about simply disappearing from Lore's Haven. He was sure they were wondering where he was.

"Go back?" Bothan asked. "Lad, you know as well as I that there's no way back. We're both stuck here, and all we can do is try to make the best of it."

"No. I mean back to Lore's Haven."

Bothan straightened in his chair. "Back there? Are you daft? Jason, have you already forgotten what I told you last night?"

"I know. I haven't forgotten, but I really need to go back and get some answers. Besides, my dad is still there. I can't just leave him."

Bothan bowed his head, his fists clenching and unclenching on the table top. Jason braced himself, but the big man's shoulders suddenly relaxed.

"Aye, you're right," he said. "A man has to make his own decisions and then live with the consequences. And, it warms my heart it does, to see your loyalty to your father. But I'd not be telling you the truth if I didna say I was worried about you, lad."

"I know. I have to admit, I'm a little worried myself. But I have to at least get my dad. I promise I'll be careful."

"Aye, all right. I'll send you back. But first I have two things I'd ask of you."

"What things?"

"Wait here," Bothan said, and then left the room. After a moment, he returned with a smooth, oblong stone about the size of his thumb hanging from a leather cord. He gave it to Jason.

"Wear that," Bothan said.

"What is it?"

"It's called a summoning stone. If you find that you want to come back here, just hold it tight in your hand and concentrate on me. I'll know, and I'll open a portal that'll bring you here." Bothan grasped Jason's shoulders. "I may not be able to keep you from going back, but I can make sure you have a safe way to get away when you need it. I think you'll be glad of having it."

"Um, okay, thanks." Jason slipped the cord over his head. The stone rested a few inches below the hollow of his neck, hidden by his tunic. It felt strangely warm against his skin. He looked at Bothan. "So, you said there were two things you wanted to ask me to do. What was the other one?"

"Wait until tomorrow to go back."

"What? Why?"

Bothan sighed heavily. "I've been here a long time, lad, and a good portion of that time has been spent alone. It's good to have someone to talk to again. I didn't realize how much I'd been missing simple conversation."

"Well…"

"I'd be able to tell you more about the things you really need to know. Things like as not the Circle's forgotten to tell you. And I would like to hear what our world is like now as well."

"I don't know. I'm sure my dad is worried about me."

"One more day is all I'm askin'," Bothan said. He gave Jason a sorrowful look. "I beseech ye, Jason."

He felt his resolve crumble away. "Okay," he said. "One more day. But first thing tomorrow I really have to get back."

"Splendid! Oh, lad, you have my thanks for your kindness. And first thing in the morning, I'll send you back to your father, I will indeed."

"Be on your guard," Gatlor said. "Something feels amiss here."

He adjusted his grip on his sword as they approached the outskirts of Brayden Fenn. Their group consisted of himself, Seerka, Calador, and four Warders from the Haven, which the High One had insisted accompany them. The forest was completely silent except for the soft crunch of their footsteps on the path. Not even a breeze rustled the leaves overhead. The

Warders watched their surroundings intently as they moved slowly along the path. Seerka's eyes were almost completely black, with just a ring of gold around the edge. Calador's face did not betray any expression, but he gripped his axe firmly as he brought up the rear.

The village did not have a travel portal, so they had taken a portal to Edgewood, a quarter day's journey away. Even if there had been a portal in Brayden Fenn, Gatlor would have insisted upon using the other. He did not walk into the middle of any situation without first knowing what to expect, knowledge they did not have in this instance.

He spotted the first buildings through the trees and signaled the group to stop. He scanned the village but could not detect any movement.

He turned to Seerka. "Do you hear anything?"

The cat-man's ears swiveled forward and his eyes took on a feline intensity as he focused his senses on the village ahead of them. After a few moments he shook his head.

"Blood and bones!" Gatlor growled. "We need Lenai here."

"Indeed," Seerka agreed. "Her skills would prove very useful in our present situation."

"Well, nothing to be done for it," Gatlor said. "Come on."

Cautiously, the group moved forward. There was no sign of the villagers. His eyes swept the buildings and the ground for any clue to what might have happened, but saw nothing that offered any explanation for the villagers' strange absence.

"Blood has been spilled here," Seerka said. "The smell is inescapable. There is also another odor that I am not familiar with, but it is…unsettling."

Gatlor drew in a deep breath, but his sense of smell could not equal the Ferrin's. However, he knew the feline warrior well enough to accept what he said without question.

"Spread out," he ordered. "But take no chances. If you find anything, report it immediately." The others nodded and fanned out into the village. He turned toward the center of town. Perhaps something there would explain where the villagers had gone.

He scanned his surroundings constantly as he walked. The doors to several of the houses stood open although there was no movement inside. In some of the houses, he could see patches of blood-soaked floors, but no bodies. As he turned a corner, an almost imperceptible sound from the thick foliage overhead caught his ear. At the upper edge of his vision, he saw something dropping toward him. He dove forward and rolled to his feet, spinning around with his sword at the ready. As he saw what had fallen from the trees, he felt a dizzying moment of recognition. A bloodstained child's doll stared up at him.

With an effort, he tore his eyes from the toy and looked up. Four arm lengths above him, the glazed, dead eyes of Liana stared back at him, a look of terror forever frozen on her young face. He swallowed hard as an unfamiliar twinge of sorrow ran through him. The girl reminded him of his niece. For just a moment, he imagined how he would feel if it were his niece's eyes he was looking into, then a shock ran through his body as his eyes swept over the silken strands encasing her.

"Manarachs?!" Tal could not keep the shock from his voice. "Captain Gatlor, are you certain?" As he saw Gatlor's eyebrow rise slightly, he held up a hand. "Forgive me, of course you are certain. I was simply unprepared for such a report. We have not had any incidents with Manarachs in three generations. We thought they had died out."

They were standing in the Circle audience chamber. Tal and one or two of the other Loremasters gathered there after Secondmeal each day to meet with the residents and hear their concerns, but he had ordered the chamber cleared when Gatlor strode into the room, his face grim.

"Of course, High One," Gatlor said. "I found it hard to accept myself when I first saw the trapsilk, but there is no other explanation. There were no survivors that we could see."

Tal rubbed his forehead. "The timing of this is most disturbing. Tell me, did you see any sign of Jason Bennett in your search?"

"No. But as soon as I realized what had happened, I ordered our return. Our small group could not have stood against an attack by such creatures. As we were leaving, I did see that it looked like the villagers' bodies were all hanging from the trees over the village, but I would recommend a much larger force if you wish them recovered."

Tal tried to quiet his racing thoughts. Manarachs? Where had they been all this time? And why had they chosen to reveal themselves in such a violent fashion? Why now? As he opened his mouth to speak, a Warder ran into the audience chamber.

With a hasty bow the Warder said, "High One, please forgive the interruption, but Dronnin has been destroyed."

"What?" He could not believe what he was hearing. "How do you know this?"

"The sister of one of the residents lives nearby in Water's Edge. When she went to Dronnin this morning to see her sister, she found the village burned to the ground and the people slaughtered."

"Could they determine who was responsible for this attack?"

"Yes, High One," the Warder said. "Trellin bloodfangs were found in several of the dead."

Tal's mind was spinning. First Manarachs and now more Trellin? And all apparently coinciding with the disappearance of the young Far Planer. It seemed almost inconceivable that the events were unrelated. He drew a deep breath, letting it out slowly as he forced his thoughts into order. He needed his mind clear, and he needed to reassure the Warders that he had a firm grasp on the situation. As the chaos in his mind settled, he knew what they needed to do first.

He straightened, trying to project an air of confidence. "Contact all of the villages in which we have contact portals," he said. "For the smaller villages that do not have a contact portal, contact the main village in their province and have them make contact with the villages under their jurisdiction. We must determine if this is a terrible coincidence or if there is something else at work here, and I want those reports before nightfall."

"We will begin at once, High One."

"Also," he said before the man turned, "have the commanders of the Circle Guard and the Warders come to my quarters immediately, and notify all of the Loremasters that we will meet following the evening meal."

"Yes, High One."

"One more thing. Do not speak of this to anyone in the Haven, not even your families. Consider that a direct order from the Circle. I want to know exactly what it is that we face before this news gets out."

Tal could not remember a meeting of the Circle that he had looked forward to less than this one. As he had waited for the reports to come in from the towns under the protection of Lore's Haven, he had hoped against hope that the two villages were merely horrible aberrations, rather than a sign of something larger on the horizon. His hope was short lived as he learned of two more attacks. Now he faced the unenviable task of passing this tragic and disturbing news to the other members of the Circle, and to one member in particular. As he faced the curious stares of the Loremasters, he knew he could not put it off any longer.

"Four of our villages have been attacked," he said bluntly.

A collective gasp went up from the Circle. "What?" "Which villages?" "By whom?"

He raised his hands to quiet the Loremasters. When they were silent, he went on. "The villages were Dronnin, Shandil, Heartwood," he met the eyes of the Ruby Loremaster, "and Brayden Fenn."

All of the Loremasters turned to Brin. He stood slowly, his knuckles white on the arms of his chair. It was clear that it was taking every ounce of his self-control to maintain his composure.

With just a slight tremble in his voice, he asked, "Were there any survivors?" His eyes begged for an answer that he clearly knew Tal could not give.

Tal had never had a more difficult time saying one word. "No."

Brin closed his eyes and clenched his fists, letting out one soft moan. Then he opened his eyes. "And do we know who is responsible?" he asked.

"Dronnin was attacked by Trellin, as was Heartwood. Shandil apparently disappeared into the earth. We can only assume the Grithor are involved in some way." Tal paused for a moment, and then continued. "Brayden Fenn fell to Manarachs."

Brin grabbed at the arms of his chair, and then carefully lowered himself back into his seat as other voices spoke up. "Manarachs?" "Are you sure?" "How do we know it was Manarachs?"

Seated to either side of Brin, Seryn and Kalen laid sympathetic hands on his shoulders as he bit down on one knuckle of his clenched fists, his eyes once more tightly shut, silently mourning the loss of his son.

With a glance at Brin, Chon stood up. "High One," he said, in a more subdued voice than was normal from him, "how do we know it was Manarachs? No one has seen one in over a hundred years."

"I sent Captain Gatlor and some of his men to investigate this morning after receiving a disturbing report from one of the inhabitants of the Haven. It was he and his men who made the discovery and determined that Manarachs were responsible."

"This morning?" Delani asked. "High One, please do not take offense, but why were we not told of this earlier?"

"Perhaps that would have been the best course," he said, "but I did not want to raise any concerns until we knew more certainly what the situation was."

T'Kel spoke up. "How did we find out about the other villages?"

"While the captain was giving me his report, one of the Haven Warders came to me with news of Dronnin. It was then that I instructed the Ward commanders to make contact with the villages under our protection." He met each Loremaster's eyes. "Looking back, I see now that I should have notified you at that time, but I was blinded by the hope that we would discover these were the only two incidents. As you can see, it was a futile hope. I ask your forgiveness and understanding for my actions."

Jarril stood. "What do you propose we do now, High One?"

"I have already ordered the Ward commanders to start sending out regular patrols of the surrounding areas so that we are not caught unaware should an enemy decide to attack here. I have also given orders for the Circle Guard to increase their patrols of Lore's Haven, and that the patrols are to consist of a minimum of three guards. I do not want a repeat of what happened to Lenai to occur again."

"All of this without notifying the Circle?" Chon asked.

"I felt time was of the essence," he said. "I gave these orders as soon as I received word of the third and fourth villages. By then I had already called for a meeting of the Circle." Chon did not look satisfied by his answer.

"Has the Shanthi regained consciousness yet?" T'Kel asked. "Perhaps she could provide additional information."

Seryn shook her head. "Lenai still sleeps. I do not know how much longer it will be before she awakes."

"And there is still no word about the Far Planer?" Delani asked.

"No," Tal answered. "The Warders and the Guard have searched all of Lore's Haven and the surrounding countryside. No sign has been seen of him."

"I told you we should have killed him," Chon said. "None of this would have happened if the Circle would have listened to me."

Reyga stood. "There is no proof that Jason was behind this! Your accusations are unwarranted."

"You blind yourself, Reyga," Chon returned, rising to his feet. "One of our Circle Guard is attacked, one of our most promising students dies as a result of that attack, and four of our villages are destroyed along with everyone who lived in them. All apparently since the mysterious disappearance of this Far Planer. I suppose you would have us believe this is nothing but coincidence."

"I would have you withhold your judgment until we have more facts," Reyga snapped.

Brin spoke up unexpectedly, eyes burning. "The *facts* are that the prophecy says 'The last to arrive, he will already be here.' And the *fact* that his father somehow came to our world before him would appear to fulfill that part of the prophecy. I see no reason to ignore the rest, no matter what your personal feelings may be toward this boy."

"Aye," Chon added. "His destruction is our hope."

"Loremasters," Tal broke in, "we have already had this discussion, and agreed to a course of action. Whether the decision we reached together," here he looked pointedly at Chon, "will bode well or ill for us, it is a decision with which we have to live. Now please, take your seats and let us deal with the matter at hand."

As Chon and Reyga sat down, Jarril stood and said, "Then I will repeat my question, High One. What do you propose we do now?"

Tal looked into the eyes of the Loremasters. He did not want to pursue this course, but felt he had no choice. "Four villages being attacked at apparently the same time is not a coincidence," he said. "It is a blatant act of aggression. I do not wish to wait until we hear the reports from the scouting parties, only to find that the reports came too late." He gripped the edges of the podium as he continued. "Loremasters, I believe we must prepare for war."

The quiet room was abruptly abuzz as the Loremasters murmured to each other.

"War?" Jarril asked, his feline eyes focused on the High One. "Against whom? Unless there is more you have to tell us, we do not yet know who is responsible for these attacks."

"I do not need to see the hand wielding the blade to know that I am bleeding," he said into the silence that followed Jarril's question. "I need only know that I have been attacked, and prepare myself for the next blow as best I can. Those responsible will be revealed in due course. However, I do not believe it wise to wait until then to begin our preparations."

He scanned their faces. A mixture of emotions warred on their features.

"A day we had hoped would not come now appears to be on the horizon," he said. "I must confess, never in my life have I hoped to be wrong until now. But I would rather be wrong by preparing for something that does not happen, than to be wrong by failing to prepare for something that does."

Jason was dreaming he was back in the High One's chambers. He turned to see the shimmering being.

"High One, I would speak with this one."

Once again, Jason found himself inside the sphere, staring into the creature's starry eyes. This time, however, the being spoke. Its voice seemed to echo inside his head.

"Don't be afraid, Jason," it said. *"My name is Nyala, and I'm not going to hurt you."*

He released the breath that, until that moment, he hadn't realized he'd been holding.

"Okay," he said. "Uh, no offense, but what are you?"

"The question is...what are you?"

"What do you mean? I'm just a seventeen-year-old kid. Wait a second." He thought for a moment, mentally counting on his fingers. "Make that eighteen. I just had a birthday."

The creature shook its head. *"Oh no, Jason, you are much more than that."*

"I am?"

"Yes," Nyala nodded. *"You are Jaben. You are the hope of this world."*

"Oh," he said, looking down. Nyala's shining eyes and sparkling skin were a bit unnerving. "You mean that prophecy the High One was talking about. Are you sure about that? I mean, c'mon, I just turned eighteen." *And I didn't even get to celebrate it*, he thought. "How can I be the hope of your world?"

"That is what you must discover. That is why we are here."

"You're gonna tell me?"

"I will tell you what you need to know. I will teach you as much as I can, so that you will be able to do what you must. But, in the end, you will have to make a choice."

"A choice? What choice?"

"Patience, Jason. All of your questions will be answered, but you will not remember the answers until the proper time."

"Why not?"

"Because your choice must be made freely, and a choice based only upon what someone else has told you is not truly free. There are things you must learn and experience on your own. People you must meet and judge for yourself. Paths you must follow based solely upon your own truths, without any interference from the knowledge I will give you."

"So how will I know when this choice has to be made? Will I just suddenly remember everything?"

"You will remember parts of what transpires here as the time is right. When the time comes for you to decide, you will have the knowledge you need to choose."

"To choose what?"

"To choose what will become of our world."

"What? Hold on. Wait a minute." He shook his head as the full impact of the words struck home. "I…I…no. No! I can't decide the fate of your world. I'm eighteen, for crying out loud. Half the time I can't even decide what to watch on TV. The fate of a world? Forget it!"

"I am sorry this has fallen on you, Jason, but you cannot avoid your destiny. You must make this choice."

"Sure, that's easy for you to say," he shot back, forgetting his fear. He waved his hand at her. "You're some kind of…of super being or something. You probably decide the fates of worlds before breakfast. But I'm just a regular human being. We don't usually make those kinds of decisions, before or after breakfast."

"I understand how you feel."

"Yeah, right. How could you?"

As he watched, the sparkles surrounding her faded, until he was looking at a woman about his mother's age, with russet-colored hair and dark brown eyes. She gave him a slight smile. "Because we're not as different as you think."

"Wake up."

He looked around, trying to locate the source of the new voice.

"Wake up!" the voice repeated.

His eyes popped open. His ancestor stood over him.

"Jason, it's time to get up, lad."

"Wha..?" He rubbed his eyes. It had been a dream? Or had it been the first memories coming out, like she'd said would happen? He took a deep breath, trying to clear the fog from his head. If it had been a memory, then he could expect this sort of thing to happen again. *I'll just have to wait and see*. Then another thought occurred to him. The Altered were human? He didn't know if that was significant or not, but it was an interesting piece of information.

"I've got Firstmeal prepared, lad, as soon as you're ready," Bothan said, interrupting his contemplation.

"Okay, I'll be out in just a second."

Bothan nodded and left the room.

He laid there thinking about the things he and his ancestor had discussed the night before. Bothan had told him that he was stronger than any Loremaster on the Circle. Jason asked why Bothan didn't simply take over and set things right, if the Circle was as corrupt he had said.

"Well, lad," Bothan had answered, "while I'm sure I could handle any one of them alone, perhaps even two or three together, I canna stand against the combined power of the entire

Circle. Besides," he added, spreading his hands, "I'm not wanting to pick a fight with them. No one wins something like that. I tried to reason with them, but they would have none of it. The only reason I left was because I had come to fear for my own safety."

And now Jason was about to go back to the place his ancestor had left out of fear for his life. He didn't know if it was the best idea he'd ever had, but he wasn't about to leave his dad there if what Bothan said was true.

When he came out of his room, Bothan was already seated at the table, a plate piled high in front of him. He looked up as Jason walked in.

"After we eat, I'll send you back to Lore's Haven and your father," he said. He started to turn back to his meal, and then stopped. "That is, if you're still wanting to go."

"Yeah. If nothing else, I have to make sure Dad's okay."

"Aye, all right then," Bothan said. "Well, let's eat, and then I'll send you back. I still dinna like the thought of you bein' back in the hands of the Circle, but I'll respect your wishes. You still have the summoning stone?"

He pulled the amulet out of his shirt. "Right here."

"Good. Keep it close and keep it out of sight. I hope you'll not be needing it, but I'm thinking you'll soon be glad you have it."

"Why do I need to keep it out of sight?"

"If any of the Loremasters see it, they'll know it for what it is, and like as not they'll know who gave it to you. You won't be keeping it long if any of them see it, so keep it tucked away."

He dropped the stone back inside his shirt.

Bothan nodded. "Good. Now let's eat. I'll not be sending you back with an empty belly," he said with a grin and a wink.

Bothan watched the portal blink out of existence, taking Jason back to Lore's Haven.

"Do you think it wise to send him back to the Circle?" a sibilant voice said from behind him. "*His power, untapped though it may be, is greater even than yours."*

Bothan turned to look at the shadowy figure that had appeared after Jason's departure.

"He has power, 'tis true," he said, "but he doesn't know how to use it. Besides, he'll be back soon enough. And when he returns, he'll be more than willing to take up our cause against the Circle."

"You have a plan, then."

"Oh, aye," Bothan grinned. "I do indeed."

13
Homecoming

Gatlor scowled and slapped the blade in front of him aside with his sword.

"If you swing your blade like that in battle I will gut you myself," he snapped at the recruit.

The training yard echoed with the ring of steel as the group of men and women practiced. Following the orders of the Circle, he was conducting training drills for the new recruits. The word had gone out from the Haven at first light that volunteers were needed. Men and women began arriving within hours.

He grabbed the man's wrist and straightened it, clamping his other hand on the trainee's forearm. "Control the sword. Do not let the sword control you."

He turned away and shouted above the din in the yard. "Everyone *stop!*" Almost at once, the bladesong faded as the fighters lowered their swords and turned to face him. As he waited for silence, Gatlor noticed one of the Warders enter the training yard, apparently looking for him.

Once he was certain he had their attention, he said loudly, "You must never think of your sword as something you are simply holding in your hand." He began weaving his sword in an intricate pattern as he spoke, the sunlight dancing along the length of the blade. "It must become part of you, an extension of yourself and of your will. Just as you use your muscles to control your arm, so must you also use those same muscles to control your blade." With a final sweep, he sheathed his sword.

One by one, he met each gaze. "Listen to me very carefully, for I will only say this once. The first time you allow your blade to control you in battle…" He gave them a hard look. "You will die. Remember that. Now back to work."

As the group resumed their training, he walked over to the Warder.

"You have something?" he said.

"Sir," the man said with a salute, "we have found the Far Planer."

"Jason Bennett?"

"Yes, sir."

"Where?"

"He was on the road approaching Lore's Haven."

"What condition is he in?"

"He appears whole and unharmed."

"Indeed. And where is he now?"

"He is waiting just outside Lore's Haven with the gate Warders."

The muscles in Gatlor's jaw clenched as he glowered at the ground in front of him. "Go get two of your best men, and return here. Then we will take the Far Planer to the Circle chambers."

"Two men, sir? Do you believe he will resist?"

"No, I do not believe he will resist. You and the other two will be there to make sure I do not do anything unwise before we get him to the Circle."

The man raised an eyebrow, and then nodded. "I know just the men. I will get them at once." With a salute he turned and strode away.

While he waited, Gatlor thought about Jason Bennett. The young Far Planer was a bit of a mystery, and he did not like mysteries. Mysteries meant uncertainty, and, as a warrior, he had no room for uncertainties in his life.

He made it a personal rule not to trust Far Planers. His original impression of Jason Bennett had been that the youth was cocky and ignorant, a dangerous combination. Had he and his squad not been under the direct orders of the High One, he would have graciously suggested that Loremaster Reyga find another escort for their journey.

The incident with the Trellin had forced him to re-evaluate his position. While he had yet to decide whether the boy's actions were born of courage or foolish ignorance, he could not deny that, had Jason Bennett not acted when he did, Lenai would have been killed. Not that he and Lenai were close friends, but they had developed a professional relationship based upon mutual respect, something he did not give freely. He had no doubts about the Shanthi's honor, and considered her a valuable member of his squad. For that reason alone, he felt uncomfortably indebted to the Far Planer.

But then he disappeared, leaving behind an unconscious Lenai, who had later been found to be a lethal trap. Gatlor had grown up with Tor's older brother, and knew Tor and Elira well. Elira's sudden death hit him hard, and devastated Tor. He intended to see that whoever was responsible paid for their actions, and at the moment, all clues pointed to Jason Bennett. His teeth ground together at the thought that he could have been deceived.

And then there were the four villages that had been destroyed after the boy vanished. He did not believe in coincidence. What the Far Planer's part was in all of this was yet to be determined, but he was going to find out.

He looked up as the Warder entered the training yard accompanied by two other men. He shook his head as they reached him. "These are the two you had in mind?"

The Warder shrugged. "They seemed to be the best choice, sir."

Seerka gave him a wink. "Who better to keep you from doing something unwise?" he said with a feline smirk.

"Indeed," added Calador.

Gatlor rolled his eyes and began walking toward the opposite entrance, the three others falling in behind.

Jason stared out his window. The portal that brought him back to Lore's Haven had placed him about two hundred yards from the front gate, giving him his first view of the keep from the outside.

It rose from the earth like an extension of bedrock. The walls were made from massive blocks of white stone marbled with gray. The road led to an iron portcullis twenty feet high and equally as wide, flanked by two large gate towers with a walkway running between them. At each tower, and spaced along the parapets, were flags of iridescent material with a white starburst in the center, outlined in royal blue. As the flags waved in the breeze, the sunlight reflected from them in all the colors of the spectrum. He could see Warders stationed at the towers and at intervals along the wall walk.

Before he was within a hundred yards of the keep, shouts rang out from inside. Four armed Warders came out and stopped him just outside the gate. About twenty minutes later, Gatlor, Seerka, Calador, and another Warder appeared and escorted him inside. As they walked through the corridors, he couldn't help but feel the tension in the air.

The first time he'd walked through the halls of the keep, everyone he'd met seemed relaxed and welcoming. Now, the smiles and greetings, while still given, were subdued. Gatlor seemed even more on edge than before, if such a thing were possible. He didn't know what had changed, but the conversation with Bothan ran through his mind again and again. For his part, Gatlor had remained silent, telling him that the Circle would answer any questions he might have. Seerka, Calador, and the other Warder had not offered any information either.

Then he was in front of the Circle…

"I don't know what you're talking about," he said.

Confronting him was a rather short, stocky Loremaster with a staff made from woven strands of metal. The stone at the top of the staff was dark, with pearlescent streaks of color running through it. The Loremasters had all been civil enough, until this man stood up.

The man snorted. "So you would have us believe that your disappearance, and the subsequent destruction of four of our villages, is nothing more than a coincidence?"

"It's the truth!" Although shocked to hear about the villages, those feelings were quickly overwhelmed by his feelings of dislike toward this man. It was obvious that the feeling was mutual. "I don't know anything about any villages or anything else," he said. "All I remember is walking through the corridor with Lenai, and then waking up in the woods."

Bothan had suggested that he not mention his stay with his ancestor to the Circle, and until he knew more about what was going on, he thought that was probably a good idea.

"Well that's convenient," the man said. "You disappear, our villages are attacked, and you tell us you took a nap for a couple of days. I trust you are well rested?"

Reyga stood. "Chon! He said he knows nothing about it, and I, for one, believe him."

"Oh, I am certain of that, Reyga," Chon said. "And I have no doubt you would also believe it if—"

"Enough." The High One stood. "Both of you sit down," he ordered. Reyga and the Loremaster named Chon slowly settled back into their seats.

The rest of the meeting had gone downhill from there, until the High One declared an end and asked Jason to return to his quarters and remain there. He understood that it wasn't a request, and reluctantly agreed. Two Warders had accompanied him back to his room.

An insistent knocking on his door interrupted his reverie. *What now?* He opened the door and saw his father standing outside.

"Dad!" His reasons for returning flooded back.

"Jason," his father said. "Are you alright? These Warders weren't going to let me see you until I explained a few things to them about fathers and sons."

Jason couldn't quite suppress a grin. He knew how well his father was at explaining things to people.

"I'm okay, Dad," he said, as the elder Bennett wrapped his arms around him.

After his father let go, Jason closed the door, shutting the Warders outside.

"Dad, you're not going to believe what happened."

His dad frowned. "I thought you told the Circle that you didn't know what had happened," he said. "At least that's what Reyga said when he told me you had returned."

"I couldn't tell them, Dad, but I was with Bothan McFarland."

"Bothan McFarland? Our Bothan McFarland?"

"Yeah. The one who was supposed to have fallen in the well."

"So he did come here," his father whispered. "Amazing. But why couldn't you tell the Circle?"

"There's something going on between Bothan and the Circle. I'm not exactly sure what, but according to Bothan, the Circle is trying to control all knowledge, and keep all of the power to themselves and whoever they think should have it."

"I find that hard to believe. I've been here thirty years and I've never heard anything like that even hinted at."

"I know, but I guess Bothan used to live here at Lore's Haven too, and was even friends with the Loremasters. Now he says the Loremasters want to kill him."

His father pursed his lips. "That doesn't sound like any of the Loremasters I know."

"Well, people are different," Jason said. "I know it doesn't sound like Reyga, but that Chon doesn't seem like such a nice guy. How do you know they're all like Reyga? For that matter, how do you know Reyga is even like what he seems? How do you know it's not just an act?"

"Jason, I've known Reyga for longer than you've been alive," his dad answered. "So let me put the same question to you. How do you know Bothan is telling the truth? Maybe he's the one that has plans to attack the Circle, and not the other way around."

He frowned as he considered that. For some reason, the possibility that it was Bothan who might be lying had not crossed his mind. Before he could reply, a knock at the door interrupted their conversation. He opened the door and saw Reyga, Tal, and Seryn standing outside.

"May we come in, Jason?" Reyga asked.

He knew Reyga was trying to be polite, but couldn't help his irritated response. "Like I have a choice?"

"Jason," his dad said.

"Sorry," he muttered. "Sure, come on in." He moved back to the center of the room as the Loremasters entered.

"I am certain you have many questions," Tal said. "We will answer your questions as best we can, but first Loremaster Seryn needs to examine you." He looked at Jason's father. "I am sorry. I must ask you to wait outside."

The elder Bennett showed no sign of moving. Reyga placed a gentle hand on his shoulder.

"Please, my friend," Reyga said. "I promise nothing will be done to Jason, and I will explain everything later."

Bruce held Reyga's eye. "Fine," he said, "but I'm holding you responsible, old friend. He's my son and I don't want anything happening to him."

"Have no fear."

His father turned to him. "We'll talk more later." Then, with a glance at the three Loremasters, he walked out. Reyga closed the door behind him.

"Why do you need to examine me?" Jason asked. "I'm fine."

"Please, Jason," Reyga said. "It is necessary."

He wondered what they would do if he refused. As he looked at their faces, he saw that, once again, they weren't really asking. "Fine," he sighed. "What do I need to do?"

Seryn stepped forward. "Please lie down," she said. "It will be much the same as when you were in the healing area."

Once he was lying down, the Loremasters moved into position beside the bed. Seryn stood in the center, with Tal and Reyga to either side, their hands resting lightly on the Diamond Loremaster's shoulders. The two men raised their free hands, and Jason saw Tal's hand begin to glow with a milky white light, while green sparks danced on Reyga's fingers.

"Wait a second," he said. "I don't remember you two doing that before."

"Peace, Jason," Reyga said. "You will not be harmed, but this is a necessary precaution."

He tried to relax as Seryn's hands blossomed with the same soft argent light as in the healing area. That had been a pleasant experience, but he didn't know what to expect with the other two Loremasters displaying their power as they were.

"Please try to relax, Jason," Seryn said. "This will not harm you, but I must probe a little more deeply than when you were injured."

"Does this have something to do with what Reyga felt when I was at his place?"

"Perhaps," Seryn said. "That is yet to be determined. Now, please try to remain still and silent."

Seryn moved her hands to just above his head. Tal and Reyga seemed tense, which made him nervous. He closed his eyes and tried to focus on staying calm.

After a moment, he heard Seryn say, "Nothing unusual yet. I am going to probe more deeply now."

Jason opened his eyes and looked at her. Her eyes were closed, and her face showed her concentration. The *dimsai* danced on the other Loremasters' fingers as they focused on Seryn.

A tiny line furrowed the space between her eyes. He wondered what she was looking for. Then her eyes opened suddenly. "Oh!"

Instantly, a barrier of energy sprang up between Jason and the three Loremasters. He flinched away at the sudden appearance of the crackling shield, almost falling off the other side of the bed. The glow left Seryn's hands and she grasped the men's wrists.

"No," she told them. "There is no danger here." Tal and Reyga looked at her then extinguished their power as well.

"What's going on?" he asked. "What was that all about?"

"My apologies, Jason," Tal said. "There was an incident during your absence which has required us to take certain precautions."

"What kind of incident?"

"I think that would be best discussed another time," Tal answered. "For now, suffice it to say that I do not believe it necessary for you to remain in your quarters."

"So I can go out and walk around?"

Tal nodded. "Yes. My only request is that you tell the Warders where you are going whenever you leave. They will remain posted here at your door."

"Why?"

"You were abducted once, Jason. I would hate to see that happen again."

He thought it was a pretty flimsy excuse, but didn't want to make them mad and possibly risk being confined to his room again, so he didn't say anything.

Tal seemed satisfied with his silence. "I would also like to talk with you again," he said. "I will send for you tomorrow."

"Okay."

"Then we will wish you a good evening," Tal said. "Loremasters, we have matters we need to discuss."

Seryn nodded to Jason, with Reyga adding a wink to his nod, and the three Loremasters left him alone in the room.

The next morning, Jason woke up still unsure whether the Circle was telling the truth or his ancestor. He needed to talk with his dad some more. He opened the door and saw two Warders stationed outside.

"You wouldn't happen to know where my dad is, would you?" he asked.

One of the Warders nodded. "He came by earlier and requested that we tell you when you woke that he would be in the training yard.

"Where's that?"

After the Warder explained how to get to the training yard, Jason went to find his father. Ten minutes and two wrong turns later, he found the entrance.

As he opened the door to the training yard, a cacophony of clashing metal, shouting trainers, and the grunts of men and women swinging their weapons met him. The smell of sweat and leather hung in the air, joined by smoke and ash from the forges at one end of the yard. The sound of the smiths' hammers formed a ringing cadence winding in and out of the other sounds.

The balcony ran around the yard, broken occasionally by steps leading down to the training area. There were also several entrances to the yard at ground level. A small set of sturdy benches stood along the far wall.

Jason saw Gatlor barking orders at a group of swordsmen, while a short distance away, Seerka was a blur as he fended off three men attacking him with blunted sticks.

Dominating one corner of the training area, Calador was studying a scroll of some sort. *Just as well,* Jason thought, *who's going to spar with him?* No sooner had the thought crossed his mind, when a second Dokal warrior ducked through the entrance in Calador's corner. Laying the parchment aside, Calador stood and greeted the newcomer, and then picked up two large clubs. An instant later, the two were engaged in a furious exchange of strikes and parries. Jason watched for a few moments, fascinated by the battle dance of the behemoths, and then observed, with some amusement, the men closest to the two giants decide to train in another section of the yard.

He saw his father standing at one end of the benches. Reyga was there as well, seated at the opposite end talking with one of the Warders. Jason waved to get his dad's attention, and motioned for him to stay put while he came down.

Steps led down from the balcony close to where his father was standing. Rather than try to cross the yard, he decided to walk around the balcony. He was about halfway there when what sounded like a clap of thunder rang out. Everyone stopped and looked around for the source. Then, from an entrance behind his father, Chon stepped into the yard.

"Hear me!" the Loremaster shouted. "And heed my words well." His voice echoed from the stone walls. "I serve Teleria! I serve the prophecy." He took another step into the yard. Chon's was the only movement. His audience was frozen, waiting for his words.

"What I do, I do for Teleria and for the prophecy." Another step, and still no one moved. "The prophecy says 'His destruction is our hope.'"

Jason noticed Chon's steps were bringing him closer and closer to his father. Suddenly, he knew what was about to happen. "No, no, no…" he whispered as he started walking, and then running, for the stairs.

"His destruction is our hope!" With one hand, Chon grabbed Jason's father and spun him to face the yard. His other hand lifted a wickedly curved dagger over his head. The curves of the blade burned into Jason's mind as it hovered above his father. For an instant, the sunlight flashed off the blade, piercing his eyes.

"For Teleria!" Chon shouted, and plunged the dagger into Bruce Bennett's chest.

"No!" Jason screamed.

As Bruce Bennett's body sank to the ground, the Loremaster yanked the dagger out and disappeared into a portal that opened and closed before anyone could react.

Without knowing how, Jason was on his knees, cradling his dad's body. "Dad! Dad!" he pleaded, as tears burned hot trails down his cheeks. "C'mon, Dad, wake up. Wake up! It's gonna be okay. Please don't leave me. Please be okay. Please, please, please…" His father didn't move. He buried his face in his father's shoulder. "Dad, no…"

A small part of him noted that no one had moved yet. The rest was too overcome with grief to care. Then he felt a hand on his shoulder, and Seerka's voice intruded upon his loss.

"Jason—"

"GET AWAY FROM ME!" His grief exploded into rage. "Don't *touch* me!" Blinded by his sudden fury, he barely noticed Seerka flying through the air away from him. His dad was dead at the hands of a Loremaster! He let his father's body slide to the ground. It was just an empty shell now. But he wasn't empty. A wrath like none he had ever known filled his soul. Even his skin felt like it was on fire.

He stood and faced the yard. The men and women there squinted against a glare that threw their shadows into sharp relief upon the walls. He didn't know where the light was coming from, nor did he care. He scanned the faces until he found the one he was looking for: Reyga.

He pointed a finger at the Loremaster. "Bothan was right," he grated. His voice sounded alien to him. "He told me not to trust you. He told me about the prophecy, and what it really meant."

He looked at his dad's body. The suddenness of his loss tore at him again. Then the rage returned. He glared at Reyga. "But I didn't want to believe him. I wanted to see for myself. My dad didn't believe him either, and now he's dead. Killed by one of *you!"*

Reyga raised a hand. "Jason, please—"

"No!" Now it was Jason's voice echoing from the stone. "I gave you a chance, and it cost me my father. I won't make that mistake again."

He reached inside his shirt and pulled out the summoning stone. He gripped it tightly and concentrated on Bothan as hard as he could. Almost immediately, a portal opened up beside him.

"Don't try to find me," he said coldly. "Don't any of you try to find me. I promise you'll be sorry if you do."

Then he turned and stepped through the portal.

Reyga was stunned. So much had transpired within the last few minutes that even his disciplined mind was finding it difficult to know what to focus on first.

When Chon stabbed Bruce Bennett, Jason had reached his father with a speed only possible with *dimsai.* Then, when Seerka attempted to comfort Jason, the Ferrin was blasted into the air by a corona of power that erupted around the young man.

Only Seerka's feline reflexes saved him from injury when he hit the ground.

Reyga replayed the events in his mind. The question about what Reyga felt in Jason had been answered in dramatic fashion. In its place, new questions arose. Was Chon a traitor? Why did he kill Bruce Bennett? Where was Jason now, and how would he respond to his father's murder, apparently at the hands of a Loremaster? Jason had said his ancestor was right. Another question answered that gave rise to even more. What were Bodann's plans for Jason? What had he told Jason about the Circle? Was Chon in league with Bodann?

His thoughts turned to the Obsidian Loremaster. Certainly Reyga and Chon saw Teleria through different eyes, and had even had their share of tense moments during meetings of the Circle. But there had ever been an underlying current of mutual respect between them. For all of Chon's blustering, he often made observations that caused the Circle to rethink its position. Reyga found it difficult to believe the man capable of what he had just witnessed. But, then again, events over the last sixday had Reyga questioning his own judgment on more than one matter.

He wiped a hand over his face. That was all for another time. For now, there were other matters to which they must attend. He knew one of the Warders would already be hurrying to notify the High One, so he focused on the one question that might lead to answers to several others. He turned to find Gatlor at his elbow.

"We must find Loremaster Chon," Reyga said. "Have the Warders conduct a thorough search of the Haven. If he is not found, be prepared to alert all of our villages to notify us if he is seen, should the High One order it."

Gatlor nodded. He started to turn away, then stopped. "Loremaster Reyga," he said, "I know you thought well of Jason Bennett, but even were he not an enemy before, we must certainly consider him one now."

Reyga stared at the body of his friend. "Aye," he said at last. "Unless we can prove the Circle is not responsible for this atrocity, that would be the prudent position to take. At least for the time being."

A Warder ran up to them. "Loremaster Reyga, the High One has summoned all Loremasters to an immediate meeting of the Circle."

"Of course," he said, "where we will discuss and debate yet more questions to which we do not have the answers."

"Loremaster?" the Warder asked.

He shook his head. "Pay no heed," he said. "Thank you for notifying me. I will go there at once." He nodded to the Warder and Gatlor, and then headed for the Circle chambers.

14
More Questions

"There you go," the young woman said. "That arm should be fine now."

The boy sitting on the treatment table cautiously flexed his arm, and then smiled as he realized there wasn't any pain.

"Thanks, Meryl," he said. "You are the best."

Meryl smiled at her little brother. "You say that now, Cord, but when I get my tasks at home done before you, you will be saying something else." She ran a fond hand through his curly hair as he slid off the table. "Now go home and let mother see that you are healed. And get ready, because she has told you before that you were going to break your arm climbing that wall. Now that you did, you will never hear the end of it."

The boy scuffed at the floor with his toe. "I know," he said. "All right." He gave her a quick hug and headed out the door. Before she could turn away, he poked his head back around the doorjamb.

"And if anyone asks, I never hugged you!"

"Not a word," she chuckled. "Now get going!"

Cord flashed her an impish grin and disappeared into the hallway. Shaking her head with a smile, she turned back to the figure on the bed. Her smile faded as she looked at the Shanthi girl. Lenai was completely motionless. The only sign of life was the slight rise and fall of the sheet.

Meryl was a fourth year student in the Diamond Order, and she had never seen or heard of anything like this. No one had. What had been done to Lenai struck at the very heart of everything the Diamond Order stood for. They were healers, using their talents to mend broken bodies and spirits. Whoever had done this to Lenai had used her as an instrument of death, violating her in a way that no healer in the Order could ever hope to repair. Meryl knew how highly the Shanthi valued honor. She did not envy the person who would have to tell Lenai about what had been done to her, and the terrible results that followed.

She studied the still figure, but did not see any change, so she turned and walked back to the table where she had been grinding herbs before Cord arrived. While the healers could always use *dimsai* to mend major injuries, the intimate nature of their power was something they preferred to avoid when treating minor cuts, scrapes, or pains. In these instances, they used herbs and other plants for treatment, using their *dimsai* abilities to infuse the elixirs, salves, and powders with extra potency.

She gave the ground up leaves in the bowl a few more turns with the pestle, and then reached for some dried berries to add to the mixture. A loud gasp caused her hand to jerk, sending berries rolling across the table. She spun around, expecting to see that someone had entered the room. Instead she saw Lenai, awake and blinking as if in a daze. Potions forgotten, she hurried over to the bed.

"Lenai?"

The Shanthi girl turned toward her, but was clearly having a difficult time focusing.

"Lenai, are you well?" When Lenai still did not answer, Meryl tried again. "Lenai, can you hear me? Do you understand my words?"

Lenai's gaze wandered across the ceiling. "Where…?" she whispered.

"You are in the healing area in Lore's Haven. You have been here for two days."

The Shanthi's brow furrowed as she closed her eyes again. "Thirsty."

Meryl filled a mug and slid her hand underneath Lenai's neck. She gently lifted her head so she could drink. After a few sips, she laid her head back.

"Where is Jason Bennett?" Lenai asked.

"No one knows," Meryl said.

"I must speak with the High One." Lenai struggled to sit up.

Carefully pushing down on her shoulders, Meryl said, "Lenai, no. You must rest. Please. I will send someone with word that you are awake, but you must stay here until Loremaster Seryn can examine you."

After a moment of struggling against Meryl's grip, Lenai gave up and settled back onto the bed. Her heavy breathing betrayed her weakened state.

"Lenai," Meryl said, "the Circle is meeting as we speak. If you will give me your word that you will stay here and rest, I promise I will send someone immediately to tell them you have awakened."

For a moment she thought Lenai was going to refuse, but then the Shanthi closed her eyes and nodded. "Very well," she said. "It would appear that I am too weak to do otherwise."

Meryl breathed a sigh of relief. "Good," she said. "Rest and I will go find someone right now to notify the Circle. I will return shortly to check on you." Then she turned and left the room, calling for someone to take a message to the Circle.

"Loremaster Chon must be found and held accountable for his actions!" the Amethyst Loremaster demanded.

"Of that there is no question, Loremaster Delani," Tal said. "But his actions may have exposed an even more serious problem which must be addressed." He looked around the Circle. "We have lived in relative peace for generations. During that time, although we have occasionally had disagreements, this body has always acted as one. Now, we are faced with what is undoubtedly our gravest hour, and one of our number has taken matters into his own hands. This must not happen. If we are to face and survive the events implied by Taleth's prophecy, we must remain united."

The Circle murmured their agreement. Then the Amber Loremaster stood.

"Perhaps Chon was not in control of his actions?" Jarril suggested. "He has ever been outspoken, but he has also always accepted the Circle's decisions, even when differing from his own beliefs. His actions were out of character, even for him."

"That is, of course, one possibility," Tal said. "However, we all know how strong Loremaster Chon was. In truth, he was one of the strongest among us. If he was being controlled, the one doing the controlling must have considerable power."

Kalen stood. "High One, that would suggest that others among us may also be susceptible to such control."

"Or perhaps are already being controlled," T'kel added as Kalen sat down.

The Loremasters looked at each other. "How would we know?" Reyga asked. "Chon seemed himself until this morning."

Tal did not answer immediately. Jarril and Kalen offered a disturbing possibility, one that had not crossed his mind. If a Loremaster could be controlled, the Circle itself would be compromised, and the one doing the controlling would be privy to everything said in this chamber.

Just then there was a knock. Tal motioned and the door swung open, admitting one of the Warders. He entered and bowed quickly to the Circle.

"High One, we have found Loremaster Chon."

"Where?"

"He was in a store room on one of the lower levels," the Warder said. "But—"

"Did you bring him with you?" Delani interrupted.

"He is dead."

"What? Dead? How?" Tal asked.

The Warder shook his head. "We do not know. He appears to be unmarked."

Tal stroked his lower lip as he studied the floor. First Bruce Bennett, and now his apparent murderer, Chon. That would mean yet someone else must be involved, that being the person who had killed Chon. But unless he had been taken by surprise, whoever killed Chon must be very powerful indeed. He knew Chon well enough to know that, if at all possible, the man would have fought back with all of the considerable power at his disposal. That no one reported anything unusual could only mean he was unable to respond to his attacker.

He looked at the Warder. "Have Loremaster Chon's body taken to the healing area. I assume Bruce Bennett's body is already there?" The Warder nodded. "Very well," Tal said. "See to Loremaster Chon's body."

"Yes, High One."

Tal turned to Seryn. "Loremaster Seryn, we need to ascertain the cause of Loremaster Chon's death, if we can."

"Of course, High One," Seryn said. "With your permission, I will go to the healing area now."

Another knock on the door to the Chamber interrupted them. Without waiting for an answer, the door opened, and another Warder stepped inside. He bowed quickly.

"My apologies for the intrusion, High One, but Lenai has awakened."

"When?"

"Just now," the Warder answered. "The healer summoned us immediately, and we came directly here to notify you."

Tal turned to the Circle. "Loremasters, I am certain you will understand when I say I think it best if we cut this meeting short?"

Several of the Loremasters nodded. "Of course, High One." "Certainly."

"Thank you," Tal said. He turned to Seryn. "Loremaster Reyga and I will accompany you to the healing area." Reyga moved to join the High One.

"High One," Brin said, standing. "I would like to come with you."

Tal hesitated. "Loremaster Brin—"

"My son is dead," Brin said. "I believe I have paid the price for whatever information Lenai may be able to give." He held Tal's eye while he waited for an answer.

"Of course," Tal said. He motioned for Brin to join them and the four Loremasters headed for the healing area.

The conversation with Lenai had been brief. She was still very weak from her experience, although she was able to confirm the sequence of events relayed to the Circle by Jason. Seryn insisted they continue the discussion later, after Lenai regained her strength. The High One dispatched a messenger for the Loremasters to have their strongest students set wards about the Haven to prevent any portals other than the main ones from opening from outside the keep.

Now they stood over the Obsidian Loremaster's body. Reyga ran his eyes over it. "Something is not right," he mused. Something about Chon's body disturbed him, but he could not decide what it was.

"Look at his face," Tal said. The dead Loremaster's features were frozen in a grimace of unmistakable fear.

"He was afraid," Brin said.

Reyga shook his head. "I have known Chon to be many things, but 'afraid' is not one of them."

"Nevertheless," Seryn observed, "he was clearly terrified at the moment of his death."

"What could have frightened him like that, and yet kill him without leaving a mark?" Brin asked.

Reyga could not imagine anything that would have had that effect on Chon. The other Loremasters shook their heads as well.

"Yet another puzzle we must decipher," Tal said.

One of Seryn's students approached. "Loremaster Seryn," she said, "may I have a word?"

Seryn nodded. "Please excuse me," she said to the three men. "I will be but a moment." Then she followed the young woman out of the room.

Tal motioned to a healer standing nearby.

"Yes, High One?" the man said.

"You examined Loremaster Chon's body?" Tal asked.

"Yes, High One, I performed the initial examination."

"Were you able to determine the cause of his death? Were there any marks on him?"

"We believe he had his air supply cut off in some way," he said, "although we cannot find any external evidence to support that belief. There are no marks or injuries anywhere on the body. Our conclusion is based solely on our *dimsai* examination of the internal organs." He shook his head. "We are at a loss to explain it, High One. I apologize for our lack of answers."

"No apology is necessary. I am certain you did a thorough job," Tal said. "It is just another mystery among the many that have been born this past sixday."

Reyga was only half listening to the conversation. He was looking at Chon's body, still trying to determine what was wrong with it. He looked up as he heard a door open, and saw Seryn re-enter the room, a look of perplexed consternation on her face.

"You look puzzled," he said when she reached them. Considering the events of the day, he was not sure if he really wanted to know the source of her dilemma. The questions were piling up too quickly, with no answers in sight.

"Indeed," she said. "'Puzzled' would be a mild description."

"How so?" Tal asked.

She indicated the door through which she had entered. "The body of Jason Bennett's father was taken to that room."

The three men nodded.

"Is there something unusual about Bruce Bennett's body?" Brin asked.

"I do not know," she answered, "for the body in that room is not that of Bruce Bennett."

"What?"

"What do you mean it is not Bruce Bennett?" Tal asked.

"High One, the body in that room has been fashioned to appear to be Jason Bennett's father, but not only is it not Bruce Bennett, the body in that room is not even human."

Reyga closed his eyes and pinched the bridge of his nose. Another question, another mystery. He could feel a headache coming on.

15
Puzzle Pieces

Jason was back in the bed at his ancestor's home, his emotions swinging from overwhelming grief and loss to barely controlled fury and back again. When he first came to Teleria, he'd thought he was alone. Then they found his father. Now he was alone again, his dad murdered at the hands of that obnoxious Loremaster Chon. All he wanted was to wake up and realize this had all been nothing more than a dream.

The image of the dagger plunging into his dad's chest ran through his mind again and again. They would pay for what they'd done. He didn't know how yet, but they would pay.

He thought about Bothan's reaction when he used the summoning stone…

The tears blurred his vision as he stepped out of the portal. Then he felt Bothan's strong hands on his shoulders.

"Laddie, what's wrong? What's happened that's brought you back to me so?"

He could barely stand. "They killed my dad!" he sobbed. "The Loremasters killed him."

"Oh, no. Oh, Jason, I'm so sorry." He felt Bothan's arms surrounding him. "Go ahead, lad, let it out. Bothan's here for you."

Grief wracked his body as he buried his fists in his ancestor's robes. Eventually, the spasms subsided. He let go of Bothan and stepped back, wiping his face.

"You were right," he said, looking at the ground. "Everything you said. I should have listened to you."

"Now, now, we'll talk about that later," Bothan said. "Right now you need to rest, and take time to deal with this."

"I don't want to rest," he said. "I want to get even. I want them to pay for killing my dad."

"Aye, lad, I'm sure you do," Bothan nodded. "But there will be time for all that. Right now you need to get some rest and let this all get sorted out in your head."

Jason looked at the ceiling over the bed. The wild swinging of his emotions had stopped, at least for now, leaving him cold and empty inside. He didn't see how he could possibly sleep, but as he lay there staring up into the shadows, he felt his eyelids getting heavier. *At least if I'm asleep I won't have to think about it.* He didn't try to fight as his eyes closed.

A dark-haired woman was smiling at him. "Because we're not as different as you think," she said.

"You're human?"

"Once. Now we're something else, a combination of human and *dimsai*."

"We? You mean everyone in Teleria?"

"No, only the Altered," she said. "I imagine you'll have been told of us by the time you remember this. Let's just say we've been here since this all began and leave it at that for now."

"But why was the High One so surprised to see you if you've been around that long?"

She shrugged. "Most people have forgotten about us. We've kept to ourselves for quite some time," she said. "At least until now."

"What's different now?"

"I can't say, other than to tell you that things have changed recently. Forces are at work that want to reshape Teleria."

"So why don't you just stop them?" he asked. "Why do you need me?"

"The Altered agreed long ago not to interfere in human affairs. That agreement is still binding."

"But aren't you interfering now?"

"I have no choice. I'm taking a great risk, but if I don't, this world will never be the same."

"Why?"

She looked at him for a long moment before answering. "When we first became Altered, we suddenly found we had powers beyond anything we could imagine. But we didn't have control of our newfound powers. In spite of this, some of us started thinking we were higher beings, even gods, and began changing things to suit ourselves." She shook her head. "The results weren't always pretty. Then we started fighting as we disagreed over matters that seemed to get more and more petty every day. Finally, in an all too brief moment of sanity, we realized that the only way we could get along, and the only way we could keep from tearing this world apart, would be to promise not to use our powers to affect this world at all. We formed a Covenant. It's the only thing that's kept the peace between us."

"Let me guess," he said. "Someone wants out of the agreement."

She nodded. "One of the other Altered has been moving behind the scenes to orchestrate our return into this world to be worshipped as gods."

"So why not just tell the others?"

"We rarely speak to each other anymore. But if my actions, or the actions of the other one, are discovered, I don't know how the rest will react. It could trigger a war between the Altered that would make the Devastation look like a children's spat. That's why, when you begin to remember, you must not tell anyone, not even the people you trust the most. To reveal anything before you have remembered everything could place you, and possibly others, in grave danger."

He thought about what Reyga had told him about the Devastation. He wondered exactly how much power the Altered had.

"So how do I fit into all of this?" he asked.

"You have, within you, the ability to use *dimsai*," she said. "In fact, you have the potential to become more powerful than any Loremaster or *saiken lo* in Teleria, maybe even as strong as we are."

"What? No way!" he exclaimed. "I don't have any power."

"Yes, you do, and I'm going to teach you how to use it."

With a start, he sat up in his bed. The morning sun sent streamers of light through the window, and he could hear Bothan in the other room. He looked around, half expecting to see Nyala, but the dream memory was over.

He absently stroked the covers as he thought about what she'd said. She had to be wrong. He knew he didn't have any power. Then a fragment of memory came to him, of Seerka flying away from him as he held his father's body. And the people in the training yard had been squinting against a bright light. Had it been coming from him? Had he sent Seerka flying through the air? Could it be possible?

He shook his head. It was just too weird. But if she was right, and he really did have that kind of power, maybe he could make the Circle pay for what they'd done to his dad. He'd bring down Lore's Haven, stone by stone. No, that wouldn't work. If he brought down the keep, people could be hurt, or maybe even killed, that hadn't had anything to do with his dad's death. He'd have to come up with a way to avenge the loss of his father without hurting anyone except the Circle. Otherwise, he'd be no better than them.

The one thing he was sure of was that, until he knew whether or not he really had the kind of power Nyala said, he wasn't going to tell anyone about his dreams.

"Jason," Bothan called. "You up yet, lad? Firstmeal is ready!"

"I'm up," he called back. "I'll be right there." Yeah, he'd keep all of this to himself for now. He struggled out of bed and went to get some breakfast.

"Uh, Bothan, can we talk? If you're not busy, that is," Jason asked after they had finished their morning meal.

"Of course, lad. I'm never too busy for a kinsman." He motioned for Jason to follow him into the next room. When they were seated, he said, "Now, what's on your mind?"

"Well..." He wasn't sure how to ask his question. He was a little afraid his ancestor might take it as an accusation. He decided to just blurt it out and hope for the best. "When I was at Lore's Haven, they told me that four of their villages had been attacked while I was here. Have you heard anything about that?"

Bothan didn't say anything. Jason started getting nervous, but then the big man nodded. "Aye," he said. "I'd heard something of the sort. I suppose I was hoping it was nothing more than a rumor until you asked about it."

"So, what happened?"

"Well, as I hear it, there were three different races that had the undoing of those villages."

"Three?"

"Aye," Bothan said. "Two were attacked by Trellin. That'd be the lizard men that attacked your party on the way to the keep. Two different races attacked the other villages."

"What races?"

"I, uh, haven't heard the others mentioned by name," Bothan said.

"Why would they attack those villages?"

"Well, lad, resentment toward the Circle has been growing for a number of years now, and not just among humans. And those particular villages have always been among the strongest supporters of the Circle."

"But why not just attack Lore's Haven and the Circle, instead of villages where innocent people and children would get killed?"

Bothan shrugged. "Who knows how other races think?" He leaned forward. "But I'll tell you this, it would take a fair sized army to have even the slightest chance to take the keep directly, it bein' at the top of a small mountain as it is. And since that's where those Loremasters are always hiding, that leaves innocents to take the brunt of the wrath that should rightly be directed at the Circle. Bunch of spineless cowards they are, if you ask me."

Jason thought about children in the hands of the Trellin. Images of the Rodinn children Lenai had played with and the little boy on his father's shoulders ran through his mind. Then he saw the dagger again, descending towards its target.

"So," he said, "what would happen if something were to happen to the Circle? Like if there wasn't a Circle anymore?"

Bothan's eyebrows rose. "Why, I suppose all the knowledge the Circle has been hoarding would be available to everyone. People could start governing themselves instead of bowing to the Circle." He studied Jason. "But, lad, the Circle has been in power for centuries. They're not just going to up and leave."

"I guess not," he said, going over the idea in his head. "But what if someone could get all of the other races to join together and demand that the Circle step down and give the knowledge to the people?"

"Well now, that's an interesting idea, Jason, my boy," Bothan said. A slow smile crossed his face. "Aye," he nodded, "that's a very interesting idea indeed."

Tal sat in his quarters, with Gatlor and two Warder commanders sitting across the table from him.

"Captain Gatlor, how goes the recruiting?" he asked.

"So far, we have received upwards of four thousand recruits, with more still arriving," Gatlor said. "At the moment, we are only accepting men and women sixteen years of age and older. If we add those from thirteen to sixteen, we probably add another seven hundred, perhaps eight. We have also received pledges of aid from several other races, most notably the Ferrin and the Dokal. All told, if it were necessary to field an army today, and if the races held true to their pledges, we could probably field an army of six to seven thousand. However, recruits are still arriving. Another sixday may bring that number closer to ten thousand."

"Very good," Tal nodded. He turned to the Warders. "Commander Jorik, Commander Garyn, our army does us no good if we do not know at whom to point it. All of the villages that were attacked are to our south. I want scouting parties sent out across our southern borders and beyond. We must know if there is an enemy army gathering, and how big it is, if that is indeed the case."

"Yes, High One," the two men answered.

"And," Tal added, "see that no scouting party has less than four soldiers. Additionally, each party should have a *saiken lo* with them. We know the Manarachs have made their presence known once more. A *dimsai* adept would give a scouting party their best chance of escape from such creatures. The Amethyst Order will be sending out hawks to assist in searching the more difficult terrain. Please coordinate your efforts with Loremaster Delani and her students."

"We will meet with the Amethyst Loremaster and begin forming the parties at once, High One," Commander Jorik said. The two men stood and left the room.

Tal turned to Gatlor. "So, Captain, tell me. What are your thoughts on this situation?" he asked. "Do you believe we have a war on our hands? And if so, what do you think we will be facing?"

Gatlor took a deep breath before answering. "High One," he began, "I do believe we will soon be at war. Four villages attacked by three different races means only one thing in my mind. As to what we will face, we will only know that when we find their army. Most certainly Manarachs, Grithor, and Trellin, at the very least. There may also be other races as well, but without question, the Manarachs will be the most dangerous. Trellin are strong, but not very intelligent, and the Ruby Order should be able to find any traps set by the Grithor." He spread his hands. "Other than that, we will have to wait for the reports from the scouting parties."

"And the preparations?"

"Going well. The Amber and Emerald Orders are coordinating efforts to create bows and arrows, with help from the Amethyst Order for the fletching. The Obsidian and Ruby Orders are making armor and weapons. Emerald and Sapphire students are growing crops and laying up food supplies, should we find ourselves in need of them."

"Very good." He was hesitant about his next question, but he wanted to know the warrior's feelings. "And what are your thoughts on the situation with Jason Bennett?"

Gatlor's fingers drummed the table as he studied its surface. Finally, he looked up. "The situation is most confusing, High One. Loremaster Chon, while always outspoken, has never acted rashly, nor against the wishes of the Circle. I know he felt the prophecy called for Jaben's death, but I do not understand what he hoped to accomplish by killing the boy's father. All it appears to have done is to convince Jason Bennett that we are his enemy. If the boy is Jaben, and has the power the prophecy implies, I can only hope Loremaster Chon's actions do not come back to plague us later."

"Indeed, Captain," Tal said. "I add my hopes to yours."

Lenai was numb and the healing area seemed very cold. She woke the day after speaking with the Loremasters already acutely aware of her failure to safeguard Jason Bennett. Now, to find out that she had also been used as an instrument of death directed against the very people she was sworn to serve was almost more than she could bear. She looked at the three Loremasters standing at her bedside. She knew they were waiting for her, but she didn't know what to say. Then her eyes stopped on the Diamond Loremaster, and she knew one thing that needed to be said. She only hoped she could get the words out without losing her composure.

"Loremaster Seryn," she said, "I am deeply sorry for your loss. I ask your forgiveness for my part in the death of your student."

Seryn shook her head. "Lenai, no forgiveness is required. You share no fault in what was done. Please do not accept blame where none is given."

"But had I reacted more quickly—"

"Nothing would be different," Reyga broke in. "There was nothing you could have done."

She started to protest, but the High One stopped her. "Lenai," he said, "Loremaster Seryn and Loremaster Reyga are correct. Whoever did this possesses more power than any Loremaster on the Circle. Not even the most highly trained warrior could have prevented what happened. We are simply relieved that you are well once more, as much as we mourn the loss of Elira."

Well. She looked down at the sheet. She would have laughed if there were any laughter left in her. It would be long before she was well.

If she had ever taken pride in anything, it was in her service to the Circle. Only in that service did she feel that she was, in some small way, helping to redeem the honor of her people. That honor had been stained by the *rishna kel*, those Shanthi who used their abilities as thieves and mercenaries and worse. Now, even here in the one human place where no one looked down on her race, her service had been tainted. She had failed to fulfill her responsibility regarding the Far Planer, and she had been the weapon that struck down one of the Diamond Order's finest pupils. For the first time since she had left her telosh, she felt lost and unsure. She needed to get away from the eyes that accused her with sympathy rather than scorn.

"Loremaster Seryn," she said, looking up from the sheet, "I am feeling stronger. May I be released from the healing area?"

"Not just yet. I would like you to stay for another day, perhaps two," Seryn said. "I do not know what effect your experience may have on you."

"Then, would it be acceptable for me to rest in my quarters? I would prefer to be alone if you would allow it."

Seryn studied her, a look of concern clouding her features. "I understand. If you will remain in your quarters, I would have no objection."

"I will stay in my quarters."

"Very well. I will send someone to check on you in the morning."

"Thank you." She swung her legs over the side of the bed, and stood. A wave of weakness threatened to send her to her knees, but the tattered remnants of her pride forced her to remain steady. She was not as strong as she claimed, but she simply could not remain here anymore. Only in the solitude of her quarters could she allow herself to feel the full brunt of her failure. She nodded to the three Loremasters and left the room.

Gatlor studied the map. A series of small discs marked areas that had already been searched. Each time a patrol reported in, he placed another disc on the map, gradually narrowing the possibilities for the location of an army. Each time he added a disc, he mentally adjusted plans for deploying the Circle's own forces, taking into account the terrain of the remaining choices.

Patrols had been searching for four days now. Since nothing had been seen within striking distance of Lore's Haven, the scouting parties were searching around the destroyed villages and beyond. So far, none had seen anything suspicious, let alone an entire army. He scanned the map again. There was still much left to investigate. He looked up as Commander Garyn walked in and saluted.

"Captain Gatlor, we have found the enemy army."

"Where?"

Garyn pointed to an area between Faedor Woods and The Riftlands to the east. "Here, in the Scorched Plains."

He looked where the commander was pointing. That would put them about ten days away from Lore's Haven, assuming they did not use portals to show up at the gates. "How many forces?"

"By the patrol's estimate, no more than three thousand."

He wondered if the patrol had estimated low. "Who reported this?"

"Warder Than and Warder Cole."

Those were two of his best. If they said three thousand, it would probably be accurate to within two hundred. With the men and women that had arrived over the last sixday, that gave Lore's Haven a three to one advantage. Perhaps this would not be as difficult as he had initially thought.

The door opened again, admitting Commander Jorik.

"We have found the enemy army, sir," Jorik said.

"Yes, Commander Garyn was just telling me. Perhaps this will not be the epic war we had feared."

Jorik looked confused, but said, "Yes, sir. We appear to have them clearly outnumbered."

"Almost three to one," he nodded. "That is, if the estimate of three thousand is correct."

"Three thousand, sir?"

"Yes. The estimate given by Warders Than and Cole."

"But sir, my report is not from Warders Than or Cole," Jorik said.

"What?" He felt his gut tightening.

"Sir, my report comes from Arden of the Amethyst Order. Her hawk found an army encampment, perhaps the same one, but her estimate puts the enemy at seven thousand."

He was silent, one finger slowly tapping the tabletop. The Amethyst Order worked with animals, and could form links to the minds of their creatures. This allowed them to see what the animal was seeing. If the hawk had seen an army, then Arden would have seen it as well. He hoped she had just vastly overestimated the number of forces, but his warrior's instinct told him otherwise.

"Where did Arden's hawk find the army?"

Jorik pointed. "Three days southwest of Brayden Fenn, in Barrenrock," he said.

That was almost two sixdays from the encampment found by the Warders. Portals or no, there was no way they were the same army. And if the girl's estimate was correct, their forces were now evenly matched.

The door opened again. Gatlor sat back and waited for more bad news.

16
Revelations

Jason watched the bird circling high overhead. The yellow color told him it was a fortunewing, but it was too high for him to tell if it was the same one that seemed to be following him.

He looked at his surroundings. Bothan's home was considerably larger than Reyga's, and was in the middle of a forest. A warm breeze blew from the south, carrying an odd odor that Jason didn't recognize. It seemed familiar somehow, and mildly unpleasant, but he just couldn't place it.

He walked back into the house. He missed his dad. The initial pain that had torn at his soul was now an empty place inside, where memories of his dad occasionally tried to punch holes in the walls of his heart. A tear started, but he wiped it away quickly. Bothan said to store up the pain. Keep it for when he would face the Circle again.

He sat down in one of the padded chairs and leaned his head back. He'd had another of the dreams last night. He closed his eyes and remembered…

"Yes you do, and I'm going to teach you how to use it."

"Why? Why do you need me? Why not just let things happen the way they're meant to and leave it at that? Besides, how do you know I won't just make things worse?"

"Jason, I understand your confusion, but there really is no other way. If you don't use your power, for either side, one of two things will happen. If the Altered stay out of it, the people of this land will be at war for years. If the Altered get involved, this world could be torn apart." She shook her head. "You must choose. No matter which side you decide to take, the results will be better than the alternatives. You can't deny your place in this."

"I don't get it," he said. "How come none of the other Altered seem to care? Why is it so much more important to you than them?"

"They don't know about what's going on, and..." Nyala bowed her head, staring at the ground without saying anything for several seconds. Then, in a quiet voice she said, "Because it's my fault." She raised her head, and he could see the pain in her eyes.

"What do you mean? What's your fault?"

She waved her hand. "All of it. Everything you see. The way this world is now. It's all my fault."

"I don't understand. How can the way the world is be your fault?"

She ran a hand through her hair. "I suppose you deserve to know. Reyga's already told you about the Devastation, right? About the weapons that were used? The ones that created openings to other realities?"

"Yeah."

"Well," she said, "I was the one that created them."

"What? You made those weapons?"

"Well, I didn't actually design the weapons themselves. But I was the lead researcher on the team that developed the technology behind them."

"You were... Wait a second. That would make you, like, fifteen hundred years old!"

"Pretty well preserved for my age wouldn't you say?" she asked with a wan smile. "We've learned that the more *dimsai* ability a person has, the longer they live."

"Wow," he said. He wondered how strong they had to be to live that long. "So you were trying to open holes to other universes? Why?"

"That wasn't what we were trying to do. We were trying to find a way to break down organic material. We called it protophasic technology." She gave a bitter laugh. "Well, we figured it out all right. The only problem was that it only worked on living tissue."

"What did it do?"

"The process essentially disintegrated organic material into its elemental components, while leaving inorganic material unharmed. When we realized it only worked on living tissue, we tried to shut down the project immediately."

"Tried? What happened?"

"Part of our funding came from the military. Even though we'd been at peace for generations, we still kept our military strong. 'Just in case,' the leaders said. When the High Command found out what the technology did, they came in and took all of our research." She shrugged. "Naturally, someone leaked it to the other side. Two years later, protophasic weapons, the ultimate clean bomb. A year after that, the Devastation."

"How did that cause the rifts? Did your research cause any?"

"No, but our tests were conducted on a small scale, affecting a very limited area. Nothing in our calculations pointed to anything like that."

"Then it really isn't your fault," he said, "if the military took your research away. You tried to shut it down. Who knows what they might have changed?"

"I appreciate the thought, Jason, but I was the one who conceived the idea of protophasics. If I had never thought it up, the military would never have gotten their hands on it."

He didn't agree, but he knew he wasn't going to be able to say anything that would change her mind if she'd been blaming herself for fifteen centuries.

"So a rift opened up and this *dimsai* stuff came through?"

"Yes."

"But how come you and the other Altered are so much stronger than anyone else? Did you just learn how to use it first?"

"I suppose you could say that, at least in part. We didn't have any choice. We had to learn, and quickly. What happened to us went far beyond just learning how to control this new power." She laughed a little. "Ironic as it is, I became a victim of my own creation."

"What do you mean?"

"Do you really want to hear this?"

"Yes."

"Alright," she said, and took a deep breath. "My family had gone on a picnic with some friends of ours."

"Family?" Jason asked. "You had kids?"

"One. A son. He was about your age when it happened. Anyway, we were out in the country when everything started. We didn't even know the weapons had been fired until we looked up and saw one dropping toward us. We tried to run, but it was no use. We hadn't even made it back to our vehicles when it detonated. My own invention had tracked me down."

"What happened?"

"The weapon went off, and then the protophasic wave hit us. Even if I'd known what to expect, I wouldn't have been prepared for it. The pain was beyond anything you can imagine. I could feel my body coming apart. I was horrified."

"How did you survive?"

"I'm not entirely convinced we did. But this rift just happened to be the one where the *dimsai* came in. The only thing I can think is that, as our natural cellular bonds were destroyed, they were replaced with *dimsai*. We all passed out from the experience. When we woke up, we were changed. Altered. It didn't take long for us to realize we weren't strictly human anymore. It did take us some time to figure out what we had become. But none of that matters if you don't learn to use your power. And I have to make sure none of the others find out I'm teaching you."

"How are you going to do that?"

She smiled. "By taking you someplace that none of them will ever think about looking."

He opened his eyes. The memory ended there. He thought about what it would be like to have that kind of power. Part of him was eager to have it, but another part was afraid of what he might do. His dad always told him that revenge was a waste of energy, but even though the fires that had raged within him before had died down to ashes, there were still embers smoldering underneath that could flare up without warning.

That was the part that scared him.

Tal sat back in his chair, his fingers idly tapping the armrest. "Three armies," he said, repeating what Gatlor had told him. "What are their total forces?"

"Between the three encampments, we estimate twenty thousand," Gatlor replied.

Twenty thousand. The Haven forces were outnumbered two to one. An enemy army of twenty thousand was bad enough, but to have it in three different locations complicated matters even further. Attack one with enough force to have a chance for victory, and the other two would be free to move.

"Where are they?"

Gatlor spread a map out on the table. "Three thousand two days east of Dronnin in the Scorched Plains, seven thousand three days southwest of Brayden Fenn, and ten thousand three days south of Dronnin along the Shonta." He pointed at each location as he named them off.

Tal leaned forward and studied the map. His eyes went from one location to the next, then to Lore's Haven to the north, and back to the armies' locations.

Without looking up from the map, he asked, "Do we know the makeup of the armies? What races we will be facing?"

"From what the scouts could see, the Scorched Plains force is mostly Trellin with a small number of Manarachs. The two armies in Barrenrock are a mixture of Trellin, Manarach, human, and a sprinkling of other races," Gatlor answered. "Bear in mind, High One, that some of the races, such as the Grithor, avoid light, so would not be seen by the scouts during the day."

"Which would mean the force we face may be even larger than we believe."

"Unfortunately, yes."

"Why have they suddenly banded together? Ordinarily, these races would be at each other's throats."

"I have no answer for that, High One, but, intending no disrespect, the question is meaningless. Regardless of the 'why,' we face what we face. Such questions can be discussed afterwards."

Tal laid his hand on the map, as if trying to feel the armies moving underneath his palm. "Captain, I am not a warrior. As the head of the Pearl Order, my areas of expertise are history and legend, neither of which will give us an advantage in the coming battle." He looked at Gatlor. "I would like you to begin drawing up plans. Consult with Loremasters Delani and Brin as well as

Apprentice Borin of the Obsidian Order, as he will be Chon's successor once the Circle can confirm him."

"Of course, High One," Gatlor said. "In truth, I have already begun."

"I expected nothing less, Captain."

Jason wandered through the house, bored. Bothan had been gone several hours, and hadn't said when he would be back. He idly picked up odds and ends, examined them, and then discarded them.

When Bothan left that morning, he'd told Jason that he liked the idea about getting the other races together, and had arranged to meet with some of them. He'd said he would like to take Jason with him, but some of the races could be a little unpredictable when it came to strangers. Jason didn't mind. In the time he'd been here, Bothan had never been farther away than the next room. He was ready for some time alone.

His roaming brought him to the back of the house. He'd been through the house more than once, but this time something made him look around a little more carefully. A hairline crack in the stone wall caught his eye. *Wonder if this world has ants*, he thought. He followed the crack upward until it took a sharp right turn. *That's kind of odd.* A few feet over the crack turned downward again.

"This isn't a crack," he said. "It's a door."

He put his hand on the stone and pushed. It didn't move. He tried a little harder, still with no success. He put his shoulder against the stone and pushed as hard as he could. The stone didn't budge. He looked for a handle, or some way to open the door, but he didn't see anything.

"Crud." He turned away, defeated. He'd only taken a few steps when he heard a click. He looked back over his shoulder. The door stood open a few inches. He could see a small sliver of another room through the narrow opening. Craning his neck, he scanned as much of the room as he could, looking for any sign of movement.

"Hello?" he called out. No answer.

He pushed the door open a little more, ready to spring back at the slightest motion. When the door's movement provoked no reaction, he pushed it open further. Still nothing. He opened it all the way and walked into the room.

It was a medium sized room, with a table set against one wall and shelves lining the opposite wall. A single well-upholstered chair sat in the center, facing a small portal hanging on the wall opposite the door. A square table sat beside the chair, holding a couple of scrolls, a candle, and an empty metal chalice.

Scrolls, and an assortment of vials and bottles filled the shelves. Papers, cloth, and other items covered the table. As his gaze roamed across the clutter, he saw a cylinder of twisted metal strands almost hidden underneath a fold of brown fabric. He walked over and pushed the cloth back, feeling barely healed wounds tearing open.

"That looks like the staff Chon had," he said. The thought brought the image of the blade plunging into his father's chest out from the dark place where he had pushed it. *Do they all have staffs like this?* No, he knew that wasn't true, because Reyga's staff was made of wood. *Maybe it just looks a lot like it.* He hoped that was all it was. He pulled the staff out from underneath the cloth.

As he pulled, he heard a metallic scraping sound. He dragged the fabric off the table. A blood-stained dagger lay on the table, its curves an exact match for the curves that had burned into Jason's mind as he watched his father die. His heart pounded against his ribs. *No!*

"Now how did you get in here?" a voice behind him said.

He dropped the staff on the table and spun around. Bothan stood just inside the door. The staff slid off the table, clanging to the ground. Questions and accusations filled his thoughts, too entangled for him to express any of them. He stared at his ancestor, his mouth filled with words that wouldn't come.

Bothan looked at the staff on the ground, and then his eyes moved to the table.

"Well and well," he said. "I suppose I should have done away with that, but I have ever had a weakness for trinkets with memories attached to them."

Jason felt like he couldn't get enough air. "He was working with you?" His emotion threatened to choke off his words.

Bothan gave him an odd look, and then a slight smile appeared on his face. "Aye," he said. He appeared unmoved by Jason's outrage. "He was working with me."

"Why? Why did he kill my dad?" He wished for the power to come, begged for it, so that he could avenge his dad. But whatever power he supposedly had didn't answer.

"He released your father! And he released you. The Circle had bewitched your father. Now he knows the truth."

"The truth? The only *truth* I care about is that you helped kill my dad, and you made me believe it was the Loremasters."

"It *was* the Loremasters!" Bothan roared. He closed his eyes and took a deep breath, then continued in a lower voice. "If they would have listened to me none of this would have been necessary. But as always, as has been for centuries, the Circle knows best, and none can gainsay them."

"It was you," Jason said, suddenly understanding. "You were the one that wanted to keep all the knowledge, and only the people you thought should have it would get it."

"There's a bright lad. Aye, that's the truth of it. How better to be sure that those with the knowledge wouldn't use it against you?" He waved his hands around. "But these bletherin' Loremasters think everyone should have it. They call themselves caretakers of knowledge and of Teleria. They're fools."

"No," Jason said. "You're the fool if you think I'm going to stay here now that I know the truth."

A tight smile crossed Bothan's face. "I'll give you one chance to change your mind, laddie. You may have power, but you can't use it. Join me and I'll teach you. With your help, this whole affair can be done and over quickly, with as few lost as possible. Without your help, I'll still win, but the war will drag on, bodies will pile up like snow during Landsleep, and the Shonta River will run red with blood. You don't want that on your head now, do you?"

"No."

"Good. Then it's settled. You've made a—"

"I mean," Jason interrupted, "no, I'm not going to join you."

The big man eyed him. "You sure about that, lad?"

"Definitely."

"Well then," Bothan said, "you leave me no choice. 'Tis a shame, really, all that power goin' to waste." He raised his hands.

"So you'd kill a kinsman? I thought that meant something."

A smirk twisted Bothan's lips. "I may have overstated my feelings of loyalty toward my kin. Goodbye, lad."

Jason suddenly felt as if his entire body was in a vice. The pressure drove the air from his lungs. He could feel the crushing force over every inch of his body. Then he felt a tickle deep inside of his mind, which quickly grew to a tingle spreading throughout his body. His lungs screamed for oxygen, even as the tingling grew stronger. He was certain that he was about to either explode or be crushed to death, but he didn't know which.

"Stop." A new voice broke in. The pressure vanished. He sank to his knees, bracing his hands on the cold stone floor as he desperately drew breath into his tortured lungs. The tingling he thought would turn his body into a shower of sparks faded as well, gone back to the secret place from which it had sprung.

"What are you doing?" He heard Bothan protest. "He needs to be done away with!"

He forced his head up, blinking his eyes to clear the spots from his vision. The new arrival looked like nothing more than a roiling black shadow with two eyes blazing at him from the darkness. *My hero?*

"Yes, he must be killed," the figure said, dashing his hope for a rescue. "*But you do not have the power to do it."* The voice shifted and swirled in Jason's ear.

"Not have the power? He canna resist me! The pup canna use his power. I was just about to finish the job when you showed up."

"No," the shadow countered, "*you were just about to die. Not being able to control the power and not having any are two very different things. In your attempt to kill this boy, the backlash would have destroyed you."*

Bothan's eyes narrowed as he looked at Jason. "Fine then. So what do we do now?"

The fiery gaze turn to Jason. "*I will destroy him."*

"You will not," a familiar voice said. Jason turned to see the sparkling form of Nyala.

"Nyala," the shadow said. *"Do you think to gainsay me? How? Even you know I am the stronger between us. You cannot stop me."*

"Perhaps not, Regor," she said. *"But if you touch this one, I will see to it that the others know. They would not be pleased."*

"How do you know I don't already have their support?" he asked.

"If that is the case, then do what you will," she said. *"But are you so certain of that support as to test it?"*

For several tense moments, no one moved as the two Altered faced each other. Jason didn't know how long the standoff would last, but he knew who he was rooting for.

Finally, Regor stepped back. *"Very well,"* he said, *"he is yours. Take him."* Jason breathed a sigh of relief. *"But be warned, my dear,"* the shadow continued. *"The time is fast approaching when that support will be assured. If we have not reached an understanding between us by then, I cannot vouch for the results."*

"I believe you understand my position perfectly," Nyala said. *"It will not change."* She turned to Jason and held out her hand. *"Come."*

"Watch your back, laddie," Bothan said. "Chon might not be the only one in the Haven working for me."

Jason took Nyala's hand and stood up. Then they left Regor and Bothan behind.

Reyga stared at the texts, hoping to see something missed the numerous times he had studied them before. *His destruction is our hope. His denial is our doom.* Histories and legends were not his strong point, being the purview of the Pearl Order, but he hoped to find something that would give them some direction. Did the prophecy require Jason's death to save Teleria? And what, or whose, denial would doom Teleria? He pushed the papers away and rubbed his burning eyes. If the High One was unable to find anything useful, he certainly was not going to find anything new. His thoughts turned toward Lenai.

It had been more than a sixday since she had learned of Elira. In that time, no one had seen her other than the healer that checked on her each day. Reyga tried to visit her the day after she left the healing area, but she told him through the door that she was tired and wished to rest. He said he understood and would come back in the morning. The next day she gave the same answer to his knocks. After three days of this, he decided to leave her be and let her deal with what had happened in her own way.

He idly swirled the contents of his mug, breathing in the warm, soothing aroma. *She was too calm,* he thought. He had seen Lenai angry, confused, delighted, and even frightened once. He knew her better than he knew anyone else at the keep, and he was certain he knew how she would react to how she had been used.

When they told her what had happened, he fully expected to see shocked outrage, or perhaps a wrathful vow of vengeance. Her quiet acceptance of what they had said worried him, a concern only aggravated by her refusal to see anyone, not even her *ch'tasa*.

A slight sound behind him interrupted his musings. He turned in time to see a sparkling form appear. His chair clattered against the floor as he jumped up.

"Nyala!" He had never seen an Altered before. His experience was limited to what he read in the texts and what the High One had told him. Now she was in his quarters, for reasons he could not begin to fathom.

"Loremaster Reyga," she said, *"I return to you that which was lost."* Then she was gone. In her place stood Jason Bennett.

"Jason?" Reyga said. Jason stared at him without speaking. Reyga wasn't sure if he should approach the young man or not. Then the stoic expression on Jason's face crumbled and he sank to his knees without a sound, tears beginning to flow down his face.

She drew a deep breath of the crisp air blowing across her high vantage point. He would come. She was certain of it.

"You opened that door," he said from behind her.

She didn't turn. "Yes," she answered. Nothing more.

"Why? What do you hope to accomplish? He doesn't know how to use his power."

She smiled to herself. "Then why are you so afraid of him that you would kill him and risk exposing yourself?"

When he didn't answer, she put on a calm expression and turned to face him. He studied her.

"You're up to something," he said after a moment. "Even after fifteen centuries, I still know you well enough to tell that."

She feigned innocence. "No more than you. If you will withdraw from this little game, so will I."

"Why do you care? If you don't want to be worshipped then don't be. Just stay up here brooding for all eternity. What difference is it to you if the rest of us decide we're tired of being confined to legend?"

"Because I know what we've become, and it isn't difficult to picture what this world would be like with gods and goddesses like us." She shook her head. "You still don't get it, do you? This is still our world, no matter how much it and we may have changed. I don't want to see it turn into what it would become."

As he looked at her, a grin crossed his features. He laughed. "You do realize you're wasting your time, don't you?" he asked, when his laughter died. "The boy doesn't have enough time to learn how to even tap into his power, much less control it."

"Then he's no threat to you or your little puppet," she answered. "There's no need for you to concern yourself with him."

He looked puzzled. "You've changed," he said. "You were always a strong woman, but you were never this…" He searched for a word. "I don't know," he said with a shrug. "But you were always open with me when we were together. Now you're different."

"I suppose a person can change over a millennia and a half."

"I suppose so," he said. Then, as if settling something in his mind, he nodded. "Fine. The boy has nothing to fear from me…for now." He pointed a finger at her. "But if it looks like he may somehow sway the outcome of our 'little game,' as you call it, I will deal with him personally."

Her jaw clenched. "If you try to do anything to Jason you will have to deal with me first," she snapped back.

"Jason? Wh—?" Then he stopped and put a hand over his mouth, his eyebrows rising. After a moment, he dropped his hand. "Now, I see. I didn't understand before, but now I do."

"What do you mean?"

"You do know this boy isn't Kevin, right?"

That stopped her. Kevin? Their son, Kevin? Of course she knew Jason wasn't Kevin. Just because they were close to the same age, and had similar looks... A shock ran through her. Was it possible? Was that why she had gotten involved? Because Kevin didn't need her anymore and Jason did? *No,* she thought, *that's ridiculous.* But the thought, once planted, refused to leave, and the pain it brought surprised her.

He was still watching her, apparently wanting to see how she'd react to his statement. She forced herself to laugh. "Don't be ridiculous," she said. "Of course, Jason isn't Kevin." Then she stopped laughing, and her brows lowered. "There is no more Kevin," she said.

"Of course," he said, rolling his eyes. "There is only Nivek."

"That's right," she nodded. "And Nivek is not Kevin."

"You keep telling yourself that, my dear," he said, "and maybe someday you'll even believe it."

Then he was gone, leaving her alone with only the chill breeze for company.

17
The Best Laid Plans

"Where are they?" Gatlor asked no one in particular. He held his hand above his eyes to shield them against the sun's onslaught. Even through the shimmering waves of heat rising from the parched ground, it was clear there was no sign of an army anywhere. And where was the scout party sent ahead?

Eight thousand forces from Lore's Haven stood at the eastern edge of Faedor Woods, ready to engage the army in the Scorched Plains. Seeing through their animals' eyes, teams of *saiken* from the Amethyst Order had opened multiple portals from Lore's Haven large enough for columns of fighters to pour through. The plan was to use the element of surprise to destroy the smallest of the enemy forces before they could call for reinforcements. But the Plains were empty.

"Captain!"

He turned to see four men carrying a stretcher accompanied by one of the healers. He kneeled down as they set the injured man on the ground in front of him. Brennon, one of the members of the scout party sent out two days before.

"He insisted he see you immediately," one of the men said. He nodded and motioned for them to stand back.

As he looked the man over, he did not need to see the healer's bleak expression to know Brennon was on the verge of death. The soldier fought for each breath, sweat pouring from him, and his skin was a pale ashen color where it wasn't covered by reddish-brown streaks of half-dried blood.

"Brennon, what happened?" he asked.

At first, Gatlor thought he was too far gone to answer his question, but then the blood-rimmed eyes opened slightly. His lips moved soundlessly as he struggled to speak. Gatlor leaned down closer to hear.

"They knew," Brennon whispered. "They knew…we were coming…" He coughed harshly, the exertion sending a small trickle of fresh blood from the corner of his mouth. “Ma...Manarachs… Trellin… As soon as the portal closed…they attacked.” His eyes closed again.

Gatlor looked to the healer, who shook his head. “There is nothing I can do,” he said. “He has been injected with Manarach venom. If we had found him sooner, perhaps, but…" His voice trailed off.

Gatlor looked at the soldiers who had carried the dying man. “What of the others?”

They shook their heads. “He was the only survivor, sir,” one said. “The others…"

“The others what, soldier?” he demanded.

“They were torn apart, sir. This man was the only one left whole and alive.”

So they meant for us to find him, he thought. *But why? As a warning? To taunt us?* He felt an icy fury building within him at the thought of the brutality his men had endured.

“A message…” Brennon rasped, somehow finding the strength to grasp his arm. “They gave me…a message.”

Gatlor forced his anger aside. He gently pulled his arm free, ignoring the streak of red left behind from Brennon’s hand. “What message, Brennon?”

“They sa…said we cannot stop them.” He coughed again, sending more blood down his cheek. “They said they know ev…every move we make.” Then his body contorted from the venom, the muscles in his neck standing out like ropes, pulling his face into a rictus of agony.

Gatlor looked at the healer, who shook his head again. There was only one thing to do. He drew his long dagger from its sheath. He looked at the other warriors and saw their expressions of horrified understanding. They knew what he was about to do, but also knew that it would be a kindness. As one they saluted their fallen comrade. He turned back to Brennon, still writhing in pain.

“Be at peace,” he said, and drove his blade home, ending Brennon’s suffering.

He felt the rage building again as he looked at the blood on his dagger. This time he let it come. He had only ever had to deliver the killing blow on one of his own twice before, and each time, those responsible had paid with their lives. He intended to see that the same thing happened this time as well.

Even through his anger, his warrior's mind was still calculating odds, considering tactics. He began pacing as he searched for answers. How did they know about the scouting party? Did they really know, or had the enemy gotten lucky, and this message was all talk? Where was the enemy army? What about the other men he had sent to watch the other two armies?

He stopped. If the message were true, if the enemy really did know their plans…

Shouting from the woods at the back of the Haven forces answered his unfinished question. The army, which had been facing the Scorched Plains, scrambled to reorient itself. Even as Gatlor ran toward the shouting, he knew they had to get out of the woods.

If Manarachs were among the attackers, as Brennon's death attested, his army would be at a major disadvantage underneath the canopy of branches and leaves. Not only could the deadly creatures attack from above, the woods would also conceal the enemy's numbers, making it impossible to know how many they faced.

"Retreat to the Plains!" he shouted as he ran. "Ware the trees! Regroup on the Plains!" He spotted one of the *saiken lo* and grabbed her arm. "Erynn, get two other *saiken lo* and come with me. Have the rest ready to open portals from the Plains to Lore's Haven on my command." Erynn nodded and ran off, shouting to get the other *saiken* adepts' attention. In a moment, she was back with two more *saiken*. Together they ran toward the sounds of the battle.

As he ran, he saw the majority of the fighters running as fast as they could for the open plains. Those at the back of the army, however, did not have the luxury of retreat. They were fighting for their lives. Bodies littered the ground as far as he could see into the dense trees.

The warriors slowly gave ground as they backed toward the Plains. As he skidded to a stop, two of the fighters were jerked into the trees above. Another managed to cut the trapsilk before being raised off the ground, but his sword got entangled in the net and he was quickly cut down by Trellin. Gatlor turned to the *saiken*.

"I need fire. There, there, and there," he said, pointing. "On my mark." They nodded and readied themselves.

"Retreat to the Plains!" he shouted. Then he turned to the *saiken*. "Now."

Instantly power shot from their hands, causing explosions of flame where he had pointed. The fiery blasts engulfed some of the enemy immediately. The rest hesitated as they saw the fire. The Haven forces took that opportunity to turn and run.

"Again," he ordered. The *saiken* sent another wave of explosions, filling in the gaps between the first.

"Retreat to the Plains!" he shouted again at the fighters, even though most of them were already dodging among the trees as fast as they could.

He waited until all of his fighters passed him before running himself. He saw another net drop down and pull one of his men off the ground. Without breaking stride, he jerked a dagger from his bandolier and sent it streaking toward the shadowy figure in the branches above. The Haven fighter dropped back down, with the Manarach falling right after, Gatlor's dagger buried hilt-deep in its chest.

He slowed to cut the man free of the trapsilk, and the two of them ran for the openings in the trees ahead. Looking back as he ran, he saw the flames vanish. He was not surprised. He expected them to have *saiken* of their own. The fire had been a momentary diversion to give his fighters a chance to break for the Plains.

As they burst from the trees, he shouted for his soldiers to keep moving to put more distance between them and the forest. The further they could get into the Scorched Plains, the more of the enemy army they would be able to see. The nearest fighters turned and ran, shouting his orders to the others.

Up ahead, two lines of archers stopped and turned back toward the trees, the front row dropping to one knee. He nodded in approval. The archery commander, Revin, had assessed the situation and had his archers ready to give the trailing fighters a little more time.

When the first of the enemy forces cleared the trees, the front row of archers let fly a barrage of arrows. A split second later, the second row released their arrows, and then the archers ran after the rest of the army.

He stopped to see the results. The archers had been brutally accurate. At least two score of the enemy was either dead or wounded, but it was clear that those numbers were insignificant compared to what was emerging from the tree line. For a span of a thousand paces, Trellin, Manarachs, humans, and other races erupted from the forest, a torrent of death and destruction pouring across the Plains after the fleeing fighters.

He turned back toward his army just as large sections of ground crumbled away, dragging scores of warriors into the pits that opened up under their feet. Dozens more tried to stop but either could not slow in time, or were struck from behind by others unaware of the new peril. *Grithor!* he thought. The warriors adjusted their retreat to avoid the pits, but too late to save those already swallowed by the earth.

For the first time in his life, he was uncertain. It was clear that the enemy had known they were coming, and had sent the bulk of their forces here to destroy the Haven army. He estimated that they were already outnumbered two to one, with more still emerging from the trees. He sprinted after his retreating fighters, who, even with the unexpected appearance of the pits, had opened up a sizable gap between themselves and the enemy.

"Portals!" he shouted, when he had closed some of the distance.

On Revin's order, the archers stopped again to give the *saiken* time to open the way back to Lore's Haven. The *saiken* worked in teams of three to create portals large enough for a score of fighters to run through side by side. He heard Commander Jorik shouting over the commotion, and then the commander and his company of three hundred men moved into position behind the archers, ready to try to give their forces more time once the enemy got too close for the archers. As Jorik's men prepared, he saw four portals spring into existence behind the Haven forces.

"Through the portals to the Haven!" he ordered. "Tell them to be ready in case any of the enemy gets through!" He joined the fighters preparing to make their stand. "Revin, have your archers fire at will until the enemy gets too close or they run out of arrows. Once either happens, do not hesitate. Run for a portal." Revin nodded and turned to his bowmen.

"You heard the captain!" he barked. "Make them pay for their approach! Any *saiken* you see is a priority target!"

Immediately the archers sent a wave of arrows into the air. Again, scores of the enemy fell. Although that temporarily slowed the approaching horde, it was obvious that it would not slow them very much.

Gatlor saw that the volley of arrows was having an unexpected effect. The arrows struck mainly in the center of the approaching army. This was allowing the enemy to flank the retreating warriors on both sides as they waited to go through the portals. Unless something was done quickly, the Haven forces would be decimated within a matter of minutes. Though he was loathe to leave, he knew he had to deal with this new threat.

"Hold here as long as you can," he told his commanders. "I must see to our flanks." Jorik and Revin nodded as they saw what was happening.

"None shall pass while we draw breath," Jorik said.

Gatlor ran toward the portals, looking for the three *saiken* who had provided the fiery delay in the forest. They would not be among those who had run ahead to open the portals. He spotted them and ran to them.

"We need protection on our flanks. I need you three on one side, and we will have to use three portals instead of four so that the other side will be protected as well."

The *saiken* looked at each other. "Captain," Erynn said, "there is another way, but it will require dropping two of the portals."

He looked back to see the archers running for the portals, their quivers empty, while Jorik and his men braced for the onslaught. He turned back to her. "If it will save my fighters, then do it!"

She nodded. "Have the army use the two center portals. We must drop the outside ones." She turned to the men with her. "We must shield. Belk, tell the north portal. Gavin, the south. Meet at the back of our forces." Then all three ran in different directions.

Gatlor raced toward the army, shouting as loud as he could, "Use the two center portals! We close the north and south!" Even as he shouted, he saw the nearest portal vanish, then the far one. Seconds later, he saw the *saiken* running toward where Erynn waited.

The nine adepts formed a semi-circle facing outward. Each put one hand on the shoulder of the *saiken* between them and Erynn, at the center of the formation. As they took up position, Commander Jorik and his men engaged the enemy. He heard the sharp ring of steel. Unless the *saiken* worked quickly, Jorik and his men would not survive long.

"Seventy paces!" Erynn shouted.

As one, the nine *saiken* bowed their heads for a moment, then their heads jerked up and they thrust their free hands, palms outward, toward the enemy. Instantly, a multicolored shield sprang up between the Haven fighters and their attackers, encircling the Haven forces back to the two remaining portals. The seventy pace distance sent the crackling energy surging through the enemy force, cutting the leading attackers off from the main body of the army, and instantly killing any unfortunate enough to be exactly seventy paces from the adepts. The shield sparked and flashed as the enemy tried to breach the wall of power.

The barrier extended fifteen paces beyond where Jorik's men were fighting. As they realized that, instead of the thousands they expected to face, they were now only fighting a few score, they fought with even greater intensity. Gatlor could see that Jorik's men had been reduced by at least a third. He did not see Jorik anywhere.

When the enemy fighters inside the shield realized they were cut off, they hesitated. Then they charged toward the semi-circle of adepts. The soldiers at the back of the Haven forces were quicker, however, and moved to intercept them before they could reach the *saiken*. In a matter of minutes, no enemy fighters remained alive within the shield.

Even with the shield in place, Gatlor knew they could not relax, even for an instant. The opposing *saiken* were throwing bolts of power at the shield, while the fighters continued to attack it with their weapons. Deafening concussions filled the air from the *dimsai* attacks. Beads of sweat ran down the faces of the Haven *saiken*, and they were breathing heavily. He did not know how long they would be able to hold. He hoped it would be long enough.

"Keep moving through the portals! Run!" he yelled.

Moving as quickly as possible, the men and women of Lore's Haven made their way through the portals. After what seemed an eternity, the last ones staggered through. The only ones remaining were the *saiken* holding the shield and the two portals, along with what remained of Jorik's company. From where he stood, he saw that Commander Jorik had fallen along with his men. The *saiken* were at the end of their endurance. Several swayed on their feet, supporting themselves with the hand on the shoulder of the next in line.

"You men!" Gatlor shouted at Jorik's remaining fighters. "A score of you prepare to help the *saiken* get to the portal when the shield drops. The rest check among your fellows to make sure we do not leave any behind who are merely wounded and not dead." Then he turned to the *saiken* at the portals. "Drop the portals. I need two of you to open a portal fifteen paces behind the shielders. The rest return to the Haven as soon as that portal is open."

Before the two larger portals could close, Revin and a score of his archers returned, followed by seven of the remaining members of the Circle. The only Loremaster missing was Seryn. Obviously she had stayed to tend to the wounded.

Revin ran to Gatlor. "Captain, we are restocked and ready."

He clapped Revin on the shoulder. "And well come you are," he said. "How many Deadmarks have you?"

Revin turned to his men. "Deadmarks! Front and center!" Eight archers ran forward.

Gatlor motioned toward the shield. "Mark where those *dimsai* blasts are coming from and take out those *saiken* as soon as the shield drops. The rest of you, aim at the largest of the front attackers. If you can take out a Manarach, so much the better. Fire one shot and then run for the portal. One shot only, and make it count."

The archers nodded and took up their positions, as the High One and the other Loremasters came forward.

"What would have you us do, Captain?" the High One asked.

"The shield *saiken* will only last a few more moments," Gatlor said. "We need to give them, and the men bringing the wounded, time to get through the portal."

The High One nodded and turned to the other Loremasters. After a quick discussion, they moved into position behind the archers.

Each shield *saiken* had two of Jorik's men behind them, ready to help them through the new portal. More men carried wounded. The archers were in firing position, and the High One turned to Gatlor and nodded, indicating that the Loremasters were ready. He didn't waste any time.

"Ready! Drop the shield!"

The shield vanished as the adepts collapsed into the waiting arms behind them. The soldiers carried their burdens as quickly as they could toward the portal. Immediately, the archers sent their arrows into the horde, then turned and ran past the Loremasters toward the portal.

Five of the Loremasters sent blazing bolts of power into the enemy ranks. Kalen Dristal waved his arms and a blistering desert wind drove grit and sand into the attackers' eyes, blinding them momentarily. Then Brin Jalasar, his face bearing a terrible grin of vengeance, stepped forward. "*For my son!*" he roared, thrusting his arms at the approaching creatures. The stone underneath the front ranks of the enemy exploded upwards, sending bodies flying into the air and forming granite obstacles the rest of the enemy would have to go over or around.

"Now back to the Haven!" Gatlor shouted.

The Loremasters sent one more volley of fire into the horde and then turned and ran through the portal. After a last glance at the enemy, Gatlor and the two remaining *saiken* ran after them.

18
Starting Over

Jason tossed in his sleep, turning his head from side to side as he dreamed…

"Where are we?" he asked. He and Nyala stood at the edge of a forest. After her strange pronouncement about where she was going to take him, she'd opened up a portal that led here. The sky above was overcast, and occasional flashes of red and purple streaked overhead. Many of the trees bordering the forest, their trunks snapped like kindling, rested amongst their fellows like drunks after an all-nighter. He could see murky columns of smoke in the distance, and here and there across the plain, patches of scorched and blasted earth lay open like raw wounds.

She surveyed the vista, a bleak look in her eyes. "Well," she said, "it's not so much a question of 'where' as a question of 'when.'"

"Huh?"

"Right now, we are almost fifteen hundred years in Teleria's past. I picked this time because the *dimsai* is at full strength, but the other Altered and I haven't learned how to control our powers yet. This way they won't be able to detect you as you train."

"Wait a second. You can go into the past?"

"If you have a clear image in your mind of where and when you wish to go," she answered, "and if you have the power."

"So why not just go back and take care of your problem in the past, before it becomes such big deal? Or for that matter, why not just go back and tell yourself to stop working on your new technology?"

"I wish it were that simple," she sighed. "I did try, when I realized I could open portals into the past. But I've found that if you go back past a certain point, the timeline is set. Even if you change something, events reshape themselves so that the present is still essentially the same. It's like tossing a pebble in the middle of a lake. The ripples last for a little while," she shrugged, "but at the shore the lake remains unchanged. And I can't take the chance of changing anything that's happened since the Covenant for fear of triggering a war between the Altered. As far as telling myself to stop my research, well, I can only go back to when the *dimsai* first entered our world. By that time it's too late."

"Oh." He scanned the desolate landscape. "This is what was left after the Devastation?"

"This is one of the more untouched areas. The survivors won't find this forest for another year or so."

"So, the *dimsai* created the Altered. Did it create the other races too?"

"Most were created by *dimsai*. The energy had very erratic effects when it swept through our world. Some of the races are combinations of two different species, while in other cases only certain traits from one creature were imprinted upon another. A few of the races, like the Dokal, came here through the larger rifts, most of which collapsed after a time, leaving those who came through stranded."

"But not all of the rifts collapsed."

"No, not all," she said. "The area where the remaining rifts are is named, rather appropriately, the Riftlands. It's a very unpredictable area, and *dimsai* doesn't always work there. Because of that, even we Altered avoid the area, since we can't be certain we would survive should the *dimsai* that's become a part of us fail."

He wondered what it would be like to find that the force that was holding you together was slipping away.

"Come." She turned toward the tree line. "It's time to begin your training."

He followed her as she led the way into the forest. Five minutes later, they entered a clearing. A small cottage sat at one end.

"Who lives here?" he asked.

"You do," she said. "Your training will take some time, and I can't go back and forth between times again and again without being noticed. So, we'll stay here until you've learned what you need to know."

"Here? But what if whatever it is I'm training for is over by the time we get back?"

"We'll return just shortly after we left. No one will know we've gone anywhere."

"Ah," he nodded. "So how long will this take? Are there spells to learn, or hand gestures or stuff like that? Am I gonna need a staff or something?"

She smiled a little. "The first thing you have to learn is that the *dimsai* power is not summoned by staffs, jewelry, or gemstones. Nor is it controlled by drawing mysterious symbols in the air." She held out her hand and a small crackling ball of light appeared, hovering above her palm. "The Loremasters use those devices and trappings to help them focus on what they want the power to do, but that's not what summons the power. The only reason such rituals are necessary for them is because they believe they are necessary." The glowing ball winked out.

"So what makes it work?"

"Passion and focus," she answered. "Either alone can call the *dimsai*, but passion without focus can be dangerous. That's why children must be taught how to use their power. Fortunately, a child's attention span is limited, so their passion is fleeting, usually not on any one thing long enough to do any real damage until they begin their studies.

"On the other hand, focus without passion is weak. The *dimsai* may respond, but not with enough strength to do much. You must learn, as any *dimsai* user, how to use your focus and your passion together. Those who attain the rank of *saiken lo* do so because of their great passion for what they do, and because of their determination to master their power. Only when you have both passion and focus will you be able to accomplish your goals."

"Uh, huh," he said. "So what are my goals?"

"That is something only you can decide."

"Y'know, that answer is getting kind of old."

"I'm sorry, but it's the only answer I can give you."

He opened his eyes. A pale pre-dawn light gave the room an eerie luminescence. He tried to roll over and go back to sleep, but the memory from the dream filled his thoughts. Passion and focus.

He slipped out of bed and walked over to the window. Staring up at the fading stars, he played her words over again in his head. Passion for what? Focus on what?

Then he thought about his ancestor. Why had he told Chon to kill his dad? What did it accomplish? He leaned his head against the cold stone frame of the window. The questions kept coming faster and faster. Even though Bothan had Chon kill his father, was Bothan right about the Circle? And if Chon was working with Bothan, were there others at Lore's Haven too? Maybe others who might try to do something to Jason? Or maybe even pretend to be his friend and then betray him when the time was right? At this point, he didn't know who to believe. For all he knew, even Nyala could have her own agenda, just using him as a pawn in some game between her and the other Altered.

Last night, Reyga had told him about the pitched battle in the Scorched Plains. All those people dead and it was his fault. He had been the one to suggest getting the other races together. Even though he hadn't meant an army, it had still been his idea. He thought about the man with his son on his shoulders and wondered if he had been among those killed. Even if that man hadn't been there, Jason was sure some of the fallen had left now-fatherless children behind. He knew how it felt to lose his father. The thought that he could have caused others to feel that kind of pain mocked him.

He walked back to his bed and sat down, pulling the cover around him to ward off the morning chill. He didn't move until the sun had fully risen and a voice at his door told him that Firstmeal was ready. Then he and his crowd of questions went down to eat.

Tal entered the dining hall as he did every morning, nodding in answer to the greetings he received. He scanned the room looking for Reyga. He saw him speaking with some students on the other side of the room and started in that direction. As he drew closer, Reyga glanced up. The Emerald Loremaster excused himself and came over to him.

"Greetings, High One," Reyga said with a bow.

"Good morning, Reyga. How fare you this morning?"

"As well as could be expected, given the circumstances. What were our losses?"

"According to Captain Gatlor's estimate, we lost over nine hundred men and women," he said. "Were it not for his quick thinking, it could have been much worse." He glanced around the room and spotted Jason coming in, the Warder assigned to him waiting at the door. "So, young Jason has returned to us," he said, wanting to change the subject. He watched as Jason sat down and was brought a plate of food. "And in a most unusual way."

"An apt description, High One," Reyga said. "It would appear that Jason continues to attract some interesting attention."

"Most interesting," he agreed. "You had a chance to speak with him last night?"

"Briefly."

"Tell me what he said."

He listened as Reyga relayed his discussion with Jason from the night before. Reyga had not spoken long when Seryn joined them. After greeting the Diamond Loremaster, Tal motioned for Reyga to continue. When Reyga mentioned the Altered showing up to assist Bodann, Tal stopped him.

"Are you certain Jason said Regor?" he asked.

Reyga nodded. "Yes, that is the name Jason gave me. He was fairly certain that was the name Nyala used."

Tal only half listened as Reyga finished his tale. If he had to pick just one of the Altered that he would prefer to avoid, Regor would be the one. The texts made ample mention of the propensities of the Shadow Lord, and the fact that he had not been averse to using his power in whatever way suited him. Of the seven, he was one of the strongest. The thought of Regor supporting Bodann could complicate things a hundredfold.

He realized Reyga had stopped talking and looked up to see Reyga and Seryn watching him. He shook his head. "This does not bode well. Bodann's power was formidable before. With Regor aiding him, his hand is considerably stronger."

"But if Nyala can hold him off..." Reyga let his sentence trail off.

"Let us hope she can," he said. "But then there is also the matter of Jason Bennett."

"What do you mean?" Reyga asked.

"He has turned his back on us once already. If he does possess the power that the prophecy implies, and if he learns how to use his power and joins up with his ancestor again, I do not see how we could stand against them."

From the look on Reyga's face, it was clear that he could not accept such an appalling thought.

"If I may, High One," Seryn spoke up.

"Of course, Loremaster Seryn."

"As you know, the duties of the Diamond Order often require us to use *dimsai* on others. And with that use sometimes comes an intimate knowledge of the patient being treated, even with our training to prevent it."

He nodded.

"As you also know, the oath we take upon entering the Diamond Order prevents us from revealing anything we learn about the patient, except under the most dire circumstances."

"And I would never ask you to violate your oath."

"I know, High One," Seryn said with a smile. Then she turned serious. "You should know that the last time I examined Jason, I did learn something about him, something I dare say he has not yet learned himself. While my oath prevents me from telling you what I learned, I can tell you this: When the time comes, I will stand with Jason Bennett."

Jason picked at the food on his plate. Much to his discomfort, he'd been escorted to the hall by one of the Warders posted outside his door. The people they passed in the corridors nodded politely, but then watched out of the corners of their eyes as he and his escort walked past. He breathed a sigh of relief when the soldier stopped at the door. The thought of eating with an armed man looking over his shoulder didn't appeal to him.

He saw Reyga on the other side of the room, speaking with the High One. They both wore solemn expressions. Considering what Reyga had told him the night before, he understood why. Then Seryn walked into the room and joined them. He turned back to his plate, pushing the food around without any interest in eating it.

He thought about his encounter with Bothan and the other Altered. Obviously, that had been the one Nyala had spoken of in his dream memory, the one that wanted to be a god. He wondered what the shadowy figure had been like before they had all changed. What would it be like to be at odds with someone for over a thousand years who used to be a friend?

"Watch your back, laddie." Bothan's parting words came back to him. Did his ancestor really have someone else in the keep working for him? If so, then he hadn't really gotten away from him after all. He wondered who it might be. A crafter? A soldier? For all he knew, it could be the Warder waiting for him at the door. Or even one of the Loremasters. They'd kept information from him too. He hunched slightly over his food, feeling suddenly very vulnerable.

"Jason."

He jumped at the sound of his name. He turned to see Reyga standing behind him. He looked across the room to where Reyga had been, but the High One and Seryn had already left.

"I seem to have a talent for startling you," Reyga said.

He tried to still his heart, which had jumped into his throat when he'd heard his name. "Yeah, seems like it," he replied.

"The High One would like to meet with you after you have finished eating."

He looked at his still half-full plate. "It may be a few minutes." He didn't really feel like talking with the High One. He knew the man would ask questions he wouldn't want to answer. On the other hand, he had a few questions himself.

"That will be fine. Just let me know when you are finished. I will be sitting over there." He pointed to where he had been speaking with the High One.

"I'll be over as soon as I'm done."

Reyga dipped his head, and then turned and walked back toward his seat.

Although he wasn't that hungry, he picked up his fork and started eating. The High One may be waiting for him, but he wasn't sure if the High One was ready for him.

The High One and Gatlor looked up from a map when Jason and Reyga entered the room. The warrior looked even more dour than usual.

"Should we come back at another time, High One?" Reyga asked.

"Not at all, Loremaster Reyga. We were just finishing." He nodded to Gatlor, who quickly rolled up the map and tucked it under his arm. On his way out, the warrior inclined his head to Reyga. "Loremaster Reyga," he said. Then, after a moment's hesitation, he also nodded to Jason. "Jason Bennett." Then he left the room.

That was odd, Jason thought. It was certainly a far cry from how Gatlor had acted toward him the first time he had returned from Bothan's.

The High One motioned to some chairs around the table. "Please. Be seated."

Once they had taken their seats, the High One looked at him. "Jason—"

"Did you find Chon?" One of their own had killed his dad. He didn't feel like listening to anything they had to say until they explained why.

The High One stopped, clearly not used to being interrupted, but then nodded. "Yes, but—"

"Did he tell you why he killed my dad?"

He saw a touch of irritation flash in the High One's eyes. Frankly, at this point he didn't care. They owed him answers.

"Loremaster Chon did not kill your father," Tal said.

His jaw dropped. How could they deny it? Did they think he was stupid? "I saw it myself!" he exclaimed. "I watched him kill my dad! How can you sit there and tell me he didn't do it? He—" Jason stopped as he felt a hand on his arm.

"Jason," Reyga said, "Loremaster Chon is dead. In fact, he was already dead when we were in the training yard."

Jason stared at him. "What?" Chon was dead? "But I saw him." *Already dead?*

"You saw someone who appeared to be Loremaster Chon, as did I," Reyga answered. "But we found Chon's body shortly afterwards wearing the same clothing he had on the previous night, not the clothing we saw in the training yard. Upon closer examination, we discovered he had been dead for several hours, most likely killed the previous evening."

He couldn't think. If that hadn't been Chon… "Then who killed my dad?"

Reyga glanced at the High One. "Actually," he said, "we do not know if your father is dead or alive."

"What?"

"Jason, after the incident in the training yard, the body was taken to the healing area for examination," the High One said.

"Were they able to heal him?" he asked, ready to jump up and run to the healing area.

The High One shook his head. "No. The body was quite dead."

"The body? That's my dad you're talking about."

"Actually," the High One said, "it was not."

"Huh?" He knew what he'd seen. What he didn't know was what they were talking about.

"Loremaster Seryn examined the body," Reyga told him. "It was not your father. In truth, it was not even human."

"How is that possible?"

"Apparently, whoever, or whatever, was killed in the training yard had been altered to look like your father."

"But why? Where's my dad now?" A spark of hope leapt up inside him.

Reyga shrugged the spark away. "No one has seen him."

"So who killed Chon? Whoever did that has to know where my dad is."

The High One shook his head. "We cannot be certain," he said, "but whoever did possesses a great deal of power. We do have our suspicions, however."

Bothan. His ancestor's words came back to him. "*I'm sure I could handle any one of them alone.*" But was it him, or was it someone else here working for him? Or was there even anyone else at all? What about Regor? How much of what Bothan had told him was true, if any?

He looked around the room as the thoughts swirled in his head. *Where's my dad? Why would someone want to make it look like he'd been killed?* His gaze passed over the shelves and decorations without seeing them.

"Jason?" Reyga asked.

"Hmm?" he said. "Oh, sorry. I was just thinking about what you'd said." If his dad hadn't been killed, then that meant he had to be somewhere. "It's a lot to take in," he added. It was almost too much. He needed to change the subject.

"Is Lenai okay?" He remembered the night Bothan grabbed him, and the sound of Lenai's shout just before a blast of power blinded him.

Reyga glanced at the High One, who nodded.

"The night you were abducted we found Lenai unconscious," Reyga said. "Nothing we attempted would revive her. Loremaster Seryn's pupils healed all of her physical injuries, but she still did not awaken.

"Under Seryn's supervision, her most experienced student, Elira, conducted a deeper probe of Lenai. During her examination, she apparently triggered a reserve of power that had somehow been placed within Lenai. Elira was struck by *dimsai* from Lenai's body."

"What happened to her?"

"Elira did not survive the attack," Reyga said.

Bothan again. *How many more?* "I'm sorry. What about Lenai?"

"Seryn and her students were able to treat her. She has recovered from the ordeal."

"Does she know about Elira?"

"Yes."

"How'd she take it?"

"Not well, I am afraid. She has not left her quarters for over a sixday." Reyga hesitated, and then went on. "You should know also that she blames herself for your abduction."

"What? That's crazy," Jason said. "Why would it be her fault?"

The High One spoke up. "Lenai feels she failed in her duty to protect you, and has thus failed the Circle. She believes this has dishonored her."

"But what else could she have done?"

"Precisely what we have tried to tell her," Reyga said. "She still believes she failed."

He thought for a moment. "Do you think I could talk with her?"

Tal shook his head. "She refuses to see anyone save the healer assigned to her."

"Actually, High One," Reyga said, "she might see Jason."

Tal's expression invited Reyga to continue.

"As a Shanthi, Lenai will feel compelled to ask Jason's forgiveness for her failure to safeguard him, just as she asked Loremaster Seryn's forgiveness for the death of Elira. Her sense of honor will demand it of her. In truth, Jason may be the only person Lenai would see."

The High One nodded as Reyga finished. "Perhaps. I leave it to your discretion then, Loremaster Reyga. When we are finished here, if you wish to show Jason to Lenai's quarters, I have no objection." He turned to Jason. "Now, young man, since we cannot answer all of the questions surrounding the events in the training yard, let us focus on those questions that we can answer."

"Like what?"

"Well, to start, after the incident in the training yard, you said your ancestor was right. Can we assume that he was your initial abductor, and the person to whom you returned?"

He thought about denying it, but he knew what he'd said. *Besides, what difference does it make now?* He nodded.

"So, you were not entirely truthful with us when you first returned to Lore's Haven. In fact, it would not be inaccurate to say that you lied to the Circle. Is that correct?"

He took a deep breath and let it out noisily. "Yes, I lied," he said. "I didn't know who I could trust. To tell you the truth, I still don't."

"You feel Bodann is preferable to us?"

"Preferable? No. Whatever happened to my dad is his fault, and Elira's death, and most likely Chon's. He would have killed me too if Nyala hadn't shown up. But you've both lied to me too, so I'm not so sure I want to be on your side either. Maybe me and whatever power it is I'm supposed to have should just sit this one out."

"I realize we withheld the knowledge of the *dimsai* from you," the High One began, "but—"

"I'm not talking about the *dimsai*. That I can almost understand. What I'm talking about is the prophecy. You forgot to mention certain parts that I might have had a couple of problems with."

"What did Bodann tell you?" Tal asked.

"He told me that my destruction is your hope. He told me the prophecy says for your land to live, my land must die." He crossed his arms. “If you plan to invade my world, you better just kill me now, ‘cause if I do have power, and if I can learn how to use it, I’ll do everything I can to stop you.”

“Jason—” Reyga began.

“Loremaster Reyga,” the High One said, holding up a hand to forestall Reyga’s comment. Tal sat back, resting his elbows on the arms of the chair and lacing his fingers together. “Very well,” he said, “it is time for total candor, since we see where caution has gotten us. Yes, we withheld certain information from you. While that is not actually lying, it is also not completely telling the truth.” He leaned forward. “So, first of all, the prophecy. In its entirety, the prophecy says

“From a far land, Jaben shall come.
The last to arrive, he will already be here.
Powerful and powerless,
Our hope and our doom are in his hands.
His destruction is our hope.
His denial is our doom.
For our land to live, the far land must die.”

“See?” Jason said. “’His destruction is our hope.’ ‘For our land to live, the far land must die.’ Seems pretty straightforward to me.”

“On the surface, yes,” the High One said. A tight smile crossed his face briefly. “You might find it interesting to know that Loremaster Chon’s interpretation of the prophecy was much the same as yours.” Jason’s mouth clapped shut when he heard this.

“Fortunately,” the High One went on, “we are not quite so hasty in our interpretation as Loremaster Chon was.”

“So what do you think it means?”

“We are still studying it,” the High One said. Then his gaze softened a bit. “Jason, I am telling you the truth when I say that no one here has any designs against you, and we are not planning on invading your world, even had we the ability to do so, which we do not. The prophecy is not so clear when you begin to truly study what it says.” His eyes hardened again. “But in the interest of complete truth, know this: If it turns out that your destruction is required for me to save my world, I will do whatever is necessary to achieve that end, even should it cost me my own life. I can do nothing less."

For a few uneasy moments, they stared at each other. Finally, Jason spoke. "Okay. I believe you. And believe it or not, I appreciate you being truthful with that last part too. So you should know that I don't want to see anything happen to your world either. And to be totally honest, I have no idea how I'm going to make a difference, one way or the other. I just don't see what I can do."

"That remains to be seen," the High One said. "So, we are agreed then. No more half-truths or withheld information?"

"Sounds good."

"No more withheld information, either way?" the High One asked, raising an eyebrow.

"Either way," he agreed. "I'll tell you whatever I can."

The High One stood. "Very well," he said. "I would like to continue our discussion, but at the moment I have matters to which I must attend. I will send for you later."

Jason nodded, and the three of them filed out of the room.

19
Visitors

Brin Jalasar sat by his window, staring with unseeing eyes at the scenery below. *Cale is gone.* The thought dropped endlessly into the empty chasm of his soul, leaving echoes of its passing as it fell. *Cale is gone...is gone...gone...* The strike against the enemy army had provided only a temporary respite from the pain. The satisfaction he drew from seeing the creatures blasted into the air quickly dried up and blew away like the dust on the arid wind the Topaz Loremaster had created.

He drew a ragged breath as the realization hit him once more that he would never see his youngest son again. Then a tingle on the back of his neck told him he was not alone.

"Behold the noble Ruby Loremaster, master of stone and earth," a whispery, shifting voice said.

Brin turned, and then stood as he saw a mass of shifting shadows in the corner.

"Who are you? What do you want?" he demanded.

"Who I am is not important. What is important is this."

Every inch of his body suddenly felt as if it were on fire. He tried to cry out, but no sound would come. The intensity of the pain drove him to his knees. He reached for his own power, but not so much as a spark answered.

"Do I have your attention?"

He managed a nod, and then gasped as the burning agony disappeared as abruptly as it began.

"Remember this."

He struggled to his feet, drenched in sweat from the brief ordeal. The breeze from the window, which before had been cool and pleasant, now felt like the icy winds of Landsleep. His muscles twitched and jumped with the memory of the pain.

"What do you want with me?" he whispered between clenched teeth.

"I have a small task for you, Ruby Loremaster. A task you may even enjoy."

"What kind of task?" His muscles slowly unclenched, the spasms easing.

"I want you to kill Jason Bennett."

"What? Why?"

"That is of no concern to you. Do not forget, Jason Bennett is to blame for what happened at Brayden Fenn. He is to blame for the death of your son."

"That has yet to be proven," he grated. How dare this creature use the memory of Cale's fate in such a way? Although he had been ready to condemn the Far Planer when he first learned of his son's fate, he had been in too much shock to be rational. Later, he realized that even though the boy was the most logical suspect, his guilt must be proven first before justice could be carried out. "I will not murder anyone, not even Jason Bennett, simply because you order it. Why not deal with him yourself?"

"Because I choose to have you do it."

"I will not."

"Do not be hasty, Loremaster. You have already lost one son. Do not forget that you have two others."

His two elder sons appeared before him. As he watched, the stone of the floor encased their feet, creeping up their legs. He heard their cries of pain. They cried out to him to save them. He was the Ruby Loremaster, keeper of stone lore! Surely he could rescue his own family from its grip? He called on his power, but nothing came. He was helpless to stop the horror he saw before him. *No, no, no...* He beat and clawed at the stone, but it moved higher. Their voices became hoarse whispers as the stone constricted their chests. Then they were unable to speak at all as the stone covered their mouths. All he saw now were accusing looks of betrayal from their eyes, and then those were gone also. Only columns of grey stone stood where his sons had been.

"No!" he sank to his knees once more, sobs tearing at his chest. It felt as if his heart must surely burst. Not his family too! He looked up to see their encased bodies again, but they were gone.

"This is the fate that awaits them, stone master, should you defy me."

He could not allow that to happen. Losing one son was bad enough. To lose all three would destroy him. Nevertheless, he was horrified to hear himself whisper, "When do you want it done?"

"Your wisdom serves you well, Loremaster," the shadow said, making his title sound like an insult. *"Anytime within the next two days will suffice."*

His gaze dropped to the floor, but he nodded.

"One more thing, Loremaster. Do not tell anyone of our conversation. If you mention a single word..." He saw the columns of stone again. *"...not even the combined power of the Circle will be enough to save them."*

Jason followed Reyga through the halls of Lore's Haven. They were quieter than ever, the people going about their business quickly, or clustering in small groups sharing subdued conversations.

As when he'd gone to breakfast, after the polite greetings, the people watched as he and Reyga walked by. He saw some of them whispering to each other, their eyes never leaving the pair.

"Here we are," the Loremaster said at last. "These are Lenai's quarters." He turned to Jason. "I believe she will see you," he said in a low voice. "I would ask this of you, please help her to see that she shares no blame in the recent events. I know she feels that she has failed in her service to you and to Lore's Haven. From your earlier remarks, I believe you know this to be untrue?"

Jason nodded.

"Then help her to accept it as well," Reyga said. "I would not see her continue to punish herself in this way." He turned back to the door and knocked. "Lenai, it is Loremaster Reyga. May I speak with you?"

There was no answer at first. Jason thought she either wasn't there, or she wasn't going to acknowledge her visitor. Then he heard her voice.

"Loremaster Reyga," she said through the closed door, "please forgive me, but I still have not recovered fully from my ordeal. Perhaps another time?"

Reyga turned to him. “This is the same answer I have received each time I have come,” he whispered. Then he turned back to the door. “Lenai, I have Jason Bennett with me.”

This time, the silence from the other side of the door lasted so long Jason was sure that Lenai wasn’t going to answer at all. Just as Reyga raised his hand to knock again, the latch turned and the door opened slightly.

“Loremaster Reyga,” she said, still concealed behind the door, “if you would, I would speak with Jason Bennett alone.”

Reyga looked as if he’d expected her reply, but hoped for another. He gave Jason a meaningful look and walked back the way they’d come.

Jason waited for some sign from inside the room. Seeing none, he cleared his throat. “Uh, Lenai?”

“Please come in, Jason Bennett,” she said in a flat, dull voice.

He pushed the door open and stepped into the room. It was a small room, sparsely decorated. A bed sat against the wall across from the door. Dark curtains covered the lone window. Sconces on the walls at either end of the room provided light, and a small table by the bed held a pitcher, a mug, and a small charcoal sketch of a man, woman, and three children. A wooden stool sat in the corner opposite the bed. He turned as Lenai closed the door behind him.

Her appearance shocked him. It wasn’t so much that she looked different from before, as much as it was her demeanor. Where before she had been confident and sure of herself to the point of aloofness, she now seemed diminished somehow. When she had shown him around Lore’s Haven, she had always met his eyes almost defiantly. Now her gaze wandered across the floor, only occasionally jumping up to him, then just as quickly away. Her eyes were rimmed with red, and her skin had a distinct grayish pall to it.

“Lenai—”

“Jason Bennett,” she said in a tone that reminded Jason of their first meeting, “I will be brief.”

“I thought we agreed you’d call me Jason.”

She wouldn’t meet his eyes. “Just as I failed to safeguard you, I am afraid I must also fail in this regard.”

“But—”

"Jason Bennett, I apologize for my inability to protect you. I failed you, and for that I ask your forgiveness."

"Lenai, there was nothing you could have done." He was getting an idea of how frustrated Reyga must be.

She gave a harsh shake of her head, still not looking at him. "Jason Bennett, I have given you my apology. Now I must ask you to leave me be."

"Help her to see that she shares no blame." Reyga's words echoed in his head. How could he do that if he couldn't even talk to her? If she wouldn't even listen to him? He searched his mind for a plan. What could he do?

"No," he said, as a sudden inspiration flashed through his thoughts. "I don't accept your apology."

Her head snapped up, a spark of anger in her eyes. "No? Do you believe the apology of one who has failed, as I have, to be beneath you? Or is my disgrace not enough for you, that you feel you should shame me more?"

Well, that got her attention. Now what? He didn't know what to say next. He forged ahead, hoping the right words would come out.

"No, nothing like that. Lenai, there's nothing wrong with your apology. It's just that it's not needed. You don't have anything to apologize for."

She stared at him for a moment, and then turned away. "I would not expect a Far Planer to understand."

"So explain it to me," he shot back, putting as much sarcasm as he could into his voice. "From what I hear, no one could have stopped what happened. What could the mighty Lenai of the Shanthi have done that no one else could have?" He was trying to keep her just a little angry, anything to keep her talking.

She clenched her fists, then relaxed them as her shoulders sagged. "I…I do not know," she replied, shaking her head. "But—"

"But nothing," he interrupted. "Lenai, the person behind all this has more power than anyone on the Circle." He didn't know if she knew about Chon, but he decided to tell her anyway. Maybe it would snap her out of her self-condemnation. "He even killed Loremaster Chon."

She turned back to him. "Loremaster Chon is dead?"

"Yes. Apparently killed by the same man that took me, and would have killed me too. The same man who used you. My ancestor, Bothan McFarland." He took a deep breath. "You know him better as Bodann."

She didn't move, but Jason saw a sudden tenseness in the line of her shoulders and neck. "Bodann is one of your kinsmen?" she asked, an edge to her voice.

"Yeah," he said. "After he found out we were related, he wanted me to join up with him. I was gonna do it too, until I found out he was behind what happened to my dad. When I told him no, he tried to kill me."

"Yet you live," Lenai said. "Is your power greater than his?"

"No," he said, shaking his head. "I haven't even figured out how to use my power yet, if I even have any. For some reason, the Altered are involved in this whole mess. Nyala stopped Bothan and another Altered she called Regor from killing me. She brought me back here."

She searched his face, then her gaze dropped to the floor. "Still," she said, the edge gone from her voice, "if I had chosen another passageway, or if I had returned you to your quarters sooner…"

"You still don't know what might have happened," he said. "Listen, I'm not going to accept any apology, because nothing that happened was your fault." He held up his hand as she opened her mouth. "If you still think you have to make something up to me," he moved over to the stool and sank down on it, "then tell me who I can trust around here."

She frowned. "I do not understand."

"Look, my ancestor may have done some pretty bad things, but he told me stuff that Reyga and your High One held back. He also said things about the Circle that, if true, I can't agree with. The fact is, I don't know who's telling the truth, who I can believe. There's so much stuff going around in my head that I can barely even think."

"I see." She stared at him, secret thoughts lurking behind her dark eyes. Then she said, "I believe I may be able to help you in that respect, Jason Bennett, but you may not like what it will involve."

The chair slammed against the wall, splinters flying in all directions from the force of the impact. Pieces of wood and ceramic that had once been décor and mugs littered the floor around the chair. Gatlor glared at the wreckage, and then looked around for something else to throw. He had thought the cold rage from the day before was gone, but today, after his discussion with the High One, it filled him again. A knock at the door stopped him before he could find another projectile. Without waiting for an answer, the door swung open.

"Forgive me," a smooth voice said, "but I sometimes find human rituals confusing. Does destroying your quarters make it easier to accept what happened yesterday?"

He scowled at Seerka as the cat-man stepped into the room. "No, but the punishment I deal out to my belongings does not get passed along to my men."

Calador ducked into the room. "For which, I am certain, your men are grateful," he said.

"I am quite certain." He ground his teeth. "Is there a point to this intrusion, or should I just add you two to the pile?"

"A point?" Seerka asked. "Perhaps it is merely two soldiers checking on their commanding officer."

"Or perhaps," Calador added gently, "it is just two men checking on a friend."

He looked at them without answering as his breathing gradually slowed to a more normal pace. Then he walked over and closed the door behind them.

Still facing the door, he balled his hand into a tight fist and lightly punched the hard wood. "All of the scouting parties were killed," he said without turning. "All told, almost a thousand men and women were lost yesterday."

"A terrible thing," Seerka said.

"War is a terrible thing," he answered, turning to them. "A terrible thing that destroys even the best of men."

"All soldiers understand the risks of what they do," Calador said. "Just as the members of the scouting parties understood the—"

"I have lost men before!" he snapped. "I understand duty and honor and risk as well as any man." He sat heavily in the chair he had kicked. "But I have never lost so many in such a short time. And never to an enemy who seemed to know my plans as well as I did."

"Aye," Seerka said, "that is most disturbing."

"Which?" he asked bitterly. "That we lost so many, or that we apparently have a spy among us?"

"Both, of course," Seerka answered. "But only one can we change."

"Even so," Calador said, "but only if we can determine who the spy is. Do you have any suspicions?"

He shook his head. "No. It would have to be someone privy to our plans, and I mean *all* of our plans. That would only be the Circle and my officers." He stood and began pacing the room. "But I cannot imagine anyone in either of those groups being a traitor." He kicked a broken mug out of his path.

"Perhaps someone in the Amethyst Order?" Seerka suggested. "They could observe the meetings of the Circle through the eyes of a small animal, perhaps a mouse."

"That is another possibility," he agreed, still pacing.

"I do not envy the one who suggests that possibility to Loremaster Delani," Calador said.

He grunted but didn't answer. The Amethyst Loremaster would almost certainly see even the mere suggestion as an affront to her and her Order. She handpicked her students, and then only after a series of tests and interviews more rigorous than any other Order.

"Although, if that proves to be the case," Seerka mused, "the guilty one may need more protection from Loremaster Delani than from you."

He stopped pacing, thinking again about the men and women whose blood still stained the ground at the edge of the Scorched Plains. He looked at the Ferrin from under lowered brows as the cold invaded his soul once more. "Not by half," he said in a voice that promised retribution.

20
Soul Searching

Jason and Lenai sat cross-legged on two cushions she had dropped on the floor. They faced in opposite directions, with his knee by her hip, and her knee by his hip. He felt his pulse quicken as she drew out her dagger and laid it across her lap.

"Before we begin, know this," she said, holding his eyes with hers. "What we are about to do is *Sho tu Ishta*, the Ritual of Clarity. For generations, my people have practiced it in time of need. Ordinarily, a Shanthi would do this alone, although in needful circumstances two may perform it together." Her gaze sharpened. "It is rarely done with those who do not have Shanthi blood in their veins.

"Be warned, Jason Bennett. This ritual will bare your soul. You will find yourself in a place where there are no lies. And because I am the one aiding you, I will be there as well. If I find that you are false and intend ill to Lore's Haven and Teleria," she laid her hand on the dagger, "I will end the ritual and kill you immediately." She paused for a moment, letting her words sink in. "Knowing this," she said, "do you still wish to proceed?"

He thought about what she'd said. What did she mean by a place where there are no lies? He didn't think he had anything to hide, but he also knew he wasn't exactly a saint. Plus, his feelings about the Circle were confused. What if he found out that his ancestor was right? Or what if she misinterpreted his confusion? If she thought he might go back to Bothan, he doubted he'd get a chance to explain himself.

"What is your answer?"

"What about you?" he asked, to give himself a little more time to think. "Since you're doing this too, will I see your soul bared?"

For the first time since they'd taken their positions, she looked away. "Yes," she answered, "my soul will be laid open for you to see as well. There is no way to hide during *Sho tu Ishta*."

"So why are you offering to do this? Not that I don't appreciate your help, but if your people are so private, why open yourself up like this to an outsider?"

She turned back to him. "I too am uncertain of you," she said. "In this way, my questions will have answers. If you are false, I will have removed a threat to the people I have sworn, and failed, to protect. This may redeem that failure in some small way. Or, it may be that you are honorable. If that is true, then allowing you to see me as no one else has may serve to redeem my failure to you. I am beset by shame on all sides. By doing this, mayhap I can cleanse some of it from me."

"So this is just as much for you as for me."

"Make no mistake, Jason Bennett. If I could fathom another way to accomplish the same ends, I would not offer this. But as this serves both of our purposes, *Sho tu Ishta* seems a fitting choice."

"So what should I expect? What will happen?"

"I cannot say. It is different for each person. You will see and experience what is needful for you to find the clarity you seek. You may not like what you see. It can sometimes be a painful experience."

"Painful?"

"Not bodily pain," she explained. "Pain of the soul and spirit. The *Sho tu Ishta* can be harsh. It does not forgive."

He took a deep breath. "Okay, let's do it."

"Very well. Raise your hand." She raised hers to show him, holding her upper arm level with the floor and her forearm and hand pointing toward the ceiling. He imitated her position. Then she opened up her hand. He saw her fingers elongate, the folds of skin under the knuckles opening up to reveal sucker-like structures. Before he could react, she grabbed his hand in hers, wrapping her lengthened fingers about his hand. He expected to feel a slimy or sticky sensation from the suckers, but was surprised when they only felt warm.

She dropped a loop of fabric over their clasped hands, letting it fall loosely about their wrists. Then she picked up her dagger and held the blade against her own forearm.

"Move your arm against the dagger so that it is held in place," she said.

Gingerly, he did as she asked. Once his arm was against the edge of the blade, she let go of the dagger, and pulled the loop of cloth down firmly on their forearms, causing both of their arms to press against the blade.

"Wait, what are you doing?"

"Since you do not have Shanthi blood, we must share mine," she said. Before he could protest, she jerked the dagger out.

He winced as the hot bite of the blade opened up his forearm, then gasped at an electric tingle that shot up his arm as her blood mingled with his. He would have pulled away, but her grip and the cloth held his arm solidly in place.

"Close your eyes," she ordered, "and clear all thoughts from your mind. Think only on my words. You may feel light headed. Do not be afraid."

As he closed his eyes, she started chanting in her native tongue. He didn't think he would be able to clear his mind, but as he focused on the strange words, he felt his other thoughts slipping away. Within moments, his entire being rode on the current of words flowing from her lips. He felt as if he was floating up from the floor, buoyed by the rise and fall of her voice. Inside his eyelids, he started seeing swirls of color that reminded him of his arrival. This time, however, he was not afraid.

Then her words sucked the soul from his body.

Sitting high in a tree outside of Lore's Haven, the fortunewing raised its head. Jason Bennett and the Shanthi girl were joining in some sort of ritual. Perhaps this was the time it had been waiting for. It lifted from its perch and flew to the top of one of the towers of the keep.

Down below, the bird saw one of the humans on the wall glance up and then call to one of the other humans, gesturing toward it. The bird's name was Crin, and it had never understood why humans acted as they did when they saw him. Crin flapped his wings once and settled his feathers more comfortably. This appeared to agitate the humans even more. Crin ignored them as he turned his attention back to the ritual inside.

Jason found himself on an empty plain, the sky overhead filled with colors swirling wildly in a wind he couldn't feel. Watching the churning sky made him dizzy so he looked away toward the horizon. There was something standing on the plain in the distance. It was the only thing he could see other than the flat surface on which he stood, so he started walking toward it. Then it occurred to him that he was alone.

"Lenai?" he called. There was no answer, so he kept walking toward the distant object. As he got closer, he realized that it wasn't one object, but three. Three mirrors stood in a semi-circle on the empty plain. He kept walking until he stood in the middle of them.

The mirror in front of him showed the empty plain behind him, but he was not represented in its reflection. He reached out his hand, thinking perhaps it was a portal rather than a mirror. His fingertips touched a hard, smooth surface. It was a mirror, but one that didn't acknowledge him.

Looking at the one on his left, he saw himself, a malevolent grin on his face. Every so often, his image laughed silently. Suddenly, it lunged at him. He instinctively stepped back, but the image never left the mirror. When it saw him flinch, it started laughing soundlessly again.

He turned to the mirror on his right. His image there was serene, looking back at him calmly. It smiled and nodded to him, and then resumed its quiet study of him.

This is seriously weird, he thought. He turned back to the center mirror.

"So what now?"

Lenai's voice answered him. "If you truly seek, you must enter."

He looked around, but she was nowhere to be seen. "Enter?" he called. "Enter what?"

His question fell into the silence, unanswered. Then the center mirror began to shimmer. *Step into the mirror?* How was he supposed to do that? He'd just touched it and it was solid. *Oh well.* With a little shake of his head, he stepped forward…

...and found himself facing Julie Peterson, a girl he'd known in school. She'd been his first kiss, and he'd been hers. It happened at a friend's party one Saturday night. Now, as if seeing the experience as a passenger, he relived the following Monday.

He watched as she came up to him at his locker at school, all smiles and giggles. She told him how glad she was that he was her first kiss, how much she'd always liked him, and how special he had made her feel. He listened for a few minutes, embarrassed at the glances they were getting from students walking past. Then he blew her off, telling her she was nice and all, but he wasn't interested in having a girlfriend.

He saw the hurt in her eyes, just for an instant. Then she shrugged and told him she was okay with that. Without waiting for an answer from him, she turned and walked away, pushing through the students crowding the hallway. Shortly afterwards, her family had moved away. He never saw her again.

Then the scene began again, only this time he saw it through Julie's eyes. He felt her excitement at seeing him in the hallway, felt her relive the kiss in her mind as she approached him. He shared her tingling anticipation of walking hand in hand with him, and going to games and dances with him. For that moment, he was the only boy in the world that mattered, and she could only think about the two of them together.

Then he felt the crushing weight of his callous words as they shattered those feelings. He felt her struggle to put on the same careless expression he had worn, trying to pretend it didn't matter, when it felt like her world was crumbling.

As she turned away, he came back to himself, shaken by what he'd learned. *I was a jerk.* They hadn't spoken again before she moved away, but he'd told himself she was fine. Her pain had been so intense, and he had never given it a second thought.

Without transition, he saw himself arguing with his mother a couple of years later because she wouldn't let him go to a different party. She was being completely unfair! She acted like he couldn't take care of himself! What did she know about parties? He heard the angry words that he'd said just before stomping off to his bedroom and slamming the door behind him.

Again, the scene replayed, with him reliving it from his mother's perspective. He felt her concern and worry for him.

She'd been to plenty of parties and knew, just because of who was throwing this one, what to expect. He was surprised at the sadness he felt from her. She wanted to let him do the things he wanted, but knew this party wasn't a good idea. Even if he didn't understand her reasons, her responsibility as a parent was to do what was best for him, even when it made him angry with her.

Then, as with Julie, he felt the hurt his words and actions caused her. But even through her pain, he felt her love for him shining through. Her pain was a price she was willing to pay as long as she knew he was safe. She would love him forever, no matter what he might say or do to her.

As the memory faded, he swallowed hard, fighting back tears. *Have I always been this selfish?* He wanted to apologize, but knew he would never have the chance.

Another scene began. *No, not again. I can't do this.* His protests were meaningless, as he relived time after time where he had been in conflict with another. Friends, girlfriends, parents, all were presented to him without mercy, showing him what he'd done, and how his actions and words affected others.

Eventually, the scenes became more recent. He saw his anger with Reyga on the journey to Lore's Haven; replayed his initial conversation with the High One. He felt again his fury at the Circle for the death of his father, and his rude behavior toward the High One afterwards. He relived his encounters and conversations with his ancestor, and his experiences with Nyala.

In each instance he saw both perspectives. A glaring difference was that in his encounters with the Loremasters, he came to understand that they were dealing with an unknown in him, and the prophecy made them afraid of what he might do.

The ritual showed him that the decisions they made were based solely on their duties to those under their protection. He felt Reyga's distress at having to withhold information from him, and the High One's discomfort, even though the High One had truly felt he'd had no other choice. He saw that, no matter how he had acted toward them, they had never acted the same way in return. With the exception of Loremaster Chon, he had always been treated with courtesy and respect, even when he didn't deserve it. *And now Chon's dead.* He hoped that was nothing more than an unfortunate coincidence.

Then he saw that Bothan was hiding something from him. He realized that his initial encounter with his ancestor, and his final one, were far closer to the truth about the man than anything in between. Even the fact that he had told Jason what the Circle had kept from him was surrounded with ulterior motives and deception.

He was shaken to the core. *I owe so many apologies. I've only ever thought about myself.* As the thought appeared, he found himself slumped over on his knees in the middle of the mirrors, his cheeks wet. He looked up at the center mirror…and saw his teary-eyed reflection looking back at him.

He looked at the mirror on his left. That Jason was furiously screaming at him without a sound. As he watched, the angry figure slowly grew fainter, until only his own reflection stared back at him.

He turned to the mirror on the right. The Jason there grinned at him and nodded, giving him a wink and a thumbs up before also fading away.

He looked up and saw that the roiling colors had disappeared, replaced with a cloudless blue sky.

"It would appear you have your answers," Lenai's voice broke into his thoughts.

Instantly, new images flooded his mind. As he struggled to understand the confusing scenes, he realized that these images were from Lenai's past. He tried to focus on what he was seeing from her memories and what he was feeling in her emotions.

He saw memories from her childhood. He felt her pride at being a Shanthi, and her confusion and disgust as her father told her about the *rishna kel*. He saw her interactions with other races, particularly humans, as she grew older. He felt her anger and resentment at the treatment she received from those who based their opinion of her on nothing more than her race. Then he saw her first meeting with Reyga.

She had been young, untrained, and curious about humans, even though her father warned her repeatedly that they were not to be trusted. One night she slipped into one of the larger villages, wanting to see for herself. The village was a confusing jumble of twists and turns. How did humans live like this? She made her way toward music and raucous laughter she heard coming from somewhere ahead.

She ended up in a filth-strewn, dead-end alley. She turned to go back the way she had come and found a group of drunken men behind her, having just come out of a rundown tavern.

They had backed her up against a wall, intent on having their way with her and then killing her. She tried to climb the wall, but it was slick with grease and slime. She could not get a grip. She pulled her dagger and slashed at the men, but her fear worked against her. Her wild swing missed and one of them grabbed her arm, twisting the dagger loose. She fought them until something struck her across the back of the head, and the world skewed sickeningly.

She felt them throw her on top of a crate in the alley, heard their taunts and insults, felt hands tearing at her clothes. She wanted to struggle, but her limbs wouldn't respond. Through her blurred vision, she saw one of the men leaning over her, leering at her. "Yer a pretty one fer shifter scum," he slurred. She felt his rough hands on her, then a hot flash of light, and he was gone.

Blinking hard, she saw a man with white hair and a pale green robe move between her and the drunken throng. He tried to reason with them, but one of the men drew a sword, and managed to land a grazing blow across the newcomer's arm before another blast threw him against the wall.

After that, the rest of the crowd scattered, not willing to be the next on the receiving end of the stranger's welcome. She tried to raise her head. The effort was too much, and she blacked out.

When she came to, she was propped against the wall, a cloak placed over her body. Kneeling beside her was the white-haired stranger. She flinched away, remembering what had happened, but his voice stopped her.

"Be at peace. The men are gone. You are safe…for the moment."

She studied him warily, pulling the cloak more tightly around her as she remembered the sound of her clothes ripping.

"My name is Reyga," he said. "You are a Shanthi. What are you doing in a human city, and especially in this part of town? It is not safe here for one such as you."

"I…I was curious," she said. "I wanted to know more about humans. Why do humans hate us so?"

He sighed. "I am afraid such misguided emotions cannot be adequately explained. I can only say that not all humans feel that way toward your race."

"You do not think ill of us?"

"No. I value the person inside, regardless of what the outside looks like." He smiled. "What is your name?"

"I am called Lenai."

"Well, Lenai, it is an honor to meet you. Can you stand?"

She nodded and struggled to her feet. She touched the back of her pounding head gingerly. Her fingers came back sticky with blood.

"You took a rather nasty blow," he said. "Can you make your way back to your people, or would you like to come with me to Lore's Haven where a healer can treat you?"

"You live at Lore's Haven?"

It was his turn to nod. For the first time, she noticed his staff, and the fist-sized emerald adorning it.

"You are a Loremaster."

"Yes."

She knew there was only one decision she could make. Even her father, with his distrust of humans, would have made the same choice. She bowed her head. "I must come with you," she said. "You risked yourself to save me. I can only hope my service to you will repay at least a small part of that debt."

He shook his head. "I cannot accept such service, for there is no debt to repay." Then, more formally. "I release you of your obligation. You are free to go back to your people or come with me, as you wish."

She started to protest when he raised a hand to stop her.

"If you wish to serve, my dear," he said, "then serve the Circle. For my part, I only desire your well-being, and perhaps, your friendship."

At that moment, the old Loremaster had become *ch'tasa* to her, and she had agreed to join the Circle Guard, the first Shanthi ever to do so, to honor what he had done for her.

Then the memories changed. Jason felt her shame at her failure to prevent his abduction. He felt her shock and horror, quickly turning to self-loathing, as she learned of Elira's fate and her own unwilling part in it. He felt her sense of self-worth crumble and fade as she faced the extent of her failure in her service to the Circle, to him, and to the people of Lore's Haven. There the visions ended.

He wiped his face and turned to see her sitting on her knees behind him. This time her appearance did shock him. Her hair was matted and tangled, hanging in her face as she blankly studied the ground at his feet. Dark circles weighed down her eyes, and her clothing was tattered and dirty.

"What is this? What happened to you?"

She didn't look up. "This is my truth."

"No. This isn't truth, Lenai. This isn't how any of the Loremasters see you. I doubt it's how anyone in Lore's Haven sees you. I know it's not how I see you."

"Nevertheless."

"You told me this was a place where there are no lies," he said. "You may see yourself this way, but this is a lie."

"No."

"Yes," he insisted. From somewhere he couldn't identify, he felt a presence join him, showing him what to do. "Tell me one thing. Do you really believe in this whole *Sho tu Ishta* thing? Or don't you?"

She looked up at him through the strands of hair hanging in her face. "*Sho tu Ishta* is an honored tradition among my people. None doubt its worth."

"Then you have to accept the truth too," he said, closing his eyes. He brought back up her feelings of pride at being a Shanthi. He remembered the warmth he'd seen between her and Reyga. He thought about her warrior spirit during the battle with the Trellin, and then later, the fierce determination she showed in the healing area. He remembered her playing with the children at Lore's Haven, and finally her willingness to sacrifice herself to defend him.

All of these feelings and images he took and, with the guidance of the other presence, he impressed them onto her. Overriding her self-condemnation, he forced her to see herself how others did, as the proud, honorable Shanthi warrior they had come to respect, and in some cases, to love.

He opened his eyes and saw her as she had first appeared to him, strong and proud. She was looking down at herself as the last shadows of the tattered clothes faded away. She looked up at him, her eyes wide.

"How did you do this?" she whispered.

"I don't know," he admitted, "but this is the truth. This is how I see you, how the Loremasters see you."

"But my dishonor…"

"Lenai, if you've done anything dishonorable, it's been to shut out the people who care about you. Nothing else."

"But…I failed in my duties," she said, but there was a note of uncertainty in her voice.

"Y'know, my father loved old sayings," he told her. "One of his favorites was a Chinese proverb that said 'Failure is not falling down, but refusing to get up.'" He shrugged. "You fell down. Everybody does. That doesn't dishonor you. Staying down does. And it dishonors everyone who cares about you and believes in you." He took a step forward and held out his hand. "It's time for you to get up."

Her eyes never leaving his, she reached up and took his hand, slowly standing to her feet.

"I thought this would repay some of my debt," she said. "But I find it has increased it." She laid her hand on his chest as he started to protest. "I accept this willingly and gladly. I believe I understand you now, Jason. I have seen your soul..." She dropped her hand and bowed her head. "…and you have restored mine. For that, I will ever be in your debt." She looked at him, once again the proud Shanthi warrior he had first met. "Whenever you have need, you have but to ask."

He didn't know how to answer. The fact that she'd called him 'Jason' hadn't escaped him. "I'm glad I could help," he managed.

Without warning, they were back in Lenai's quarters, sitting on the floor. The sudden change disoriented him for a moment, then the world righted itself. Lenai released his hand and undid the cloth tying their arms together. He was almost afraid to see what kind of damage her dagger had done, but when he carefully wiped away the blood, all that showed was a hairline scar across his forearm. *Wow.* He lightly traced the scar with one finger.

"That was a little rough," he said as they stood up.

"The first time is always difficult. But past incidents, once resolved, do not appear again."

"How much of that was real?"

"All of it," she said. "But I understand your question, so I will say it once again. Whenever you have need, you have but to ask."

"So, you're okay now?"

She smiled at him, the first smile he had received from her. "Yes," she said, "thanks to you. I have regained myself once again."

"Well then, I know of at least one Loremaster who would really like to talk to you. Reyga's been very worried."

"Then perhaps we should go to him."

He nodded, and the two of them went to go find Reyga.

21
Bird's Eye View

To say Reyga had been pleased to see Lenai would have been an understatement of epic proportion. Jason smiled again as he remembered the expression on the old Loremaster's face when he opened the door. Although they both protested, he excused himself, saying that he needed time to recover from the ritual. While that was true, he really thought they needed some time to talk without him around.

Now, alone in his room, he thought about what he'd seen and felt. Seeing firsthand how his words and actions affected others had been a sobering experience. At least now he knew which side he was on, even if he didn't yet know how he was going to make a difference.

"Jason."

"Huh?" He looked around. Then he realized that he hadn't heard the voice with his ears. It had resonated in his mind. "Nyala?"

"No, not the sparkling one."

He twisted around, scanning the room. He jumped up when he saw a fortunewing staring at him from the sill of the window.

"Where'd you come from?" he asked it, then continued his inspection of his room while watching the fortunewing out of the corner of his eye. He was waiting for someone or something to appear.

"I came from outside," the voice said. "*I've been sitting in the trees waiting for you."*

He slowly turned back to the window. *No way,* he thought.

"Yes," the voice said. "*Don't you remember me yet?"*

"Are you talking to me?" he said to the fortunewing.

"Of course," the voice sounded amused. Then he got an impression of sorrow. "*You do not remember me."*

Just when I thought things couldn't get any weirder. "Okay, let me get this straight," he said. "The voice I'm hearing…in my head…is coming from you. A bird."

"Yes, but I'm not just any bird. I'm Crin. Your Crin."

"My Crin? What do you mean, 'my' Crin?"

Jason felt the mental equivalent of a sigh. "*The sparking one said you would forget me for a while. I was hoping when I helped you with the Shanthi that you would remember.*"

"The sparkling one? You mean Nyala? Did she send you here? Wait a second. That was you I felt during the ritual? You showed me what to do?"

"So many questions," came a laughing reply. "*Just like when we first met.*" The bird settled its feathers. "*Yes, the one you call Nyala is the sparkling one. No, she did not send me. And yes again, I joined you during your ritual. The Shanthi girl is important to you, so I helped you help her.*" Crin cocked his head at him. *"Is she to be your mate?"*

"What? Mate? No! I mean, she's pretty and all but… Y'know, I really don't think that's any of your business." He rubbed his forehead. *I'm arguing with a telepathic bird on another planet about whether or not a human chameleon is my girlfriend. I think my weird-o-meter is broken.*

"I like her." The bird still sounded amused.

"Well, I'm glad. I guess." He wasn't sure how to respond, so he decided to change the subject. "So, meeting you is one of the things I don't remember? How did we meet?" Then he had another thought. "Can you show me how to use *dimsai*?"

Crin didn't answer right away. Jason got the impression the bird was listening to a voice that he couldn't hear.

"I am sorry. I'm not allowed to help you remember yet. I'm told it is not yet time." Crin was silent for a few moments. "*One thing I am allowed, though. Before you forgot, you were able to see as I do. I am permitted to give that back to you. I'm told you have need of that now."*

"Told by who?"

"By the sparkling one. She says she is being watched and so cannot speak with you directly, but tells me what needs to be done."

"But my eyes are pretty good," he said. "You mean being able to see long distances or something?"

"No. It is difficult for me to explain, but you will understand soon."

He felt a tickle inside his head.

"There. It is done."

He glanced around the room. Nothing was different. He moved to the window and stared at the forest below. It looked just the same as every other time he'd looked at it. He focused on a bird circling high overhead. Nothing.

"I must go now."

"Why?"

He felt frustration from Crin. *"It was not time for you to remember yet. I do not like having to wait. The ritual was unexpected, but useful since it allowed me to help you."* Crin launched himself into the sky. *"One more thing the sparkling one says to tell you. Do not mention me to anyone. At least not yet."*

"Wait!" he called, then realized that he might be overheard. *Will you come back?*

"Of course. But not until it is time." Crin answered as he flew toward the trees. *"I am told it is not safe for me to speak with you too much until you remember everything, so I will not. But I will be watching."*

Wait, he thought as Crin disappeared into the forest. But there was no answer.

"A spy? That is a strong accusation, Captain." Tal was taken aback at Gatlor's blunt declaration. When Gatlor asked to speak with him, he assumed the captain planned on discussing strategies or defense plans. Instead, the veteran warrior opened the conversation with the last thing he expected to hear.

"I know, High One," Gatlor answered, "but I can come up with no other explanation for what happened on the Scorched Plains. Lore's Haven is warded against intrusion from outside *saiken*, so only someone already inside the keep would be able to learn of our plans."

Tal could think of at least a few beings that the wards would have little effect against, but did not see the necessity of mentioning them. Other than those notable exceptions, he had to admit, Gatlor's theory seemed to be the most plausible. The wards were only to keep portals created outside from opening up inside the keep. A spy already inside would have no difficulty reporting any plans to an outside accomplice.

"Do you have anyone in mind, Captain?"

"Regrettably, High One, I do. That is why I asked to speak with you alone."

"I do not understand. Should this not be a matter for the full—" He stopped mid-sentence as he understood Gatlor's meaning. "You believe the spy to be a member of the Circle?"

"High One, I believe we must at the very least consider the possibility."

"I see." Even as he looked at Gatlor, Tal was mentally running through the Loremasters, picturing each as a possible spy, and just as quickly discarding the thought. "And are the Loremasters your only possibilities?"

"No. I must also consider my own officers, as well as anyone else who may have known of our plans."

"Who else other than the Circle and your officers would know?"

"The *saiken* from the Amethyst Order who opened the portals for us."

"Of course. They would have known as well. Have you spoken with Loremaster Delani about your suspicions?"

"No, High One. I wanted to discuss my thoughts with you first."

He considered what Gatlor had said. Certainly someone had been inside Lore's Haven; otherwise Loremaster Chon would still be alive. Loremaster Delani would be outraged, but they had to consider all possibilities. Then his thoughts turned to Bodann. Did he have enough power to penetrate the wards? He had been formidable when at Lore's Haven. Had his power grown? Or was Regor or one of the other Altered aiding him?

"This must be brought before the Circle," he said. He held up a hand to forestall Gatlor's protest. "I know, Captain, the members of the Circle are among your suspects. But I am afraid we must risk this. I have known each Loremaster on the Circle for many years. If one of them is a spy, I will step down from my position."

Jason studied the forest below, trying to get a glimpse of the fortunewing, but he couldn't see past the thick leaves. A knock on his door pulled his attention away from the window. A Warder stood outside.

With a brief bow, the man said, "The High One requests you attend the meeting of the Circle which is to begin shortly."

"Yeah, okay."

"Do you need time to prepare?"

"No, we can go now."

He followed as the Warder turned and began walking down the corridor. A few minutes later, he walked into the Circle chamber, apparently the last to arrive. The Loremasters were standing in twos and threes immersed in quiet conversations. He noticed that only eight Loremasters were present, and then, with a pang of guilt, realized who the missing one was. Gatlor and two other men he didn't know sat in the chairs facing the Circle.

As he entered the room, the Loremasters turned and nodded greetings to him. All except for one. The Loremaster named Brin wouldn't look at him at all. Bothan's parting words echoed again in Jason's memory. Was Brin working for Bothan?

"Ah, Jason," the High One said. He indicated the open seat next to Gatlor. "Please be seated and we will begin."

The High One stepped to the podium as the Loremasters took their seats. "Loremasters, as you know, we suffered significant losses on the Scorched Plains. In addition to that, the members of the scouting parties were also killed. Aside from the tragic loss of life, what is most disturbing about this is that the enemy apparently knew of our plans." He paused for a moment, and then continued. "Captain Gatlor and I have discussed this matter. It is the captain's belief that we have a spy in our midst."

At this pronouncement, the Loremasters began whispering among themselves. Gatlor remained motionless, his face impassive. Jason watched the Loremasters' reactions. All seemed equally surprised by this remark, again with one exception. Brin was staring at Jason with a strange look on his face, but when Jason looked at him, the Loremaster quickly looked away.

The High One raised his hands for quiet. "As detestable as I find the thought of one of our own betraying us, I must confess, I can see no other credible possibility. The wards set about the

Haven prevent outside portals from opening here, but do nothing to stop portals opened here from reaching outside. A spy would have no difficulty reporting to someone outside of Lore's Haven."

Delani stood. "High One, do you or Captain Gatlor have any suspicions as to who this spy may be?" She looked ready to go out and apprehend the guilty party herself.

"Unfortunately, nothing specific. We do, however, have possibilities." He looked around the Circle. "If a spy is behind this, then they must have had enough advance knowledge of our plans to give the enemy forces time to prepare. This limits the possibilities to three groups."

He clasped his hands and rested them on the podium. "There is, of course, ourselves, the Circle." At this, the Loremasters looked around at each other. Most wore expressions of skepticism. The High One again raised a hand. "Please," he said. "I do not give this suggestion credence. I merely mention it as one of the logical possibilities. I have already told Captain Gatlor that if one of us is a traitor, I will step down from my position as High One." This seemed to satisfy the Loremasters, and they settled back in their seats.

"The next group is Captain Gatlor's officers. This, too, I find difficult to believe, although the captain certainly knows his officers better than I." He turned to Gatlor.

Gatlor stood. "High One, I would trust each of my officers with my life. But when it comes to the safety of Lore's Haven, I rule nothing and no one out." Then he sat back down.

Jarril stood. "And who is the third group, High One?"

"Concentrate," a voice whispered in Jason's mind. *"See the unseen."*

Crin? he said in his head. No answer. *Nyala?* Still nothing. Just the cryptic remark. See the unseen? What did that mean? He looked around the room, not knowing what it was he was looking for.

The High One turned back to the Loremasters. "The final group that must be considered…" He looked at Delani. "…are those *saiken* who opened the portals for our forces."

Concentrate. On what? *A little more information would be helpful!* he yelled in his head. But there was still no answer. He saw Loremaster Delani stand up so he tried focusing intently on her. Her eyes were blazing, but when she spoke, her voice betrayed only the slightest hint of tension.

"High One," she said, "the *saiken* who opened the portals were all members of my order. Is it your belief that the traitor is in the Amethyst Order?" This time she didn't sit down.

"Loremaster Delani, please do not take offense," the High One said. "If we do indeed have a traitor in our midst, we can do no less than to consider all possibilities, no matter how distasteful they may be. The blood of a thousand men and women cries out for it from the dust of the Scorched Plains."

Concentrating intently on Delani, Jason felt the same tickle in his brain that he'd felt with the fortunewing. Then, a brilliant purple aura blossomed around the Amethyst Loremaster. He blinked and looked again, but the glow was still there.

After a moment, Delani nodded. "Of course, High One," she said. "I apologize for my unwarranted reaction." She didn't seem aware that anything had changed as she retook her seat, although she still looked irritated.

As he looked around the room, he saw that everyone was surrounded by a glow, each a different color. A sparkling green aura surrounded Reyga, while Seryn glowed bluish-white. *Just like their hands when they examined me,* he thought. The High One had a cream-colored aura, and the rest of the Loremasters glowed red, orange, yellow, and blue.

Jarril stood, surrounded by an orange halo of color. "High One, do you or Captain Gatlor have any ideas as to how we may ascertain the identity of the spy? Or of how we may prevent them from obtaining any more information that may hinder our efforts?"

Do they all see this and I'm just now seeing it? he wondered. *Or am I the only one that can see the auras? Is this the unseen?* He forced himself to relax so that he wouldn't draw any attention to himself. He casually glanced around the room as the High One answered the question. Even Gatlor and his commanders had faint glows, although their auras were not nearly as intense as the Loremasters'. *Does the brightness have anything to do with how much power they have?*

"At this time," Tal said, "we do not have any ideas on how to identify the spy, if indeed there is one. However, in order to minimize potential damage a spy may do, we will be limiting the number of people who have advance knowledge of any plans we make. Captain Gatlor will explain."

He kept scanning the room as the High One talked. Then, just behind the seated Loremasters, almost obscured by the light surrounding them, he saw a faint outline against the wall. It was as if someone's aura had remained behind after they'd left the room. He blinked his eyes, thinking it might be an afterimage of one of the other Loremaster's auras, but it was still there. There was someone else in this room.

He looked away. He didn't know why the mysterious guest was here, but he didn't want the figure to know it had been discovered. He tried to turn his attention back to the podium.

"Of course," Gatlor said, "the Circle will be included in planning any actions, but only myself, Commander Maton, and Commander Garyn," here he indicated the two men with him, "will be involved. We will prepare any forces we may need, but we will tell them only what they need to know. Likewise, no *saiken* we use for portal travel will be told where we are to go until it is time for them to open the portals." He looked around the Circle. "In this way, we will limit the number of people who know in advance of our plans to no more than twelve. Unless the spy is among those twelve, these measures should prevent the enemy from gaining any more advantages over us."

Jason pretended to look around the room again, his eyes sweeping without stopping across the figure against the wall. It hadn't moved.

Delani stood again. "And what if we have students or instructors in our Orders whom we trust as much as you trust your commanders? Are we to be allowed to share such plans with them in order to prepare, as you and your commanders will be able to prepare your forces?"

"With all due respect, Loremaster Delani," Gatlor answered. "If such preparations can be done without the aid of others, or at least without their knowledge of precisely what we plan, that would be preferable. However, I am not a Loremaster. I do not know the intricacies of your position. If you feel you must share your knowledge with others in your Order, then that is entirely your prerogative. But please bear in mind, each additional person who knows of our plans is one more potential threat to the men and women who will be risking their lives." His hands clenched into fists as they rested on the podium. "I do not want a repeat of what happened yesterday."

"Nor do we, Captain Gatlor," the High One stepped back to the podium.

Gatlor inclined his head and took his seat.

"Loremasters," the High One said, "as it is almost time for Secondmeal, we will conclude this meeting. Please consider what has been said here and what you can do to help ensure the safety of the people of Lore's Haven. We will meet again on the morrow. May the mantle of wisdom ever rest upon your shoulders."

"May your power be exceeded only by your honor, High One." They all stood and began filing out of the room.

As he stepped into the Corridor, Jason heard Reyga calling his name. He stopped and waited for the Loremaster.

"Jason," Reyga said as he came out of the Circle chamber, "I was wondering if you would join me for Secondmeal. I would like to speak with you."

"Sure, I guess. Is that where you're going now?"

Reyga nodded, and the two of them headed for the dining hall. Looking at the people they passed, Jason saw that everyone was surrounded by a glow. The auras came in all different colors and intensities. By the time they finally reached the dining hall, he felt like he was in the middle of a pastel river. He was sure he'd seen every color in the rainbow, plus a few new ones he'd never before experienced.

They found seats and were about to sit down when Reyga said, "Please excuse me for just a moment, Jason. I must speak briefly with one of my students."

Jason took his seat while Reyga made his way toward a group of students on the other side of the room. Reyga began speaking with one of the students. Jason noticed that the boy's aura was the same color as Reyga's, although not as strong. *It must have something to do with what they're good at,* he thought. A plate of food was brought to him, and he began eating. He put his spoon down as an idea struck him.

Looking around, he spotted a young woman sitting nearby in an animated discussion with some other young men and women. The glow surrounding her was silvery white. He went over to them, stopping beside the girl.

"Excuse me," he said.

With a questioning glance at her companions, the girl turned to him. "Yes?"

"I'm sorry. I don't mean to interrupt, but are you one of Loremaster Seryn's students?"

"Yes, I am a member of the Diamond Order." She bowed her head slightly. "I am Meryl. You are the Far Planer, Jason Bennett. It is an honor to meet you." Then she turned solemn. "I am sorry for the loss of your father."

He looked at the floor, unsure how to respond. When he raised his head, he noticed the others in the group looking at him curiously. "Well, I didn't mean to int—"

"How did you know I studied under Loremaster Seryn?"

He hadn't planned that far ahead, and he didn't want to mention the auras. He needed to find out if everyone saw the auras, or if it was only him. "Oh, uh, well, I think Reyga mentioned you once."

She looked surprised. "Loremaster Reyga spoke of me?" She looked at the Loremaster across the room.

"Actually, it may not have been Reyga after all," he said quickly, afraid she might ask Reyga about it. "I think it might have been someone else. I can't remember who."

"Oh."

"Yeah, well, like I said, sorry for interrupting. I guess I'll get back to my food. It was nice to meet you." He turned and walked quickly back to his seat.

As he ate, he thought about what he'd learned in their brief conversation. The girl acted like she didn't know how he knew she was one of Seryn's students. That meant that either no one here could see the auras, or, as a Far Planer, she didn't expect him to be able to see them. He needed more information.

Just then Reyga returned and sat down.

"Um, Reyga?"

"Yes?"

"I was just wondering, is there any way to tell how strong someone is with *dimsai* by looking at them?"

Reyga shook his head. "Would that there were," he said. "But we can only determine that while the child is being trained and tested. Why do you ask?"

He shrugged. “No reason,” he said, picking up a spoon full of food. “Just curious.”

Well, that was one question answered. Now all he had to do was figure out what Brin was up to.

After the meal, during which Reyga thanked him several times for what he’d done for Lenai, Reyga asked him what he planned to do that afternoon.

“Um, well I’ll probably just hang out in my room. Maybe take a nap or something.”

“Hang out?” Reyga asked. “Not the window? Jason, that would not be safe!”

He had to laugh. “No, I mean I’ll probably just stay in my room. We call it ‘hanging out’ back home when we plan to stay somewhere for a while.”

“Ah,” Reyga shook his head with a chuckle. “You certainly have odd sayings in your world. Well, I am going to the market area, which is in the same direction. With your permission, I will accompany you for a while.”

As they walked through the halls of Lore’s Haven, he thought about the strange figure. At first he wondered if it could have been Bothan, but dismissed the thought. It hadn’t been nearly large enough. None of them had acted like they knew it was there. If no one else could see these auras like he could, that would mean no one else would know about an invisible lurker.

He glanced around the corridor, but didn’t see any other disembodied auras. “Reyga,” he said, “are there any other races in Teleria besides the Shanthi that can make themselves invisible?” He hoped the fact that Reyga had spoken so much about Lenai over lunch would make the question seem innocent.

Reyga shook his head. “None so far as we know. To the best of our knowledge, the Shanthi are unique in their abilities of concealment.”

He nodded. If that was true, then that meant that their unseen guest had to have been a Shanthi.

He stopped in the middle of the corridor. “Hey,” he said, “do you really need to go to the market right now?”

Reyga turned back to him, a puzzled look on his face. “No, I can get what I need later. Why do you ask?”

“I think we need to go see the High One.”

22
Deceptions

Gatlor smiled with grim satisfaction. He was staring at the back of the enemy army from the top of a rise behind which he, a hundred archers, and a score of *saiken* waited. Although initially skeptical of Jason Bennett's claim, he had been convinced when Jason was able to identify the Orders of several students presented to him. Then the High One summoned Lenai and she confirmed the presence of two unknown Shanthi within the keep.

His first impulse had been to capture the spies and get what information they could from them, but Jason had suggested another plan. From what he was seeing now, the scheme was working perfectly. The enemy forces waited in a low plain, facing away from them. Their attention was on the unmistakable glow of portals over the next set of hills. They expected the next Haven attack to come from that direction. They expected it from there because that was what he and the Circle had deliberately discussed for the benefit of their unseen visitors.

After the initial battle, it had been clear that the Haven forces could not survive a head-to-head war with this massive horde. Now they hoped to reduce the enemy numbers with as many quick strikes and withdrawals as possible.

He signaled the archers. The men and women moved forward until they were just below the top of the ridge. A hundred drawn bows mirrored the motion of his arm as he slowly raised it, keeping his eyes on the enemy. The initial volley would strike in the heart of the mass of fighters below.

He watched the army as it milled about. They needed to be sure the enemy did not see the source of the first attack. Now. He dropped his arm, and the soft thrum of a hundred bowstrings answered. With a quiet hiss, the arrows soared into the air. The archers nocked another arrow into their bows and waited for his next signal.

He watched the arrows' descent. Even from this distance, he could hear the fatal sounds of their arrival. Almost immediately, a roar went up from the center of the army. The fighters at the back strained to see what was happening, their attention fixed on the shouting.

He signaled again. The archers moved up to the top of the ridge and fired another volley into the nearest ranks. Then they turned and sprinted down the back of the ridge toward two portals. The *saiken* not holding the portals stepped to the top of the ridge and sent blazing bolts of *dimsai* into the confused army below. They sent a second blast of power into the mass just as a bolt of *dimsai* detonated against the ground just below them. That was their signal to run for the portals, as the enemy surged up the ridge, roaring and howling in outraged fury.

He waited for the last *saiken* to clear the ridge, and then he sprinted after them. The archers had already gone through the portals and the *saiken* were just a few steps away. As the first *saiken* entered the portal, the enemy crested the ridge and sent arrows flying after them. The last *saiken* was ten paces from the portal when he fell, an arrow in his shoulder. Gatlor dragged the man to his feet, and the two of them stumbled toward the portal.

He glanced over his shoulder. One of the Trellin, faster than the others, was bearing down on them. Gatlor gave the *saiken* a shove toward the portal and drew a dagger from his bandolier. An instant later, the lizard man crumpled to the ground, the hilt of the dagger protruding from one eye socket.

Gatlor grinned fiercely. Their blood could stain the plains just as his warriors' had. Time for the second part of the attack. The archers would be coming back through the other portals. Their orders were to move to the crest and fire at will into the rear of the army, which had originally been the front.

He heard a fresh roar from the enemy forces. The Haven archers were pouring as many arrows into the ranks as they could. The leading edge of the horde slowed as they heard the new commotion, looking behind them, and then back at him, clearly not sure where their rage should be directed.

Their confusion was short-lived as commanders in the ranks bellowed orders. Most of the enemy turned back toward the new attack. Three score renewed their charge toward him.

He wanted nothing more than to bury his blade in as many enemy fighters as possible, but he knew today was not the day for such things. There would be another time.

He drew his sword and held it to the sky as he shouted his defiance at the approaching creatures. Then he turned and ran through the portal. Today did not make up for the first attack, but it was something…it was something.

Brin stared at the dagger lying across his knees. Troubled eyes stared back up at him from the reflection in the blade. *How can I do this?* The thought of what he was going to do tore at very soul. *How can I not?* The possibility that the shadowy being might carry through on its threat was even more unbearable.

When his wife, Sharyn, died fifteen years ago, his sons became the center of his world, followed closely by his duties to the Circle. He remembered how proud his family had been when he told them he was to be Loremaster Farris' apprentice. His sons could not wait to tell their friends. The love and pride in Sharyn's eyes made every minute of tedious study, every hour of practice and lessons, worth the effort he had put into them twice over.

He thought about his predecessor, Loremaster Farris. He remembered sitting by the old man's bedside as his final moments approached. Even on the brink of death, Farris' eyes gleamed with pride in his Order, and in his apprentice.

"The honor of the Ruby Order now lies on your shoulders, Brin," he whispered. "I have given you all of my wisdom. I have faith that you will make me proud." He had smiled at Brin, and then he was gone, his wisdom going to join those who had gone before. Although Brin had thought himself prepared for it, the finality of his master's passing seemed to suck some of his own life away as well. He vowed then that he would prove worthy of Farris' faith in him.

While not as vocal as Loremaster Delani, he was just as fierce in his determination to serve the Circle and to uphold the honor of his Order to his dying breath. But now, what he was about to do would cast a stain on everything he had ever done. It would sully the Ruby Order for generations to come. Worse yet, it would betray the faith and pride of the one person who had mattered most, his beloved Sharyn.

The eyes in the dagger hardened as he thought again about how the being had used the memory of his son. *There must be a way out of this!* He searched for possibilities, probing and prodding even the most outlandish ideas thoroughly before discarding them. He had trained his mind for decades to look at every situation from as many different angles as possible. If he could just find the right way of seeing this, he knew he could find a way to keep from committing murder, and yet save his sons from a hideous fate.

His breath caught. That was it. He knew what must be done. He could almost hear Loremaster Farris' voice in his head asking, "*Are you certain of this course?*" He nodded to the memory of his previous master. It would be risky, and he could only hope that it would work, but he could see no other way.

"And did you kill *any* of them?" Bothan's voice trembled as he glared at the Trellin leader. The creature writhed inside a cocoon of *dimsai*.

"We…wounded…one," it managed to rasp through the pressure.

"Ah. Well then," Bothan said. "As long as you wounded one."

The creature made a strangled sound as the pressure increased.

"You wounded one?" Bothan roared. "One? I lose over three hundred of my army, and you tell me you wounded one? *One!*" The Trellin's feet lifted off the ground as the pressure increased with Bothan's rising fury.

"Pleeasssz…" the lizard man hissed. A trickle of blood trailed from one nostril. "The ssspy told usss they would attack from the north, not the sssouth."

"And did the idea of sentries never cross that pea-sized brain o' yours?" The *dimsai* flared as, with an expression of disgust, he tossed the creature aside. It landed a short distance away, thin plumes of smoke rising from the scorched corpse. He absently watched the smoke rise while he thought about its report and its implications.

"What will you do now? If they continue to attack like this, they will chip away at your forces until they can defeat you."

He turned to the shadowy figure behind him. "Aye," he said. "Like as not they've discovered our spies." He shook his head. "Sure and I'd like to know how. Clearly, they used them against us."

"Why don't you simply attack the keep directly and be done with it?"

"Why don't you?" he snapped back, his anger flaring.

The eyes in the shadow blazed. "*Do not forget to whom you speak.*"

He forced his anger down. "Forgive me, Lord Regor. It was my frustration speakin'. It's just that I don't see why the others are opposed to this. You're working to bring the glory they once had back to them."

"It is not that they are opposed as much as it is that they are unaware. We are bound by an ancient agreement."

He'd heard this before, even if he didn't understand it. "And you cannot even—"

"I cannot," Regor said. "*I risk much even being here, and even more by giving you the power that I have. If the others realize what I'm doing, they may take action against me.*"

"Well then," he said, "to answer your question, no ordinary army could take Lore's Haven. Built as it is on the plateau, and with all of the *saiken* and power at their disposal, we would have a better chance fighting the wind."

"So what will you do?"

"Whether they intended it or no, they sent us a message," he answered. He looked at the corpse again. "We send one back."

Jason scanned the Circle chamber, looking for any disembodied auras. It had taken no small amount of concentration, but he'd discovered he could turn the vision off and on. He was very pleased about that. If nothing else, it meant that he could walk down a hallway without feeling like he was drifting through a psychedelic fog. When he was convinced there were no unseen guests, he nodded to the High One.

"Loremasters," Tal said, "it would appear that our strike yesterday was successful. Captain Gatlor tells me he estimates the attack eliminated several hundred of Bodann's army while we escaped with only one injury. Pell, from the Topaz Order, was wounded, but I am told he is recovering in the healing area."

Kalen nodded. "Thanks to the expert care from Loremaster Seryn's students, he should be back to his duties within two days," he said.

"Excellent," the High One said. "Clearly, these deceptions will only be effective temporarily. Jason has assured me that this room is clear for the moment, so let us plan our next attack." He turned to Gatlor. "Captain Gatlor, do you have any ideas regarding our next move?"

Jason was only half listening to the conversation as Gatlor began discussing his next plan of action. His attention was on the Ruby Loremaster.

Brin was agitated, his eyes moving from the podium to Jason and just as quickly away. His jerky gaze crawled across the floor, jumped to Jason, and then away again. All the while his fingers picked and worried at a fold in his robe.

What's going on with him? In his time in Teleria, Jason hadn't seen anyone acting like this. The only time that had been close was after Nyala's first appearance in the High One's chamber. Even then, after the initial shock, the High One had quickly composed himself.

Gatlor was answering a question from Loremaster Jarril when Brin stood up.

"No," Brin said, almost as if speaking to himself. He shook his head. "No."

Gatlor stopped speaking as the High One stepped back up to the podium.

"Loremaster Brin, do you have a question?"

Brin stared at the High One. "A question?" His gaze jumped to Jason and then back to the High One. "Yes, a question." He blinked at the floor, his lips moving without a sound. Then he looked to the podium. "Why are we here?" He raised a hand to his mouth, stroking his lips absently. "Why are we here? Is that the question I want to ask? I can't…I can't remember." His other hand was buried in his robe.

The Loremasters exchanged glances as Brin took a hesitant step toward the dais. Gatlor moved to the side, frowning as he watched the Ruby Loremaster's strange behavior. Seryn was studying Brin intently.

"Loremaster Brin," she said, "are you well?"

Brin looked at her as if surprised to see her in the room. "Well? Of course I am well. Why would I not be well?" His gaze wandered across the room. "Of course. Why would I not be well?" He looked at the High One. "But you asked…yes…I have a question. A question. It was…it was…"

His eyes leapt to Jason's face, fixing him with a glare that set Jason back in his seat. "Yes, a question. Now I remember." He raised one hand, pointing a shaking finger at Jason. "Why is he here?"

"What? Me?" Jason gaped at the Loremaster.

"What? Me?" Brin mimicked Jason's voice. "Yes, you! You are the reason for all of this."

Several of the Loremasters rose to their feet. Gatlor's hand dropped to the hilt of his sword. "Loremaster Brin," the High One said. "What are you—"

"Chon was right! All of this is your fault!" Brin shouted at Jason. His raised hand, still pointing at Jason, shook violently and his eyes were wild.

Jason stood and moved so that his chair was between the two of them.

"You are the reason my son is dead. Why are you still alive?" Brin's robe flared out as he pulled a long dagger from underneath it. With his free hand he gestured toward Gatlor, who was drawing his sword. With a rasping ring of metal, the sword ripped out of Gatlor's hand and slammed back into its scabbard.

"Brin!" several voices shouted.

"No more!" Brin shouted back, and lunged toward Jason.

Jason couldn't move. *He's going to kill me*. He felt like he was in a trance. He couldn't even raise his arm to defend himself. The thought of his impending death immobilized him. Suddenly, everything seemed to move very slowly. He saw the light sliding along the blade in Brin's hand. He saw Gatlor pulling futilely at his sword. The High One and the others surged forward, but he knew they were already too late. He watched the dagger carve a gleaming arc through the air as Brin raised it over his head.

Then Brin was lying at Jason's feet, a pool of blood spreading underneath him. With a strangled sound, Jason stumbled backward until the wall of the Chamber stopped him.

"What the...? What happened?" he blurted, his heart pounding. He wrapped his arms over his chest, tucking his hands away to stop them from shaking.

For a moment, no one answered, no one moved. Then the High One rushed to Brin.

"He tripped and fell on his own dagger," Gatlor said, looking confused for the first time Jason could remember.

"Brin," the High One said. He grasped Brin's shoulder and rolled him onto his back. Brin's eyes were closed and the hilt of his dagger stood up from underneath the ribs on his right side. The metallic smell of blood filled the air as a dark stain spread on Brin's tunic.

"Seryn," the High One said, but she was already moving to Brin's side, her hands flaring with power. She knelt and moved her hands over the wound.

"This must be done delicately," she said. "Backlash from a *saiken lo* could be deadly." She focused on the wound. After a moment, she quenched her power and sat back. "I have stemmed the flow of blood somewhat," she said, "but we must get him to the healing area without delay. He is fortunate the blade entered where it did or he could easily be dead already."

Bent over Brin as he lay on the table in the healing area, Seryn focused on her work, using her power to mend torn muscle and flesh back together. She worked with precision, using as little *dimsai* as possible in order to prevent revealing any secrets Brin may have. The Ruby Loremaster was not an unfriendly man, but he did tend to be a rather private man. While members of the Diamond Order often had to use *dimsai* on their patients, they did their best to respect the privacy of those under their care. There was also the potential for backlash, which became more of a concern the more power a patient had. With a *saiken lo*, extreme care had to be taken.

"There now, Brin," she murmured as she finished, "that should do it." She did not expect an answer. Brin had not moved since they carried him in and laid him on the table, so she was startled to hear him whisper her name. She looked up at the High One, standing on the other side of the table. He was watching Brin intently.

"Brin?" she said. His eyes were barely open, but he was looking at her. "I apologize. I did not realize—"

"Deeper…" he whispered.

"Deeper? I do not understand."

"Probe…deeper…"

"Are you in pain? Is there damage that I missed?" she asked, her power flaring up on her hands once more.

"Deeper. Please." Then he was unconscious again.

She thought the damage repaired, but he had come as close to begging as his weakened state would allow. While Brin always graciously accepted aid when it was offered, it was extremely rare for him to ask for it. There had to be something she was missing.

She focused her power on the wound, sending her senses past the repaired flesh, deeper into his chest. No other damage. She cautiously increased her power. Still nothing.

She stepped back, going over the sequence of events again. He was here because he fell on his dagger. He fell on his dagger because of his irrational behavior in the Circle chamber. *Perhaps he meant something other than the wound.* Something had to have caused him to act as he did.

"I do not see any more damage. But something else must be wrong for him to ask for a deeper examination. With your permission, High One, I would like to check for any other trauma that may have affected his actions."

When the High One nodded, she moved up and placed her hands above Brin's face. She hesitated for a moment, and then called up her power. *I hope he understands*. She sent her power into his head, looking for anything unusual that could have caused his actions in the chamber.

Her initial probe revealed nothing, so she focused her power more deeply. She still did not see any sign of damage or… She gasped as his thoughts filled her mind.

"Seryn?" the High One asked.

She did not answer, focused on what she was seeing. This was unthinkable! The images, and what they implied, shocked her. This was what he wanted her to find. She waited until they finished, then let her power drop.

"Oh, Brin," she breathed, laying her hand on the sleeping man's shoulder.

"Seryn, what did you see?"

Brin stirred, his eyes opening slightly. He looked at Seryn. Seryn nodded. "I saw," she said.

"Tell them," he whispered, then slid back into unconsciousness.

"Tell us what?" the High One asked.

She looked around the room. "We need to find Jason Bennett," she said.

"Why would Brin deliberately fall on his own dagger?" the High One asked.

They were back in the Circle chambers. Jason was there to make sure no unseen visitors were around. At Seryn's request, several of the strongest *saiken lo* also held a ward around the room to prevent any intrusions.

"He felt it was the only way to save both his own sons as well as Jason," Seryn answered. "One of the Altered threatened to kill his other sons unless Brin killed Jason."

As he heard Seryn's description of what she'd seen, Jason knew who the shadowy figure was. Regor. The scene in the chamber had been nothing but an act in case Regor was watching. Regor would see Brin try to kill Jason, but fail due to his own clumsiness.

Delani stood. "So, already faced with a war we may not win, we now find ourselves in the midst of a conflict between the Altered?"

Nyala! he shouted inside his head. He didn't know if she could hear his thoughts, but he had to try. *Nyala! Can you hear me?* No answer.

"So it would seem," the High One answered. "From what Jason has told me, Nyala stands between him and the Shadow Lord. Apparently Regor has decided to use others to commit his crimes."

Not getting an answer from Nyala, he tried a different tack. *Crin! Are you listening?* Although he still didn't get an answer, somehow he knew Crin heard him. *Crin, you have to tell Nyala what Regor is doing.* He relayed what Seryn had discovered, hoping the bird would be able to pass along the message.

"What are we to do?" T'kel was saying. "We cannot stand against one such as he."

"But if Jason is important enough to attract the attention of the Altered, we cannot simply give him up either," Reyga said.

"Are you saying we should defy Regor?" Kalen asked.

"You don't have to," Jason said. Crin was relaying Nyala's response. "Regor is bluffing. He can't actually touch anyone without making the other Altered angry."

"Jason," the High One said, "do you know something you have not told us?"

"Yes and no," Jason answered. "I didn't know about the bluff until just now, but there are some things that I haven't mentioned."

The High One frowned at him. "I thought we agreed there would be truth between us."

"I know," he said, "and I'm sorry. But I was ordered not to tell you anything by someone who…well…they outrank you."

"An Altered," Reyga said. "Nyala?"

"Yeah. I'm still not sure if I'm supposed to say anything or not, but I think you need to know." He could feel Crin's disapproval. *I'm tired of hiding*, he thought to the bird. *They have to know.* He sensed the mental equivalent of a sigh, but Crin didn't protest.

"Jason," Reyga said, "will revealing this place you in any danger? I can only speak for myself, but if that is the case, I trust you without it."

"As do I," Seryn added.

Seryn's agreement startled him. Reyga's he had expected, but Seryn's profession of faith made him wonder what she'd seen when she examined him. While he appreciated their confidence, he hoped it wasn't misplaced. He still didn't know how to use his power.

"I appreciate that, Reyga, Loremaster Seryn," he said, "but I'm tired of secrets. I want you to know what's going on."

23
Knocking on Doors

Tal sat in his chambers, staring blindly at the candle on the table. He had not gone down for Firstmeal this morning. The conversation with Jason Bennett the night before filled his mind, pushing thoughts of food aside.

Jason had told them about his dreams. He also said there were still some things that he could not yet reveal. It boggled Tal's mind that so much had taken place in the time Jason had been in the sphere with her. The power of the Altered was even more impressive than he could have imagined.

With Regor aiding Bodann, and with the forces Bodann had somehow managed to assemble, their only hope was deception and misinformation. Unless they could pare down Bodann's army, he could not see any way for them to prevail. But even faced with almost certain defeat, he would fight until his last breath. He knew that every man and woman in Lore's Haven felt the same way.

He looked up at a knock on the door, and tried to blink away the afterimage of the flame dancing in his vision. He gestured and the door swung open.

"Come in," he said.

Gatlor stalked into the room, a scowl darkening his face.

"Captain Gatlor, is there a problem?"

"Arynn has been destroyed."

His heart sank. Although he was afraid he knew what the answer would be, he had to ask. "Were there any survivors?" He braced himself for the answer he knew was coming.

"There was one. The village elder."

A survivor? This was unexpected. "Where is he? Is he able to speak?"

Gatlor nodded. "He is unharmed. He waits in the corridor."

"Unharmed?" He wondered at that. "Bring him in."

Gatlor stepped to the door and motioned. A white-haired man limped into the room, aided by one of the Warders. Once the man was seated, the Warder bowed and left.

"High One," Gatlor said, "this is Thoris, Arynn's village elder."

As Thoris struggled to stand, Tal came around the table and placed a hand on his shoulder. "Please," he said, "remain seated. You have been through a terrible ordeal."

He moved back around the table and sat down, studying the old man. Thoris' weathered hands trembled as they rested in his lap, and deep wrinkles carved his face. The haunted look in his eyes told Tal much about what had happened at Arynn. He regretted having to make Thoris relive what he had endured, but they needed anything that might give them any hope of victory.

"I am truly sorry to have to ask this," Tal said, "but I need to know what happened."

Thoris closed his eyes and nodded. "I know, High One, and I will tell you. If I may have but a moment."

"Of course. When you are ready."

Thoris sat for a moment with his eyes closed, and then took a deep breath as he opened them. His voice shook as he spoke.

"A man came into our village. He said he was looking for the village elder. When I introduced myself, he sent a blast of *dimsai* into sky and grabbed my arm." He looked at Tal, the pain clear in his eyes. "He made me watch as all manner of foul creatures killed the people of my village. When everyone was dead except me, they burned everything to the ground." A tear traced its way down his furrowed cheek. "It is not right that I should live while everyone I knew was killed."

"I am sorry," Tal said. "I know this is difficult. I only have a few questions." Thoris took a shaky breath and nodded. Tal went on. "What did the man look like?" he asked. He was sure he knew who it was, but it was best to be certain.

Thoris wiped his face. "He was a big man, with dark red hair," he answered. "His eyes were as green and hard as emeralds."

Tal nodded to himself. That was almost certainly Bodann. "Did he say why you were spared?"

"I am to deliver a message," Thoris said. "The man said to tell you, High One, that your deceptions will no longer work. He said that unless the Haven army meets his army at Landscar one sixday from today, they will destroy village after village until there are none left."

The murmur of subdued conversations hung in the air like dusty cobwebs as Reyga entered the chambers. He looked around at the others in the room. In addition to the Circle, Captain Gatlor and Jason were also present. An old man Reyga did not recognize was there as well, staring at the floor in front of his chair. Reyga saw Lenai enter the room and move to take a seat beside Gatlor and Jason. Reyga smiled as he saw the smile she gave Jason. Yet another debt he owed the young man, but one he was most happy to accept.

He looked over to one side at another young man who would soon be named the Obsidian Loremaster. Borin fidgeted as he stared at the chair that, up until a few days ago, had been filled by his predecessor, Loremaster Chon. Reyga walked over to him.

"Greetings, Borin. Welcome to the Circle chamber."

Borin jumped a little at Reyga's voice. "Oh, Loremaster Reyga," he said, bowing hastily. "Thank you. It is somewhat overwhelming. While I knew I would be here one day, I did not expect that day to come so quickly."

"None of us did," Reyga said. "You join the Circle during trying times and under most difficult circumstances. It cannot be easy for you."

Borin lowered his voice. "Loremaster Reyga, what if the Circle elects not to confirm me? To choose someone else for this position?"

Reyga shook his head. "Highly unlikely," he answered. "The Loremasters select their own successors. Unless there are very compelling reasons, the Circle abides by those decisions. It is only our present situation that has prevented us from confirming you already."

Borin let out a shaky breath. "I am not certain I am ready for this."

"I am afraid you have little choice." Reyga put a comforting hand on his shoulder. "Just remember what you have learned from Loremaster Chon and you will do well."

"Thank you, Loremaster Reyga. I will do that."

The High One stepped up to the podium. With a last squeeze of Borin's shoulder, Reyga moved to his chair.

"Greetings, Loremasters," the High One began. "I will dispense with the formalities and come straight to the point of this meeting. It would appear that Bodann has discovered our ruse. Arynn has been destroyed."

Reyga closed his eyes. More innocent lives lost. He could hear the other Loremasters murmuring as they absorbed the news. He opened his eyes as the High One continued.

The High One indicated the old man. "This is Thoris. He was the elder of Arynn, and is the only survivor. Bodann spared him so that he could deliver a message to us." He gripped the sides of the podium. "Unless we meet Bodann's army at Landscar a sixday from today, he will continue his attacks on our villages until they have all been destroyed."

A stunned silence filled the room. All of the Loremasters knew the size of Bodann's army. Most had seen firsthand during the ambush at the edge of Faedor Woods. Reyga knew what their chances of success were against such a massive force.

Gatlor stood. "High One, I will say what everyone in this room is thinking. We cannot win against the army that Bodann has amassed. Not without more forces of our own."

"Nevertheless, Captain, we must try," the High One answered. "If we do not meet him, thousands of innocent lives will be lost, while we sit within the safety of Lore's Haven. That is unacceptable."

"Then we need no longer keep up the pretense with the spies within our walls. I suggest we capture them and find out what they know."

"Agreed," the High One said. "Lenai, can you tell us where they are now?"

Lenai stood. "I will try, High One." Reyga watched her eyes take on a faraway look as she sent her senses ranging for Bodann's spies. After a moment, she shook her head. "I am sorry, High One, but they are no longer within Lore's Haven. I do not sense them anywhere."

"Of course. Once Bodann knew we had discovered them, there would be no need for them to remain."

Delani stood. "Can we not ask for more aid from the Dokal or the Ferrin? Or perhaps the Yellowtooth, or the Shanthi?"

The High One turned to Lenai. "Would your people be willing to aid us, do you think?"

"High One, as you know, my people prefer to remain neutral in such matters, and they have little love for humans," Lenai answered.

Reyga stood as an idea popped into his head. "And yet we know there are Shanthi aiding Bodann."

Lenai turned to him. "That is true, Loremaster Reyga. However, it is almost certain that those aiding Bodann are *rishna kel*." She spat the words as if trying to get a bad taste out of her mouth.

He had expected her answer, and had an answer ready. "And as it is primarily the fault of the *rishna kel* that the Shanthi are a mistrusted people, would not that very fact help to sway at least some of them to aid us?"

Lenai considered his words. Then she nodded slowly. "Perhaps," she said. She looked at Jason. "If Jason were to accompany me, and I told them of what he did for me, that may help persuade them as well."

Jason looked surprised, but didn't say anything. The High One looked at him. "Jason, would you be willing to go with Lenai to ask her people for aid?"

Jason looked around at the Loremasters watching him. "Yeah, I guess. If you really think it would help."

"I would like to join them as well, High One, if it is allowed," Reyga said.

The High One looked at Lenai. "Would that be acceptable, Lenai?"

"Loremaster Reyga is *ch'tasa* to me. I would welcome his company."

"Then it is decided," the High One said. "You will leave at first light. We will also send an emissary to the Yellowtooth, in the hopes of enlisting their aid as well."

Jarril stood. "High One, while I hope otherwise, the Yellowtooth may decline simply because they know my people are aiding you. The Ferrin and the Yellowtooth, while never coming to open hostilities, have never been on amicable terms."

"I understand," the High One said, "but we must make the attempt. We have a sixday to find as much aid as possible, or Teleria may fall under the control of Bodann and Regor." He turned to the Loremasters. "Whether our requests for aid are granted or not, we must use our time to prepare. The next time we face Bodann, the fate of Teleria will hang in the balance."

Jason, Lenai, and Reyga stood in the middle of a small clearing in Ambrewood Forest. They had used a portal that morning to travel to the village of Brynden, where Reyga found horses for them.

The man they got the horses from had trained at Lore's Haven with the Amethyst Order. When Reyga told him where they were going, he told Reyga to simply let the horses go once they arrived. His link with the animals would guide them back safely.

Their ride took them across the Shonta River. Once they crossed the narrow bridge, Lenai pulled her horse to a stop.

"Welcome to the land of my people," she said. "Loremaster Reyga, I must tell you that the Circle holds no sway among the Shanthi. There is no danger here, but you should know that we will be watched for the remainder of our journey. When we arrive, do not speak until I tell you. There will be some that will be displeased that I bring outsiders among them, and will not welcome the sound of your voices."

When they nodded, she turned back to the path and they continued on. As he swayed along the trail, Jason thought about using his special vision to see how many Shanthi were around, but then decided he wasn't sure if he really wanted to know. When they reached the clearing, they dismounted and turned the horses back toward Brynden.

Now they stood in the clearing, the horses gone, almost certainly surrounded by who knew how many invisible Shanthi. Although Lenai had assured them they would be safe, he couldn't help but feel a nervous fluttering in the pit of his stomach.

She took a couple of steps away from them and said something in her native tongue. Jason looked around, but didn't see or hear any response. She spoke again, a little more forcefully. For several uncomfortable moments, there was still no reply. Then a disembodied voice answered her, speaking Shanthi. She said something else, and again the voice answered.

Jason leaned toward Reyga and whispered, "Can you understand—"

"Silence, human!" a voice ordered, right at Jason's shoulder.

Lenai spun around. "*Bena sin rish!*" she snapped. She turned back to the clearing. "Is this the honor of the Shanthi? These humans come willingly among you, unarmed and accompanied by one of your own, and this is the welcome you give?"

Without warning, a man appeared in front of Lenai. He was several inches taller than her, lean and muscled. Occasional strands of grey streaked his ebony hair. He wore a simple headdress and an unmistakable aura of authority. As soon as he appeared, Lenai crossed her spread fingers in front of her face and bowed. When she straightened, he fixed her with a stern gaze.

"They are outsiders, Lenai. Surely you did not expect us to welcome them as our own?" He looked at Reyga's staff. "They may be unarmed, but this one is a Loremaster. He needs no weapon."

Lenai put herself between the man and Reyga. "Yes, he is a Loremaster. That in itself should be enough to convince you of his honor. However, if that will not suffice," she raised her chin, "he is also *ch'tasa*."

The man glanced at Lenai, and then appeared to reappraise Reyga. "This is the one?"

"Yes. This is Loremaster Reyga, the one I told you about." She turned to Reyga. "Loremaster Reyga, this is Baruun, the leader of my people."

Reyga bowed. "It is a privilege to meet you, Baruun. The honor of the Shanthi is well known among those who value truth."

Baruun inclined his head. "Well spoken, Loremaster Reyga. Be welcome among the Shanthi. What you did for Lenai is known to me, and I am pleased to have the opportunity to offer you my thanks after so many years."

"What of this one?" the voice by Jason demanded. A muscular man appeared, gripping a spear pointed at Jason's stomach, which he instinctively sucked in. "He is not a Loremaster. What speaks to his honor?"

"I do," Lenai countered.

"And what if you are deceived?" the man snapped.

"Then *Sho tu Ishta* is a lie."

"*Sho…*" the spear tip wavered as the man looked uncertainly at Baruun.

Jason heard whispering around the clearing, and here and there he caught brief glimpses of Shanthi as their concealment wavered. Lenai had apparently taken them by surprise with her statement.

"Lenai," Baruun said, "you shared *Sho tu Ishta* with an outsider?"

She dropped her gaze. "Much has happened since last we spoke," she said. She looked back up at him. "If I may be allowed to show you, I believe you will understand."

After a moment, he nodded. "Very well." The man beside Jason took a stance a few steps away as Baruun raised his hands so that his palms faced Lenai. Then, as had happened with Lenai during the ritual, he stretched out his hands, elongating the fingers. Lenai spread her hands and placed them palm to palm against Baruun's. Then the two of them bowed their heads, eyes closed.

Jason didn't know how long they sat there. No one moved. Not Lenai or Baruun, not Reyga, not the man with the spear. After what seemed an eternity, Lenai and Baruun opened their eyes and lowered their hands. Baruun wore an expression of confused wonder.

"*Ch'nai?*" he said quietly.

Lenai ducked her head, and then nodded, staring at her feet.

"And this human? Bodann?"

She looked back up at him, eyes burning. "He used me to hurt those I am sworn to protect."

Baruun hesitated a moment. "Does he know?"

She flashed a glance at Jason, then looked back at the ground at Baruun's feet and shook her head.

Jason wondered why Bothan wouldn't know he'd used Lenai. Or were they talking about something else? The way she'd looked at him. Was there something about Bothan that he didn't know? He would have to ask her about it sometime. Before he could give it any more thought, Baruun walked over to him.

Baruun bowed his head. "Jason Bennett, I have seen what you did for Lenai. I extend my thanks to you as well. While Loremaster Reyga protected her from bodily harm, you restored her soul. Ask a boon of me, and if it is within my power, I will gladly grant it."

Jason looked at Reyga, unsure how to respond. Before Reyga could say anything, Baruun went on.

"However, before we discuss such things..." He turned to the clearing. *"Shani ko rin!"* Suddenly, they were surrounded by dozens of Shanthi, as the hidden watchers ended their concealment. "Hear me," he said. "These men are welcome here. Prepare a feast, for tonight we will show them the hospitality of the Shanthi."

Around the clearing, the Shanthi bowed to the three visitors, crossing their fingers in front of their faces as they did. Then they scattered in various directions.

Baruun turned back to the three. "Be welcome in our telosh. Please, come to my home, where you may rest before the feast."

Jason looked at Reyga. Reyga bowed to Baruun once more. "You honor us beyond words, Baruun. In truth, the hospitality of the Shanthi would gladden any heart. However, we come on a mission of some urgency, and would speak with you of our need."

"I understand. Speak, and I will hear you."

Quickly, Reyga told Baruun of the recent events. Baruun's face darkened as he heard of the Shanthi spies in Lore's Haven. Reyga finished by summing up the situation with the Haven forces and Bothan's ultimatum.

"So you see, Baruun, we have come seeking your aid. In less than a sixday, we must face an army it would appear we have little hope of defeating. Emissaries have been sent out in the hopes of garnering more forces. We have come to you. I believe Jason would agree that, if he could ask one boon of you, it would be that you and your people would stand with us against Bodann." Jason nodded as Reyga finished.

Baruun looked at them for a long moment without answering. Then he shook his head. "What you ask, I am unable to grant. As the leader of my people, I could order this, but I will not." He looked at Reyga. "Loremaster Reyga, you, perhaps more than any other outsider, should understand this."

"I do," Reyga sighed. "But I must confess, I had hoped for a different answer."

"I know," Baruun said, "and I wish I could give you the answer you seek. But the mistrust among my people towards humans runs deep. As their leader, I must respect those feelings." He looked back and forth from Jason to Reyga. "I will pass your words along to my people. I will also tell them of what you both have done for Lenai. Perhaps some will feel that such deeds are worthy of their aid," he placed his hands on Jason's and Reyga's shoulders, "as I do. Whether my people choose to aid you or no, I will be there. But you must stay for the feast tonight. After that, you may return, or you may stay with us for the night and return in the morning."

"Baruun," Reyga said, "you honor us greatly, but we—"

"Loremaster Reyga," Baruun interrupted with a twinkle in his eye, "surely you would not have my people believe you refused their hospitality?"

Reyga hesitated. "Ah…what I meant to say, Baruun," he said at length, "was that we might lose ourselves in such hospitality and forget our reason for coming."

Baruun grinned. "Well said. You have my word. We will see that you do not forget your purpose."

Jason stared at the forest from his window at Lore's Haven. It had been three days since the visit to Lenai's telosh and they still hadn't seen or heard any sign of the Shanthi. A contingent of Yellowtooth, the race that Jason had originally thought of as werewolves in the marketplace in Drey's Glenn, had arrived two days ago. They agreed to join the Haven forces only with the assurance that they would not be taking orders from any Ferrin. More human, Dokal, and Ferrin fighters had arrived as well, but even with the additional forces, they were still badly outnumbered.

The amphibious F'aar sent word that, since the battle would be in the arid Scorched Plains, they would be unable to take part. Instead, they sent loads of materials for weapons and armor, as well as food for provisions.

The disparity between the two armies wasn't all that had Jason worried. The battle was tomorrow, and he still didn't know how to use his power. He didn't see how he could be so important if he couldn't do anything. He hadn't had any more memories, and Nyala and Crin had both been conspicuously silent over the last few days. Had revealing what he had to the Circle made them angry with him? Or had it changed things some other way? He hoped he hadn't gotten Nyala in trouble with the other Altered.

When they'd returned to the keep the day after the feast, the war preparations were in full swing. Between sessions of the Circle, Lenai showed him what the *saiken* were doing to make sure the Haven forces had the arms and supplies they would need.

"The Orders work together making weapons and armor, and laying up any supplies the Circle thinks we might need," she'd said.

As they walked the plateau behind the keep, he saw groups of *saiken* handling various tasks, with the Rodinn scurrying back and forth on numerous errands. *Chipmunks serving as gophers,* he couldn't help but think with a touch of amusement. He used his vision so he would know what Orders he was seeing. In one group, *saiken* from the Emerald Order used their power to accelerate the growth of plants, while Amber students guided the growth into perfectly straight stalks.

"Here they are making shafts for arrows," Lenai told him. "In other parts of Teleria, members of the Ruby Order use their abilities to find the metal ore needed for the Obsidian craftsmen to create weapons and armor. Emerald students will also grow crops when necessary, with members of Topaz ensuring the fields receive adequate rainfall. Amethyst students train hawks for surveillance, horses and charnoths for battle, and also create any leather goods that may be needed."

As Jason went over the things he'd seen, a knock on his door interrupted his thoughts. When he opened the door, he saw Lenai standing outside.

"Would you like to see more of our preparations before this morning's meeting?" she asked.

"Sure," he said. "What will we see today?"

"I thought you might be interested in watching the Obsidian Order crafting the armor and weapons. Then, after the meeting..." She stopped, her face taking on a distant expression. Then her eyes widened.

"Come!" She grabbed his arm and pulled him into the corridor.

"Where are we going?" he asked, trying to keep up with her insistent grip.

"Baruun has arrived," she said. She wouldn't tell him anything else in spite of his persistent questioning. After numerous turns and a couple of staircases, Lenai opened a door and they walked out onto the wall of the keep. The sudden openness and height gave him a moment of vertigo until his senses adjusted.

A short distance out on the wall, Jason saw Baruun. The Shanthi leader turned as they approached.

"Ah, Jason Bennett, good. I was hoping Lenai would sense my presence and bring you. I have requested that Loremaster Reyga and your High One join us as well. Come." He turned and began walking along the wall toward the front of the keep.

As they neared the front gate, Jason saw Reyga and Tal coming from the other direction. When they met, Reyga bowed. "Baruun, it is good to see you again. May I present Tal Vardyn, Pearl Loremaster and High One of the Circle of Nine." He turned to the High One. "High One, I give you Baruun, the leader of the Shanthi."

Baruun inclined his head. "If Loremaster Reyga is any example of your influence, High One, then it is an honor to meet you."

Tal bowed in return. "The honor is mine, Baruun. You are most gracious. Be welcome in Lore's Haven, where all who seek truth, knowledge, and wisdom are welcome."

"Thank you, High One. In truth, at times it can be difficult to be a Shanthi. At other times, such as now, I cannot conceive of being anything else." He looked at Reyga, and then at Jason. "Loremaster Reyga, Jason Bennett, for what you have done for Lenai, we are in your debt." He waved his arm toward the road leading to the front gate. "Behold how the Shanthi repay." He turned to the road and shouted, *"Shani ko rin!"*

The gate Warders jumped back in surprise as wave after wave of armed Shanthi warriors suddenly appeared on the road. The column extended down the road as more and more warriors became visible. Jason watched, slack-jawed, as the ranks of Shanthi grew until it disappeared around a bend in the path. He heard Reyga and Tal gasp in surprise. He looked at Lenai. Her eyes were shining as she watched the warriors appear.

Baruun turned back to them with a triumphant smile. "High One, Loremaster Reyga, Jason Bennett, behold the deadliest warriors in all of Teleria. We are at your service."

24
Landscar

The two armies faced each other from opposite ends of Landscar, a jagged arc of rocky hills at the edge of the Riftlands. Shimmering waves of heat rose from the cracked earth, and the sun was not yet at its zenith. Jason, Seryn, and a number of students from the Diamond Order sat atop a hill behind the Haven forces. Gatlor was with them, surveying the battlefield from horseback. In the distance, they could see the seething mass of Bothan's army. Behind the enemy, past the other end of Landscar, the air was discolored and turbulent, with occasional flashes. The Riftlands.

"His army has grown," Gatlor said. He sounded like he was observing the weather.

Jason wondered how he could sound so calm. From what he could see, Bothan's army was well over twice as large as the Haven forces, and that didn't take into account the races that Reyga said would be hidden. Reyga had also told him they didn't understand why the races were working together. At this point it didn't really matter.

Gatlor turned in his saddle. "Jason Bennett, if I may suggest, now might be a good time to remember what the Altered taught you."

"I wish I could." He'd been trying to dredge up any little scrap of the time he'd spent with Nyala. Sometimes he felt like he was on the verge of remembering something, then it would slip away, leaving him grasping at the thought like trying to catch smoke on a breeze. The sick feeling he had in the pit of his stomach when he saw the size of Bothan's army wasn't helping either. He knew there was no way the Haven forces could win without help of some kind.

"I've tried," he said. "There's nothing."

"Well," Gatlor turned back to the battlefield, "try to remember something before we are all dead."

Oh good, no pressure, he thought with a grimace.

Gatlor glanced over his shoulder at him. "Stay here. You should be safe with Loremaster Seryn and the other *saiken*, at least for a while." Then he turned and spurred his horse toward the army waiting below.

He watched Gatlor gallop down the hill. *Nyala!* he shouted inside his head. No answer. He closed his eyes tightly, bouncing his clenched fist against his leg as he struggled to remember something, anything, that might help them.

"Peace, Jason," Seryn said. "I do not believe Nyala would have shown you what she did only to allow you to fail when you are most needed."

He knew she was trying to encourage him, but the word 'fail' echoed loudly in his mind. He'd come to understand that the people of Lore's Haven, and of most of Teleria, were good people. The last thing he wanted to do was sit on the top of this hill and watch thousands of them die, especially if somewhere inside of him was the power to prevent it.

He saw Gatlor reach the front of the army. The warrior shouted something that he couldn't make out. Then the Haven forces began a slow march toward the enemy.

Bothan grinned. He was standing on a hill behind his army overlooking the battlefield. If this was the best they could come up with, he would be home in time for a good meal. Or perhaps he would eat in the dining hall at Lore's Haven. He laughed as he pictured the shocked expressions at the keep when he and his forces marched through the blasted-open gates. This land would soon be his.

"You are amused, Bodann?"

"Aye, Lord Regor, I am. I was thinking of how different the world will be once it is ruled properly and overseen by you, as it should be."

"I am not a fool, Bodann," Regor said. *"I know you only think of me as a means to an end. For now, I will allow you that illusion, for you are useful to me. But when this day is done, make no mistake, you will rule Teleria, but I will rule you."*

They would see about that. He could play act as well as anyone. The young pup had been completely taken in until he'd found the dagger "Chon" had used to kill his father. Even then, the little fool hadn't figured out that he had been the one to do the deed, rather than that pathetic Loremaster. Oh yes, he would bow and scrape to Regor's face, but when the Shadow Lord was not around, he would run things his way.

"Meaning no offense, my lord, but you have me wrong," he protested. "I look forward to the day when you and the other Altered return to rule Teleria as gods. I will be your strongest supporter and most willing servant!"

"Of course you will," Regor said. *"Just remember. I reward my servants according to their service."* Then the Shadow Lord vanished.

He turned his attention back to the battlefield. He saw Gatlor raise his sword and then the Haven army began slowly moving forward. With a thought, he commanded his own forces to advance as well. As he watched the two armies close on each other, a messenger ran up the hill.

"We have found the Far Planer, my lord," the man said.

"And?"

"He is on the hill behind the enemy."

He peered across the battlefield. He could just make out a small group of specks on the hillside behind the Haven force. If the boy was still sitting there, with the two armies about to attack each other, it could only mean one thing.

"He still hasn't learned how to use his power," he chuckled.

"Do you want us to kill him?"

He shook his head. "No. Let him watch and learn what it means to refuse me. Afterwards, we shall see."

Tal gripped his staff tightly as they moved toward Bodann's army. Although he had hoped otherwise, inside he had always known this day would come, ever since Bodann had been expelled from Lore's Haven.

At that time, Tal served as Loremaster Rake's apprentice in the Pearl Order. Bodann had been Loremaster Madin's apprentice in the Amethyst Order, and was on the verge of being confirmed as the next Amethyst Loremaster once Madin stepped down. He had been one of the most talented students in the history of Lore's Haven, and could easily have mastered any of several disciplines. The fact that he was a Far Planer made this even more astonishing, as no Far Planer before had ever shown any abilities with *dimsai*.

When the Circle became aware of Bodann's beliefs, they confronted him. Bodann brushed aside their protests, insisting that knowledge was a weapon, not a gift. He argued that it should only be given to those who pledged their loyalty to the Circle. The Loremasters tried numerous times to convince him otherwise, but he was stubbornly insistent that he was right.

After several very vocal meetings, the Circle decided that the only solution was to banish Bodann from Lore's Haven. If there had been a way to remove his power from him, they would have. Unfortunately, that was not possible. Delani had been chosen to serve as the next Amethyst Loremaster in his stead.

Now they faced him and his forces, with the fate of Teleria hanging in the balance. He didn't know how Bodann had managed to unite the different races, but with his Amethyst training and power, if anyone could do it, it would be him. If Regor decided to show up as well, the battle might not last very long.

His thoughts turned to Jason Bennett. The young man still did not know how to use his power. Tal had no doubts that he had power, simply because he was able to see *dimsai* auras, something no one else in Teleria was able to do. He was further convinced by the attention Jason had been receiving from Regor and Nyala. Regor definitely considered Jason to be a threat, while Nyala obviously felt Jason was Teleria's only hope.

He did not understand why Nyala had chosen to shroud Jason's memories. If the boy had been able to use his powers earlier, they might not be here now. Then it occurred to him that if Jason had use of his powers when he thought the Circle had betrayed him, they might not be here now either, but for an entirely different reason. He sighed in frustration. They would simply have to trust in Nyala's wisdom and hope that Jason remembered what he had been taught before it was too late.

Gatlor surveyed the creatures as the distance between the armies dwindled. From here, he could make out humans, Trellin, and Manarachs, the latter standing head and shoulders above the others. Baruun, walking nearby, assured him that, although there was a small number of *rishna kel* in Bodann's army, none were close enough to be an immediate threat. He knew somewhere underground the Grithor would be found as well. The High One and several members of the Circle rode nearby, along with a number of *saiken* from their Orders. The rest of the *saiken* were scattered among the Haven forces.

"What are your thoughts?" Calador asked, walking beside him. Even on foot, the Dokal warrior was at eye level with him on his horse. Seerka walked on the other side of Calador. His eyes were forward, but his ears betrayed that he was listening closely for Gatlor's response. He did not answer at first. Many things were running through his mind, not all of which he felt he should share.

As a warrior, he did not believe that any situation was completely hopeless, but the one in which they now found themselves was as likely a candidate as any. Nor did he believe this would be a long, drawn out war. They had mustered all of the forces they could. If they lost today, there was little hope of gathering more for another try. At least not anytime soon. This one battle could decide the fate of Teleria, and unless something unexpected happened, the future of Teleria did not look good.

The surprising addition of the Shanthi was a small source of hope. He had not expected the mission to Lenai's people to succeed, and he was glad to be proven wrong. Once again, Jason Bennett had proved his worth. Baruun told them that, although Reyga was greatly respected because of his protection of Lenai, it had been Jason's actions during the *Sho tu Ishta* that had moved the Shanthi to join their cause. He shook his head. The young Far Planer was a constant source of amazement and irritation.

If anyone but the High One had told him that hundreds of Shanthi were at the gates of Lore's Haven, he would not have believed them. Even with the news coming from the High One, he had to see them for himself. When he saw the ranks upon ranks of the new arrivals, he immediately began thinking of possible ways to use their unique abilities. He had fought beside Lenai more than once. He knew the leader of her people would be a kindred soul. The two of them, along with their most trusted men, discussed possible options most of the night.

They now fielded a force of over ten thousand. Even with the addition of their new allies, however, he was afraid it would not be enough to change the outcome of the battle. Although the Shanthi were deadly warriors, he knew that some of the creatures they faced could be even deadlier. He also knew enough to keep such thoughts to himself.

He saw that the cat-man's ears were still cocked his way. "I think we may be more popular than I had realized," he said for Seerka's benefit.

Seerka looked over at him, his eyes bright with amusement. "Well! There may be hope for you yet," he said with a wink.

In spite of their situation, Gatlor could not completely suppress a grin as he shook his head. The Ferrin's confidence bordered on arrogance.

Loremaster Brin moved up beside him. "Captain Gatlor, there are a number of weaknesses in the stone ahead. Cavities have been hollowed out underneath the surface. Enough weight on them will cause them to collapse."

"Traps," he said.

"Aye, it would appear that the Grithor have been busy."

From Brin's other side, the High One said, "Can you shore up the earth so that we may pass safely?"

"Under ordinary circumstances, yes, but I have no doubt that there are Grithor *saiken* watching those areas. They would counteract any moves we might make to strengthen the stone."

"Then can you go ahead and collapse them instead?" Gatlor asked. "At least that way we would be able to see them and go around."

"We could do that," Brin said, "but we will need to be closer."

Gatlor estimated the distance between the two armies. "Can you do it now? We will need to adjust our approach to avoid the pits."

Brin looked toward the enemy. "Yes, but we will need to hurry."

Brin and three of his students rode out ahead of the Haven army until they were midway to the enemy. Then they split into pairs, one pair moving to the left, with the other moving in the opposite direction. When they stopped, one student from each pair moved a little ahead and raised a shield between them and the approaching horde. As Brin and the remaining student extended their hands toward the ground, the shields flashed and popped where occasional arrows flew into them.

Gatlor heard a barely discernible rumble, and then the ground in front of the Ruby Loremaster and his students crumbled and disappeared with a crashing roar, leaving gaping holes in the parched earth. As thick clouds of dust rose into the air, the students dropped the shields and the four wheeled their horses and charged back toward the Haven army. One of the horses squealed and stumbled as an arrow struck it in the flank. The woman got her mount under control and they made it safely back to the army.

Brin pulled his horse to a stop by Gatlor. "There are more cavities around their army. Further proof that there are Grithor *saiken* working to prevent any collapse unless we are above."

"Is there anything else between the traps you exposed and where we are now?"

Brin shook his head.

"And the traps still hidden, is there a way through them?"

"From what I could see, yes," Brin answered. "But any attempting it would need members of my Order guiding them."

"Have some of your students prepare for that," he said. "We may need to send horsemen around to flank them if possible. Also, if they can, have them collapse the traps as they pass so that we may see them as well."

"I will lead them myself. I have much to settle with Bodann and his ilk," Brin grated as he turned his horse away.

Gatlor nodded. If Brin had not chosen the path of a Loremaster, he would have made a fearsome warrior. He looked to the High One. "High One, if you would?"

The High One raised his staff and sent a flare of *dimsai* into the air. The army came to a halt. Gatlor moved his horse out a little ahead and turned to face them. He looked out over the men and women, all prepared to fight to the death to save what they loved. Human, Dokal, Ferrin, Yellowtooth, all stood side-by-side watching him expectantly. Even a few Rodinn. He did not know how useful they would be in the battle to come, but had not felt he had the right to refuse them the chance to fight. A warrior's heart was not determined by the size of the body in which it beat.

"Warriors, hear me!" he shouted. "Yes, I said warriors, for that is what you are. Some of you have trained your entire lives for just such a moment as this. Others had not raised a blade until just a few days ago. But you are all warriors nonetheless. For a warrior is not defined by the weapon in his hand, but by the passion in his heart." He rode across the front of the ranks as he spoke. "And that passion, the willingness to fight for those who cannot fight for themselves, the desire to protect those you love, the fire to strike at those who would destroy all that you know, burns in all of you, from the largest to the smallest." He raised his sword over his head. "Today, our enemies will feel the heat of that blaze!"

The fighters raised their voices and weapons into the air as they shouted and cheered. He waited for the noise to die down, and then went on. "Today we fight, not just for victory, but for the future of our land. Remember what you have learned, and hold nothing back. Today will decide all of our tomorrows. I am honored to go into battle with you, for I know that your actions today will be such as what legends are made of. Now, let the ring of our steel echo throughout the land as a warning to those who would come against us! Let us go and make our mark upon the ages!"

The army roared its approval and surged forward as the *saiken* sent blazing bolts of *dimsai* into the air overhead. The battle for Teleria had begun.

25
Battle for Teleria

Gatlor wheeled his horse toward Bodann's army and charged forward, the Haven forces right behind him. An instant later, the enemy began their own roaring, hissing charge. He watched the enemy ranks spread out, as the leading creatures opened space between them and the ones behind. When they were within three hundred paces of each other, he looked over his shoulder.

"Now!" he shouted.

Kalen sent a flare of yellow *dimsai* skyward. The Haven fighters halted their charge. Across the front of the Haven army, Topaz *saiken* ran forward and created scorching winds, blowing dust and grit into the faces of the advancing creatures. Gatlor knew this would be countered by the opposing *saiken*, but he only needed a few moments. Two hundred archers ran out and sent arrow after arrow high into the air. The Trellin, Manarachs, and other creatures would not see their death approaching as they shielded their eyes from the dirt-laden wind. The front of the enemy army fell into disarray as the arrows fell among them.

Bodann's *saiken* responded quickly, sending up a shield overhead to protect the fighters from the falling arrows, which flared into ash as they hit the shield. When he saw that the arrows had been countered, he turned and signaled. Reyga raised his staff and sent a green flare of power into the air.

Gatlor called to Delani. "Loremaster Delani, I need to know exactly how this tactic fares."

Delani nodded, then looked to the sky, her face taking on a distant expression as she linked her mind to the hawk flying far overhead.

Bothan watched the clouds of dirt and grit envelope the front of his army.

"Poor little Loremasters. What do they think a wee bit of dust will do?"

He sent a mental command urging his fighters forward. Peering through the haze of dirt, he could just make out figures rushing forward from the Haven army. Then a cloud of another kind soared up over the dust and arced toward the leading edge of his army. The front ranks wavered, as scores of fighters stumbled or fell under the attack. Then he saw flashes of light as a shield sprang up over his forces.

"Aye, well done, lads. Well done. Now they'll have to fight like men, face to face."

A man scrambled up the hillside toward him, his frantic feet sending rocks and scree flying in all directions. "Lord Bodann! Lord Bodann!"

"What is it?"

"My lord," the man panted, "they have Shanthi."

"What of it?" he sneered. "We have Shanthi too."

The man shook his head sharply. "Meaning no disrespect, my lord, but you misunderstand. *They have Shanthi!*"

His attention jerked back toward the battlefield as a new roar went up from his forces.

Jason watched the arrows flash into nothingness against the shield. Then a green flare of *dimsai* soared into the sky. He knew what was coming next. He concentrated intently and a rainbow of auras appeared across the battlefield. On the hillside opposite where he stood, he saw a sickly glow like a diseased star. *That must be Bothan.*

To the right of Bothan's army, Jason saw what looked like fog as a mass of disembodied auras approached the enemy fighters. He heard a roar rise up as the concealed Shanthi carved into their ranks. Scores, and then hundreds, of the enemy fell against the invisible onslaught of the Shanthi warriors. He remembered the look on Lenai's face when the Trellin had attacked them. He shuddered to think what it would be like to face an army of warriors like that.

But for all the damage the Shanthi were doing, it was still just at the fringe of the massive force. Their attack was taking its toll, but it would take much longer to do any significant damage.

It was just a matter of time before the enemy came up with a way to counter the tactic. Then it happened. He saw Manarachs forcing their way toward the perimeter of the army, shoving other fighters aside. When the creatures reached the edge, they began throwing silken threads and nets into the empty air. As they descended, some of the threads caught on invisible bodies. The Manarachs and Trellin furiously attacked the Shanthi entangled in the webbing. More were caught as the Manarachs cast their silk again and again. As the Shanthi died, their broken and slashed bodies became visible in the grit of the battlefield.

He was vaguely aware of a pain in his jaw as he clenched his teeth. "Get out of there," he whispered.

He pounded his fist against his leg in frustration at his own helplessness, and wondered if Lenai was one of the Shanthi in the attack. Then another green flare lit up the sky, and he saw the fog begin moving away from Bothan's army. They were calling the fighters back. The relief he felt was short-lived. Once they realized their nets weren't catching anything, Trellin and Manarachs poured after the retreating forces.

Without warning, great sections of earth collapsed and vanished into a chasm in front of the retreating Shanthi. The fighters changed direction, moving parallel to the abyss as they ran. This allowed the enemy pursuit to close the gap between them and the Shanthi. More silken threads flew out, and more Shanthi bodies appeared on the ground. Moments later, a column of horsemen charged out from the Haven ranks toward the fleeing Shanthi, a bright red star leading the way. *That must be Brin*. As the horsemen charged around the flank of Bothan's forces, the main section of the Haven army surged forward

It was too much for him to take. His heart pounded in his chest and his thoughts were an incoherent jumble. Then one thought stood out clearly: If he really did have power, he needed it now.

He looked skyward and raged at the heavens. "*NYALA!!*" Then his eyes went wide as a flood of memories washed everything else from his mind.

Brin watched Delani as she monitored the attack through the eyes of her hawk. At the first sign of trouble, he and his *saiken* would lead the mounted warriors to the aid of the Shanthi. His desire for vengeance and retribution warred with his self-control as he waited.

"The Shanthi are attacking, and many of the enemy are falling," Delani said.

Brin looked at Bodann's army. Their advance had slowed as they looked toward the commotion behind them.

"Wait," Delani said. "Manarachs are casting trapsilk and ensnaring the Shanthi. They cannot fight back. The Shanthi are falling and more Manarachs are coming."

"Loremaster Reyga," Gatlor said, "signal the Shanthi to fall back."

Reyga nodded and sent a green flare of *dimsai* into the sky.

After a moment, Delani nodded. "The trapsilk is now falling empty to the ground. The Shanthi have withdra— Traps! A pit has opened up behind where the Shanthi were. I cannot tell if any fell, but the enemy is pursuing."

"Loremaster Brin," Gatlor said, "take the mounted warriors to help the Shanthi. Once you have gone, we will press the attack from here. Perhaps we can pull their attention back to us and away from the Shanthi."

Brin nodded and kicked his horse into motion. "Ruby *saiken*, mounted warriors, to me!" he shouted as he rode across the front of the army.

Within moments, they thundered around the far end of the southernmost pit. Up ahead, he could sense a concealed pit to the right, with the open chasm to the left, leaving a narrow strip of solid ground in between. They charged toward the ribbon of ground to keep the enemy from attacking before they could flank them.

"Ride along the edges," he told his students, "so that the riders behind can see the safe way. If you can, collapse the weakened earth so that the pit can be avoided by others." When they nodded he pulled his horse to the side and slowed.

"Watch where the *saiken* ride," he called to the warriors as they passed him. "Do not stray outside their path."

After the last of the riders had passed, he fell in behind. A subterranean rumble told him his students were triggering the trap. He saw dust rising from the earth to the right side of the column of riders, and then the ground crumbled away, leaving a deep ravine. The riders at that side of the column fought to keep their mounts under control as the horses shied away from the chasm that suddenly appeared beside them.

Ahead to his left, he could see the enemy chasing the invisible Shanthi. He saw dust rising from the ground, but could not tell if it was due to unseen feet or the shaking earth. He hoped the pit between them and the Shanthi ended soon so they could turn and aid the retreat.

Then the creatures noticed the riders and altered their course toward them. He nodded to himself. Better to chase a foe that can be seen than one that cannot. At least if they were coming after the horsemen, the Shanthi could make their escape. Now it was just a matter of where the fissure between the two forces ended that would determine the next move.

Shouts from in front of him grabbed his attention. He had to rein in sharply to keep from running into the horses ahead of him that were sliding and skidding to a stop. Thirty paces ahead, a horse reared, its rider frantically trying to bring it under control. Because of the suddenly crowded conditions, the horse came down on the back of another, causing that one to jump. The first horse reared again, and fell backward into two other horses behind it. Before Brin could do anything, all three horses and riders plunged into the yawning gulf.

"What happened?" he shouted. "Why have we stopped?" He looked toward the front of the column of riders and saw the group milling around uncertainly. Meanwhile, the leading creatures from Bodann's army had reached the edge of the crevice. It would only be a matter of moments before they started sending arrows or blasts of *dimsai* into the midst of the riders.

He carefully urged his horse forward through the mass. The soldiers moved aside as best they could. Glancing to his left, he saw that more and more of Bodann's creatures were lining the chasm, hissing and grunting as they looked for a way to get at the Haven fighters.

He saw the reason for their halt before he reached the front of the column. The crevices to either side had curved away and then toward each other to join at the front. The ground they stood on was an island in an ocean of emptiness. All that joined this platform to solid ground was the narrow stone bridge they had ridden across. He gritted his teeth in frustration. They would have to go back. He hoped their distraction had been enough to allow the Shanthi to escape.

He turned his horse around and saw that going back was no longer an option. The creatures had reached the entrance to the spit of land and were now blocking it. He watched as they advanced toward the trapped riders while more gathered behind them. He heard a cry from his right. One of the riders, caught by a line of trapsilk cast across the chasm, was desperately trying to keep from being pulled over the edge. Brin blasted the Manarach with a bolt of *dimsai,* then sent two more blasts in rapid succession toward the rock just below the opposite edge. As the power exploded against the rock, it crumbled away carrying several Trellin with it. He forced his horse around once more.

"Beryk!" he shouted to one of the senior *saiken* that had accompanied them. "Open a portal back to Lore's Haven. Hurry!"

A blast sent splinters of rock into the air as one of the enemy *saiken* returned Brin's greeting. The edge underneath two of the horsemen began to crumble. He used his power to shore up the rock long enough for the riders to move their mounts.

"Sara," he called. "Help Beryk with the portal. Tam, Keryn, shield this side while the riders go through." As soon as he was certain the *saiken* understood his instructions, he guided his horse toward the back of the column. "We are opening a portal to Lore's Haven," he told the soldiers as he passed. "The *saiken* will shield you while you wait for your turn to go through."

They had to hurry. He saw some of Bodann's forces running for the other side, where the Haven fighters would not be shielded, and the creatures advancing up the causeway were getting closer by the second. He had a plan, but he needed to be sure the riders and *saiken* were safe first.

"Riders! Hurry through the portal!" He looked back as he heard Beryk shouting. Beryk and Sara stood at the edge of the platform. The portal hung in space two paces off the edge of the rock. There had not been enough room to place it on solid ground because of the press of horses. The riders would have to jump the gap to reach it. As he watched, the first rider went through, while more moved into position.

"Loremaster Brin, why do we not fight?" one of the warriors asked him.

"We are at too great a disadvantage here," he answered. "Our purpose was to draw the enemy's attention away from the Shanthi, and we have accomplished that. However, we are now beset on two sides, and will no doubt soon be surrounded. We can aid our cause more by escaping this trap through the portal, and then returning to fight again." He did not mention that he fully intended to strike a blow once the riders were safe.

The ground trembled as he finished, followed by the sound of an explosion from the chasm. He jumped off his horse and looked over the edge. Grithor *saiken* were attacking the base of the rock, obviously intent on collapsing it before they could escape. Brin focused his power into a brilliantly glowing sphere and sent it down into the shadows. The Grithor shielded their eyes, retreating back into tunnels in the opposite wall.

He looked up at the creatures approaching along the narrow bridge of land. They had apparently noticed their prey escaping, and were advancing more rapidly. He sent a bolt of power toward them and watched as his attack sent several into the abyss to either side.

He looked back toward the portal. The horses were moving more quickly as space opened up where they could maneuver. A concussion filled the air as one of the enemy *saiken* attacked the shield. He looked at Tam and Keryn. Both were breathing heavily as the strain of maintaining the shield took its toll on them. He hoped they could last long enough, but more *saiken* were beginning to attack.

Another tremor shook the ground. He looked into the crevice and saw that his *dimsai* orb had failed. The Grithor *saiken* were attacking the base of the rock once again. He sent another brilliant crimson orb into the depths, and then threw two more blasts at the approaching creatures. His first volley sent more over the edge, but the second detonated against a shield that appeared in front of the approaching mass. He looked back toward the portal. Just a score of riders remained. Tam and Keryn were clearly at the end of their endurance. He waved at a rider who was looking toward the creatures on the bridge.

"You. Get another rider and take the shield *saiken* with you," he said. The man nodded and called to another warrior. A blast threw Brin to the ground as a *saiken* on the bridge attacked. He threw a shield up just in time to catch the next bolt. Looking over his shoulder, he saw the horsemen in place beside Tam and Keryn.

"Tam! Keryn! Drop the shield!"

Instantly the shield disappeared. The two riders hauled the exhausted *saiken* across their mounts and sprinted for the portal, just making it through as arrows began streaking after them. Brin climbed to his feet and sent another flare of power toward the force on the bridge.

"Sara! Beryk! Go back to the Haven!" he shouted.

"Not without you!" Beryk yelled back.

"I will make another way! Now go!"

Sara and Beryk looked at each other and then moved to get a run for the leap. Sara started first and then staggered as an arrow pierced the back of her thigh. Brin knew she would not make the jump.

Beryk ran to catch her. He did not slow as he wrapped his arm around her waist and leaped with all of his strength for the portal, which winked out of existence as they passed through.

Now, he thought, facing the creatures coming toward him, *now Cale will be avenged!* With a cry from the depths of his soul, he raised his hands. A scarlet corona of power erupted around him. All of the grief, fury, and outrage he had been holding inside since learning of the death of his son now poured forth in a paroxysm of vengeance and retribution. Arrows intended to pierce his body disintegrated as his power consumed them.

He sent a barrage of *dimsai* across the chasm, the volleys exploding just underneath the ledge or blasting through the crowded mass of bodies. As he threw bolt after bolt, he watched the creatures approaching on the narrow ridge of stone. He needed them closer. A tremor tickled the bottom of his feet. The Grithor had returned and were once again attacking the base of the platform.

The fighters on the bridge saw that he was alone and surged forward. When they were ten paces from the platform, he threw out his hand, casting a shield across the end of the bridge. As had happened with the horses, the creatures in the back did not realize their charge had been stopped until they found themselves pressed up against the leaders. The smell of burning flesh filled the air as the leading bodies pressed against his shield.

With his other hand, he gave free reign to his fury, continuing to throw power across the abyss. Sweat stung his eyes and his breath was labored, but he did not, would not, stop. In a few moments, several hundred of the enemy crowded the bridge, unable to move forward while his shield held.

When he was certain no more could fit onto the bridge, he turned his full attention to them. He brought back up the emotions that had threatened to overwhelm him in the Circle chamber; dredged up the indignation he had felt during the Shadow Lord's visit. He poured all of his outrage, all of his pain, into one massive surge of power and focused it on the bridge. His senses sought out weaknesses in the stone, and he sent his power to attack those points. Fractures appeared. Cracks streaked through the base of the bridge.

When the creatures on the bridge realized what he was going to do, they tried desperately to reverse their course. As they pushed and jostled to escape, some fell tumbling into the shadows below. Shouting Cale's name, he pulled more power from within. With a groan of tortured stone, the bridge collapsed, carrying all of the enemy unable to make it back to solid ground plummeting into the darkness.

The platform, now deprived of the support from the bridge, shuddered underneath his feet. He could feel it beginning to sway, and the Grithor's attacks came constantly. He had known this would happen. As he felt the platform begin its fall, he threw a few more bolts of power into the enemy. Then, his mind filled with thoughts of his son, he ran for the edge and leaped out into empty space.

"Jason! Are you well?"

Jason barely heard Seryn as he stood frozen, staring blindly at the battlefield. The two armies were little more than an afterthought as the memories rushed back. Passion and focus…

"Passion can come from emotion or desire," Nyala said. "Either alone is sufficient. Together they can be a formidable force. You must be careful, though. *Dimsai* called by emotion alone can be unpredictable, often guiding, rather than being guided by, the user. You must learn to focus your desire, tempering emotion when necessary. The more you use the *dimsai*, the more easily it will respond to your call..."

Jason saw the two armies come together, the stars that represented the *saiken* sending off sparks of power in all directions. He saw the ground crumble away beside the column of horsemen as they rode to the aid of the Shanthi…

They started small, with Nyala trying to teach him how to create a ball of power as she had done. Over and over he tried. Time and time again he failed.

"Keep trying, Jason," she said.

After hearing it for what seemed like the hundredth time, he lost his temper.

"I am trying!" he snapped, and then gasped as a sparkling sphere appeared, floating over his open palm.

The shock at the ball's appearance broke his concentration, and it winked out almost immediately. But he had done it. His anger vanished, replaced by giddiness. He had done it! He felt the same way he'd felt after Tracy Jacobson agreed to go out with him. He had to stop himself from giggling…

The column of riders was trapped, Bothan's forces cutting off their exit. Jason saw the warriors escaping through the portal. Once all were gone, the red star exploded with power like a supernova. A few moments later, the bridge, and then the platform, crumbled and the star disappeared into the depths…

Six months they had been in the past. Jason practiced for hours every day. He learned quickly. Even Nyala had been surprised at his progress. With her help and guidance, he learned in months what took other students years. She taught him how to move objects and how to reshape them. She taught him how use his power to see the strengths and weaknesses of the things around him.

He learned to accelerate and guide the growth of plants. She explained how to heal injuries, although there was no way for him to practice. She taught him how to open portals, and how to use his power to move quickly from one place to another. Then she taught him how to use his power in battle…

The Haven army engaged Bothan's forces. The ring of steel and shouts of the warriors rang faintly in his ears. *Dimsai* flashes reflected in his unblinking eyes. The ground rumbled as the riders that had been on the platform charged past, racing back to the battle…

"You've done well," Nyala said, "we are ready to return. However, for reasons that I will explain to you after we go back, I must block all memory of this from your mind."

"Huh? Then why teach me all this stuff? If I'm just going to forget it?"

Nyala smiled. "If I tell you my reasons now, you won't remember them. Don't worry. I promise you will remember at the proper time."

He'd learned that arguing with her was pointless. "Fine," he said. He looked around the clearing. Blasted trees and rocks surrounded them from his battle practice. "Wait, I missed one," he said as he spotted an unblemished tree. He sent a bolt of power crashing into the trunk.

A bird's scream startled him. He looked up to see a fortunewing launch from the branches above as the tree shuddered. The bird was clearly agitated, trying to get back into the waving limbs and leaves.

He sent his senses searching through the branches. There was a nest halfway up the tree. As he focused, he saw an egg teetering on the edge of the nest, bounced there by the shaking limb. Then it rolled off, plummeting toward the ground.

He reached out with his power and caught the egg before it hit any of the branches. In the grip of the *dimsai*, the egg began to crack. He could tell the chick inside was too young to survive if it hatched now. But the egg was already cracking open. He didn't think, just sent his power into the chick, encouraging its growth. Within seconds, a fully grown fortunewing appeared, shaking bits of eggshell off its feathers as he set it gently on a branch. Then his eyes went wide as he turned to Nyala.

"He says his name is Crin."

Jason blinked dust from his dry eyes as the memories came to an end. He looked to the skies. *Crin!*

"Jason! You remember me!" A surge of joy accompanied Crin's answer.

Jason grinned. *Yes, I remember you, and I will never forget you again.*

"That is good," the bird answered. *"But the battle has begun. You must hurry."*

He looked toward the battlefield. There was something different about it. Besides the *dimsai* auras, there were hundreds of thin lines, almost like a ghostly mesh blanketing the armies. Movement at the base of his vision caught his attention. Looking down, he saw an ethereal thread extending skyward from his chest. Following it with his senses, he discovered that it led to where Crin circled high above.

He looked back at the armies. The threads all converged on the sickly star on the opposite hill. *That's how he got them all to fight together*. Somehow, Bothan had made connections to the creatures fighting against the Haven forces. If he could break those connections…

"Jason, are you well?" Seryn laid a hand on his shoulder.

In answer, he turned and created a small orb of iridescent light. "I've remembered my power," he said. Like the reflections from the globe of light, he saw hope and anticipation begin sparkling in her eyes. "I have to get to Bothan," he said. Then he turned and sprinted toward the battle, using his power to speed his way.

As he descended the hillside, he saw a bright green star in the midst of the battle. Reyga. He ran toward the Loremaster. At the edge of the battle, he stopped and focused his power on the nearest Trellin, trying to break the connection between it and Bothan. The creature started toward him, and then hesitated as the thread vanished. It shook its head, and then turned and attacked a nearby Manarach.

He nodded in satisfaction, then focused his power again. More of the threads vanished, but only those that were closest to him. The creatures began fighting whatever happened to be the closest target. After a few moments, the threads re-established themselves. The creatures were once again under Bothan's control.

He would have to get to Bothan. If he could cut all of the threads at once, they might have a chance. But he wanted Reyga with him. Using his power to blast a way, he ran toward the emerald star.

26
Confrontation

Reyga sent a green flare of power at a hissing Trellin before it could bring its sword down on the back of an unsuspecting warrior.

"My thanks!" the man gasped, as he turned and realized what had happened.

Reyga turned his horse away, swinging his staff in a wide arc, the blazing emerald at the end leaving a crackling trail of green hanging in the air. A cry to his left caught his attention. Another warrior caught in trapsilk. Reyga incinerated the thread, and then sent a blast toward the Manarach that had thrown it.

He had been separated from the other members of the Circle as the two armies collided. Now he was using all of his power in an effort to keep the warriors around him alive. An arrow grazed his sleeve. He realized sitting on his horse made him a more visible target, but he was loathe to dismount; this vantage point allowed him to view the battle. Another arrow flying past made his decision for him, and he slid to the ground. He slapped the horse's hindquarters, sending it barreling through the throng.

He sent power flying into the mass of enemy fighters. In the chaos it was difficult to know which way to attack first. A Trellin leaped toward him, bringing its sword down in a lethal arc. Reyga deflected the blow with his staff and then slammed the end of the staff into the side of the creature's skull. As it staggered backwards, he threw a flare of *dimsai* at it, sending it crashing into the creatures behind.

He felt something wrap around his legs, jerking him off balance. His staff bounced away as he hit the ground, stopping just outside of his reach. He rolled over to see a Manarach looming over him, ready to impale him with a spear.

A blast of power sent the creature flying away. Another flash cleared a small area around him, which was suddenly encompassed in an iridescent curtain.

"I figure I owed you that one," a voice said, as the trapsilk around his legs dissolved into ash.

He looked up to see Jason holding his hand out to help him up.

"Jason, you have your power!"

Jason pulled him up. "And I know what I need to do with it. I have to get to Bothan. Will you come with me?"

"Do you believe you can defeat him?"

Jason shrugged. "I won't know until I try. But even if I can't beat him, I think there's one thing I can do that might help."

Reyga looked at the battle raging outside the shield. He could stay here, hoping to protect the handful of warriors he could see, or he could go with Jason, perhaps to save them all. He had been there when this all began, when Jason first arrived. It seemed only fitting that he should be with Jason if it was coming to an end.

He nodded. "I will come with you."

Gatlor jumped from his screaming horse as it went down, several Trellin bloodfangs broken off in its flanks. He landed beside Seerka and Calador, who had stayed near him as they charged the enemy. The battle raged around them as he and Seerka took up positions shoulder to shoulder. Behind them, Calador's axe and maul kept the creatures there at bay. Between the clashing of blade and shield, and the hissing and roaring of the enemy, he could barely hear himself think.

"I suppose popularity has its price," he yelled over the din, yanking his sword from the Trellin he had just dispatched.

"Naturally," the Ferrin shouted back. "It is difficult to go anywhere without being noticed."

A thread of trapsilk landed on his arm. He sliced through it with his dagger before the creature could pull him off balance. The Manarach gave ground to avoid the slash of his sword. He could see flashes of *dimsai* in the throng surrounding them, but was unable to determine if it was coming from Haven *saiken* or the enemy. A reptilian body thudded against him. Before he could react, it slid to the ground, blood pouring from the gashes in its neck.

"You owe me an ale," Seerka laughed as Gatlor shot him a look.

"Aye," he answered. "Perhaps more than one."

He heard Calador roar from behind. Sparing a glance over his shoulder, he saw that two of Manarachs had the Dokal warrior entangled in trapsilk. They were unable to pull the giant off balance, however, and for the moment, his armor-like skin was deflecting most of the damage from Trellin swords.

With a flurry of flashing steel, he gained just enough space between him and his attackers to allow him to spin and slash at the silken threads entrapping Calador. His maneuver freed the giant from one of the Manarachs and loosed the arm wielding the maul. Heaving on the remaining threads, Calador pulled the other Manarach close enough to bring his maul down, crushing the creature's skull. With a backhanded sweep of the weapon, Calador sent several Trellin flying into their comrades, clearing a small space in front of him.

Gatlor looked around as he slashed and parried. They were completely surrounded. While they could fend off the enemy for a moment, they would not be able to keep it up for much longer.

A streak of pain flashed across his shoulder as a Trellin blade slashed him. He ducked under the next swing and rammed his dagger up under its breastplate into its heart. He tried to pull the blade free as the creature sank to the ground, but it was knocked aside by others pushing forward. The sudden sideways motion yanked the dagger from his hand. He parried another blow with his sword as he pulled a dagger from his bandolier.

A backswing laid open a Trellin throat just as another line of trapsilk landed on his sword arm. He pulled as hard as he could and sent the dagger flying toward the other end of the line. The Manarach hissed in pain as the blade buried itself in its shoulder. Before the creature could react, he pulled another dagger out and cut away the strand, just managing to bring his sword up in time to block a blade intent on separating his head from his neck.

The bodies pressed in closer and closer, making it difficult to swing his sword. He could feel the first subtle signs of weakness in his arms as he spared a look at Seerka. The cat-man bled from several shallow wounds, but his ears laid back and his fangs were in full display as he growled at his attackers.

"It has been an honor fighting alongside you, my friends," Gatlor shouted.

"And with you," Seerka called back. "Although I would have enjoyed sharing another ale or two with you."

"We are not dead yet!" Calador bellowed. "Down!" Gatlor and Seerka dropped to the ground as the giant spun in a circle, the axe and maul swinging over their heads. His sudden tactic caught several of the Trellin and one of the Manarachs. They crashed back into the throng, allowing a small space to open up around the three of them.

A flash of *dimsai* blinded him. He raised his sword instinctively as he tried to blink the spots from his vision. As his eyes focused, he saw a glimmering shield of power surrounding them, sparking and flashing as the creatures attacked it. Standing in front of them, with his arms spread, was Jason Bennett. Reyga stood behind him.

"Well," he panted, "your timing is excellent. It would appear that you have finally remembered how to use your power."

Jason nodded. "Finally," he said. Then he swung one of his hands in a circle around his head. The flashes from the shield stopped. Gatlor wiped gritty sweat from his face with his sleeve and looked at the surrounding creatures. They looked dazed. Then they began attacking each other. The Manarachs threw silken strands in every direction, killing any creature they could snare. The Trellin attacked the Manarachs and each other. The ground outside the shield was soon littered with bodies.

"What did you do?" he asked, not sure he could believe what he was seeing.

"These things are all connected to Bothan somehow. That's how he's controlling them. I broke the connection for the ones around us. Without Bothan's control, they go back to fighting each other, but it won't last long."

"Can you break all of the connections? If the army began attacking itself, we might have a chance."

"That's what I was thinking too. But I've got to get to Bothan. I can only break them when I'm close to them. To break them all, I'll have to do it at his end. Come on." Jason opened up a path with a blast of power, and then ran into the mass of creatures. Reyga nodded at Gatlor's unspoken question, and then went after Jason.

He didn't hesitate. "Follow them. He goes to confront Bodann, and perhaps end this battle." He ran after Jason, the others falling in behind.

Jason stood at the base of the hill, looking up at his ancestor. To his vision, Bothan looked like some demonic octopus out of a nightmare. Thousands of ethereal arms radiated out from his malignant aura toward the battlefield. The big man grinned down at him, his hand resting on the pommel of the sword at his hip.

"Well, lad," Bothan said. "I see you've got your power, right enough. No matter. Unless you'd be coming to join me, I'm thinking you and your friends will live longer if you turned around and walked away right now." He looked to Jason's side. "Greetings, Reyga, my old friend. It has been a while, hasn't it? I trust you are well?"

Gatlor stepped forward. "Let us finish this." With a blur of leather, he whipped out a dagger and hurled it at Bothan. Almost negligently, Bothan flicked his wrist, reversing the dagger's course. Gatlor ducked to the side as the dagger sliced open the shoulder of his tunic.

"You'll have to do better than that, Gatlor," Bothan sneered. "You always were too headstrong for your own good." He held up a hand as Calador raised his axe. "Hold, giant. Not even a brute your size is any concern to me. Why don't you two take your pet cat and let old friends chat?" With a gesture, he wrapped the three warriors in a cocoon of power and sent them flying across the parched rock. Jason couldn't tell where they landed, but it looked like it would take them a while to get back, assuming they were even able.

"Bodann," Reyga said, "why are you doing this? You would destroy Teleria? Why?"

"Teleria is not the target, Reyga. It is the prize. To win it, I will break the Circle and all who are loyal to them. Any who will not pledge themselves to me will pay the price."

"Then let me give you my first payment." Reyga sent a blast of *dimsai* that exploded at Bothan's feet, sending him stumbling backward. As Bothan fell, Reyga turned to Jason.

"Jason, listen to me," he said. "I cannot defeat him. His power surpasses mine. But I can distract him. While I do that, you must break his hold over his army. Give our people a chance."

"But—"

"Please, Jason." Reyga turned back toward Bothan and started walking up the hillside.

"Now, Reyga," Bothan said, getting up, "that was a trifle uncalled for wouldn't you say?"

"Not at all, old friend," Reyga said. "If you will not cease this foolishness, then I must." He sent another volley of power, but the big man was prepared this time. Reyga's power detonated loudly, but harmlessly, against a shield that now surrounded Bothan.

Bothan sighed heavily. "Ah, Reyga. I had truly hoped you would change your mind once you saw which way the wind was blowing. But, just as the others, you have ever been blind to what should be." He threw his power at Reyga, who just managed to put up a shield to deflect it. Even with the shield, Reyga staggered, and had to struggle to retain his balance.

Reyga shot Jason a look before throwing another blast at Bothan. Jason turned his attention to the threads overhead, trying to ignore the explosions of power a few yards away. He focused on a particularly thick cluster of strands and sent his power upward. As the power sliced through them, the tendrils frayed and faded away.

Satisfied with the results, he began severing more of the connections. He looked over his shoulder at the two men. Reyga threw bolt after bolt at Bothan, but it was clear that it was an effort in futility. The blasts detonated impotently against the shield protecting Bothan, who appeared mildly amused.

He turned back to his task, working as quickly as he could. Half of the strands were gone now, and he could hear a subtle difference in the sounds coming from the battlefield. He risked a quick glance. Sections of the battle had dissolved into chaos as the creatures no longer under Bothan's control attacked anything within reach.

"What are you doing, boy?"

He turned just in time to catch the back of Bothan's hand across his face as the big man stormed down the hillside. The blow knocked him backwards, and he landed on his back, stunned. As he shook his head to clear it, he saw Reyga lying motionless a short distance away at the base of the hill. A small trickle of blood wandered from the corner of his mouth through the dust on his face. *Oh, Reyga.*

"I asked you a question, boy. What do you think you're doing?" Jason looked up to see Bothan towering over him. He struggled to his feet, coughing as dust clogged his throat.

"I'm stopping you," he managed to choke out.

"What? You're….you…stop….?" Bothan looked taken aback for a moment, and then he roared with laughter. "You? You're going to stop me? Oh, that's rich that is." His laughter cut off abruptly and his eyebrows lowered. "The only thing you're going to stop doing today, lad, is breathing."

Once again, Jason felt the icy loop constricting around his throat. He forced himself not to panic and focused on his power. A moment later the pressure disappeared.

Bothan scowled. "Aye, lad. That's a nice trick," he said as he slowly paced around Jason. "But you'll need more than that to walk away today." He glanced at the battle, and then waved his hand toward it. Jason saw the threads he had destroyed spring back into being. With Bothan's control restored, the creatures again focused their attention on the Haven forces. Bothan turned back to him.

"Actually, lad, I'm glad you've found your powers. Here and I was thinking this might be a dull afternoon." He threw a glowing blast of *dimsai* at him.

He had been expecting something like this, and was ready with a shield. Even prepared as he was, the force of the impact drove him back a step. But just one. Bothan frowned as he saw him still on his feet.

He smiled at his ancestor. "My turn," he said. A bolt of power shot from his hand, shaking the air as it exploded against Bothan's shield. The big man staggered back as a second bolt rocked him. Jason waited to see his reaction, but the sheer hatred blazing from his ancestor's eyes stunned him more than had the man's attack.

With a howl of rage, Bothan sent a flurry of volleys at Jason. Although none of the blasts penetrated his shield, the unrelenting intensity of the attack drove him down to one knee.

Then he remembered his father. The fury and pain that he'd felt in the training yard came pouring back into his soul. And now he had a target for it.

Teeth bared, he sent a bright flare of power streaking toward Bothan. As Bothan threw another blast toward Jason, the two bolts collided in a thunderous explosion that knocked the big man backwards.

Jason stood up and started toward his ancestor. "*What*...did you *do*...to my *dad?*" He punctuated his words with blast after blast of *dimsai*. Bothan staggered backward with each bolt, suddenly looking uncertain. Along with his rising passion, Jason felt a rush of power coursing through his soul. Almost as an afterthought, he threw power at the tendrils radiating from Bothan, severing them all instantly. Then he reached out and wrapped Bothan in a cocoon of *dimsai* like the one Bothan had used on Gatlor and the others. *Time for you to see how it feels.* Then everything went white as a concussion of power threw him backwards.

"I warned you not to interfere."

Jason tried to get up, but his tingling limbs refused to obey. He could only lay there blinking at the sky, trying to breathe air that seemed to get thicker by the moment. A dark shadow leaned over him, eyes blazing. The dusky aura drowned out everything around it, like an eclipse cutting off the sun.

"You should have listened to me, boy. Now it's too late, at least for you."

Regor. Jason's mouth went dry. Where was Nyala? Was she just going to let Regor kill him? Pushing aside the surge of fear, he focused on his power, trying desperately to resist the mounting pressure building in his chest. It felt like he was trying to pull molasses into his lungs. If he didn't get some air soon, he wouldn't last much longer.

Just as the edges of his vision began to darken, he felt a minute easing in the constriction, allowing the barest whisper of air to seep into his starving lungs. If he could just manage to break free, maybe he could use his power to get away.

But if he ran, he would be leaving all of the people of Lore's Haven, and who knew how many others, at Bothan's mercy. He remembered the Rodinn children, and the sounds of their laughter as they played with Lenai. He thought about the woman who had given him, a complete stranger, a beautiful piece of craftsmanship, and about her husband and son. The pride in her husband's eyes still touched him. He thought about all of the people he had encountered since he'd arrived, and how welcoming, how polite, how nice they all were. If he'd had any air in his lungs, the realization that struck him would have taken it away. Somehow, without knowing how or when, he had come to love this world.

Then he thought about the world he'd come from. Bothan surely fit better in that world than this one. If he ran, all of the people here would suffer, and this world might take a step toward becoming more like his own. He couldn't allow that to happen if there was any way he could prevent it. He didn't know if he could take Regor, but he wasn't going to just run away and let him and Bothan win. He let go of his fear, and let his newfound passion blossom within. As he did, he felt another surge of power. The constriction eased enough for him to take a deep breath of dusty air. Then, from where he lay, he poured his soul into a blast of *dimsai* he sent at Regor.

The impact staggered the Altered, and for the briefest instant, the ebony cloak shredded. In the center of the dark aura, he caught a glimpse of a man with wavy blonde hair, a look of surprise etched on his face. Then the darkness returned, the edges of the shadow shifting and flowing. The eyes blazed even brighter than before.

"That the best you got?" Jason challenged, standing up. Like his dad always said, better to be hung for an eagle than a dove.

"Oh, you have no idea," Regor said. *"You were just a minor irritation before, boy. Now you have my full attention."*

Within Regor's shadowy silhouette, a globe of utter blackness began forming. The intensity of it was almost painful to Jason's vision. It was as if Regor held a ball of concentrated nothingness that was growing stronger by the moment. He focused all of his power into his shield, but he didn't know if it would be strong enough to resist the destruction that Regor was preparing.

Regor sent the black energy flying toward him. He braced himself for the impact. At this point, he just hoped he would survive. The dark globe detonated against the shield, the sound of the explosion almost deafening him…but it wasn't his shield that took the blow. A wall of sparkling iridescent force stood between him and Regor. His head snapped around, and he almost fainted from relief. Nyala stood behind him.

"I said you would have to deal with me if you wanted Jason," she said.

Regor didn't answer, as he and Nyala faced each other. At last he said, *"Are you certain you want to do this, my dear? It doesn't have to be this way."*

"I'm afraid it does."

"Very well," he said. *"Then let's not waste time."*

Almost simultaneously, the two beings threw concentrated blasts of power at each other. The explosion as they met sent Jason flying backwards. He got a glimpse of Bothan sailing in the opposite direction. Then everything changed.

He didn't know where he was, but the multi-colored glare was almost blinding. Squinting until his eyes were mere slits, he could just make out vague shapes. There were other people here. He realized that the glare was coming from their *dimsai* auras. He stopped using his vision and blinked rapidly as everything seemed suddenly dim.

As his eyes adjusted, he saw that he was in a room. The walls and ceiling constantly shifted colors and patterns. Looking at them too long gave him a queasy feeling in the pit of his stomach. The floor was the only thing that stayed one color and texture. Nyala stood beside him, with Regor on her other side. Facing them were five figures that Jason could only assume were the other Altered.

There was a tall, matronly lady wearing a white shawl. One of her eyes was solid black, while the other was pure white. As he watched, the eyes changed colors. Blue, green, red, violet. Always one solid color, but always changing. Beside her was a figure that constantly shifted from one appearance to another. Now a teenage boy, now a stocky lady, now a frail old man, and so on, no two ever the same. Next was a woman that looked to be in her twenties, but her skin, hair, and eyes were solid gold, almost like a living statue. Beside her stood a human shape made up of whirlwinds. The last figure was made entirely of flame.

Even without his vision, the power present was potent enough to make his skin crawl. It wasn't doing his nerves any good, either. He wished they would drop the disguises. Maybe then, this wouldn't feel so much like a trial. Or an execution. He looked at Nyala.

"These are the other Altered, Jason," she said. "They are Airam, Nivek, Haras, Ekim, and Darnoc." He noticed her voice sounded normal in this place, losing the shifting quality it had before.

"Altered have attacked each other for the first time since the agreement," the matronly woman said, ignoring Nyala's introduction. "Apparently because of this boy. Would either of you care to explain?"

"Do you break the Covenant, Nyala?" the golden woman asked.

"No, Haras, I don't," Nyala answered. "I merely seek to retain the balance upset by Regor."

"Regor?" the whirlwind said. "In what way does Regor upset the balance?"

Jason looked at Regor, but the dark figure remained silent.

"He gives his power to a man called Bodann," Nyala said. "He does this with the intention of becoming a god to the people of Teleria."

"Is this true, Regor?" the whirlwind asked. "You gave your power to a mortal?"

Jason didn't think Regor was going to answer at first. "Yes," Regor said abruptly, clearly irritated. "I lent some of my power to Bodann."

"Why?" Haras asked.

"Because I am tired of being relegated to myths and legends. The Covenant was fine when we first gained our powers. It prevented us from destroying this world, and maybe even ourselves. But now we've mastered our power. It's ridiculous for us to still be bound by something that no longer serves a purpose." He turned to the flaming figure. "Darnoc, you remember. We discussed this."

"Yes, I remember," Darnoc said. "But as I recall, we agreed to let it be."

"That was over two hundred years ago," Regor said. "I got tired of waiting."

"It was not your decision to make," said the matron, both eyes bright red. "While I understand your frustration, Regor, you had no right to act on your own." She turned to Nyala. "And what of you? You said you sought to retain the balance. Did you give your power to this boy as well?"

"No, Airam," Nyala said. "Jason's power is his own. I merely showed him how to use it."

Regor laughed. "I doubt that. If any of you had felt his attack on me, you would find that statement highly questionable."

"His attack was self-defense, and you know it," Nyala shot at him. "You attacked him first. He was trying to survive."

"Still," Airam said, "it would be very unusual for a boy of his age to possess the kind of power Regor describes."

"I believe her," the shifting one spoke up. "Nyala and I have had our disagreements over the years, but she's not a liar." He looked at Jason. "I'm Nivek," he added. Jason nodded to him, grateful that at least one of them acknowledged him. If he was Nivek, that would make the whirlwind Ekim.

"Nyala, why didn't you come to us when you learned of Regor's actions?" Haras asked.

"We haven't spoken as a body in centuries," Nyala said. "I was afraid it might lead to unnecessary confrontations among us. My hope was to deal with the situation quietly, and keep the rest of you from ever knowing it had happened."

"Understandable, even if mishandled," Ekim said.

"So, what do we do about the situation?" Darnoc asked. "Is the Covenant broken?"

"No," Airam said. "Bent, perhaps, but not broken. Although Regor brings up valid points regarding it. It may be that we need to discuss…other options."

"Other options?" Nyala asked. "You can't be considering Regor's plan."

"I didn't say that, Nyala. I said other options, one of which may or may not be Regor's idea. Just because we haven't met as a group, doesn't mean there haven't been individual discussions.

Considering the situation, I think it's time we all get back together and decide if we want to continue the Covenant, or explore other possibilities."

Jason saw several of the group nodding in agreement. Nyala shook her head, but didn't say anything further.

"So what do we do now?" Nivek said.

"I say we let the situation play itself out, without any further interference from either Nyala or Regor," Darnoc said. "If the boy's power is indeed his own, and if Regor has been giving his power to this Bodann character, it should resolve itself rather quickly. Then we can focus on the future."

Airam looked at the others. "Is that acceptable to everyone?"

The other four nodded in agreement.

"Very well. Nyala, Regor, your part in this is over. Do not interfere again." She turned to Jason. Her eyes turned white and gained a blinding brilliance. "It's time to send you back, young man."

Jason landed on the packed earth with a thud that drove the air from his lungs. He rolled to his hands and knees, disoriented by his sudden change in location. The last echoes of the explosion still hung in the air. He looked up the hill and saw Bothan struggling to his feet. From one side he heard coughing. Looking to his right, he saw Reyga trying to prop himself up on one elbow. A surge of relief poured through him.

"Where's Regor?" Bothan shouted. "What did you do?"

Jason looked up the hill. "I didn't do anything," he called. "Regor's gone. It's just you and me now." He saw that the threads connecting Bothan to his army were all gone, apparently a product of Regor's borrowed power. He looked over at Reyga, who was sitting up and looking around dazedly. Since it looked like the Loremaster would be okay, there was some cleaning up to do.

He turned back to Bothan just in time to see him throw a bolt of power. He caught the blast on his shield as he stood up, but another blast at his feet knocked him backwards.

A third bolt flew past him. He heard it detonate behind him followed by a rumbling crash. He glanced over his shoulder to see that a large pit had opened up in the ground about ten yards behind him.

Another explosion at his feet threw him off balance, sending him closer to the pit. He looked at Bothan, standing halfway up the hill. His ancestor was throwing blast after blast of *dimsai*, driving him back toward the edge of the pit. He was spending too much time trying to catch his balance to be able to focus on a counter attack.

Yet another blast, and his feet landed a few inches from the edge. He looked up to see another bolt flying toward him. He managed to catch it with his shield, but the impact made him take another small step back. *Oh man, this is really gonna suck.* He windmilled his arms frantically, trying to regain his footing, as the ground crumbled underneath his feet. As he started to fall, he grabbed for the edge. His fingers brushed against the rim, but immediately slipped off. Then he was falling into the pit.

He tried to twist to see how deep the pit was when a jerk wrenched him around and slapped him against the rock wall. He hung in midair, something holding onto his arm. Then Lenai appeared, her feet braced on the side of the pit, one hand grasping the edge, the other wrapped firmly around his wrist.

He thought he might have a heart attack. He said the first thing that popped into his head. "So," he gasped, "does this make us even?"

A smile bent one corner of her mouth. "Perhaps," she said. "But we can discuss that another time."

She hauled him back up so that he could hook his hands over the edge. He struggled out of the pit and looked up the hill. Bothan had mounted a horse and was riding through a portal at the top. Before Jason could stand up, Bothan had disappeared. Just before the portal winked out, he saw a streak of yellow zip through.

After a few moments, an image appeared in his head. "*Jason, he is here.*"

Crin, have I ever told you you're the best?

Crin sounded amused as he replied, "*Yes, but it's always nice to hear it again. Now you must hurry. He rides toward the Riftlands.*"

He turned to Lenai. "I have to go after Bothan. Can you stay here and take care of Reyga? He's been hurt."

"I will tend to him," she said. She laid a hand on his shoulder. "Jason, be careful."

"Don't worry. I will." Then he opened a portal to the location Crin showed him and stepped through.

Reyga saw Jason disappear through the portal. Then Lenai jogged over to him.

"Loremaster Reyga, are you injured?" she asked, as she kneeled beside him.

"Nothing that will not heal, my dear," he said. "Where did Jason go?"

"He goes after Bodann."

"Where?"

She shook her head. "He did not say."

He looked toward the battlefield. It appeared that Jason had been successful in breaking Bodann's hold over the creatures in his army. Less than half of the enemy remained, and the creatures were attacking each other more than they were attacking the Haven fighters. Most of the Haven forces had actually withdrawn to a safe distance, only intervening when any of Bodann's fighters tried to escape. The battle would be over soon, with the Haven forces achieving a shocking victory.

Then he saw Gatlor, Seerka, and Calador walking toward them. Although Gatlor bled from several scrapes, and Seerka had a slight limp, they did not look seriously injured. He breathed a sigh of relief. When Bodann cast them away, he had not known whether their departure would be permanent or not. Lenai helped him to his feet as they walked up.

"Loremaster Reyga," Gatlor said. "Are you well?"

"I am well, Captain. A few bumps and bruises is all."

"Where is Jason Bennett?"

"Bodann fled," he said. "Jason went after him. We do not know where."

Suddenly, an image appeared in his head. Along with it, he felt a presence in his mind.

"Loremaster Reyga."

He stiffened as he heard the voice in his head. Nyala? Jason? No, it did not sound like either of their voices.

"Loremaster Reyga, can you hear me?"

"I hear you," he said.

Gatlor looked at the others, who shook their heads. "Loremaster," he said. "No one spoke."

He waved his hand, shaking his head. "Not you."

"Loremaster, Nyala bids me show you where Jason has gone. Bodann leads him to the Riftlands. He needs your help, and the help of the warriors with you. You must follow."

"Who is this?"

He saw the warriors exchange puzzled glances, clearly wondering about his sanity. "Loremaster Reyga…" Lenai began, before he shushed her.

"My name is Crin." The location faded, replaced by the image of the fortunewing they had encountered outside his home. *"I am Jason's companion."*

"You are the fortunewing?"

"Yes," the voice said. *"Now you must hurry. Bodann is leading Jason into a trap. Jason will die without your help."*

"Why does Nyala not protect him?"

The voice sounded impatient. *"Nyala and Regor have been removed from this conflict. They are no longer allowed to interfere. Nyala risks much asking me to relay this information to you, but feels it is necessary. You must hurry."*

The original image filled his thoughts again, and then the presence was gone.

He blinked the dust from his eyes. Then he took a couple of steps away from the others and began creating a portal.

"Loremaster Reyga, what are you doing? Where are you going?" Gatlor asked.

"You mean where are *we* going," he said. "Bodann is leading Jason into a trap with the intention of killing him."

"Loremaster," Lenai said, "how do you know this?"

"I will explain later," he answered. "We must go now. Jason's life depends upon it."

The portal sprang into existence. Through it could be seen the turbulent atmosphere of the Riftlands. He looked toward the Riftlands in the distance. Somewhere out there, Jason Bennett was going to die unless they could get there in time to prevent it. At his urging, the others ran through. He looked at the Riftlands once more. *We are coming, Jason. I just hope we are not too late.* Then he stepped through and the portal vanished.

27
Turning the Tables

Jason stepped out of the portal, looking around to make sure Bothan wasn't waiting to spring another trap.

"This way, Jason."

He saw his ancestor in the distance, riding at an easy trot toward the most inhospitable area he had ever seen. The clouds seemed almost malevolent as they roiled and churned overhead. Massive distortions twisted the atmosphere, creating disturbing voids in the landscape, and the chill wind blowing out from the storm had a bite to it that went beyond mere physical discomfort. It was as if his nightmare that first night had come to life. *Nothing like walking into your own bad dream*. But he had no choice. If he was ever to confront his ancestor, now was the time.

He started running toward Bothan's retreating figure, using his power to enhance his speed. Soon he could tell that he was closing the distance between them. He studied the big man as he ran. Bothan held the reins with one hand, while a globe of *dimsai* enveloped his other. He prepared to throw up a shield in case Bothan suddenly turned and attacked.

He had closed the gap between them to a hundred yards when the glowing globe vanished. He slowed. *Be ready, Jason*, he told himself. Bothan turned and looked over his shoulder. When he saw Jason chasing him, he grinned as if he'd been hoping to see his young visitor. He kicked his horse up to a gallop, opening up some distance between them. Not far from one of the rifts, he pulled his mount to a halt and jumped off, the grin still on his face.

Jason slowed to a jog. *What's he up to?* He scanned the area constantly as he approached, waiting for his ancestor to spring the surprise.

"Jason, you must be careful," Crin sent. "*The Riftla—"* The inner voice cut off.

Crin? He looked up. Crin sailed overhead, adjusting his wings constantly to compensate for the blustery winds.

Crin? Still no answer. He didn't know why his friend wasn't answering, but as long as he could see that Crin was okay, there were other things to deal with.

He watched Bothan as he drew closer. Considering the events at the battlefield, the man seemed unconcerned. *He can't be waiting for Regor, can he?* He hoped Regor really was out of the picture. He stopped when he was within fifty feet. He could feel his anger building again, but something was different this time.

"Well, lad," Bothan said, "welcome to the Riftlands. Lovely place, isn't it?"

"Definitely," he said. "It's where this will finally end."

"Aye," Bothan said, glancing at the sky. "That it will, lad. That it will." He squared his shoulders and looked Jason in the eyes. "Well, do what you must." He made no further move, simply stood there.

Jason hesitated. Something wasn't right. Bothan suddenly pointed his hand toward him. Acting on reflex, Jason threw a blast of *dimsai*. Or at least he intended to. Nothing happened. He tried again. Still nothing. *What?* He stared at his hands and then thrust them at Bothan yet again, watching as they stretched out impotently. Then he heard Bothan chuckling.

"What did you do?"

Bothan just grinned at him.

"What did you do??"

Bothan laughed and started walking in a wide circle around him. "Didn't Nyala teach you anything? You're in the Riftlands, laddie. Where *dimsai* may or may not work." He stopped when he was between Jason and the Scorched Plains. "As it happens, where we're at, it doesn't."

Jason backed a couple of steps away. He wanted to kick himself. Nyala had told him about *dimsai* and the Riftlands. He'd been too intent on catching Bothan to think about it.

He jumped as Bothan's horse snorted behind him. He glanced back to make sure nothing was coming out of the rift, and then looked again. A sword hung from the side of the saddle. He lunged for it. He didn't expect to beat Bothan with the few lessons he'd been given at the keep, but maybe he could maneuver around him and make his way back to where his power would work again.

He turned around to see that Bothan had drawn his sword and was watching him with a little smile.

"Aye, lad," Bothan said, "it always comes down to this. A man lives and dies by the sword. Always has, always will. Whether it's made of treachery, magic, steel, or wits makes no mind. It's still a sword in the end."

He stepped toward Jason. "Let's be about it then."

Jason got his sword up to block Bothan's overhand swing. The shock ran up his arm all the way to his teeth, almost making him drop the weapon. He jumped back to avoid the next sweeping attack. He managed to get a firm grip again just in time to parry Bothan's backswing. He backed off another couple of steps and moved to the side, hoping to get into a position to move around Bothan, but the big man moved sideways with him, blocking his route.

A streak of yellow sliced through the air, but, unlike the Trellin ambush, this time Crin's attack failed to hit his target. With a flick of his sword, Bothan slapped Crin to the ground. Jason's anger surged as he looked at the unmoving body of his avian friend. He lunged at Bothan, but the man knocked his sword sideways, laughing as he did.

Movement behind Bothan caught his attention. He saw five figures approaching. *Reyga.* A flood of relief went through him. Now if he could just hold out until they got there.

His emotion must have shown in his face because Bothan gave him a strange look, then came at him with a slicing attack. He stumbled backwards, feeling the sword pass just inches from his throat. Bothan glanced over his shoulder toward the Plains.

"Well," he said. "I was wondering if they might show up. Good. I would have hated for them to miss this."

He turned and attacked again. Jason managed to parry one blow, but Bothan's attack was much faster and harder than before. His next blow numbed Jason's hands, and the one after that sent Jason's sword flying. *He's been playing with me.* He felt the cold blade exit his back before his brain registered that it had entered his front. He looked down at the length of metal sticking out from just below his ribs, his eyes following the blade back to Bothan's hand. It didn't hurt as much as he would have expected, but it was suddenly very hard to breathe again.

Bothan leaned toward him. "Sorry, lad. We could have ruled together. You just chose the wrong side."

Bothan yanked the blade out, and the searing pain came. He clutched at the wound and sank to the ground, fighting for each breath. Odd. It sounded like someone was calling his name. He looked down at his hands. So much blood…

The portal vanished behind him as Reyga stepped out.

"This way, Loremaster Reyga," Gatlor said pointing toward the Riftlands.

Reyga looked where Gatlor was pointing. In the distance he could see two figures facing each other. Jason and Bodann. He started moving toward the two as quickly as his bruises would allow.

"We must hurry." He pushed through the pain and managed to break into a halting jog. It still was not enough. "You go ahead," he told them. "I will be there as quickly as I can."

"I will help you," Lenai said, slipping her hand under his arm as Gatlor, Seerka, and Calador began running toward the two in the distance.

As they got closer, Reyga saw Jason squaring off with a sword. He shook his head and forced his legs to move faster. Bodann, while not being a master, was still an accomplished swordsman. Jason would not win this fight.

"Faster, faster," he told himself, putting his head down and willing more speed from his aching legs.

"Jason!"

He jerked his head up at Lenai's scream, just in time to see Bodann pull his sword from Jason's body. *No*. Reyga looked at Lenai's tortured face as she watched Jason sink to the ground.

"Go," he said, pushing her forward. "Go."

She squeezed his arm and then sprinted toward Jason's still body.

Bodann had mounted his horse and was riding hard toward the Plains, one hand held out in front of him. He rode at an angle from them, keeping as much distance as possible between him and the approaching warriors. Reyga saw Gatlor and Seerka stop. Gatlor grabbed his bow and pulled an arrow from the quiver. Bodann's hand flared with *dimsai*. He turned and threw a bolt of power toward the two warriors. Then it seemed to Reyga like time slowed down.

Gatlor sent an arrow streaking toward Bodann. Seerka leaped in front of Gatlor into the path of the *dimsai* blast. The power threw him backwards, knocking Gatlor down in the process. Bodann opened a portal out in front of his racing horse. Just as he reached it, he jerked in his saddle. The arrow had found its mark. Then Bodann was gone, and the portal disappeared.

Reyga turned back and saw Calador and Lenai kneeling beside Jason. He stopped when he reached them, gasping for air.

"Jason! Jason, can you hear me?" Lenai said. Blood covered her hands as she pressed them over the wound.

A weak groan answered her. The knot in Reyga's stomach eased slightly. At least he was still alive. For now. The blood spreading over the ground cried out that they needed to get him to a healer quickly. Not far away, a bundle of yellow feathers lay on the ground. Crin. He saw one of the wings move.

"Calador, bring Jason," he said. "We must get out of the Riftlands so I can open a portal back to the battlefield. Loremaster Seryn will be there."

Calador gently picked Jason up as Reyga walked over and scooped up the injured fortunewing. They half walked, half jogged toward the border of the Plains. They met Gatlor, who was carrying Seerka. Wisps of smoke still drifted up from the cat-man's scorched leathers.

"Gatlor?" Reyga said.

"He took an attack meant for me."

"Will he live?" Calador asked.

Gatlor shook his head. "Not much longer." He said nothing more, but his eyes betrayed his feelings.

"What happened?" Jason's voice was a whisper.

"Jason, you should save your strength," Lenai said.

"Tell me."

"Seerka has been injured," Reyga said. "We must get you both to Loremaster Seryn."

"Let me see him."

"Jason, you are in no condition—"

"Let me see him."

Reyga nodded to Gatlor, who carried Seerka over to where Jason could turn his head and see the Ferrin.

Jason reached out a shaking hand and laid it on Seerka's chest. He closed his eyes as his hand began to glow. Then his hand slid off, hanging limply from Calador's grasp. Reyga hurried to check him. He was still breathing, but faintly. They had to hurry.

A sudden gasp startled him. He looked over to see Seerka staring up at Gatlor.

"What happened?" Seerka said. "Why are you carrying me?"

Reyga could see that Gatlor was struggling to hold his emotions in check. "Because you decided to fall asleep in the middle of a battle," Gatlor said. "I thought about leaving you out here, but knew I would never hear the end of it."

"Well," Seerka said, looking around at the rest of them. "Do you think you might put me down? This is rather undignified." As Gatlor put him on his feet, Seerka saw Jason in Calador's arms. "Does he live?" he asked.

"For the moment," Reyga said, opening a portal. "We must find Loremaster Seryn immediately."

Then the small group stepped through the portal back to the battlefield.

Jason opened his eyes to see a circle of faces looming over him. Seryn, Reyga, Lenai, and behind them, the three warriors.

"What?" Then he remembered, and clutched at his wound. The pain was gone.

Reyga smiled. "Bodann nearly killed you, but Seryn was able to heal your wounds."

He looked at Seryn. "You keep saving my life," he said. "Thanks. I guess this is another one I owe you."

Seryn shook her head. "No, Jason, it is we who are in your debt. Your actions today saved thousands of lives. Any feelings of gratitude are ours."

"What about Bothan?"

"He managed to escape," Reyga said. "But not before Gatlor put an arrow into him."

"Is he dead?"

"We do not know. For now, what is important is that his army is destroyed. Lore's Haven and the people of Teleria are safe."

"And you live," Lenai added.

He closed his eyes. Yeah, everything was fine for now. But if Bothan was still alive, he would try again. He remembered the hate in his ancestor's eyes. Hate that wasn't just directed at him, but at the Circle as well. And there was still Regor. He might have had to sit out the final showdown, but that didn't mean he was out of the picture for good.

"Jason."

He grinned as he heard Crin's voice in his head. *Crin, are you okay?* He looked up and saw the bird soaring overhead.

"Yes. The Loremaster healed my injuries as well. I am pleased that you are well once more."

Do you know where Bothan went?

"No."

So, he really had gotten away. If Gatlor's arrow didn't finish him, it would just be a matter of time before they heard from him again. He started to get up.

"Jason, you should rest," Seryn said. "You lost a great deal of blood." But she didn't make any other effort to stop him.

"I'm okay," he said. Lenai held his arm to steady him. When the world stopped spinning, he looked out over the battlefield. Bodies littered the earth, turning what had been dust into a blood soaked quagmire. Men and women from Lore's Haven made their way through the fallen, looking for any others that were still alive. Here and there he could see people kneeling on the ground, mourning over a fallen friend. Many might have been saved, like Seryn said, but many had died as well.

Looking at the mourners, his thoughts flashed back to the scene in the training yards. He knew how the ones out on the field felt. He wished there was something he could do to help them, but it was too late.

But the body Chon left behind hadn't been human. They still didn't know what had happened to his dad. Didn't know if he was alive or dead.

He went over his time in this world. So much had happened in such a short time. The training with Nyala in Teleria's past.

His experience in the meeting of the Altered. Bothan's attack on his father. His wild swings of emotion and confusion until Lenai helped him see clearly in the Shanthi ritual. Wait. Bothan's attack. Something…there was something about that. His eyes went wide.

"Jason?" Lenai asked. "What is it?"

He looked at her, a small glimmer of hope coming to life inside of him. "I think I know where my dad is," he said.

"Jason?" Reyga said.

He grinned at Reyga and began running toward the battlefield.

28
Surprise

"But I thought Nyala told you the past could not be changed," Reyga said.

"That's just it," Jason said. "I didn't change the past, because what we thought happened didn't really happen."

"Well, all I know is that I thought I was a dead man," Bruce Bennett said. He was sitting at the table with Tal, Reyga, Seryn, and Lenai, with Jason standing behind him, his hands on his father's shoulders. "I looked up and saw the dagger start down. Then everything stopped and I saw Jason standing there with…with me."

"Let me make certain I understand," the High One said. "You took a body from the battlefield, altered it to look like your father, and then went into the past to exchange it so that Bodann, disguised as Chon, would think he had killed your father?"

"Yeah," he said. "When I was looking at the bodies on the ground, I started thinking about all of the stuff that had happened since I'd been here. Then it hit me: If Nyala could go fourteen hundred years into the past, maybe I could at least go back a few days."

"So, the reason the body I examined wasn't human, was because you had exchanged it," Seryn said.

Jason nodded. "I didn't bother with anything on the inside because it just needed to convince Bothan that he'd killed my dad."

"Remarkable," Reyga said. "Truly remar—"

Jason was surrounded by an expanse of white. A dark haired woman smiled at him. He smiled back.

"Nyala."

"Jason, I wanted to thank you. You saved the people of my world from a dark future."

"Well, I couldn't have done it without you."

"I only showed you how to use your power. You chose the ways in which to use it."

"You did more than that," Jason said. "You saved my life a couple of times. If Regor would've had his way, I wouldn't be here now."

"Then we helped each other," she said. "If you like, I may be able to help you again."

"How?"

"I think I can help you get back home."

"What?" Her words almost made him dizzy. Home? He could go home? "You can send me home?"

"I can't," she said. "My power is not strong enough. But if we were to join our power, I believe that, between the two of us, we could open a portal back to your world. Of course, it would have to be to a time after both you and your father came to Teleria. Otherwise the effects on the timeline would be unpredictable, perhaps even disastrous."

His thoughts were a confusing blur. For some reason, the idea of going home didn't excite him as much as he thought it would. He had been through so much here, met so many good people. Here, with his powers, he could actually make a difference. But he had friends back home. And after all, it was home. He needed time to think.

"Nyala…"

"I know," she said. "Teleria has its appeal." She smiled at him again and laid a gentle hand on his cheek. "Give it some thought, Jason. When you decide, think of me and I will come."

"—kable," Reyga said. "Jason, I know you are happy to have your father back, but I am equally pleased to have my friend back. You are truly an extraordinary young man."

"Yes, he is," his dad said, laying a hand over Jason's. Jason's mind was racing as he thought about what Nyala had said. He almost didn't notice his father's touch.

Reyga turned to Lenai. "And what of Baruun? I have not seen him since before the battle."

"Baruun was injured, but will recover," she said. "He has returned to our telosh."

"I am pleased to hear that," Reyga said. "Please give him my regards the next time you speak with him."

"And also our thanks for the aid from your people," Tal added.

"I will relay your words to him," she said.

Jason's thoughts had turned back to the battle. He looked at Tal. "I'm sorry I didn't remember my power sooner. I saw Brin fall into the pit."

"Actually," Tal said, "Loremaster Brin is in the healing area."

"What? How?"

Tal shook his head with a smile. "That man astonishes me sometimes. After he jumped off the ledge, he opened a portal back to the Haven as he fell. He was still severely injured when he flew through the primary portal and crashed into the opposite wall, but the healers were able to treat him in time."

"That's amazing," Jason said.

"Indeed," Tal agreed. "I could not have said it better myself."

The small group sat around the table for another hour, talking about the events of the last few days, and discussing the future now that the war was over. Eventually, everyone began saying their good nights until only Jason, his dad, and Lenai were left.

"Well," Bruce said, standing up and stretching, "I think I'll retire too. These old bones need their rest."

"Wait," Jason said. "Dad, Nyala told me she thinks she can help us get back home. I thought I would be more excited than I am at the thought of going back. What do you think?"

His dad took a deep breath. "Home. Funny how the meaning of that word can change. I've been here for thirty years. There's nothing left for me back on Earth." He laid a hand on Jason's shoulder. "This is my home now, and I've come to love this place, but if you want to go back, I will go with you."

He didn't answer as he pondered his dad's words. If they went back to just after his dad left, like Nyala had said, all of Jason's friends would be almost forty years old. They could always move somewhere else, and he could make new friends, but…

"I know there's a lot more on Earth for you than there is for me," his dad said. "Why don't you sleep on it? Whatever you decide, I'm with you. Good night, son." His dad hugged him and kissed his cheek before shuffling out of the room.

He watched his dad leave, and then turned and looked at Lenai.

"What would you do?" he asked her.

She shook her head. "Only you can answer that, Jason, for only you know where your heart truly lies."

"Yeah." He only wished it were that simple. Right now, he didn't know where his heart wanted to be. He stared blankly at the table. He had friends back home even if they would be twenty years older, but he'd made friends here too. And what about Crin?

"Yes, what about Crin?" Jason smiled as he heard the fortunewing.

"What is it?" Lenai asked him.

"Oh, Crin is just giving me his opinion."

"Ah." Lenai stroked the tabletop. "Jason."

"Hmm?"

She seemed hesitant. "Jason, I do not wish to make your decision any more difficult than it already is, but there is something I must tell you."

He waited for her to continue.

"When we performed *Sho tu Ishta*, something happened."

"What happened?" he asked. "Did I become *ch'tasa* like Reyga? If that's it, Lenai, you don't have to worry. I won't ask you to tell me anything you don't want to."

"No," she said, "you are not *ch'tasa*."

"Oh." He felt an odd tinge of disappointment. "Well," he said, trying to make light of it. "Whew! That was close." He forced himself to chuckle.

"You are not *ch'tasa*," she repeated. "But when you restored that part of me which is Shanthi to me…when you restored myself to me, my soul…you became *ch'nai*."

"*Ch'nai*? What does that mean? Is it good or bad?"

"That is for you to decide," she said. She stared at the table top. "I am bound to you, Jason. Or rather, my soul is bound to yours." Her words came pouring out as she looked up and saw his stunned expression. "Jason, I am sorry. I never intended this to happen. If I could change it I would, but *Chai na,* the

Bonding, cannot be broken." Her gaze dropped back to the table. "If you are angry with me, I will understand."

"What do you mean, your soul is bound to mine?"

She didn't look up. "It means that where you are, I must be there as well. It means that if anything were to happen to you, I could not survive." She looked at him finally, her eyes heavy with threatening tears. "It means that I would give my life for you."

He gaped at her. She was bound to him? Nothing like throwing a new wrinkle into the mix. If she was bound to him…

"Lenai, what will happen to you if I go home?"

She looked down again. "As long as you are well," she said, "I will be also."

He didn't believe her. "Tell me the truth."

Her voice dropped to a whisper. "I do not know."

He looked around the room as he tried to bring his whirling thoughts in order. How could he go back if there was a possibility that Lenai might die if he did? Could they take her with them to Earth? No, even if she agreed to go, that wouldn't work. Aside from the occasional shifting of the color of her skin, bound to draw the wrong kind of attention, he didn't think her warrior's sense of honor would be able to handle some of the things in his world. Besides, his dad didn't really want to go back either. And there was Crin. Plus, they didn't know if Bothan was really gone or not. He took a deep breath. Well. That was it then.

"Well then," he said, "I guess I'll have to stay a while."

Her head jerked up. He saw a tiny glimmer of hope in her eyes.

"Jason," she said, "do not stay if it is only because of me. What happened is not your fault. You should not have to sacrifice your world because of that."

"I'm not," he said. "Look, if I can go back now, I can go back later. So, for now anyway, I'll stick around. Bothan may still be out there, and there's a lot of Teleria that I haven't seen yet. Maybe you could show it to me?"

She smiled at him, her eyes shining. "Yes, I can show you."

He smiled back. He could think of a lot worse things than being bound to someone like her. Besides, she was prettier than Tracy Jacobson anyway.

Epilogue

In a dimly lit room, a small circle of men and women sat around a table.

"Bodann was a fool," one said.

"So what do we do now?"

"The only thing we can do. Now that the Circle has destroyed so many of our forces, we must rebuild. Fortunately, most of our *saiken* were able to escape the battlefield."

"Even with the *saiken*, it will take time."

"We have no choice."

"Bodann was a fool," the first speaker repeated.

A dark shadow stepped out of the corner.

"Bodann was not a fool," the shadow said. *"He was over confident. But even that is better than sitting around a table endlessly making plans you do not have the courage to carry out. At least Bodann acted on his plans."*

A grumble went around the table, but no one dared to challenge the Shadow Lord.

"So we rebuild."

"But now this Far Planer is with them. From what I hear, he is almost as strong as an Altered."

They waited for the shadow's response.

"Jason Bennett is strong, and we lost many of our forces," Regor said, *"but there has been some good come of this encounter."*

"What is that?"

"The other Altered now know of my feelings about the Covenant. And I have learned that I am not the only one who feels this way. It is just a matter of time."

Jason's story continues in

ALTERED INTENTIONS

JABEN'S RIFT, BOOK 2

And

SOUL OF POWER

JABEN'S RIFT, BOOK 3

Appendix

A Little More About Teleria

The Races of Teleria

Teleria is home to numerous races other than humans, most of which came about as a result of the protophasic technology used in the last world war, the Devastation. Their progenitors were created either as a side effect of the technology or came to Teleria through a rift from another world. This list contains only the most prominent of the sentient races.

Ally, Neutral, or Enemy indicates their general stance toward the Circle.

Dokal (Ally)

The first Dokal came to Teleria through one of the rifts created during the Devastation. The rift subsequently collapsed, leaving the small exploratory band trapped and unable to return home. Although a warrior race, they are also very introspective and thoughtful. After learning of the Loremasters and their quest to preserve and restore knowledge, they became allies of the Circle. The first saiken to begin working on creating portals to other worlds did so primarily in an attempt to aid the Dokal in their desire to return home.

Over the centuries, their numbers have grown, although they are still outnumbered by most of the other races. What they lack in numbers, however, they make up for in size. The average Dokal stands three heads taller than a human and the smallest weighs twice as much. Their skin is extremely thick and plate-like, serving as a natural armor. Their weapons of choice are battle axes, maces, and clubs, wielded by both male and female in battle. As Far Planers, they do not possess any *dimsai* ability.

The Dokal mentality is part warrior, part philosopher. Belying their daunting appearance, the typical Dokal has an excellent sense of humor and a quick wit when they choose to display it. Their leadership is determined by mutual debate and discussion and it can sometimes take them months to come to a consensus. The leaders rule until they either step down from their position or die due to battle wounds or old age.

F'aar (Ally)

This amphibious race is also alien to Teleria. During the Devastation, a rift opened up to their watery home world, dragging an entire F'aar village through. When the rift closed, they were unable to return. The F'aar are the only non-Telerian race where any member can use *dimsai*, similar to the humans of Teleria.

Generally human looking, their amphibious nature is clear due to the gills on the sides of their necks, slightly webbed hands and feet, and horizontally slit pupils in their eyes. They also possess an inner eyelid that allows them to see clearly when they are underwater.

As a rule, they are a pacifistic people, and it is very difficult to upset their natural composure. Threaten something dear to them, however, and their warriors, generally female, can be fearsome opponents. Their weapons of choice are poison-tipped spears and daggers.

Ferrin (Ally)

The Ferrin are a cat-like race of people. They appear to be mostly human, with their only feline features being slightly pointed ears set high on the sides of their heads, slitted pupils in their typically yellow or green eyes, and retractable claws in their fingers.

They are an easy-going race who can usually find some humor in almost any situation, even in combat, where they are masters of lethal grace and precision, employing acrobatic jumps, flips, and diving rolls in their repertoire of skills. As a rule, they disdain any form of weapons in favor of their razor-sharp claws. They also rarely wear armor other than metal bands on their wrists and ankles, as the armor interferes with their naturally fluid movement. They are one of only two hybrid races to have full use of *dimsai*, the other being the Grithor.

Ferrin warriors are generally male, although unmated females will often also take part in battle. Ferrin leaders can be male or female, with leadership determined by weaponless challenge combat. Leaders, past and present, are usually marked by multiple scars on their head, faces, and bodies. Leadership can only be challenged once per year. When multiple candidates are vying for leadership, various contests of skill will narrow the field to two candidates who will then battle for the position.

Grithor (Enemy)

The Grithor are very sensitive to light, having small, weak eyes, and have become an underground dwelling race, only coming to the surface at night or in an emergency. Although pound for pound stronger, they are shorter than humans, with squat legs and muscular bodies. Their hands are slabs with stubby fingers and powerful claws. Due to their weak eyesight, they have developed extremely acute senses of smell and hearing. Along with the Ferrin, they are one of only two hybrid races to have full use of *dimsai*.

They live in warrens underneath the Scorched Plains and further south and west in Barrenrock. Living underground, they are usually covered in a layer of dirt and grime, rarely bothering to clean themselves. Their build makes them very efficient excavators, and their preferred method of attack is to hollow out the ground beneath an enemy until the ground collapses underneath them. Any attacker that manages to make it into their tunnel system is met with swords, maces, and *dimsai* from their *saiken*. Although unrivaled in their stonelore, their overall intelligence is slightly below average in all other areas.

Leadership belongs to whichever Grithor can intimidate the others the most, either by combat or threats.

Manarach (Enemy)

The Manarach species are human/spider hybrids, with human torsos, arms, and heads on hairy, pony-sized spider bodies. They are a predator species and consider any living creature as prey, unworthy of their respect or consideration. They are very reclusive, living in the foothills of the Cauldron Mountains southwest of Barrenrock, and few who venture into their land have ever returned. Manarachs are intelligent and extremely territorial of any place they consider theirs.

From the waist up, they are human looking except for two large black orbs where the human eyes would be, and six smaller orbs circling the rest of the head. They also have two hand-length fangs, which hide within folds of skin on the neck underneath their human chins. They do not possess any *dimsai* ability.

Manarachs are a matriarchal society, with females being dominant. Leadership is determined by battle, with the loser generally slain. Their preferred weapons are their fangs and spears. They also use their trapsilk to ensnare foes and potential meals, which are synonymous to the creatures.

Rodinn (Ally)

The Rodinn are one of the smaller races of Teleria. They are a naturally polite people, and can be somewhat timid around those they do not know. Unable to use more than the basic *dimsai*, they are very good with their hands and often become skilled craftsmen. Although generally human looking, their hair never grows more than a thumbs-length long, and their eyes, nose, and ears are smaller than the typical human. They stand approximately the height of an average human's shoulder and are very quick and nimble. Other than becoming craftsmen, they often fill the roles of courier and voluntary domestic servants.

The Rodinn accept the leadership of wherever they may happen to reside. The oldest lucid resident of a Rodinn village will generally serve as the Elder of the village unless he or she chooses to decline leadership.

Shanthi (Neutral)

The Shanthi are a secretive people with the ability to change the color of their skin to match their surroundings, even down to matching patterns of leaves and walls. With proper training, they can learn to use the minimal *dimsai* available to their race to make themselves completely invisible. They are human in appearance, though their eyes are slightly larger than a human's. Their fingers and toes can extend when necessary, revealing sucker-like structures underneath the knuckles which allow them to climb and cling to walls and ceilings. Although the distance varies by individual, the Shanthi are also able to detect when others of their race are nearby.

The Shanthi do not interact with other races on a regular basis, particularly avoiding humans. In generations past, this was not the case, but some Shanthi started using their abilities as thieves, mercenaries, and assassins, selling their services to whomever had the coin to retain them. This reflected poorly on the entire race, even though those doing such things, called *rishna kel* by the majority of their people, represented only a small fraction of the race as a whole. As a result, the Shanthi have developed an extremely high sense of honor and loyalty to each other and any whom they grant the rare privilege of friendship. They can be easily offended if a remark is perceived as a slur or a question of their honor. Physical touch from anyone they do not know is unwelcome and can trigger retaliation depending upon the setting and intent of the other person.

Although they generally distrust humans, some find the Circle's intentions and practices acceptable and do not harbor such feelings toward the Loremasters or those humans living at Lore's Haven. In battle, the Shanthi males and females fight side by side. Their weapons of choice are the long dagger and bow.

The Shanthi live in multiple clans, with each clan having its own leader, and all of the clan leaders forming a Clan Council. The Council will select a *Shani tu Rish*, or Shanthi of Honor, who will lead the Council, and by extension, all of the Shanthi. When a clan leader dies, the leaderless clan will send three candidates to the Council, from which one is selected by the Council to serve as the new leader of that clan. New *Shani tu Rish* are also selected or reappointed each time a new clan leader is chosen.

Trellin (Enemy)

The Trellin are a belligerent, lizard-like race, having scaly skin, usually mottled dark green and brown. Like human fingerprints, no two Trellin will ever share the same coloration pattern on their skin. Physically, they can best be described as resembling one of Earth's Komodo Dragons if the dragon were to stand upright, lose its tail, and take on more humanoid proportions. Although very strong, they do not possess great speed or intellect. Like their lizard cousins, they are cold-blooded, which restricts them to the warmer climates of Teleria.

Trellin weaponry consists of jagged, double-bladed shortswords, and thin black daggers called bloodfangs. The bloodfangs are hollow and filled with a virulent poison. A tiny hole in the tip of the dagger slowly releases the poison into the

Trellin's victim. Although very durable while dry, once embedded in flesh, the blade material immediately begins to degrade. If it is left in the flesh for longer than a few moments, it will break off if pulled, releasing all of the poison at once.

Due to their adversarial nature toward other creatures, even those of their own kind, they rarely function well in groups larger than five, and even then only if one of the group is clearly dominant. There is no organized leadership in what passes for Trellin society. The leader of any particular group is the largest and/or strongest of the group, regardless whether they are male or female.

Yellowtooth (Neutral)

The Yellowtooth are a blend of canine and human. Surly, although not outright aggressive, they are generally human looking with short snouts, a thin layer of fur coating their bodies and short, black, fixed claws on their fingers and toes. They stand about the same height as a human, and have stocky, muscular builds, rendering them stronger and faster than the typical human. Their society runs the gamut from soldier to scholar, but they have no *dimsai* ability.

Yellowtooth warriors lean toward the males, although in a battle, the female of the species will be well represented also. The preferred weapons of the Yellowtooth are swords and maces.

While never coming to open hostilities, tension exists between the Yellowtooth and the Ferrin. It's not uncommon for a Yellowtooth to leave a room when a Ferrin walks in. The Ferrin find this rather amusing and will even go out of their way to irritate a Yellowtooth, stopping just short of the point where the Yellowtooth might lose control.

Female Yellowtooth occupy the leadership positions, which are chosen by hand to hand combat, in much the same way as the Ferrin.

****

The Orders

Agathon Saltor is credited with establishing the Circle and the nine Orders in the year 107 PD (Post Devastation).

In 97 PD, he realized that without intervention, all of mankind's knowledge not already lost in the Devastation would soon vanish. He searched for ten years until he finally found nine men and women whom he thought would be able to undertake the task of safeguarding, and in some cases rediscovering, the knowledge mankind had amassed over the centuries. He charged them with the responsibility of preserving mankind's knowledge in order to prevent the world from falling into darkness and chaos.

The nine Orders, their areas of expertise, and their current Loremasters are:

Emerald – Agriculture, horticulture, small flora.
Loremaster Reyga Falerian, Human male
Ruby – Geography, geology, and stonework (construction and artisanship)
Loremaster Brin Jalasar, Human male
Diamond – Healing, medicinal plants and herbs
Loremaster Seryn Shal, Human female
Amber – Forestry and woodcraft (including fletching and bows)
Loremaster Jarril Breth, Ferrin male
Amethyst – Zoology, animal physiology and husbandry
Loremaster Delani Morn, Human female
Topaz – Meteorology, atmospheric phenomena
Loremaster Kalen Dristal, Human male
Obsidian – Metallurgy, blacksmithing, and other metal working
Loremaster Chon Artel, Human male
Sapphire – Marine and freshwater biology and ecology
Loremaster T'kel Sho, F'aar female
Pearl – History, both factual and legend, social sciences
Tal Vardyn, Human male (Also serves as High One of the Circle of Nine)

Each Loremaster serves until they die or step down from their post for any reason. At that time, the Loremaster's apprentice is presented to the Circle to be approved. Once an apprentice is selected, it is a very rare occasion that they are not subsequently approved by the Circle when the time comes. If a Loremaster dies before naming an apprentice, the Circle will confer to determine which student of that Order will assume the position of Loremaster.

****

Telerian Calendar

The Telerian year has 360 days, and is divided into six cycles, each consisting of ten sixdays:

Cycle of Awakening
Cycle of Storms
Cycle of Growth
Cycle of Gathering
Cycle of Change
Cycle of Landsleep

Cycles are used for date keeping. A date would be said as "the twenty-second day of Growth," or "the forty-first day of Landsleep."

Other time periods include spans, which are five sixdays (12 to a year), and duals, which are two sixdays (30 to a year).

About the Author

G. David Walker was born in Ulysses, Kansas, in the summer of 1963, the youngest of four brothers and one sister. As the internet had not yet been invented when he was a young man, he instead devoured any science fiction or fantasy book that he could get his hands on, dreaming of different worlds, fantastical creatures and strange, alien beings. As an adult, he decided to forge into the realms he had only read about, creating his own worlds to explore and share.

David is also an avid Trekkie (although not rabid) and harbored a secret desire to appear on the SyFy network's short-lived series "Who Wants to be a Super Hero?"

David is a member of the Missouri Writers Guild and the Springfield Writers Guild, and currently lives in southwest Missouri with his wife and children, and whatever stray animals his children happen to bring home. For more information about David and his current or upcoming projects, visit his web page, Chasing Dragons in the Ozarks, at www.gdavidwalker.com.

A word from Dave:

Thank you for taking the time to read *From a Far Land.* I appreciate your time and I hope I've given you an enjoyable experience with this, the first book of the Jaben's Rift trilogy. I strive to write stories my readers will enjoy, and I love getting feedback (even constructive criticism) about my work. If you have any comments or questions, please don't hesitate to contact me through my website, gdavidwalker.com.

The greatest gift you can give any author is to share the word about any of their books that you have enjoyed. Tell your friends. Leave a review on your favorite book-related website, or even just a rating. Buy a copy as a gift for someone else. It's all appreciated.

Keep up with Dave online at:

Twitter: @gdavidwalker
Facebook: http://www.facebook.com/pages/G-David-Walker/115393528485341

Visit Dave's website

Chasing Dragons in the Ozarks
http://www.gdavidwalker.com